"*The Exiles of Erin* is an important book. No scholar knows Irish-American fiction as well as Fanning does. He has used his expertise to give readers interested in Irish-American history valuable insights into its development. The book held my interest with the high quality of humor and style of many of the selections." – Lawrence J. McCaffrey, Professor of Irish & Irish-American History, Loyola University of Chicago

"Of immense value to anyone interested in the Irish story in America." – *The Boston Globe*

"With voices forgotten as well as famous, Charles Fanning charts the transformation of the Irish immigrant to the Irish-American, from survival to respectability, in the pages of *The Exiles of Erin*. It is an outstanding contribution to Irish-American scholarship by its preeminent literary historian." – Maureen Murphy, Hofstra University and past President, American Conference for Irish Studies

"Fanning should be thanked for bringing 20th-century readers on a tour of 19th-century Irish-America, with all its complexities and charms." – *Irish Literary Supplement*

"Fanning has provided an extremely interesting selection of writing from novels, magazines, and newspapers that takes us part of the way into the cultural consciousness of the Irish as they sought to express themselves in their new country." – Dennis Clark, *Irish America*

"Wonderful yarns as well as vital descriptions of Irish life in America in the nineteenth century." – *Journal of American Ethnic History*

"Fanning's scholarship is exciting, his prose graceful, his subject important." – Elizabeth Cullinan, author of *House of Gold*

The Exiles of Erin

NINETEENTH-CENTURY IRISH-AMERICAN FICTION

Second Edition

Edited by Charles Fanning

Dufour Editions

Published 1997 by Dufour Editions, Inc., Chester Springs, PA 19425-0007

ISBN 0 8023 1315 9

Library of Congress Cataloging-in-Publication Data

The Exiles of Erin: nineteenth-century Irish-American fiction /
Charles Fanning, editor.
    p. cm.
  ISBN 0-8023-1315-9
  1. American fiction--Irish-American authors. 2. United States--Emigration
and immigration--Fiction. 3. Irish Americans--Social life and customs--
Fiction. 4. Ireland--Emigration and immigration--Fiction. 5. American fic
tion--19th century. 6. Exiles--Ireland--Fiction.I. Fanning, Charles.
PS647.I74E95 1997
813'.008'089162'09034--dc21   97-6244
                                                                  CIP

Printed and Bound in the United States of America

TO FRAN,
STEPHEN, AND ELLEN

There came to the beach a poor Exile of Erin,
The dew on his thin robe was heavy and chill,
For his country he sigh'd when at twilight repairing,
To wander alone by the wind-beaten hill;
But the day-star attracted his eye's sad devotion,
For it rose o'er his own native Isle of the ocean,
Where soon in the fire of his youthful emotion,
He sang the bold anthem of Erin go bragh.

> – from "The Exile of Erin,"
> traditional song

No treason we bring from Erin–nor bring we shame
   nor guilt!
The sword we hold may be broken, but we have not
   dropped the hilt!
The wreath we bear to Columbia is twisted of thorns,
   not bays;
And the songs we sing are saddened by thoughts of
   desolate days.
But the hearts we bring for Freedom are washed in the
   surge of tears;
And we claim our right by a People's fight outliving a
   thousand years!

> – from "The Exile of the Gael,"
> John Boyle O'Reilly

Contents

Acknowledgments

During the years of my research in Irish-American fiction I have received assistance from a number of organizations and institutions. For their generous support I wish to thank the American Council of Learned Societies, the Rockefeller Foundation, the National Endowment for the Humanities, the American Irish Foundation, the Newberry Library, the American Antiquarian Society, and the Cushwa Center for the Study of American Catholicism at Notre Dame. For their professional advice, encouragement, and most of all their friendship, my heartfelt thanks to Thomas N. Brown, Blanche M. Touhill, Richard F. Peterson, Lawrence J. McCaffrey, Andrew M. Greeley, Emmet Larkin, Daniel Hoffman, the late William V. Shannon, Maureen O'Rourke Murphy, and Ellen Skerrett. I am also very grateful to many others who have helped me to find and understand this material over the years, especially Jay Dolan, Shaun O'Connell, John Hench, Joyce Flynn, Dennis Flynn, Robert Rhodes, and Dan Casey. My special thanks to Bill Levin for introducing me to the wonders of word processing, to Sandy Bicknell for typing the original of this difficult manuscript so well and with such good will, and to Matt Jockers for his painstaking work on the text of this new edition. My greatest debt is to my wife Fran whose understanding and encouragement make my work possible, and to my children Stephen and Ellen who help me keep it in perspective.

Author Biography

Charles Fanning is Professor of English and History and Director of Irish and Irish Immigration Studies at Southern Illinois University at Carbondale. His publications in Irish Studies include *Finley Peter Dunne and Mr. Dooley: The Chicago Years* (Winner of the Frederick Jackson Turner Award of the Organization of American Historians) and *The Irish Voice in America: Irish-American Fiction from the 1760s to the 1990s* (Winner of the Prize for Literary Criticism of the American Conference for Irish Studies). He has edited critical editions of Finley Peter Dunne's "Mr. Dooley" columns, James T. Farrell's *Studs Lonigan: A Trilogy,* and *Chicago Stories of James T. Farrell.*

Introduction

We are still a long way from knowing all there is to know about immigrant life in nineteenth-century America. Most historical accounts of that experience have drawn upon four sources of information: demographic records, immigrant letters, the ethnic press, and, of course, reports by members of the host American culture. The present anthology collects for the Irish immigration an additional body of source material–fiction written by the immigrants and their children that describes their experience as strangers in the strange land of the United States before the twentieth century. Irish-American fiction represents a hitherto unexplored resource for understanding the human dimension of the Irish diaspora and its American aftermath. As the first large-scale voluntary influx of a non-Anglo-Saxon people into America, the Irish immigration provides valuable insights about the challenges inherent in the collision of new and established ethnic groups on shared territory. These issues continue to have relevance in our own time of intensifying worldwide migration.

Historically, the Irish have been an extremely articulate people, the creators of a richly various literature, especially impressive in proportion to their numbers. This heritage, along with their knowledge of English, helps to explain the many fascinating and accomplished Irish literary responses to American immigration. Taken together, these texts establish the existence and persistence of an Irish-American tradition of written self-expression. Rooted in the eighteenth century and blossoming in the twentieth, this is the most extended, continuous body of literature by members of a single American ethnic group available to us.

In the nineteenth century, Irish-American writers formed into three distinct literary generations: those who came before the catastrophe of the Great Hunger of the late 1840s; the Famine generation who came between 1850 and 1875, the period of greatest immigration and upheaval; and the children of the Famine immigrants, who chronicled the growth of an Irish-American middle class between 1875 and World War I. As a group these writers have embodied and documented the changing self-consciousness of the Irish in America over a period of more than a hundred years.

1

Any survey of the historical background of Irish immigration, however brief, must begin with three events around the turn of the eighteenth century. In July 1690 at the Battle of the Boyne the Protestant forces of William of Orange defeated the Catholic forces of James II, decisively setting the direction of Irish history for the next two hundred years. In 1704 the British Parliament passed "an Act to prevent the further growth of Popery" in Ireland – the first of the ferocious Penal Laws, aimed at the systematic destruction of religious, civil, and cultural life for Irish Catholics.[1] (The success of these laws through the course of the eighteenth century created the Protestant Ascendancy in Ireland.) And in 1717, when Scottish settlers in Ulster began to lose their leases due to poor harvests and high rents (rackrenting), the first wave of 3,000 emigrants left northern Irish ports for America, thus setting in motion the most significant pattern of Irish migration before the Great Famine of the 1840s. For the entire eighteenth century, Ulster Protestants, mostly of Scots Presbyterian background, went to America at the rate of 3,000 to 5,000 each year, with an increase to 10,000 in the years 1771-75 because of further severe rackrenting and a decline in the Belfast linen trade. [2]

Emigration from all of Ireland's provinces intensified after the serious potato famine of 1740-41, in which 200,000 people died. The emigration was largely from three of Ireland's four provinces: Ulster, Leinster, and Munster. (Very few people before the nineteenth century came from thoroughly impoverished Connacht.) The great majority of immigrants were men. In addition to those who paid their own way over, they included indentured servants, redemptioners (who came hoping to find "redeemers" to pay the balance of their fares), and convict transportees (perhaps as many as 20,000 before the American Revolution). Another impetus to this earliest immigration was agrarian violence within the landlord/tenant system. Guerrilla actions of barn-burning, beatings, and maiming of stock were carried out by peasant secret societies: the "Whiteboys" in Munster in the 1760s, and the "Oakboys" and "Hearts of Steel" in Ulster in the sixties and early seventies.

By 1790 nearly one sixth of the three million citizens of the new United States were of Irish birth or descent. The figures are approximate, but of some 447,000 Irish Americans, perhaps 280,000 were of Ulster Scots (mostly Presbyterian) background and 106,000 of native Irish (mostly Catholic)

1. See Maureen Wall, *The Penal Laws, 1691-1760* (Dundalk: Dublin Historical Association, 1967); T. W. Moody and W. E. Vaughan, eds., *A New History of Ireland, IV, Eighteenth-Century Ireland, 1691-1800* (Oxford: Clarendon Press, 1986), 16-21, 37-39, 91-97.

2. See R. J. Dickson, *Ulster Emigration to Colonial America, 1718-1775* (London: Routledge and Kegan Paul, 1966), 21-31, 52-81; David N. Doyle, *Ireland, Irishmen and Revolutionary America, 1760-1820* (Dublin and Cork: Mercier Press, 1981), 51-74; J. G. Leyburn, *The Scotch-Irish: A Social History* (Chapel Hill: University of North Carolina Press, 1962), passim.

background from the other three provinces. The remaining 61,000 were split about evenly between descendents of Irish Catholics from Ulster and of English settlers in Ulster or the South. Altogether, the Irish were easily the largest non-English immigrant group in America just after the Revolution. [3]

From 1782 until 1801, Ireland had her own Parliament, managed by an English Lord Lieutenant and Chief Secretary and populated exclusively by members of the Protestant Ascendancy. The largely Protestant Society of United Irishmen was organized in Belfast in 1791 to agitate toward democratic reforms for all of the Irish, Catholics as well as Protestants. Through the decade of the nineties this group became stronger and more radical, until, with some support from Catholic peasants and the French, the Rising of 1798 broke out. After scattered but sometimes fierce fighting, the rebellion was crushed. Trouble flared again briefly in 1803 when Robert Emmet led a last, abortive rising of United Irishmen in Dublin. The consequences of this end-of-the-century turmoil included the deaths of United Irish leaders Edward Fitzgerald, Wolfe Tone, and Emmet; the official Union of Great Britain and Ireland on January 1, 1801; and the emigration to America of a number of dynamic Irish intellectuals who later produced some of the first important Irish-American books.

The first two decades of the nineteenth century marked the rise to power of Ireland's first great modern politician, Daniel O'Connell of Derrynane, whose name and achievements were on the lips of all Ireland and Irish America right up until the Famine years. O'Connell organized the peasantry into the formidable Catholic Association, which by 1829 had pressured the English into restoring most of the freedoms lost under the Penal Laws, including the right to sit in Parliament. Subsequently, O'Connell committed himself to a campaign for repeal of the Act of Union, which reached its climax in a series of huge rallies in 1843. When O'Connell, fearing violence, canceled what was to have been the largest of these meetings at Clontarf in October, that movement ended.

The terrible watershed of the Great Hunger was preceded by several partial potato crop failures – in the years 1822, 1831, 1835-37, 1839, and 1842.

---

3. The first census of the United States (in 1790) recorded 44,000 Americans of Irish birth, but recent analyses suggest that this figure is much too low. My figures, and this historical summary, are based on the following sources: David N. Doyle, *Ireland, Irishmen and Revolutionary America*; William D. Griffin, *The Irish in America, 1550-1972, A Chronology and Fact Book* (Dobbs Ferry, N.Y.: Oceana Publications, 1973); Oliver MacDonagh, "The Irish Famine Emigration to the United States," *Perspectives in American History* 10 (1976), 357-446; Patrick J. Blessing, "Irish" entry, in *Harvard Encyclopedia of American Ethnic Groups* (Cambridge, Mass.: Harvard University Press, 1980), 524-45; Maldwyn A. Jones, "Scotch-Irish" entry, in *Harvard Encyclopedia*, 895-908.

The number of eighteenth-century Irish immigrants is still in question. In his exhaustive analysis, *Emigrants and Exiles: Ireland and the Irish Exodus to North America* (New York: Oxford University Press, 1985), Kerby A. Miller says that "at best, we can guess that perhaps 50-100,000 left Ireland in the 1600s, and 250-400,000 from 1700 to 1776" (137).

Emigration became more attractive to the small farmers with each passing year, especially as news of the canal, road, and railway building booms in America reached their ears. Thus, after 1815, with the War of 1812 ended and immigrant trade resumed, the numbers of people leaving Ireland increased dramatically over the next thirty years, even before 1845, the first Famine year. This 1815-1845 movement was much more of a Catholic and Southern Irish emigration than had previously taken place. The evidence also suggests less economic solvency and a lower literacy rate among the emigrants with each succeeding decade. The following approximation of those who went directly to the United States (certainly lower than the real numbers) demonstrates a weighty new Irish presence in America:

1815-1825:	28,600
1826-1835:	118,400
1836-1845:	289,700

Many immigrants traveled first to Canada and then south, perhaps doubling the above figures of those who ended up in the United States.

In the ever-burgeoning Irish America, a few milestones can also be noted. In 1816 in New York City, exiled Ninety-eighter Dr. William MacNeven founded an Irish Emigrant Society to help new immigrants get their footing. In 1828, Andrew Jackson, hero of New Orleans and the son of Scots Presbyterian emigrants from County Antrim, was elected president of the United States. Such hopeful signs were countered by the first violent anti-Catholic and anti-Irish responses to the increased immigration: the burning of a convent in Charlestown, Massachusetts, in 1834, and extensive rioting in Philadelphia ten years later, during which thirty people were killed and three churches destroyed.

2

There were many dramatic events in Ireland and Irish America during the thirty years of the Famine generation, 1845-1875. Of first importance, of course, is the Great Hunger of the late 1840s, the devastating effects of which can hardly be overestimated. This greatest of Irish national tragedies was the product of forces that had been building since early in the century. There was overpopulation, especially among the most vulnerable segments of the society – the cottiers (allowed a hut and a garden patch by the slightly better-off small tenant farmers), the landless agricultural laborers, and the wholly destitute beggars. There was the constant danger of necessary reliance on the potato, the single crop capable of feeding a large family on a tiny farm. And there was overall a precipitous, countrywide decline in living standards, such that a French traveler in the late 1830s found "misery, naked and famishing . . .

everywhere, and at every hour of the day."[4]

Also contributing to this perilous state of affairs were the policies and predilections of the British government in Ireland. Eighteenth-century Penal Laws discouraging primogeniture among Catholic landowners, added to the large increase in population among the tenant farmers, had forced subdivision into smaller and smaller holdings. Also, the growing desire of Protestant landlords to consolidate their lands for livestock grazing or implementation of "new farming" ideas (such as crop rotation and diversification) encouraged the eviction of tenants in arrears. There had been partial potato failures and famines every few years going back to the 1820s. The final catastrophe, therefore, was a surprise only in its duration and intensity.

The Great Hunger began with the failure of the potato crop over one third of Ireland in the autumn of 1845. A second failure, in July and August 1846, was general throughout the country and had, as Oliver MacDonagh states, "an instantaneous and unmistakable effect. For the first time in Irish history, there was a heavy autumn exodus. For the first time, thousands risked their lives on a winter crossing, ready, as one said, to undergo any misery 'save that of remaining in Ireland.'" [5] In 1847 famine and disease spread like wildfire through the country, and although it was much less blighted, that year's potato crop was still too small to stem the rising tide of hysterical flight. But 1848 brought the final stroke. At harvest-time the blight was again universal, destroying virtually the entire potato crop. This was the death blow to the Irish rural culture that had existed for centuries. From this time on, for the bulk of the Irish people, emigration was a reasonable, and often unavoidable, alternative. Contemporary observers reported that the most immediately noticeable difference in post-Famine rural Ireland was a new silence. Before 1845 there had been music at every teeming crossroads, much of it provided by beggars singing for their supper. Afterward, the land was quiet.

When the worst was over, the figures told a grim tale. An accurate count is impossible, but during the years of the actual blight, at least one million people died of starvation and related diseases and one and a quarter million fled the country. The population of Ireland had dropped from nearly 8.5 million to about 6.5 million people. As MacDonagh declares, "relatively speaking, no other population movement of the nineteenth century was on so great a scale." [6] The ten-year official figures for Irish immigration to the United

4. Gustave de Beaumont, quoted in Oliver MacDonagh, "The Irish Famine Emigration to the United States" (366). On the Great Hunger, see also Kerby A. Miller, *Emigrants and Exiles*, R. Dudley Edwards and T. Desmond Williams, eds., *The Great Famine, Studies in Irish History, 1845-52* (1956; rpt., New York: Russell & Russell, 1976); Cecil Woodham-Smith, *The Great Hunger, Ireland 1845-1849* (New York: Harper & Row, 1962); W. E. Vaughan, ed., *A New History of Ireland, V, Ireland Under the Union I: 1801-1870* (Oxford: Clarendon Press, 1989), 272-371; Cormac Ó Gráda, *The Great Irish Famine* (Cambridge: Cambridge University Press, 1995); Chris Monash and Richard Hayes, eds., *'Fearful Realities': New Perspectives on the Famine* (Dublin: Irish Academic Press, 1996).

5. MacDonagh, 407.

6. MacDonagh, 417.

States during this period are striking:

1846-1855: 1,442,000
1856-1865: 582,400
1866-1875: 645,700

The actual numbers are certainly higher. Some immigrants entered ille-
gally, and between 1846 and 1855 over 300,000 Irish people came to Canada.
Since many of these ultimately headed south, the total number of Irish immigrants to the United States in the crucial first ten years was probably more
than 1.6 million. Once established, the blood-draining habit of emigration
continued for the rest of the century and beyond, with half a million people
leaving Ireland every ten years up to World War I. The result was a continuing net decrease in the population of Ireland that was unique among
European countries and would not be reversed until the late 1960s.

There were other sad happenings in Famine-generation Ireland as well.
In May 1847 Daniel O'Connell died heartbroken, and an Irish political era
died with him. Over the next thirty years, the nationalist effort produced but
a few instances of public action, most of them ill-fated. The Young Ireland
movement of nationalist intellectuals had begun with promise in 1842 when
Thomas Davis and Charles Gavan Duffy founded *The Nation*, a journal providing respected cultural counterweight to O'Connell's practical politics.
However, the Young Ireland initiatives ended with Davis's early death at age
31 in 1845 and a hopeless, abortive 1848 rising, a pitiful echo of the tumult
elsewhere during Europe's year of rebellion.

In 1858 James Stephens in Dublin and John O'Mahony in New York
founded the Irish Republican Brotherhood and its American branch, the
Fenian Brotherhood, named for the Fianna, warrior-heroes of Irish legend.
Both groups were committed to freeing Ireland by force of arms. Thousands
of Irish immigrants formed the financial backbone and a large portion of the
membership of these organizations. Thus, one ironic result of the mass emigration from Ireland was a significant strengthening of the nationalist movement. From this point on, support from the "Great Ireland" of America was
a formidable force to be reckoned with. As Thomas N. Brown has pointed
out, the Irish nationalist movement in America "had its origins in [the] loneliness, poverty, and prejudice" of the immigrant experience. The Fenian
Brotherhood and its successor organizations gave the Irish in America something ostensibly noble and self-affirming to belong to. The American Civil
War provided training for a number of Fenian "circles," which operated openly in the Union Army. In June 1866 a few of these military units crossed the
border in a symbolic invasion of Canada, but their aim of dramatizing the
plight of captive Ireland was dissipated in the wild improbability of the venture. No less a failure was the weak, disorganized rising by the Irish

Republican Brotherhood in Ireland in March of the following year, 1867. [7]

After these debacles, the pendulum swung again to the supporters of parliamentary, or "moral," force. Their efforts were encouraged by the sympathetic leadership of British Prime Minister Gladstone, who had begun pushing for alleviation of Irish injustices in the late 1860s. Gladstone won significant victories in Parliament with the passage of acts disestablishing the Church of Ireland in 1869 and effecting Irish agrarian reform in 1870. In 1875, the Irish parliamentary party was joined by the man who was to resurrect Irish nationalism and dominate the Irish imagination for the remainder of the century – Charles Stewart Parnell.

Those who left Ireland for America in the hard years between 1846 and 1875 numbered at least 2,700,000, nearly half of them women. To the pains of leaving home were added the perils of the voyage by sea and the problems of settlement in the New World. For a total cost of five to seven pounds, an Irishman could get to America, usually by way of Liverpool, the nearest mainline port of the transatlantic trade. Living conditions in Liverpool lodging houses and then in the "coffin ships" themselves were often nearly intolerable; the ships were unconscionably overcrowded, filthy, and disease-ridden, with no proper provisions for good water, cooking, sanitation, or privacy. Many people died in these crossings and many more were scarred in various ways. In one year, the fabled "black '47," 20 percent of the Irish emigrants, over 42,000 people, died on the journey or shortly after landing.

But getting to America was only the beginning of the immigrants' troubles. In the first decade alone, 1846-1855, the Irish added a hardly ignorable 7 to 8 percent to the population of the United States. (By 1855, 34 percent of all voters in New York City were Irish-born.) These new arrivals met in the "sweet land of liberty" of their dreams a pronounced resentment and hostility. John V. Kelleher explains the polarized situation in Boston in these stark terms:

> On the one side, the Irish, fleeing from a homeland where they had been racked, robbed, and demoralized by an imposed aristocracy of Protestant, Puritan, Anglo-Saxon derivation. On the other, a Protestant, Puritan, Anglo-Saxon people who had, when the Irish arrived, just about completed a city and a society made in their own best image. More thoroughly than ever before in history the sins of the fathers were visited on the second cousins once-removed. The mutual despair and hatred reechoed from the welkin. [8]

7. Thomas N. Brown, "The Origins and Character of Irish-American Nationalism," *Review of Politics* 18 (July 1956), 327-58, and *Irish-American Nationalism, 1870-1890* (Philadelphia: Lippincott, 1966), passim. A moving account of the human dimension of the 1867 rising is in Thomas Flanagan's novel, *The Tenants of Time* (New York: Dutton, 1988).

8. John V. Kelleher, "A Long Way from Tipperary," The Reporter 22 (May 12, 1960), 46.

To be sure, immigrants who were able to travel farther than the East coast – to Chicago and the Midwest or around the horn to San Francisco – were somewhat better received. Nor was all of America insensitive to the catastrophe of the Famine. Owen Dudley Edwards points out that Americans in these years exhibited a sort of double standard. There was, in fact, a great outpouring of money to Famine relief organizations, but there was little transfer of concern to the situation of the new immigrants: "The wealthy philanthropist gladly spent hundreds of dollars on Irish relief while reluctant, in many cases, to toss a cent to an Irish-American beggar in his own street, since, if encouraged, the wretch might continue to pollute the street." [9]

As MacDonagh summarizes: "Behind the militant nativism of the few there stood a widespread distrust of 'Romanism,' a persistent fear that cheap Irish labor would drag down the general level of wages, and plain racial prejudice. A little later, two new sources of alarm appeared – Irish nationalism and the Irish political machine." [10] There was probably more rioting in America in the 1850s than in any other decade until the 1960s. The political culmination of this turbulence was the Know-Nothing movement of 1854-55, when nativists swept to victory in a number of state and local elections. Immigrants also had to reckon with the opposition of fellow Irishmen who had reached America first – the better educated, more often Protestant, pre-Famine immigrants and their children. While some of these now established and successful people helped their compatriots by publishing newspapers and guidebooks and by becoming active in immigrant-aid societies, many others turned away from their less fortunate countrymen and tried to create distance, often by resurrecting the spurious distinction of "Scotch-Irishness."

The so-called Scotch-Irish were prominent in anti-Catholic activities in America throughout the Famine generation and beyond. Much urban violence during these years pitted Irish Protestants against Irish Catholics. For example, there were terrible riots in New York City in 1870 and 1871 on the occasion of the July 12 Orange parade celebrating King William's victory at the Battle of the Boyne. [11] The Orange Order itself also spread quickly in the United States after the founding of the first American lodge in 1867, and Orangemen were influential in the American Protestant Association and its determinedly anti-Catholic successor, the American Protective Association.

Contributing to their difficulties, and to the ill-feeling against them, was the position of the Famine immigrants at the bottom of their adopted society. As MacDonagh states, "for a generation [they] constituted much of the urban proletariat of the United States, with all the sad corollaries of that condition," including poor living conditions, pauperism, alcoholism, high mortality rates,

9. Owen Dudley Edwards, "The American Image of Ireland: A Study of Its Early Phases," Perspectives in American History 4 (1970), 274.

10. MacDonagh, 433-34.

11. See Michael A. Gordon, The Orange Riots: Irish Political Violence in New York City, 1870 and 1871 (Ithaca: Cornell University Press, 1993).

and victimization as an unprotected, exploited labor force. [12] Because they arrived without skills, most immigrant men had to settle for what they could get – pick-and-shovel work on the railroads and canals or temporary jobs as urban day laborers. As for the women, 75 percent became domestic servants and the rest went into the mills and factories. Furthermore, most of these immigrants were stuck in their unskilled jobs. Occupational mobility upward became possible only for their children.

Lawrence J. McCaffrey points out that the life in urban "ghettoes," which the Irish pioneered in the American experience, was not entirely negative. While "it did nurture Irish failure much more than it encouraged Irish ambition by cultivating the paranoia, defeatism, and feelings of inferiority planted by the past," the ghetto neighborhood also "served as [a] psychological haven, preserving traditions and values and perpetuating a sense of community" among the threatened and oppressed immigrants. Moreover, "the ghettoes also functioned as halfway houses between two cultures," a service performed as well by the Catholic parish churches. And, of course, in neighborhood solidarity was the seed of the political power that the Irish were to seize in the last quarter of the century. [13]

The American Civil War was crucial in smoothing the immigrants' way, although its nurturing of Fenianism was far from helpful to the acceptance of the Irish by native Americans. Nearly 150,000 Irish-born soldiers and many sons of immigrants fought in the Union Army, and the exclusively Irish regiments from New York, Massachusetts, Illinois, Michigan, Ohio, Indiana, and Iowa did much to convince skeptics that the Irish respected and belonged in America. Famous Union generals of Irish background included Philip Sheridan, Michael Corcoran, Philip Kearny, John A. Logan, and exiled Forty-eighter Thomas F. Meagher. Similarly, the Confederate Army had an impressively large number of Irish soldiers who mustered into such recognizably ethnic units as the Emmet Guards of Virginia and the Emerald Guards of Alabama.

Unfortunately, some of the good will engendered by Irish participation in the war effort was dissipated by the terrible draft riots in New York City in July 1863. Directly incited by the institution of an unfair conscription act which allowed anyone with $300 to buy his way out of the army, mostly Irish working-class mobs roamed the city for three days, burning, looting, and attacking bystanders. Along with the economic discrimination represented by the $300 release (which few Irish could afford), the rioters were angered by

12. MacDonagh, 435.

13. Lawrence J. McCaffrey, *The Irish Diaspora in America* (1976; rpt., Washington: Catholic University of America Press, 1984), 66. McCaffrey's book is the most useful survey of the Irish-American experience. For the situation of women, see Hasia R. Diner, *Erin's Daughters in America: Irish Immigrant Women in the Nineteenth Century* (Baltimore: Johns Hopkins University Press, 1983), and Janet A. Nolan, *Ourselves Alone: Female Emigration from Ireland, 1885-1920* (Lexington: University Press of Kentucky, 1989).

disproportionately large draft quotas in Irish wards, and frightened by the threat to their jobs represented by the emancipation of African Americans. Among the enormities perpetrated were the destruction of a Negro orphanage and the hanging of several black people in the streets. The upshot was a new surge of anti-Irish feeling in New York. [14]

3

The rise and fall of Charles Stewart Parnell dominated the history of Ireland in the last quarter of the nineteenth century. Following his election as president of the Home Rule Confederation of Great Britain in 1877, Parnell played a leading role in the orchestration of events that seemed to be pushing Ireland toward a measure of self-government. These included the formation in 1879 by Michael Davitt of the Irish National Land League, which organized peasant resistance against rackrenting and evictions during the "Land War" of the early eighties. This campaign featured ostracism of abusive land agents, including a certain Captain Boycott from County Mayo, whose name came into the language to describe the technique. Parnell also cooperated with British Prime Minister Gladstone's unsuccessful attempt to get an Irish Home Rule bill through the House of Commons in 1886.

Parnell rode out the storm of criticism generated by the several manifestations of Irish nationalist violence during these same years. Debate raged in the 1870s and 1880s between those who followed Parnell in supporting parliamentary agitation, or "moral force," and the advocates of violent revolution, which included the leadership of the Irish Republican Brotherhood and its American counterpart, the Clan na Gael. In May of 1882 a band of "physical force" men murdered two of the highest ranking British officials in Ireland in Dublin's Phoenix Park. Then, in March 1883, the "Dynamite Campaign" began with explosions at Britain's Local Government Board in Whitehall and at the offices of the *London Times.* Largely financed with American money from a secret "Skirmishing Fund," this terrorist campaign went on for several years. In one 1884 foray, Cincinnati Irish American William Lomasney was killed while setting a charge at the base of London Bridge. The climax was the simultaneous bombing of Parliament and the Tower of London in January 1885. Miraculously, there were no serious injuries, but anti-Irish sentiment in England rose to a fever pitch. Although Parnell was accused of complicity in the Phoenix Park murders on the basis of incriminating letters supposedly in his hand, they were found to be forgeries. Thus vindicated, Parnell emerged as the "uncrowned king of Ireland," and Home Rule seemed near at hand. However, within two years, all was

---

14. See Iver Bernstein, *The New York City Draft Riots* (New York: Oxford University Press, 1990), and the vivid description of the riots in Peter Quinn's novel, *Banished Children of Eve* (New York: Viking Press, 1994).

changed, changed utterly.

In December 1889, Captain William O'Shea filed suit for divorce in London, naming as co-respondents his wife Catherine and Charles Stewart Parnell. A year later the divorce was granted – uncontested. The ensuing scandal resulted in Parnell's being voted out as leader of the Irish parliamentary party. He then experienced the wrath of the Irish Catholic bishops, who roundly condemned his adultery from their pulpits. Parnell had not been well for several years. He went on to campaign strenuously and unsuccessfully in three by-elections, and he died on October 6, 1891, at the age of 45. The animosities generated by the Parnell affair destroyed for a generation any hope of a solid front in the Home Rule agitation. [15]

This low point in Irish political life was followed by a significant cultural renaissance in Ireland. (William Butler Yeats, who began publishing poems and essays in the mid-1880s, argued that the fall of Parnell forced Irish intellectuals to divert their nationalistic energies from practical politics to the arts.) A major event in the new cultural nationalism was the founding of the Gaelic League in 1893 by Douglas Hyde, who counseled wholesale "refusal to imitate the English in their language, literature, music, games, dress, and ideas." The great works of the Irish literary revival followed apace: Yeats's poems, plays, and essays, the prose and plays of John M. Synge, the plays and collections of folklore and mythology of Lady Augusta Gregory, the fiction of Seumas O'Kelly, George Moore, and James Joyce. [16]

Meanwhile, 1903 marked a quiet revolution with the passage in the British Parliament of the Wyndham Land Purchase Act, which brought about a dramatic acceleration of the transfer of land ownership from landlords to tenants by encouraging landlords to sell entire estates and providing long-term loans to purchasing tenants. A piece of innovative legislation, the Wyndham Act did not, however, accomplish its chief purpose of staving off nationalist agitation for yet another generation. With the founding of the Sinn Fein party in 1908, the next, and partially successful, movement toward the political separation of Ireland from England was under way. The culmination was the Easter Rising of 1916, the Irish Revolution of 1918-21, and the establishment of the Irish Free State in 1922.

These were also eventful years in Irish America. It has sometimes been overlooked that the habit of emigration continued long after the Famine generation. Between 1845 and 1870 about 2.5 million Irish people had come to America. But between 1871 and 1921, 2.1 million more joined them. To complete the ten-year, mid-decade population summaries through the onset of

15. See F. S. L. Lyons, *Ireland Since the Famine* (New York: Scribners, 1971), 160-202; and F. S. L. Lyons, *Charles Stewart Parnell* (New York: Oxford University Press, 1977), passim.

16. F. S. L. Lyons, *Ireland Since the Famine*, 223-25. See also Philip L. Marcus, *Yeats and the Beginning of the Irish Renaissance*, Second Edition (Syracuse: Syracuse University Press, 1987), Herbert Howarth, *The Irish Writers: 1880-1940* (New York: Hill and Wang,1958), Richard Fallis, *The Irish Renaissance* (Syracuse: Syracuse University Press, 1977).

World War I, the numbers are as follows:

1876-1885: 490,400
1886-1895: 541,400
1896-1905: 394,300
1906-1915: 346,600

Augmenting the continued influx of immigrants was a network of cross-cultural connections forged by a new phenomenon – the American fund-raising tour. In 1878 Michael Davitt came to the United States to enlist support for his Irish National Land League. Two years later, Parnell himself came over seeking American aid for the Land League and famine relief. He spoke in sixty-two cities, addressed a joint session of Congress, and helped raise $300,000. [17] Not to be outdone by the politicians, the leaders of the Irish cultural revival also came to spread the light of their new movement in America. In 1903 William Butler Yeats made the first of his four American tours, lecturing from New York to San Francisco and back on the state of Irish letters, and in 1905 Douglas Hyde came seeking support for the activities of the Gaelic League.

Thus nourished by sustained immigration, Irish America continued to grow. However, the culture was changing rapidly. While most of the immigrants continued to live out their lives as working-class laborers, their children were beginning to move toward middle-class status and a measure of respectability. By the turn of the century there was a considerable white-collar and skilled-labor Irish-American population. By 1900, outside Yankee-dominated New England, the percentages for Irish-American males were roughly equal to those among native white Americans: 35 percent white-collar or farming and 50 percent skilled labor. [18]

With memorable clarity, John Kelleher has traced the emergence of an Irish-American middle class to the evening of September 7, 1892, when "Gentleman Jim" Corbett defeated John L. Sullivan, "the Boston Strong Boy," for the world heavyweight boxing championship. Kelleher sees both men as archetypes. Sullivan, boisterous, hard-drinking, and having dominated the sport by sheer brawn, "was still the meaningful symbol of what the Irish here

---

17. Thomas N. Brown, *Irish-American Nationalism*, 103.

18. Kerby A. Miller, "Assimilation and Alienation: Irish Emigrants' Responses to Industrial America, 1871-1891," in P. J. Drudy, ed., *The Irish in America: Emigration, Assimilation and Impact, Irish Studies* 4 (Cambridge: Cambridge University Press, 1985), 89. See also the fuller treatment of the period in Kerby A. Miller, *Emigrants and Exiles*. For a comparison of the American Irish with those who went to England and Australia see David Fitzpatrick, "Irish Emigration in the Later Nineteenth Century," *Irish Historical Studies* 22, no. 86 (Sept. 1980), 126-43; and Fitzpatrick, *Oceans of Consolation: Personal Accounts of Irish Migration to Australia* (Ithaca: Cornell University Press, 1995). See also Patrick O'Farrell, *The Irish in Australia* (Kensington: University of New South Wales Press, 1987) and O'Farrell, *Vanished Kingdoms: Irish in Australia and New Zealand* (Kensington: University of New South Wales Press, 1990).

had perforce to be proud of: native strength, the physical endurance that made possible the 'Irish contribution to America' that orators and writers have since sentimentalized so much." (Kelleher goes on to point out that "what they really mean is that from the 1840s on, floods of Irish immigrants gave the country what it had not had before, a huge fund of poor, unskilled, cheap, almost infinitely exploitable labor, and that this labor force was expended, with a callousness now hard to comprehend, in building the railroads and dams and mills, in digging the canals, in any crude, backbreaking job.") As for Corbett, he was "equally representative. . . . a prophetic figure: slim, deft, witty, looking like a proto-Ivy Leaguer with his pompadour, his fresh intelligent face, his well-cut young man's clothes. He was, as it were, the paradigm of all those young Irish-Americans about to make the grade." [19] Of course, this transformation had been in process for years. The inevitable separation of immigrant parents and their American children, wrought by changes in environment, education, opportunity, and aspiration, had begun as soon as the Famine Irish began to marry and raise families in the New World.

Throughout the last quarter of the century, Irish-American breakthrough accomplishments proliferated. In 1879 Terence Powderly, the son of Irish immigrants, was elected head of America's first national union, the Knights of Labor, with 800,000 members. Irish America provided numbers of outstanding journalists to the nation's press corps, and in 1884 Antrim native Samuel S. McClure established the first newspaper syndicate in the United States. In 1886 Dubliner Victor Herbert came to New York to begin a career as the most popular light-operatic composer of his day. Louis Sullivan's commission to design the Transportation Building at the 1893 World's Columbian Exposition in Chicago marked a milestone in his brilliant, innovative architectural career. In 1875 John McCloskey of New York, the son of Irish immigrants, became the first cardinal appointed to the Catholic Church in the United States. By the end of the century, half of America's Catholic bishops were of Irish background, and the Church was thoroughly dominated by Irish Americans. The leaders of the conservative wing were Archbishop Corrigan of New York and Bishop McQuaid of Rochester, and the liberal leaders were Archbishop Ireland of St. Paul and James Cardinal Gibbons of Baltimore. [20]

Another much-remarked phenomenon of this period was the coming to political power of the Irish in American cities. The 1890 census-takers counted an all-time high of 1,872,000 Americans of Irish birth, and the combination of numbers, linguistic and organizational talents, and a cohesive ghetto community made for success in urban politics. A most conspicuous creation was the urban machine, a tightly woven net of single-minded people, from the

19. John V. Kelleher, "Irishness in America,"*Atlantic* 208 (July 1961), 38-40.
20. Griffin, *The Irish in America*, 19-22. Blessing, "Irish" entry, 534. William V. Shannon, *The American Irish: A Political and Social Portrait* (New York: Macmillan, 1966), 114-30.

boss at the top to the precinct captain at the bottom, through which few votes were allowed to slip. One watershed here was the election of Hugh O'Brien in 1885 as the first Irish-born mayor of Boston. Also notable was the Irish dynastic rule in New York's Tammany Hall, stretching from "Honest John" Kelly's takeover after the fall of Boss Tweed in 1871 through the reigns of Richard Croker and Charles F. Murphy. In 1880 shipping magnate William R. Grace became New York City's first Irish Catholic mayor as well. In the same years, the wide-open city of Chicago was being run by an Irish-domi-nated council of aldermen, including "Johnny de Pow" Powers, "Hinky Dink" Kenna, and "Bath-house John" Coughlin. Writing in 1894 of "The Irish Conquest of Our Cities," an alarmed political analyst declared that "among the cities led captive by Irishmen and their sons, are New York, Brooklyn, Jersey City, Hoboken, Boston, Chicago, Buffalo, Albany, Troy, Pittsburgh, St. Paul, St. Louis, Kansas City, Omaha, New Orleans, and San Francisco." [21]

The dismay of native white Americans at this Irish sweep to urban power contributed to a new surge of nativism in the United States in the late 1880s and the 1890s. In addition, there was a renewal of anti-Catholic feeling, in response to the perceived dramatic growth and influence of the American Catholic Church. Also disturbing to the W.A.S.P. hegemony was the flood of so-called "new immigrants" from Southern and Eastern Europe, among them Polish and Russian Jews escaping pogroms and Italian peasants fleeing agrar-ian and political unrest. An organizing force in the new nativism was the American Protective Association, a Protestant group fond of disseminating "Popish plot" propaganda. Founded in Iowa in 1887, the A.P.A. soon spread throughout the United States. Its peak membership time was during the national depression of 1893, after which it faded quickly. Next came the hey-day of "Anglo-Saxon supremacy," a pseudo-scientific nativist ideology aimed directly at the "new immigrants." Its political arm was the Immigration Restriction League, founded in Boston in 1894. Thus began the movement that culminated in the 1920s when permanent immigration-restriction legis-lation slammed shut the Golden Door.

4

A useful way to introduce the three nineteenth-century Irish-American literary generations in this anthology is to consider the intended audience for the writers in each generation. The pre-Famine Irish-American community contained a large number of educated professionals, and its writers produced a significant amount of fiction in which satire and parody dominate. The tar-

21. John Paul Bocock, "The Irish Conquest of Our Cities," *The Forum 17* (April 1894), 187. See also Shannon, *The American Irish*, 68-85; James B. Walsh, ed., *The Irish: America's Political Class* (New York: Arno Press, 1976); and Steven Erie, *Rainbow's End: Irish Americans and the Dilemmas of Urban Machine Politics, 1840-1985* (Berkeley: University of California Press, 1988).

gets of this cluster of humorous writings included various kinds of literary propaganda: political campaign biographies, anti-Catholic "convent revelations,"
anti-Irish character stereotyping on the stage and in print, and the moralizing
plots of popular sentimental fiction. The audience for such works was conceived not as exclusively Irish-American, but as a wider and well-read public, appreciative of sophisticated literary effects. If the reader were Irish, it was
assumed that he was sure enough of his identity and position to be able to
laugh at himself; if a member of the host American culture, it was assumed
that he could laugh at his own stereotyping and misconceptions of the Irish.

With the coming of the Great Hunger, all such laughter stopped. Nothing
could be further from the playful sophistication of the pre-Famine satirists
than the grimly serious and didactic fiction produced by Irish Americans of
the Famine generation. The reversal is even more dramatic because the writers who emerged after the Famine of the late 1840s were not a second generation, not the children of immigrants, but a new first generation. The great
majority of these new Irish-American novelists were themselves immigrants
who had come to the United States as adults in the 1840s. The salient weakness of their generation's fiction was the constriction of the assumed audience.
As Famine immigrants themselves, these new writers wrote only for their own
kind, the traumatized refugees with whom their own experiences allowed
them to identify. Perceiving that audience to be desperately in need of guid-
ance, the writers produced conservative, practical novels, unambiguously
didactic and dedicated to helping troubled people stay Catholic and survive
in the New World. So it was that in a matter of a few years the fictional norm
was overturned: from satiric critique of propaganda to propaganda itself,
from parody of fictional conventions that have been manipulated for extra-lit-
erary purposes to the humorless embrace of those same conventions – sentimental rhetoric, stereotyped characters, simplistic conflicts, and moralizing
themes.

Echoing the wider American literary scene after 1875, the new, third generation of Irish-American writers joined the aesthetic debate between genteel
romantic fiction and the "new realism." The result was a recurrence of both
earlier conceptions of the intended audience for Irish-American literature.
The weaker writers, the genteel romancers, created a second wave of didactic propaganda fiction, aimed exclusively at the developing Irish-American
middle class. In place of the Famine generation's manuals for survival in
America, these writers attempted to provide practical instruction for the new
bourgeoisie in the importance of being earnestly respectable. Doubling as
guides to etiquette, their novels featured descriptions of drawing-room con-
versations, dinner parties complete with course-by-course menus, courtships,
and weddings à la mode. On the other hand, the stronger writers, the realists,
wrote for a wider audience of literate Americans, a readership for whom, it
was assumed, clear perspectives on an ethnic culture would be enough

reward. These pioneers made concerted efforts to count the costs and assess the damages of the previous generation's experience. And they did so from an impressive range of settings and perspectives, from New York to Chicago to San Francisco, from urban ghettoes to prairie farms.

These promising beginnings, did not, however, bear immediate fruit. In the literary generation that came of age just after 1900, no Irish-American writer built a career of consistent accomplishment based on the example of the proto-realists of the 1890s. There had been in the nineteenth century dozens of writers and hundreds of books that explored Irish immigration and ethnicity. There certainly still continued to be an Irish-American ethnic life through the first three decades of the new century. And yet, writers emerging from that background did not use ethnic self-consciousness to build careers as realistic novelists. What happened was a form of cultural amnesia.

A partial explanation lies in concrete historical events. With the approach of World War I, European ethnic identifications (other than ties to England) became positively unsavory in the eyes of many Americans. Some Irish-American organizations were rightly perceived as sympathetic to the Central Powers. (The Clan na Gael executive actually sent a secret message of support to the Kaiser.) Moreover, in the context of increasing support for United States entry into the War, the Easter Rising in Dublin in April 1916 was less than popular in mainstream America. This unsuccessful but symbolically powerful opening to the Irish Revolution ended with 3,000 casualties and the British execution of the sixteen leaders of the rising as traitors in time of war. Also, in 1914 President Woodrow Wilson made his famous "hyphenated Americans" speech at the unveiling of a monument to Commodore John Barry, whom Wilson praised as "an Irishman [whose] heart crossed the Atlantic with him," unlike "some Americans" who "need hyphens in their names, because only part of them has come over." [22] Wilson and Theodore Roosevelt became the leading spokesmen in the hue and cry over "divided loyalties" which intensified with United States entry into the War in April 1917. This public rhetoric, America's alliance with England, and the negative perception of Irish nationalism after the Easter Rising all contributed to an emphatic dampening of the fires of Irish-American ethnic self-assertion during these years.[23]

Finally, two further blows to Irish ethnicity, literary and otherwise, were the bitter conclusion of the Irish Revolution and the passage of the immigration restriction laws. First, the treaty signed in December 1921 to end the Revolution created the problematic partition of Northern Ireland and the Irish Free State, which, in turn, led to the heartbreaking "Troubles" of civil war for two more years. This prolonged strife worked to destroy the power-

---

22. Ray S. Baker and William E. Dodd, eds., *The Public Papers of Woodrow Wilson, vol. 2, The New Democracy* (New York and London: Harper & Brothers, 1926), 109.

23. See John Higham, *Strangers in the Land, Patterns of American Nativism, 1860-1925*, Second Edition (New Brunswick: Rutgers University Press, 1988), 194-233.

ful nationalist component of Irish-American self-consciousness. The war in the old country was close enough to being over to satisfy the grandchildren, and even many of the children, of the nineteenth-century immigrants. And to many, the Troubles were an extremely painful coda, much better left unexplored. Second, the agitation for immigration restriction eventually brought about severely limited quotas which affected Ireland along with the rest of Europe. A provisional measure passed by Congress in May 1921 was succeeded by the Johnson-Reed Act of 1924, which established small and decreasing quotas for admission to the United States. With new blood from Ireland severely curtailed, Irish America was transformed from an immigrant to an ethnic culture.

It was not until 1932 that the heritage of nineteenth-century Irish-American literary self-scrutiny came alive again. In that year, with the publication of *Young Lonigan: A Boyhood in Chicago Streets*, began the extraordinary career of the novelist who would give the fullest literary form to the experience of the American Irish – James T. Farrell. [24] This prolific realist's fifty years of fierce dedication to his trade would surely have been appreciated by the nameless or neglected writers in this anthology, his legitimate ancestors.

*   *   *

Along with an overall revision of introductions and notes, this second edition contains three additions to the text: in Part I, an excerpt from Thomas C. Mack's brilliant satirical novel, *The Priest's Turf-Cutting Day* (1841), in Part III, the climactic scene from John Talbot Smith's 1899 novel, *The Art of Disappearing*, and also in Part III, a greatly expanded selection of Finley Peter Dunne's "Mr. Dooley" columns.

---

24. James T. Farrell (1904-1979) created an unparalleled fictional chronicle of the works and days of Irish Americans, from nineteenth-century immigrant teamsters to twentieth-century intellectuals and artists. Irish-American characters and concerns run through his corpus of over sixty works of fiction. A collection of his short stories is Charles Fanning, ed., *Chicago Stories of James T. Farrell* (Urbana: University of Illinois Press, 1997). See also his first two fictional cycles, *Studs Lonigan: A Trilogy* (1935; Urbana: University of Illinois Press, 1993) and the O'Neill-O'Flaherty pentalogy: *A World I Never Made* (1936), *No Star is Lost* (1938), *Father and Son* (1940), *My Days of Anger* (1943), and *The Face of Time* (1953), all published in New York by the Vanguard Press. Farrell's earlier writings about Irish history and culture have been collected in Dennis Flynn, ed., *On Irish Themes* (Philadelphia: University of Pennsylvania Press, 1982).

For contextual placement and analysis of all the fiction collected in *The Exiles of Erin*, see Charles Fanning, *The Irish Voice in America : Irish-American Fiction from the 1760s to the 1990s*, Second Edition, enlarged (Lexington: University Press of Kentucky, 1997).

PART I

Before the Famine:
Satiric Voices

An Irish-American voice first sounds clearly in a broadside hawked on the streets of New York in 1769: "The Irishmen's Petition, To the Honourable Commissioners of Excise, &c."

> The humble petition of Patrick O'Conner, Blany O'Bryan, and Carney Macguire, to be appointed Inspectors and Over-lookers for the port of – And whereas we your aforesaid petitioners will both by night and by day, and all night, and all day, and we will come and go, and walk, and ride, and take, and bring, and send, and fetch, and carry, and see all, and more than all, and every thing, and nothing at all, such goods, and commodities as may be, and cannot be liable to pay duty; and whereas we your aforesaid petitioners will at all times and at every time, and no time and times, we will be present and be absent, and be backward and forward, and behind, and before, and no where, and everywhere, and here, and there, and no where at all; and whereas your aforesaid petitioners will come and inform, and give information and notice duly and truly to the matter, as we know, and do not know, and by the knowledge of every one and no one; and we will not rob or cheat the king any more than is now lawfully practised; and whereas we your petitioners are gentlemen, and value him, and we will fight for him, and run for him, and from him, to serve him or any of his acquaintances, as far, and much farther than lies in our power, dead or alive, as long as we live. Witness our several and separate hands, one and all three of us both together. [1]

The piece is signed with four names, but it had a single author, Irish immigrant Lawrence Sweeney, who was a noted character in New York City

---

1. "The Irishmen's Petition, To the Honourable Commissioners of Excise, &c." New York, 1769 (Evans 11485, American Antiquarian Society). See Michael J. O'Brien, *In Old New York: The Irish Dead in Trinity and St. Paul's Churchyards* (New York: American Irish Historical Society, 1928), 64.

journalism, known as "The Penny Post Boy" because he charged a penny for delivering mail, and as "Bloody Sweeney" for his habit of calling out gory headlines of the fighting during the French and Indian Wars. He also stirred up trouble by secretly distributing the seditious newspaper *The Constitutional Courant* during the Stamp Act agitation of 1765. Sweeney's broadside is a parody of bureaucratic jargon which satirizes the toadying of Tory office-seekers and sets the tone for Irish-American literature before the Famine. Another early contributor to this largely humorous vein was immigrant publisher Mathew Carey, who wrote hilarious satiric pamphlets, including *The Plagi-Scurriliad: A Hudibrastic Poem* (1786), an attack against a fellow Philadelphia publisher, and *The Porcupiniad* (1799), in which he accuses essayist William Cobbett (who wrote as "Peter Porcupine") of generating anti-Irish propaganda under orders from the British government. [2]

Thanks to an eighteenth-century Irish immigration of over 400,000, an Irish presence in American publishing was firmly established by the turn of the nineteenth century. Books of Irish history, folklore, antiquarianism, and popular verse were generally available, and much of the early material was reprinted from Irish or British sources. There were immediate American editions of two standard histories from Protestant Ascendancy perspectives, Thomas Leland's *History of Ireland* (1774) and Francis Plowden's *Historical Review of the State of Ireland* (1805-06). Shortly after the 1798 rising, revisionist, anti-British histories of Ireland, often penned by fugitive rebels, began to appear. A famous early example was *Pieces of Irish History*, a detailed apologia for their cause published in 1807 by exiled United Irishmen William James MacNeven and Thomas Addis Emmet. [3]

The early folktales and myths tended to exemplify what has persisted as the most marketable manifestation of Ireland in the American book trade: supposedly picturesque swatches of local color and legendry, replete with turf-fires, fairs, and fairies. All manner of Celtic flotsam and jetsam surfaced in the American periodical press in the later eighteenth century, and original

2. Mathew Carey, *The Plagi-Scurriliad: A Hudibrastic Poem.* Dedicated to Col. Eleazer Oswald (Philadelphia: Printed and sold by the author, 16 January 1786); *The Porcupiniad: A Hudibrastic Poem in Four Cantos.* Addressed to Mr. William Cobbett (Philadelphia: Printed and sold by the author, 2 March 1799 and 15 April 1799). Born in Dublin in 1760 and trained there as a printer, Mathew Carey came to Philadelphia in 1784 and became one of the most successful publishers and booksellers of his time, with Dickens, Scott, Irving, and Cooper on his list, as well as the *Douay Bible* and *Moore's Irish Melodies.* See Thomas N. Brown, "The Irish Layman" in *A History of Irish Catholicism: The United States of America* (Dublin: Gill and MacMillan, 1970), 57-59.

3. Thomas Leland, *The History of Ireland from the Invasion of Henry II*, 4 vols. (Philadelphia and New York: H. Gaine, R. Bell, and J. Dunlap, 1774). Francis P. Plowden, *An Historical Review of the State of Ireland*, 5 vols. (Philadelphia: William F. McLaughlin, 1805-06). William James MacNeven and Thomas Addis Emmet, *Pieces of Irish History, Illustrative of the Condition of the Catholics of Ireland, or the Origin and Progress of the Political System of the United Irishmen; and of their Other Transactions with the Anglo-Irish Government* (New York: Bernard Bornin, 1807).

4. Among the early anthologies are *Beauties of the Shamrock, Containing Biography, Eloquence, Essays, And Poetry* (Philadelphia: Bartholomew Graves, for William D. Conway, 1812), and *Tales of the Emerald Isle; or, Legends of Ireland*, by A Lady of Boston (New York: W. Borradaile, November 1828).

anthologies soon followed. [4] The earliest Irish-American piece may be an eight-page pamphlet, one of a number of millennial prophecies of Ireland's deliverance from her sufferings: *Old Irelands Misery at an End; or, The English Empire in the Brazils Restored* (Boston: sold at the Heart and Crown, 1752).

Poems, Irish and Irish-American, appeared in virtually every newspaper and periodical with Irish or Catholic leanings throughout the nineteenth century and into the twentieth. The stock-in-trade of such verse was the immigrant's lament for an idealized homeland and the patriot's impassioned plea for Irish freedom from British oppression. Such materials make good songs, but bad poems – poems that hover between sentimentality and bathos and exhibit in unseemly nakedness strains of pure nostalgia and righteous indignation. [5]

A similar static element informs the renderings of Irish-American experience and character in the nineteenth-century American theater. The bibulous, blarneying, and belligerent "stage Irishman" is a familiar figure, early and late. He appears as the braggart soldier in plays of the Revolutionary War, the song-and-dance man popularized by Tyrone Power in the 1830s and John Brougham in the 1840s, the intrepid, brawling volunteer firefighter, "Mose, the Bowery B'hoy," in the 1850s, and some of the Sixth-Ward New Yorkers of Edward Harrigan's Mulligan plays in the 1870s and 1880s. Irish-American drama did evolve after the Civil War to include more realistic treatments of ethnic life in plays by Harrigan, Augustin Daly, and others. The stage Irish caricature persisted through the century, however, especially on the popular stage of vaudeville and minstrelsy. Not until the late, "Irish" plays of Eugene O'Neill, notably *A Moon for the Misbegotten* and *Long Day's Journey into Night*, was the stage-Irish mold truly broken. [6]

Still and all, these two extreme, opposing portraits from poetry and theater – the melancholy figure of the suffering exile and the comic figure of the stage Irishman – have been an undeniable part of Irish-American identity from the earliest to the most recent migrations. Both portraits – "Those masterful images because complete" (Yeats's phrase) – have cast their exaggerated shadows over all the fiction collected in this book. And yet, the insistent demand on the novelist, especially the nineteenth-century practitioner, to convey a realistic world makes even the least accomplished examples of this fiction worth examining for clarification of what it has felt like to be Irish in

5. A representative nineteenth-century collection of Irish and Irish-American poetry, with a clarifying introduction by one of its best practitioners, is *The Poetry and Song of Ireland*, with *Biographical Sketches of Her Poets*, compiled and edited by John Boyle O'Reilly (New York: Gay Brothers & Co., 1887).

6. Edward Harrigan's cycle of eight plays about the Mulligan family and their neighbors on New York's lower East Side, from *The Mulligan Guard Ball* (1879) to *Dan's Tribulations* (1884), is a rich source of information about urban, ethnic working-class life. The definitive source of bibliographic information about nineteenth-century Irish-American and other ethnic drama is Joyce Flynn, "Melting Plots: Patterns of Racial and Ethnic Amalgamation in American Drama Before Eugene O'Neill," *American Quarterly* 38: 3 (1986), 417-38.

America, all along the way.

From the earliest days Irish literature was readily available in the United States, often appearing immediately after initial publication in Dublin or London. Maria Edgeworth's *Castle Rackrent* (1800), which marked the beginning of serious Irish fiction, had separate American editions as far apart as 1814 and 1904, with several others in between. Very popular in America were the flamboyantly romantic "national tales" of Sydney Owenson (Lady Morgan). Her Dublin and London bestseller, *The Wild Irish Girl* (1806), was published the following year in New York and Philadelphia in five separate editions. Also widely available in America were the works of Ireland's other nineteenth-century novelists, the Banim Brothers, Gerald Griffin, and William Carleton, whose masterpiece *Traits and Stories of the Irish Peasantry* (published in Ireland in 1830 and 1833) had American editions as early as 1833 and 1834. The novels of the two most successful nineteenth-century perpetrators of Irish caricature, Samuel Lover and Charles Lever, were also perennially popular, at least among non-Irish readers. Both received the blessing of the American literary establishment in the form of gorgeously printed, multi-volume collectors' editions from Boston's prestigious Little, Brown and Company. In addition, Irish fiction appeared frequently throughout the nineteenth century in a wide range of American periodicals, from Catholic and Irish nationalist weeklies to mainstream magazines and newspapers.

Despite its ready availability, however, contemporary Irish fiction did not significantly influence Irish-American writers in the three decades before the Great Hunger. Satire, though present, was not the strongest suit of Edgeworth, the Banims, Griffin, or Carleton, and the effect in Lever and Lover is less satirical than broad-brush burlesque in the stage-Irish tradition. And yet it was toward a habit of sophisticated satire that their American cousins gravitated. Not that this tendency was wholly unexpected. Rather, pre-Famine Irish-American satire was both a natural response to American conditions and the translation to the New World of a profoundly Irish habit of mind that had merely gone underground for a generation in Ireland. Satire has been central in Irish writing in both Gaelic and English, from the early bards whose poetic ridicule was feared for its magical power to Brian Merriman's hilarious cultural and sexual satire, *Cúirt an Mheón-Oíche* (The Midnight Court) of 1781, and from Jonathan Swift to James Joyce and Flann O'Brien. [7]

Five of the six writers in Part I of this anthology, all of them newly discovered, followed the lead of Lawrence Sweeney, Mathew Carey, and their Irish forebears by publishing fascinating books that establish satiric content

7. See Vivian Mercier, *The Irish Comic Tradition* (New York: Oxford University Press, 1969), and David Krause, *The Profane Book of Irish Comedy* (Ithaca: Cornell University Press, 1982). For clarification and extension of this tradition to include Samuel Beckett, Patrick Kavanagh, Sean O'Casey, and Brendan Behan, see Maureen Waters, *The Comic Irishman* (Albany: State University of New York Press, 1984).

and parodic form as central to the first Irish-American literary generation. *The Life and Travels of Father Quipes, Otherwise Dominick O'Blarney* (1820) and *The Life of Paddy O'Flarrity* (1834) are engaging picaresque tales which satirize the immigrant's dream of success and the venality of political aspiration by parodying American campaign biography. *Six Months in a House of Correction; or, the Narrative of Dorah Mahoney* (1835) parodies the anti-Catholic fiction of "awful disclosures" about convent life and derides the nativist impulse as manifested in the burning of the Charlestown convent the previous year. Set in Ireland, *The Priest's Turf-Cutting Day* (1841) by Thomas C. Mack thoroughly exposes demogoguery from the Catholic Sunday sermon, to Ascendancy bureaucracy double-speak, to the Irish nationalist stump speech. And John M. Moore's *The Adventures of Tom Stapleton* (1842) pokes good-natured fun at many aspects of American and Irish-American social, political, and literary life, while parodying a range of New York dialects and the conventions of popular, sentimental fiction.

All of these books also undermine native American stereotypes of the Irish by reproducing them in exaggerated comic versions, even as they display a further dimension of comic self-satire, an acknowledgment that the Irish do, in fact, drink, fight, blarney, and backbite, perhaps to excess. As a group, this cluster of entertaining treatments of sensitive subjects (Catholicism, nativism, nationalism, political corruption, and unattractive aspects of Irish identity) suggests that this first Irish-American literary generation and its audience were sophisticated, highly literate, confident, and unthreatened by the strange, new American culture in which they found themselves. This was an immigrant generation that could laugh at itself, at its foreign background, and at native American prejudices against it.

The last piece in Part I reflects the heavy early emigration from the North of Ireland. A story of Ulster immigrants to western Pennsylvania at the time of the French and Indian War, *The Wilderness* (1823) is the first novel of James McHenry (1785-1845), himself an Ulster immigrant and the first Irishman to undertake a career as an American novelist. McHenry's Irish characters in American settings (primarily in *The Wilderness*) and in eighteenth-century Irish historical settings (in *O'Halloran; or, The Insurgent Chief,* 1824, and *The Hearts of Steel,* 1825) are pioneering attempts to define Irishness for an American audience. [8]

---

8. *The Wilderness* is actually the second Irish-American novel. The first is *The Irish Emigrant* (Winchester, Va.: John T. Sharrocks, 1817) by "An Hibernian," the story of an Ulster patriot's flight from the 1798 Rising in County Antrim to a comfortable life on a Potomac River estate. A turgidly written, sentimental tale of love and adventure, this novel introduces an archetypal pattern for Irish-American fiction: the sorrowing farewell to Erin, a transitional sea-change, and the dazed, wondering arrival in the New World. It is otherwise unremarkable, except that the Ulster-born hero is a Catholic. It has been attributed to one "Adam Douglass," whose name appears on the copyright page.

The Life and Travels of Father Quipes, Otherwise Dominick O'Blarney

Written by Himself (Carlisle, Pa.: Printed for the Purchaser, 1820)

Printed anonymously, this fascinating immigrant's picaresque tale takes its hero from County Kerry to Carlisle, Pennsylvania, with stops along the way in Galway, Sligo, and (thanks to a British press gang) Ceylon. The good father's story is told with some wit and, for its time, audacious candor about country matters, and its satiric targets include the habits of the Pennsylvania Dutch, American political electioneering, and the fad for impossibly romantic novels. Only thirty of the book's thirty-two small pages survive, and all but five are reprinted here. A promised sequel – "for though old in vice, I am yet young in years" – seems not to have been written. The book has been attributed to a John McFarland.

Father Quipes is among the earliest nineteenth-century examples of the Irish-American tradition of satire, the roots of which are in eighteenth-century Ireland and Irish America. Irish examples include, in English, many works of Jonathan Swift, including his terrifying "A Modest Proposal" of 1729, and, in Gaelic, Brian Merriman's The Midnight Court, *written in 1780-81. Eighteenth-century Irish-American satirists include New York journalist Lawrence Sweeney and Philadelphia publisher Mathew Carey.*

In a short preface Quipes (who never explains why he calls himself "Father") apologizes for inaccuracies of "arrangement and punctuation," explaining that "the work was hastily compiled, and written amid the bustle of an electioneering campaign," and adding that his parents were unable "to afford me that education which the meanest herdsman in the county of Kerry, nay, through the entire province of Munster, contrive to give their children."

I was born on one of the most remote mountains of *Finnevarrah*, in the *west* of *Ireland*, but am unable to give any accurate account of my parentage, owing to the wild and savage state of that unsettled country, further than that my father and mother, held in the neighborhood a character for honesty and sobriety, which could not well be otherwise, where there was little to steal and nothing at all but clean water to drink. The first remarkable incident of my life occurred among the wilds of these mountains, and, indeed, forms the earliest occurrence of my recollection. I was one day lying under the shade of a ragged hawthorn bush, busily engaged in tracing the map of the world on my measled shins, when looking up I espied two or three strange looking men with no beards, and shoes and stockings on their legs and feet, busily engaged in rolling a barrel to the top of the hill, where, having placed it in an exposed situation, they immediately disappeared. I felt a great curiosity to discover what was in the barrel, and getting up from the ground where I lay, ran forward, and peeping into the bung-hole, which these cunning fellows had purposely left open, I saw a fine large POTATO which I lost no time in laying hold of, by thrusting my hand and arm into the hole. Having thus secured the rich and delicious prize, I endeavored to draw it out, but, alas! not all my art or strength could pull it through the devilish bung-hole; and loth to part with my plunder, yet still unable to extricate it from the unlucky barrel, I kept hauling and tugging at it, until the men who set the trap, rushed from their lurking places, and caught me in their arms with as much tenderness and humanity as the American Indians would catch a wild horse.

I at first made a most hideous outcry or wailing in such dismal notes of distress, as I had often heard from the old women who are usually hired to *keen* at our country wakes, but no assistance arriving to my rescue, I was hurried off by this merciless banditti, through innumerable swamps, heaths, and turf-bogs, until we arrived in the county of Galway, and where the country seemed to be thickly inhabited. – Here I first saw houses and barns, and women and children, with clothes on their backs. Not understanding my language, it was impossible for them to comprehend my statements respecting the villains who had me in custody, and consequently I could obtain no relief, until they found means to sell me to a Connaught drover who had come to Oranmore fair, for the purpose of purchasing cattle. This man took me home with him, and after fastening a tether to my leg with a great stone to the end of it to prevent my running away, carried me out to a bog which belonged to his farm, and set me at *turf cutting*. I shall never forget the merciless treatment I received from this hard-hearted miscreant, who gave me but *one potato* and the *tail of an herring* for my daily allowance, which I was obliged to wash down with a *noggin of dirty buttermilk.* Oh! the infatuated ingrate! I shall one day hold up his name to public scorn, and blast the infidel with the consuming turpitude of his own baseness.

In this miserable condition I remained for one year, until a happy chance of cutting the tether, released me from the incumbrance, and making a good use of my heels, I succeeded in reaching the county Sligo and town of that name, where I was immediately taken up by one of the bum-bailiffs, under some law they have in that country for apprehending vagrants, and in a few minutes I found myself sitting on the edge of a bench, elevated about eight feet from the ground, my feet sticking through two holes in a plank, and my hands thrust in a similar situation through a board nearly as high as my head, and this the finisher of the law, who officiated during the ceremony of my inauguration, called the stocks. In this uncomfortable posture I was kept for a good hour at least, without a morsel to eat or drink; but the fellow who treated me in this uncivil manner, probably relenting, came back and released me, in the very nick of time that the tenantry of a neighbouring schoolhouse had commenced a play of rotten eggs and dirt about my bare head. I then told the scoundrel that he looked like a butcher with his knife in his fist; and that the knife was the precise and horrible emblem of his countenance. In answer to this, he very unceremoniously began to apply his foot to my breech, with considerable vigor and infinite industry, and continued to amuse himself in this manner, until he fairly kicked out the seat of my buckskin breeches, and left me much battered and bruised in my lower extremities. After this, he took me before a magistrate, who gave orders to have me bound out to one Neal M'Bride, to learn the art and mystery of a *wheelwright*.

I always possessed a happy knack of making myself agreeable to the ladies; and so was not long in the house of Mr. M'Bride before I contracted an intimacy with the *genteel* Miss Biddy O'Rafferty, whom I afterwards married, and who resided with the family in the capacity of *"potwallopper"* and *"knife-scourer."* This dear creature became much interested in my welfare, and used to employ her leisure hours in combing my head and catching numerous swarms of those troublesome *"travellers"* who had accompanied me from the wilds of *Finnevarrah*, and who had established a regular form of government and administered justice on all parts of my skull.

Biddy and myself were constant companions, until it appeared from the tightness of her gowns and the increasing limp in her gait, which the dear creature was always subject to, in consequence of a sore shin and a corned toe, that something was *"rotten in the state of Denmark;"* and so to save her from the evil consequences of our mutual embraces, we entered into the connubial state. She soon after had a fine promising son, but never saw a well day afterwards, and at length died for want of breath.

Having now nothing on hand to engage my attention, I commenced reading the primer, and with the assistance of Mrs. M'Bride, soon became an adept in reading and writing. After becoming clear of my apprenticeship, I took an affectionate leave of my kind master and mistress, from whom I had received more *"cuffs than coppers,"* and shaped my course for Londonderry, where I was caught by a press gang belonging to his Majesty's ship Bellerophon, and hurried on board. I was at first in great dismay at the adventure, expecting nothing else than a wooden leg for my services, but was cheered up by the flattering expectations of prize-money and good eating, a thing that I had seldom been accustomed to at home. The ship sailed the next day for Ceylon, an island in the East Indies, and on the passage I was appointed *boat-swain's-mate*.

. . . .

From Ceylon we sailed for North America, and arrived in the Delaware river, where we were obliged to perform quarantine on suspicion of having the yellow fever on board. But this was not the case by any means, for we had but one death during the passage, and that was the Captain's dog, who jumped overboard after a shark.

On arriving at Philadelphia, I took a French leave of my worthy captain, and was much rejoiced to find myself safe and sound once more upon terra firma. Walking up the middle of the street, in order to have a better view of the houses on both sides; I was assailed by a large dog, who I would immediately have killed, but upon looking around for a stone, was much astonished to find them *tied fast to the ground.* In this dilemma, I had no other safety but in flight, but the dog running as fast as myself, he caught me by one of my legs, and very unceremoniously threw me down on the broad of my back, where I lay in the utmost consternation and misery, the dog standing over me – snarling, shewing his teeth and wagging his tail, with other symptoms of rage and passion, until a gentleman passing that way, freed me from my pitiable situation by giving the dog a smart rap over the sconce, with a large cane which he carried in his hand. From this circumstance I took the hint to provide myself with a good *cudgel,* and which I have taken pains to bear with me ever since.

This instrument of defence and attack, I have often found very serviceable, and on a late occasion when Col. M'G–s took the liberty of knocking me down in the street, I would have made a very good use of it, if the bystanders had permitted.

Finding upon enquiry that a man in Philadelphia, without wit or money, is much in the same situation and has the same prospects of bettering his fortune, that a cat has of killing mice and rats without claws or teeth, I wisely made the best of my way out of the chequerboard city as fast as possible. . . .

I travelled through Montgomery county, until I arrived at a place called Trap, where I fell in with a Justice of the Peace, which are very numerous all over the state of Pennsylvania, and officiate at the annual elections, in the capacity of drill sergeants. This man's name was Todd, and learning my forlorn condition, he kindly took me to his house and clothed me in a tolerable decent garb; he likewise found me employ at my trade, and supplied me with money and other necessaries. But after residing there for a short time I became tired of work, which indeed I never felt any great fondness for, and took a moonshine flitting from my friend Todd. Let no man blame me for this, for I claim to be blamed by no one. The *dark malignity* of the man in lending me money, his *villainous stratagems* in procuring me employment, and the *mysterious dagger of insinuation,* with which he clothed my naked body, all gave me an indisputable right to treat the wretch as he deserved.

From Trap I proceeded towards Reading, in Berks county, and travelled through a rich and fertile country, chiefly inhabited by Germans, who have many strange outlandish customs, which I was often at a great loss to account for. They have a fashion of making a number of small white balls or cakes, from the curds of milk, which they arrange on a small board and stick upon a couple of pins, drove into the sides of their houses, in a situation exposed to the sun. In this manner they lie for some weeks, again which time they smell very loud, and are covered with innumerable little things, which I remember often to have seen in our buttermilk at Finnevarrah, and there we call them "*skippers.*" Another practice prevails among these people, which I thought very queer and subject to much censure. In the fall when they lift their cabbages, they slice them down into a large vessel, shaped like an invert-ed churn, and getting into it with their *feet,* stamp it down at intervals, until they get the vessel filled. It is then set aside with a large stone on the top of it to keep it well packed, until it begins to *stink,* when they eat it and the little cakes, which they call cheese, in the same manner and with the same avidity that we do *potatoes* and *sowings.*

In travelling through this country, I was one evening about night fall, much alarmed at the strange cry of some fowl or bird of passage, which sat upon a tree directly over my head and said,

"*Whop-go-hee, whop-go-hee, whop-go-hee.*"

I hastened forward to the nearest house, and reported to the person living in it, the strange voice I had heard – when the fellow instead of answering me, set up the most hideous horse-laugh I had ever heard, full in my face. I was both angry and astonished at his rude behavior, and promptly told him what I thought of his conduct. You villain, said I, you are the main disturber of the social order of this county, you are a mean drudge, a hack, a menial, a mer-cenary slave, a very Janizary, and the reduced and squalid candidate, for the compassion of mankind. The fellow made no more ado, but slammed the door shut in my face, telling me that I was a "*verfluchter dihenker,*" and I pur-sued my journey. – The first man I met, appeared to have more politeness, for on enquiring, what the "whop-go-hee" meant, he very civilly told me it was a bird which the natives of this country called a "*whipperwill.*"

The next day, as I was trudging along the road and reflecting on the many curiosities of this strange land, I perceived a fine large eel, lying direct-ly across my way and basking in the sun. I approached towards it for the pur-pose of catching it, but the devil eluded my grasp and ran off with the agility of a horse and I after it. I pursued it for about a quarter of a mile, when a gen-tleman who met me on horseback, asked me what I was after. Och, says I – I have no time to talk to you, I want to catch the eel, the eel. "Why, you fool you," says he, "that's a black snake, it will bite you." Arrah no, replied I, that's what we call an eel in Ireland, and you are a depraved monster for attempt-ing to prevent my catching it with the mysterious stiletto of insinuation. He made no reply, but made off laughing, and the eel creeping under a huge pile of stones I gave up the pursuit.

Nothing worthy of my attention happened on the road after this, until I arrived at Reading, where I put up at the house of one Jacob Goslin, and changed my name from *"Patrick,"* the appellation I received from the rascally drover, who purchased me from the kidnappers at Oranmore, and assumed the title of *Dominick,* to which I have since added *O'Blarney,* and sometimes *Quipes*. It was at Mr. Goslins, that I first saw *apple-dumplings,* and was much perplexed in my own mind what to make of them, when Mrs. Goslin first introduced them to the table. I turned one of them over and over on my plate, and seeing no aperture or place to commence eating it, the thought struck me of giving one of them to a large dog who belonged to the house, and who was at the moment lying under the table. I reached it to him on my fork, and he snatched at it immediately, but after getting it in his mouth and finding that it burnt him, he began whining most piteously, and scratching his mouth with his forepaw. I then concluded that these things were *dogs jewsharps,* and never intended for mankind to eat.

Having obtained from the Goslin a little money, I set up my trade, and becoming acquainted with a Mr. Wormbread, who I understand has since been commissioned a general, learned from him the first rudiments of the politics of this *happy country*. I now began to see my way clear, and concluded that the speediest way to arrive at distinction in Pennsylvania, would be to make a noise in the newspapers, and bellow and brawl at elections. I immediately abandoned the wheelwright business and providing myself with pens, ink and paper, commenced writing, and the Gazettes were for some time crouded with the ebulitions of my wit and talent. I was courted by all the great men of the day, and commenced a correspondence with Lawyer Ash of York, and Archibald Bard of Franklin county, who honored me with the most flattering marks of approbation. But, alas! my success was too flattering to be of long duration, for in the midst of my golden visions of fame and glory, I was seized by what they call a constable in America, and barbarously immured in the lonesome and solitary damps of a prison.

I lay here some time before I could learn to whose friendship I was indebted for this signal expression of charity, but afterwards discovered that I was confined on *suspicion of debt.*

After remaining here for some time, I was released through the kind interference of a friend, who discharged the debt, out of his own pocket. I afterwards treated the scoundrel as he deserved, by paying him back his money and interest, with my customary gratitude.

I took my departure from Reading immediately afterwards, and passing through Harrisburg, became acquainted with one *Buck Miller,* a fat spongy man who was a great politician, and who gave me a little money for lampooning some fellow who had offended him. From Harrisburg I travelled to Carlisle, where I became acquainted with one Thompson Brown and James Bredin, and through the kind officiousness of these men I afterwards received an introduction to Mr. Andrew Boden, whose friendship and acquaintance I have cultivated ever since. From Carlisle I proceeded to Hanover in York County, where I again commenced my trade, and again quitted it for the purpose of writing politics.

During my stay at Hanover, I went in company with a friend to visit General Shearman, who resides six miles from Hanover, and who has a great number of plumb trees on his farm. When we arrived at this place it was in the dusk of the evening, and my companion mounted one of the trees for the purpose of shaking it – when, as he told me, I might gather up the plumbs as they fell. The first shake he gave, something dropped on the ground near to where I was standing which I took for a plumb, and immediately swallowed it. – Then addressing the man who was still shaking the tree, I asked him "has the plumbs legs?" "No," replied he; "arrah then by the powers, I have swallowed a *straddle bug*," I exclaimed, and he fell to laughing immoderately, telling me it was a "tree frog," which he had thrown down on his first climbing up.

Shortly after this adventure I became acquainted with Dr. William H. Crawford, of Adams county, who was then a candidate for a seat in Congress, and whose election I was very instrumental in promoting, by the many learned and wise essays which I wrote in his favor. The doctor took me home to his house and introduced me to his lady, from whom I received such flattering marks of regard and friendship as quite turned my head. The doctor went so far as to interest himself in my behalf with the Government, and I was appointed an ensign in the *hundred and twenty-fifth* regiment of infantry, and stationed to recruit at Greencastle, in Franklin county, where the Hon. David Fullerton that is, invited me to take a cup of TEA with him.–Hearing whilst at Greencastle that the British had made a descent on our coast at Baltimore, I immediately marched in defence of my country with six brave fellows, whom I had enlisted, and who would have marched to the cannon's mouth in search of – *a bottle of whiskey.* But when I arrived at Baltimore, I met with some spalpeen of an officer, who was superior to me in rank, and who ordered me immediately to return to the place from whence I came and wait for orders, so that my first campaign was rather inglorious in the end. On my return I stopped with my old friend at Hanover, where I enlisted the brother of Mr. J. Kuhns, innkeeper, who now resides in York, and who was so much irritated at me for taking advantage of his brother, who at stated periods was afflicted with *mania,* that he horse-whipped me from one end of the town to the other. I never have had it in my power to return the kindness of my friend Kuhns, but keep it in my minds eye for a future period, when I shall write a piece of scurrility against him, that will make him wish the devil had him.

I now marched my company, which by this time had increased to nine, and who were something like Falstaff's "younger sons of younger brothers," to Gettysburg, from which place I made occasional visits to the neighboring

towns of Oxford, Petersburg and Littlestown, as well for the purpose of enlist-
ing recruits as to see and converse with the pretty farmers' daughters along
the road, who were as much taken with the novelty of a uniform coat and officers "rattee," as an old maid with a pinch of snuff or dish of coffee. Amongst
these damsels I must not forget to mention the name of Miss Polly
Gaullagher, a buxom young wench, whose silly ideas of honor and virtue
were more easily tampered with than her fellows, and who became a prey to
my lust, before she had time to attend a wedding ceremony or ask the prayers
of the parson in her behalf. Poor Polly! when I am able to remunerate her for
the pains and misfortunes she has encountered through the false trust she
reposed in me, it is likely I shall call upon her.

. . . .

About this period I began to launch out in the political world, and in a
short time became very notorious as a writer, using a great many tropes and
figures, such as the "mysterious dagger," "horrible insinuation," "infamous
wretch," "reptile," "villain," "scoundrel," &c. &c. and by this means became
so notorious, that the very school-boys could point to my productions and say
"that's Dominick."

The Hon. Andrew Boden, Esq. hearing of my performances in the literary world, invited me to his house, where a sumptuous dinner was prepared
and an invitation given me to partake, which I was always very ready to
accept. One article of the fare I was a good deal staggered at, and never having seen any thing of the kind before, commenced eating it in rather an auk-
ward manner. Seeing that the dish was completely covered and crusted above
and below, I perforated it at the top, with my knife, and finding that it contained apples nicely sliced and stewed, took a spoon and carefully scraped
them all out; being very careful not to injure the crust. After I had it emptied,
I handed the dish to Mrs. Boden, saying, "please fill this again madam?"–But
she told me that what I had eaten was a PIE, and that it was customary to eat
the crust at the same time with the apples.

After dinner Mr. Boden and myself had a private *tete-a-tete*, when it was
agreed that I should uphold and protect him against all opposition, and that
his brother John should afford me his protection against the constables, especially one Mr. Erb, whose visits to my house were both troublesome and
unwelcome, as well as frequent. This treaty, offensive and defensive, has
existed ever since, whilst I have been so fortunate as to write Mr. Boden out
of *Congress*, and he has been so unsuccessful as to lose his political character,
having got in exchange for his office, the title of APOSTATE; a name he will
carry to the grave.

I am now busily engaged in procuring signers to a petition in favor of the
Hon. Andrew Boden, to the office of Prothonotary, and have every reason in
the world to expect that I shall obtain about *fifteen thousand.* But notwithstanding, from the opinion already expressed by the new Governor, that none

but the *most worthy* ought to enjoy the benefits of office; I am apprehensive that my friend will not succeed. – I forgot, in a more early part of this work, to tell the reader that I wrote all the fine speeches for Mr. Boden, that he delivered in Congress, and that my pay for that important service was the office of Marshal of Cumberland county, from which distinguished situation I have since been kicked for incapability and laziness.

The foregoing brief sketch of my life and adventures, I hereby usher to the world, merely as a foretaste of what is yet to come – for though old in vice, I am yet young in years, and the second volume of my travels, which I shall publish some five years hence, shall contain as much information to the reader, and mirth to the world, as I am capable of introducing.

Signed QUIPES.

The Life of Paddy O'Flarrity, Who, from a Shoeblack, Has by Perseverence and Good Conduct Arrived to a Member of Congress

Written by Himself (Washington, D.C.: no publisher listed, 1834)

The title indicates this short novel's aim of satirizing the rags-to-riches American dream of success, and a second title, printed on the outside cover – "A Spur to Youth, or Davy Crockett Beaten" – suggests that it parodies the Crockett autobiography, which appeared earlier the same year. Paddy O'Flarrity *is the story of a wily, amoral immigrant Irish boy's rise in the world of American politics. It is written with deliberately outlandish grammar that constitutes a form of linguistic subversion and contributes to the cynical message that traditional education and ability count for nothing in the race for political gain in America.*

Landing penniless in Baltimore, Paddy works first as a shoeblack and a barkeep, and then heads west to Missouri, where he promptly loses his brogue, buys a new suit of clothes, assumes "a modest air," and gets a job as private tutor to the children of "Judge D–." The job allows Paddy time to "improve" himself with the judge's law books, and to pick up enough Latin "to throw a superficial gloss over my learning." All runs smoothly from here. A fortuitous Indian attack, from which he rescues the judge's daughter, results in Paddy's becoming a media hero: wax effigies of his exploit go on display in St. Louis. Soon the judge is elected governor of Missouri. Paddy marries the daughter, changes his name to hers, and is himself elected to the state legislature and then to Congress. He concludes his story with ambitions for the presidency and a challenge to the reader to "guess who I am." He has "made it" by denying his Irishness, assuming a veneer of culture, and letting unprincipled ambition be his guide. Along the way, the author works authentic Irish folk motifs into the story; for example, courtship in the presence of a corpse, used here in chapter IV, and by John M. Synge in his early play, In the Shadow of the Glen *(1903). Because of such realistic touches, and because the object of the satire is American political life and perception of the Irish, not the Irish themselves, I believe the author to have been an Irish American.*

Reprinted here are the Preface and most of the first half of the book, at the end of which Paddy takes his seat in the state legislature.

Preface

In laying before the public this short history of my life, I hope it will meet with the success for which it is intended, viz. the improvement of the Youth of America. The work clearly shows that it is by *Perseverence*, avoid *bad company, care* and *industry* will cause the aspiring youth to succeed in any effort. Though it has been said that nature must endow you with genius, reader, heed it not. For take my word, God has put us all here as equal, and Art is the accomplishment of all things – which can only be acquired by *Perseverence*. Look at many of your countrymen, at the leading men of learning and education, who are at the head of government, and look at me, who during our infantine state, were pronounced as fools by our school companions, and now called men of genius, learning, &c.

Look at your Henry Clay, your Wirt, modern Demostheneses, who, like him of old, sprang from humble life, but by Perseverence acquired the pinnacle of glory they now possess. But, above all, I must not forget Patrick Henry, who, even to the age of 23 or 4 years, was considered a dunce – see what Perseverence did for him; behold how he was rejected, disappointed and laughed at for his presumption, as it was termed by the envious, and then see, notwithstanding many impediments, to what immortal fame he arrived to. And lastly, behold myself, Paddy O'Flarrity, who, from a poor Irish boy, on the wide world, without a friend, from a Shoe Black, has arisen, by Perseverence and good conduct, to a Member of Congress. Reader! go thou and do likewise.

PADDY O'FLARRITY.

Chapter I

Containing the history of my birth and education, and the difficult manner of obtaining the latter.

My name was Paddy O'Flarrity. I was born in Ireland about 46 years ago, and my parents were both what you Americans call Raw Irish, because they were begotten as well as born in that land, not of milk and honey, as you might think, but faith in the land of milk and potatoes. I was the youngest of thirty-two children, for my father, you must know, had six wives; that is, not all at one time, but one after the other. So it was; thirty-two of us he had, and all boys in the bargain, who were as thumping paddies as ever you saw and all ambitious, striving and enterprising, as the most of my countrymen are. And as daddy said, have done wonders in this big world considering how we were raised, on our scant allowance of milk and potatoes. For my father owned but a small spot of ground, containing one acre and a half, which every year he put in potatoes. He had also three cows, one horse and always raised three good fat hogs out of an old sow, which if not dead, must certainly be living yet. Ah, you old bitch, well do I recollect how often you used to slit up the back part of my leather breeches, with your old snout, and then such scorching as mammy would sure to give my back. Well, with my tale again. Daddy would first make us all work his patch of potatoes, and then good natured like, would start us off, to fish for ourselves. So away we would go, each after his own liking; some farming for the neighbors round, some at one thing, and some at another.

But there was one trade which we all, what time we had, was fond of, and that was schooling. Every Sunday we collected under a large tree, the general place of resort for the poorer class, for that purpose. It was there I am indebted for the scant knowledge of reading and writing which now I possess. Yes, and let it be a spur to ye, American youth, that you may arrive to that which now I am. Having arrived to the age of 18 years, the oppression of my country forced me to leave the home that gave me birth and take refuge in a land where LIBERTY exists and VIRTUE is rewarded.

Chapter II

I leave Ireland for America – arrive there and engage work with a Shoe Black – afterwards become a Printer's Devil, where I acquired a taste for erudition, &c.

Having give mam and dad a hearty buss, I set off for America, working out my passage, not a cent of money in my pocket; – I landed at Baltimore, where I engaged myself to a *Shoe Black,* to clean the boots and shoes at Barnum's Tavern. Finding no other employment then at hand, being in a strange country, no friends or money, and knowing the bad tendencies of an idle life, I thought that better than none. In this employment I remained for about three months, till I had accumulated upwards of 50 dollars by my wages, and money given me by gentlemen when I carried their boots to them. Feeling desirous of getting in a higher employment, I readily accepted of an offer made by an editor of a considerable paper of that place, namely, to carry papers around to the doors of his subscribers and do other little jobs that might be wanting about the office; in short I was a *Printer's Devil.* In this capacity, I had much leisure time to improve myself by reading the newspapers from the different parts of the world, thereby acquiring a knowledge of modern history which gave me a relish for that of ancient. It was here I first read Goldsmith's Rome and Goldsmith's Greece. How often did I think of the eloquence of Demosthenes, which he acquired by his unbounded perseverence, and which made him so great a man? The wisdom of Socrates, the contentment of Diogenes, the virtue of Aristides, which made them so conspicuous and immortal for their respective qualities, fired my very imagination with redoubled ardor, when I thought of the poor and humble origin they sprang from, the zenith of glory they arrived to, immortal patterns for coming ages.

[In chapter III Paddy is turned out of his job and lodging in his employer's home because of "a foolish accident." Frightened in the night, he climbs into bed with his master's wife and refuses to budge, "notwithstanding the repeated claws of the wife and blows of the husband to make me get out."]

Chapter IV

My departure and advice to young men – I arrive in the city of Washington, where I get into business as a bar-keeper.

Turned out of house and home for the above foolish account, I had nothing to do, but take my bundle on my back and stear my course for the city of Washington; for I would advise every young man so soon as he becomes notorious for any crime or bad conduct, whether falsely accused or not, to shape his course for some other place where he is not known, in order to reclaim his lost name.

Having arrived at that city in good health, I soon found employment in keeping bar for an Irishman by the name of Pat Duffy, who kept a grogshop near one of the Departments, and who was tolerably well patronised by a number of the wild young clerks of that office. Among whom there was one, who became so inattentive to his business, that many times of a night I would have to sit up doing that, which he should have done, and for which I was well paid by him for my services. In this double occupation of bar-keeper and sub-clerk, I remained two years so closely engaged, that my foot scarcely ever crossed the threshhold of the door, thereby saving my money and avoiding all bad company and its liabilities. Having at length some business in the country, which called my attention for a day or two, I was, on my return, to be again the tool used in another unfortunate predicament, somewhat similar in aspect to that which I have related in the preceding pages; that occurred at Baltimore, and which is as follows:

On my return home after feeding and rubbing down my horse, it being then dark, and feeling somewhat wearied after my ride, concluded that I would go to bed without troubling the family for my supper, and accordingly did so. On reaching my apartment I observed a candle burning on the table, and a man apparently asleep in my bed, which I thought nothing off, thinking that the family did not expect me that day, therefore put the lodger there. So along side of him I got and soon commenced thinking of the business which I had been about, as some are accustomed to do when they retire. After sometime, in came the landlord's wife and one of these young clerks, and seated themselves before the fire without observing me on the bed. Curious to know the upshot of this uncommon visit, I lay all motionless for fear of being discovered by them. But I did not wait long before they were busily engaged in courtship at the expense of my poor employer, when hearing this woman say to the man, "a'nt you ashamed to do so and a dead man in the room too," hearing this, the truth of the thing rushed to my mind like lightening, and running my hand over the dead man's face, for so he actually was, and finding it cold as ice, I gave one spring and landed in the middle of the floor. The two lovers supposing it was the dead man come to life, fled with the utmost precipitation down stairs, and I, equally frightened, followed close after, which redoubled their alarm, so as to cause the woman to faint, and the man to confess his error to the husband, who was heartily pleased at the lucky incident which snatched his wife from eternal infamy. You must know that these two lovers went to set up with the corpse, which was no other than my old benefactor, the dissipated clerk – the fruit which never fails to grow from frequenting such hellish places, and which has blasted many a youth, who might be a solace to their aged parents and an ornament to their country.

Chapter V

I am compelled to leave my employer – obtain the office of sub-clerk – leave Washington on account of another accident more fatal than any – encouragement to youth.

After this circumstance, finding no peace in the house, with a woman whom I had thus, by accident exposed, I determined once more to shift my quarters. Accordingly I applied to one of the clerks who still frequented the shop for employment, which he readily granted, allowing me one-fourth of his salary, he holding the office, and I doing the work, which I generally accomplished by three or four o'clock, granting me an opportunity to attend the debates in Congress and improving myself by reading history, &c.

In this capacity I remained for about ten months, with unimpeachable character, till another accident, which fate decreed for me to undergo, once more occurred to the utter ruin of my situation and promising hopes of the future. On a fine summers evening there was to be a great book auction, where it was supposed that they would be sold cheap – wishing to purchase some, I repaired thither, clad in a white linen roundabout, blue pantaloons,

&c. suitable to the season. After being there sometime, in came a young man dressed somewhat similar to myself, with a large black dog, which together with another dog, were very quarelsome, so much so that a man was induced to give one a pretty severe kick, which was as readily returned by the master of the dog, with such violence that sent the poor fellow reeling in the crowd. No sooner than he had recovered himself, spang he takes me right side of the head, thinking that I was the fellow who struck him, being dressed as I said in a similar garb – the master of the dog having slip out after what he had done. Finding no time to reason the case with the fellow, I set in to hard fighting, tumbling about in the crowd, till we were both taken off to jail to await our trial next morning.

There sad remorse took possession of me, and never once did I close my sobing eyes, the whole night; thinking on my sad reverse of fortune, which the great and ambitious are so susceptable of. Then I thought all my future hopes blasted, for the bare idea of being in a jail was a sufficient bar to prevent any one from rising to any eminence in this life, but how happily was I mistaken. Young men take courage from this, let not the casual accidents of a day blast the future hopes of a long and happy life. Think as I did, that how the virtuous and brave La Fayette – the wise philosopher Socrates and many others, far above the sphere in life that you may arise to, have been like us, incarcerated in the walls of a prison, and then arrived to the zenith of glory and immortal renown.

So to proceed with my story. The next day, I, together with my antagonist were ushered before a justice of the peace, to answer for our riotous conduct. – The fellow swearing that I struck him first, and I that he struck me first, the magistrate found us both guilty, bound us both over to the peace, and fined us in the sum of five or ten dollars.

My laurels being thus nipped; in compliance with my old adage, I immediately thought of leaving a place where I was thus barbarously used, to try with that unbounded perseverence, which I was always so characteristic of, my fortune in the Western states. Having packed up all my clothing, and to the amount of $400 in money, which I accumulated by care, temperance and industry, I bid adieu to Washington City, with a firm resolution of never setting my foot in it again, lest I went in a capacity which would command respect, for my good deportment, and in a situation to chastise officious magistrates, who may be, as too often is the case, detected in transcending their authority; blasting the prospect of youth; destroying the fond hopes of devoted parents, and in many instances, severing the dependent family from the father and the husband.

Chapter VI

I hear great talk of the west – I emigrate thither – meet a snake the first time in my life – scriptural knowledge essential to all – laughable anecdotes elicited from an Irishman, a fellow traveller – a lesson to liars.

At this time there was a great emigration to the west. Every body talking of the richness of the soil, so that the farmer had nothing to do, but go and scatter the corn, raise great crops and then gather it. Hens and chickens were so abundant that they became wild; hogs were running wild in the woods, and belonged to no body, but those who choose to catch them and send them down to New Orleans and get their own chink for them. But above all, was the great quantity of wild geese, which one had nothing more to do, but get an eel and tie it to a long string, holding one end in your hand and then throwing the end which the eel is tied to, among the geese, which being seen by them, will be readily caught at, and as readily, owing to its slippery nature, go out of the goose's other end – the next goose will grab it, and be caught in the same manner, and so on till you get your line strung with geese.

Having got all my effects in readiness, away I started for the land of plenty, which I have just described in the manner I was told. Travelling along I was in deep study, a thinking to what state I should go to, where I could the quickest make my fortune, and arrive to importance in the state, the bent of my determination, ever since I read of the mighty Demosthenes and all those great men that I was telling you of, when I was a printer's devil. When suddenly out came into the road, a great long black thing, with eyes glistening like diamonds, and looked right at me – I stopped and looked at it, for sometime till I thought it was one of the most beautiful creatures that I ever saw; it appeared as if I could have cherished it to my bosom and would have done it, had not by accident, a man came by at the time and prevented me; telling me it was a snake, the most poisonous of all reptiles, an animal I never saw before, for in faith we have none in Ireland. This was the shape, he continued, which the devil appeared in, when he deceived our father and mother, Adam and Eve. Hearing this, the natural heniousness of the vermin, at once discovered itself to my eyes, and after several blows, quickly put an end to his life. After this I determined to read the bible – for I found it was as essential for a gentleman to be acquainted with sacred as well as profane history.

Continuing my travels along the banks of the meandrous Ohio river, I was much amused with a countryman of mine, whom I happened to fall in with, together with several young Americans, whose principal sport was at the expense of my poor countryman, who pretended that he had seen water melons in Ireland much larger than any in this country. All of which might have been very true; for, in fact, he never saw any, before he was shown one which we had the pleasure of eating between us on our journey. From which the following anecdote occurred. Passing along a farmer's fence on which were a number of very large gourds, Pat seeing them and making no doubt but that they were of the same kind which he had been bragging about, and which he had just eaten, observed, "I wondre uf the paple wud be mod uf we were to take a watre mullan." Oh no, Pat, the young men replied, readily guessing his mistake. Pat lays hold of a large one, and begins to knaw with a face grinning wrong side outwards. How do you like it, Pat? "Why it is domb'd bittre, indade." Now, Pat, replied one of the young men, let this be a warning to you, to never tell a lie, lest some future accident may catch you in it, to your sore mortification. But this advice did not avail Pat any thing, for one of the young men, wishing to catch him in another lie for their sport, pointing Pat to a pear tree, whereon a gourd vine had run, containing a great many gourds, asked him if he ever saw such fine pears in Ireland as they were. "Oh yes, by St. Patrick, three times as large," at the same time going to pluck one, but recollecting the resemblance they bore to the water melons, thought of the advice then given him, and determined henceforward to profit by it.

Chapter VII

Part with my travelling companions – hear of a situation vacant – purchase new clothes, &c. cap-a-pie – visit the gentleman and obtain the situation of private teacher – the effects of being genteelly dressed, so important to young men – the good use I made of my leisure time in improving myself – study a little of law and latin – advice to fortune hunters.

Here I parted with my companions, and hearing that a Judge D– wanted a young man, who could teach plain reading and writing in his private family, determined me to offer him my services. Accordingly I purchased me a first rate suit of clothes, cap-a-pie, sold my old horse and bought a better, with new saddle, bridle, martingale, whip and spurs, which by this time having lost that dialect which is so peculiar to my countrymen, that I looked for all the world like an American buck – which was readily proved to me by an old negro, who doffed his hat and bowed till I passed by. Receiving such encouragement, my pride began, like all others who spring from nothing, to rise with my dress and importance, to arrogance and folly. But this passion I had the prudence to crush in the bud, knowing its bad tendencies, and pursue that old and true adage, which is, "that a gentleman is the same thing in every station," and with a modest gait rode up to the house of my intended employer, in a manner more suitable to my occupation and which in fact appeared more noble than all the pompous airs of the mushroom nobility. I was cordially received by the old Judge himself, with all the politeness and affability, so characteristic of a well bred gentleman, – the first I ever had the honor of doing business with. After knowing my business and occasionally eyeing my dress, which I could not help observing, together with the modest air I assumed, what a great effect it has in commanding respect from the old as well as young – an attention which all young men should pay the greatest regard to, particularly where they have nothing else to recommend them. Our bargain was soon closed, and the following morning commenced with the duties of my new capacity.

Here I lived as happy as the days were long; having nothing to do but teach three children their lessons morning and evening, granting me a sufficient opportunity to improve myself, with the Judge's law books, and occasionally to study a little Latin to help me along, and throw a superficial gloss over my learning, which often proved of essential benefit to me, when I happened to be in company with men of education, with whom I was very careful lest they discovered my cloven foot. My insinuating manners, which I advise every fortune hunter to assume, if he does not naturally possess them, secured me the good will of the neighbors round, and especially the Judge's family, who consisted of his wife, a most amiable daughter, of whom I shall speak hereafter, three younger children and a swarm of negroes.

Chapter VIII

Live happily – introduced to the first society – my benefactor elected Governor of Missouri – offer myself for the Legislature – I am elected – the Governor departs, with his family, for the seat of government – his daughter Maria – curious sensations on parting with her – find a billet-doux under my pillow, which explained to me the cause of my feelings, &c.

In this abode of peace, sport and happiness, I, for about four years, spent after finishing my daily duty, in fox hunting, visiting the neighbors and other recreating amusements; in which I was generally accompanied by the Judge and sometimes by his amiable Maria, introducing me to the first of society, which my correct deportment assisted me in acquiring, and which from my humble life raised me to my present station.

About this time, a great political contest ensued among the candidates for Governor of this state, among whom my worthy benefactor, the Judge, was the most prominent one. This event gave me an opportunity of becoming more extensively known, owing to the active part I took in electioneering for him. The success of whom emboldened me to offer myself, the following year, to my constituents, as a candidate for the Legislature of Missouri, the state of my adopted home.

That year, the Judge being elected Governor, in compliance with his official duties, was compelled to move his family to the seat of government, a place appropriated for his excellency; – leaving me behind to take charge of affairs, as well as attending to the accomplishment of the purpose above mentioned.

Never till then did I know the true situation of my heart. Such throbbing, such beating and bumping, up and down, the like you never felt, when I bid Maria farewell. The rosy hue that overspread her face, the faltering voice and trembling hand, as she drew it from mine, sufficiently told that sympathy rested there.

After seeing the various offices of the farm placed in proper order, I retired with a heavy heart, pregnated with the most curious sensations that I never before felt, but which quickly suggested the cause, on finding the following lines under my pillow:

> Tho' fate decrees that we must part
>   A little while, to meet again,
> Still, that while pricks deep my heart,
>   To see thy image once again.
>
> Tho' mountains high and dashing billow
>   May sever us, far apart,
> Still with this, lies under thy pillow,
>   An emblem of my wounded heart.
>
> Farewell, farewell! a short adieu!
>   May glory crown thee soon,
> With honors bright, long due to you,
>   I hope to see thee soon.

Think, gentle reader, what must have been my feelings on perusing the above flattering and encouraging lines, from one whom I loved better than myself. – Guess, then, with what double ardor I strived to place myself in such a situation as to deserve the favors bestowed on me, by so lovely an angel. Think not, that like many of my readers, transported with love and enthusiasm, I posted full after her, to lay my bleeding bosom at her feet, and return her my grateful heart. Not so, my reader. I knew my situation. I thought of my origin, my then capacity in life, and determined to place myself in a situation worthy of a Governor's daughter before I dare make any such pretensions.

Chapter IX

My joy on being elected – write a billet-doux to Maria – a scream – the Indians and Maria – I protect her, and kill the Indians – restored to her parents – the Governor espies the billet-doux, &c.

The next election for members of the Legislature came, but think what must have been my joys, on hearing that I was the first on the ticket. Think with how much joy, honor and happiness I anticipated, upon meeting my Maria in a situation, which I knew from the frequent hints of the Governor, would be acceptable to him and his worthy family.

On receiving the returns of the election, transported with joy, I sat down and wrote Maria the following but poor composition, being my first attempt at any thing of the kind. But emboldened by the remarks of some wise author, who says –

"Sure he who feels the pangs of love can write them."

Determined me to send the following stanza:

> With rapt'rous heart, in honors clad,
>   I fly, to meet thee now,
> With hopes so fond I long have had,
>   Low at thy feet to bow.
>
> There will I lie, with aching heart,
>   With panting bosom heave,
> Till thy angel's touch heals the smart,
>   My wounded heart relieve.
>
> Then with frantic joy I'll arise,
>   And seal those lips to mine,
> That angelic form, those limpid eyes
>   So heavenly, so divine.
>
> O, lovely nymph! I long have sigh'd
>   The hour, that it was near,
> To seal that pledge in wedlock tied
>   To thee, Maria, ever dear.
>
> But soon, soon that hour will come,
>   When we, no more, shall part.
> And I'll protect thee, let dangers come
>   I'll shield thee in my heart.

I had scarcely finished the last words, before the servant came running with the cry of, The Indians! The Indians! At the same time, hearing the distressing shrieks of a female voice, I seized my gun and immediately advanced to the spot from whence the sound originated. But, Oh God! what were my feelings, on beholding Maria's lovely form lying on the ground, apparently lifeless, and an Indian standing over her, in the bloody act of scalping the lovely locks which adorned her angelic person.

I raised my gun, and in an instant laid the Indian a lifeless corpse along the ground. The report of my gun awakened the senses of Maria, who had swooned away with fright. On seeing which I rushed to her and clasped her to my breast.

By this time two other Indians advanced, who had been in pursuit of the Governor, who had fled, leaving Maria, whose horse was shot, thinking that she had met with that fate likewise. One of them fired, the ball lodging in my right shoulder, doing not a sufficient damage as to prevent me from using my arm to some purpose. I rushed on the wretches, and with one blow, with the butt end of my gun, levelled one to the earth. The other raised his gun to fire, but with a desperate spring, I seized it with one hand and stabbed him to the heart with the other.

Having thus happily, by the assistance of that all powerful God, rescued the image of my heart from a cruel death, I, together with Maria, was not forgetful of the grateful thanks, due to our beneficent Creator, for the lucky preservation of our lives, which were so miraculously saved in this instance.

After fulfilling our duty in the above instance, we repaired to the house, where we were joyfully surprised, at seeing the aged Governor and family had arrived in safety, but with throbbing hearts at the loss of their Maria, whom they made no doubt was dead; the old man standing before the fire holding in his hands the paper containing the above lines of poetry, which in the hurry I had left exposed on the table, shedding over it tears of sorrow for the ideal loss of its lovely subject, the darling Maria.

The servants having told him where I had gone, concluded that I had met with the same untimely end. – But what was his joy and surprise on beholding us advancing with all the health and vivacity of life, to greet each other on our happy and wonderful escape.

[In chapter X the Governor embarrasses Paddy by reading aloud his poetic effusion to Maria. Then "old Tom," a family servant, tells a tall tale about killing a buck, a rabbit, a flock of partridges, a squirrel, and a turkey with one shot.]

Chapter XI

The Governor again speaks of the billet-doux – his approbation –

Maria – our engagement – my thanks to God for my good fortune
in life – the result of good conduct.

The length of this story I was in hopes would cause the old Governor to
forget the poetry – but not so, for no sooner were they done laughing at the
lies and ingenuity of old Tom, then he again calls to Maria, "well girl! what
hast thou to say? Come speak! don't be bashful! for your poor father is not
long for this world, and I know of none so worthy to take charge of yourself,
your little sisters and aged mother when I am gone, as Mr. O'Flarrity – never
mind his name, if that dont suit you, he shall petition to the legislature and
take mine. What say you Mr. O'Flarrity, have you any objections to taking
the name of one of the first families of Virginia, and now of the Governor of
Missouri? Speak! boy what sayest thou?" The suddeness of the question
caused me somewhat to hesitate, but recovering myself a little, I replied; –
"Your excellency but does me too much honor, particularly when accompanied with so heavenly boon, as your daughter as not to submit in every
respect to the utmost of your wishes." "Now, girl, dont you hear that? Wont
you do the same Maria?" "Yes father whatever be the will of you and my dear
mama, shall be mine, especially in this respect." "Then next Monday shall be
the day." "Then my dear papa, next Monday shall be the day." "Come Peggy
get up her clothes, for to-morrow we must be at the seat of government, being
the day when the legislature will meet. For I am determined that the first thing
done, shall be the changing O'Flarrity's name into mine. And the Monday
following he shall marry Maria in the Governor's house. "Come boy get yourself ready! there is no time to loose, on such an occasion as this."

Transported with joy, in an instant I found myself in my room, fell on my
knees and gave God thanks for the unbounded fortune and happiness, which
through his divine goodness he was about to bestow on a poor Irish boy; who
from a *shoe black* was about to raise to a rank equal to any in the Union, and
far more acceptable than the greatest title that England can bestow, whilst
linked with its chains of slavery and despotism.

Chapter XII

We depart for the seat of government – arrive there – my name
changed to that of the Governor's – marriage with Maria – I dont
choose to tell my name – warning to the American youth – the
chance offered by the free government of the United States to the
enterprising youth – enter on my legislative duties – perseverence.

Every thing being in readiness, for the governor was of that disposition,
that every thing must be done in an instant – we made the best of our way to

the seat of government, where we arrived in safety, the house having convened and waiting for the Governor's message.

After receiving which, the first thing done was the changing my name for that of the Governor's – the name I now bear, but which I dont choose to tell you, lest when you see me, you may say, "there goes the Irish Paddy, the *shoe black*; the dirty villian who came to our country to cut our noses out of joint – I guess you had better staid in your own country and eat your fish and potatoes." The first of which may be very true – therefore let it be a spur to you, and not have it said that any more Irish paddies should come from Ireland to disjoint the noses of the American youth – lest you will find that I will not be the only one, by ten thousands, who will monopolise the places of rank, which you should fill by your correct deportment and persevering energy; which no matter what may be their birth, fortune or education, by industry, sobriety, prudence and attention they may acquire the two last in a country like this; where "all men are born equal," and where the lowest mortal may arrive to the Presidency of the United States, and have the choice of the first lady in the land. – The blessings of a happy country.

Having got all things prepared; the eventful Monday arrived. Coaches and four, gigs in tandem, horses and the old nick knows what all, were dashing about, to and from the Governor's house – all anticipating the pleasures of the evening, but none more so than myself, who received into my arms the lovely Maria, wedded by all the indelible bonds of matrimony.

Things being thus over, the next day I entered on my legislative duties, to which I paid the strictest attention, in order to fulfil the wishes and confidence of my constituents – and arrive to that end, which I always had in view, notwithstanding the many vicissitudes and discouraging impediments I had to undergo; which would have had the tendency of making one half of you American youths, disheartened and relinquish your designs, which can only be overcome by perseverence.

Six Months in a House of Correction; or, the Narrative of Dorah Mahony, Who Was Under the Influence of the Protestants about a Year, and an Inmate of the House of Correction in Leverett St., Boston, Mass., Nearly Six Months

(Boston: Benj. B. Mussey, 1835)

Significant anti-Catholic and anti-Irish feeling existed in Boston well before the Famine generation. One of the earliest examples of nativist violence in America, in fact, was the sacking and burning of the Ursuline convent in Charlestown in August 1834. The mob had been incited in part by Rebecca Reed's Six Months in A Convent, *a trumped-up tale of abusive treatment of unwilling novices in the anti-Catholic tradition of "convent revelations." The Reed story, itself ghost-written, had described the Charlestown convent as a prison with "inmates." "Dorah Mahony's rejoinder,* Six Months in a House of Correction, *describes the Leverett Street jail as if it were a convent, complete with punishing penances, homilies from the jailors, and the sheriff's exhortations that his charges embrace their true vocation as prisoners. The parody is clever and close. The Reed book's clumsy attempts to make ordinary convent activities seem exotic, sinister, and subversive are echoed in Dorah's lavishly tedious, redundant, and anti-climactic descriptions of life in jail; for example, some twenty pages on the preparation of supper in the kitchen. Also presented with deadpan mock-seriousness is the full range of anti-Irish prejudices in Boston: ignorance, drunkenness, and belligerence, the eagerness of colleens to marry any American who will have them, and complicity in the papal plot to take over the United States. At the same time, the more zealous of Boston's nativist Protestant clergymen, Lyman Beecher and Jedediah Burchard, are characterized by name as ranting fanatics, and the anti-Masonic movement is skewered as perhaps even more anti-Catholic than the Masons. In the face of the trauma of the convent burning, this is an impressive response. By means of sophisticated parody, the Boston Irish community retaliates here with style.*

The excerpts here include the opening narrative of Dorah Mahony's emigration from Ireland to Lowell, Massachusetts, where she gets work as a nursemaid and teacher, several examples of the prison/convent parallel, which begins as Dorah is sentenced to six months on a false charge of being drunk and disorderly, and the "Closing Letter," which parodies the Reed book closely.

The first I can remember of the light of heaven, I was within four walls of turf; just such as may be seen along the Lowell rail-road. There were six older children than myself, eating potatoes out of a wooden naggin, with now and then a sup of buttermilk. A piece of meat was hanging up in the centre of the mud edifice, and none of the childer were allowed so much as to look at it, because why? it was saved for Christmas. My father, honest man, was lying asleep in a corner with his head bound up with a cloth, for he had tarried late at the fair, and had had his head broken with a blackthorn cudgel. The pig, the darlint, was nosing him. Clothes were not plenty in my paternal mansion; I was dressed myself in a pair of my brother's breeches, which he had out-grown, and besides this I had nothing. By living in this way the finest peas-antry in the world acquire a noble spirit of independence, and a proper hatred to the aristocracy.

I am not going to weary my Catholic readers with my family affairs. My father was an illustrious bog-trotter, rented half an acre of bog, or what the heretics here would call a swamp, fought manfully for his faction at wakes and fairs, and went duly to mass and confession. He brought all his children up in the fear of the Lord – the Priest, I mean; and when at last he was transported for swearing an alibi, he left his heavy curse upon us if we ever departed from the faith of our ancestors.

I can truly say that, until I was fifteen, I was much better off in Ireland than I have ever been in this poor miserable country. We had a cow and a pig, and the Priest once honored our humble dwelling by holding a station in it.* We never wanted for any thing, milk, potatoes or whiskey. All my coun-trymen agree with me that Ireland is much superior to America, and my won-der is that none of them ever go back to it.

I have said that my father had the misfortune to be transported. My mother was dead before. My three brothers enlisted in the royal Irish. One of my sisters, and a handsome, purty girl she was, occupied the honorable sta-tion of housekeeper to Father O'Shaughnessy. The two others were married to a pair of decent boys, who carried them to New Brunswick. So there was none left to cultivate the half acre of bog, and I went to live with my aunt Judy Reilly. It was there I fell in with Patrick Murphy, and he became my white-headed boy at first sight. We were to have been married; and were published, that is, read from the pulpit. But one night, as we were sitting late at the hagar, who should come in but Paddy, and he in a terrible fright. It seems the dear lad was a repealer and a white-boy, and had broken into a gentleman's house with several other ribbon-men, and had set fire to the dwelling and carried off the plate and money. While they were doing the job neatly, a party of the mil-

---

*[A station is a mass said outside of a church – in a cabin or the open air. – Ed. Throughout this book, bracketed notes are editorial; unbracketed notes are from the original texts.]

itary came upon them, and three were taken. One of them turned informer, and now the peelers were out after Paddy.* Every one knows that the cruel and oppressive laws by which Ireland is governed, punish arson and robbery with death. Paddy, therefore, was obliged to fly, and came to bid me farewell. But what Irishwoman was ever known to abandon a countryman, not to say a lover, because he was poor and in distress? I was obligated by the tenderness of my feelings to offer to accompany him into exile, and his share of the plunder of Squire Malone's house was enough to bring us over.

But the ways of Providence are wonderful. We passed over the banks of Newfoundland in a storm, and received no injury, and came in sight of Neversink. It was then that we came in sight of a great whale and a flock of porpesses. Paddy had not yet slept off last night's bottle, when I called him up from the cellar to look at the wild beasts of the sea. He looked over the fence on the side of the ship, and lost his balance and fell over head foremost, and took an everlasting leave of the buttermilk and the potatoes and the whiskey. Salt tears did I shed for him, for I never saw him again. He sunk like any stone. I should not have minded it so much, but that he had our purse in his pocket when he fell over, and I could not pay for a mass for his poor miserable soul.

They put me on shore at New York, and if it had not been for the mate of the vessel, I should not have known what to have done with myself. He was going to Newport, in Rhode Island state, where he had a wife, and children, and friends. He had been at sea a great while, and, in course, his clothes wanted a good deal of mending to make him decent to appear in. Among other accomplishments that I had learned in my paternal edifice, I had some knowledge of the use of a needle. My father and brothers, before they went away, would have brained me if I had been unable to repair their decencies, when they got them torn, which happened quite as often as once a week. So it seemed I was just the person he wanted; and we were pleased with each other, for he was a handsome man, and I am as Heaven made me. So he took me to Newport, and I mended his clothes, all excepting his shirts. I could not do that; and how should I know any thing about such a garment, seeing that no such thing was ever known in my father's domicil?

When I got into Newport, I agreed to help the mate's wife; for it's one good thing in America that there are no servants in it. I did not much like to work, but there was no help for it; I must do it or starve. I did not come to this country to work. I could have got enough of that at home, though, to be sure, I should not have been paid for it. It is a vile, inhospitable country, this. The people have no regard for strangers.

---

*[A "repealer" is a supporter of the movement to repeal the Union of Great Britain and Ireland. "White-boys" and "ribbon-men" are members of Irish nationalist secret societies. "Peelers" are the police, so called because a governmental police force was formed in 1814 by Sir Robert Peel, then the Irish Chief Secretary.]

I staid in this family three months, and don't know but I might have staid to this day (for I got a dollar and a half a week), only for two reasons. In the first place, the mistress insisted on my going to meeting on Sundays, to their heretical sermon shop, which went clean against my conscience; and in the second she took it into her head to be jealous of me: – of me, that would scorn any dirty Yankee; and all because she once saw her husband give me a dollar, for the work I did for him on my passage from New York! She insinuated to me that my presence was not agreeable; that is, she told me to "pack up my tatters and be out of her house." I am a girl of spirit, and I did not wait for a second hint. I put up my worldly goods in a piece of brown paper and took the stage for Lowell, which I had heard was a grand place, and that there I should find a great many of my warm-hearted countrymen, and have an opportunity to attend mass. I had the matter of twelve dollars in my pocket, that I had saved out of my wages.

The first person I met in Lowell, when I got out of the stage-coach, was Mr. Thaddeus Murrough, and I knew him out of hand; for he had been an old friend and a neighbor. Very glad he was to see me, and much talk we had about old times, and sorry he was to hear of my dear father's misfortune. Mr. Murrough had been known to our family as a poor scholar in Clonmel, and a world of learning he had. He left our neighborhood seven years before, a tall white-headed gossoon, for reasons that need not be specified. Otherwise, I have no doubt he would have been a Bishop by this time. Now he was three feet across the shoulders, for all the world like Paddy Carey, and had black whiskers, and a wife and four babies. But all that is neither here nor there. I shall best explain the obligations I am under to this excellent man in his own words.

"Dorah, my darlint," says he, "you're in a bad way. The people here don't like our folks, at all at all: and they're very petticular about character, and I do n't think you can show one from your last place, from what you tell me. Besides, they do n't think much of ignorant parsons, and it's my private opinion you can't write your own name, or read it either. Then again, Dorah, they do n't think much of a lady that dhrinks, and it's no more than natural and rasonable that any one brought up in turf smoke should like a taste in rason now and then; because why? they're used to it. And they're very unkind to sthrangers. For the laste bit of a ruction they put 'em in jail, and keep 'em there. Sorrow a sup of marcy have they for us."

I could only burst into tears at this dreadful story, which I have since found too true, and exclaimed, "What will I do? What will I do?"

Mr. Murrough replied, "I'll tell you what to do, Dorah. You must know that I have established a school here, to tache the poor, ignorint savages of this counthry larning and vartue. The *vanithee* often interrupts me, to come and rock the cradle, and bothers me entirely. Now come you to my siminiry, and take care of the babbies, and I'll pay you wages, and give you the bist of idication into the bargain. But mind, a *cuishla*, not the laste bit of the brogue is tolerated in my academy; I have a nathural avarsion to every thing that's vulgar, and you must reform your pronounceation altogether."

I went into Mr. Murrough's family, and I wish I had never left it. It was I that tended his children, and tried to learn to read and write; and if it had not been for the bad example of the Protestants, I should have made much more improvement than I did.

. . . .

[Eventually, Dorah moves into Boston "among the heretics and Anti-Masons." To avoid becoming "a burthen on society by going to South Boston, as too many of my countrymen and women did," she agrees to marry Mr. McShane, whose bad character is revealed when he gets drunk at their engagement party. A bit tipsy herself, Dorah runs away, sprains her ankle, and is picked up by the police and brought to court.]

His Excellency was sitting in a little box with a desk before him, and two clerks writing at a table lower down, as it was their place to do, and I was put into a box fronting him, with iron spikes to the back of it, and was locked up there. When his Lordship asked me whether I was guilty, I burst into tears and could not speak, upon which he spoke kindly, and told me to take my own time. After which I plucked up courage enough to tell his Majesty all about my breed, seed, and generation, and what had brought me to Boston, that very day. Upon which up jumped the two peelers and swore that they had been intimately acquainted with my father's daughter for more than two years, and that I was a drunken, lewd and lascivious person, whose only redeeming trait was an inclination to attend lectures and camp meetings; and so these two monstrous villains swore my life away.

His Worship then asked me if I had any friends to say a word in behalf of myself, upon which I remarked that I had no friend in the wide city but Mr. Mc S., and asked his Honor to send for him; but here the peeler stopped my mouth again by telling the court that Mr. Mc S. was no better than myself, but had once been in the state's employment in Charlestown; which I afterwards learned was true, though a peeler did speak it; and thus he circumvented me at every turn.

His Honor's Excellency then said to me, "Mrs. Mahony, if your name be Mahony, it is apparent from the oaths of these excellent citizens and worthy officers that you are an old offender, and that a little confinement will be of advantage both to you and to society. However, as this is the first time you have been before *this* court, and as you are not yet too old for amendment and repentance, I do not think it necessary to be severe. The sentence of this court is, that you pay a fine of three dollars thirty-three cents and costs, or in default thereof be confined at hard labor SIX MONTHS, and that this award be executed upon you in and within the precincts of the House of Correction. Officer, remove the prisoner." My readers may be assured that I was in a horrible passion with his Majesty the judge, though since that time I have come to the conclusion that he was not at all to blame, and that it was all the fault of the peelers. However, I gave him and the others the rights of the case, as well a woman's tongue could do it.

I was then taken to a stone building in the western part of the city, and introduced to a Mr. B., a large, strong man, who I was told was keeper of the jail, or jailer. He asked me if I should prefer solitary confinement or hard labor, and desired me to step into an apartment which I thought quite well adapted to my love of seclusion; but I did not like to be forced to do anything, and so I told him. He then took me by the nape of my neck, and said, "I do, by the force of these bones and sinews, and the virtue of authority in me vested by law, seclude you, Dorah Mahony, from the world for six calendar months, and place you under restraint in this house of thieves, to do whatever obedience prescribes, and to talk with no one but myself and the sheriff, and the turnkey, without permission." After this the jailer summoned two of the inmates of the house, and with their assistance conducted me into a cell, where they gave me some meat, skillygolee, and potatoes, and left me to amuse myself. Presently the jailer returned to the door, wishing to know how I liked seclusion, the stone walls, &c. Observing that I wore a pocket, he asked me if I had any worldly wealth in it, and observed that if I had he would take care of it for me; but the peelers had picked my pocket of every haperth, and I replied that if I had any money, I would not intrust it to his care. He then told me that if I behaved well he would use me well, and requested me to make no noise, upon which I instantly struck up "O, be joyful." His observation was that I should immediately commence hard work. I then left my cell, and sat down to a long table, where about twenty more young ladies were engaged in picking oakum and other ornamental work, and a hammer was put into my hand. On the next Sabbath morning, I was attended at the door of my apartment by my friend Mrs. J., who had heard of my misfortune, but they would not suffer her to enter. She was shown into the arch, and requested me to join her in her devotions, which we did and continued in the most edifying manner till the jailer made his appearance, and opened the door, and made a sign for us to follow him. He led the way into the arch below, at one end of which stood a heretical preacher, who I was afterwards informed was one of the saints, and the jailer told me that this was the time of silence. After the service was over, perceiving that my dress was torn, he gave me a new one, at the public expense, as he told me, and said it was a blessing to us poor, forlorn creatures that there was such a place as a House of Correction. This done, we were all driven back to our cells, and in mine I found a new *postulant,* or candidate for the honors of the institution, to whom I had liberty to speak, because, perhaps, the jailer thought it would be impossible to keep two women together in silence. One of the jail birds then came round with skillygolee and potatoes, and the postulant produced from her pocket two raw turnips, and began to eat one of them, inviting me to do the same, which I declined, as, having heard that the rules of the house were very strict, I was afraid to violate them. I have called this young lady a postulant, because I do not know any more suitable term; and candidates are so called in convents, as I have heard; and as their discipline is as severe, or more so, than Houses of Correction, I have thought the term would apply very well. However, she was not so regardful of the rules as I, and proceeded to eat her turnips, which the jailer ascertaining by questioning us separately, said there was no harm in it, but soon after sent her away, as he said, to take her trial before the righteous Judge T., of the Municipal Court, by whom I now know she was sentenced, as happens to a great majority of those who come before that upright man.

. . . .

The next morning, after receiving our portions, which were brought to us by a black man, the door were opened, and we were set at our daily tasks, but we were allowed to say our prayers, if we chose. Very few ever availed themselves of the opportunity. My business was pulling certain bits of tarred rope to pieces in order to make oakum, business with which I was wholly unacquainted, and which proved very distressing to my delicate fingers. I observed that it was a great pity all this work could not be done by steam, which would be a great saving of labor to us poor creatures, at which all present laughed; and I have heard that my elegant and humane saying got into the newspapers. I must remark here that the rules were very strictly enforced, being made, I suppose, by the sheriff and his deputies, to suit their own convenience, without any regard to that of the prisoners, which I take to be a rank piece of oppression and cruelty in a free country. In the morning the men were all taken to the yard and there set to work in breaking stone with large hammers, which must needs be very fatigueingly laborious. We women were seated by ourselves at a table in the arch, and employed as has already been stated. The following were the rules, which were not put into a gilt frame, or any other frame, but expounded to us by the officers verbally, that is to say, by word of mouth. It was made the duty of every prisoner to understand them all.

1. To work hard all day long and get nothing for it, which was very hard.

2. What was much harder, for us women, to work in silence, and not to speak unless spoken to.

3. When speaking to the jailer or any of the officers, to use perfect civility, and to address them by the title of Mr.

4. To make no noise or disturbance of any sort, on pain of deprivation of food and solitary confinement.

5. To obey all orders from the lawful authorities.

6. Not to make any use of our hands, eyes or tongues, but those commanded.

7. If necessary to speak to the officers during a time of silence, to approach

on tiptoe and speak in whispers.

8. Never to think of going into the jailyard without permission, or to make any attempt at escape.

9. To rise up and retire to the cells at the word of command without scruple or hesitation, in order to be locked up for the night.

10. To keep our cells clean and in good order.

The following, as near as I can remember, are the rules and penances of the institution.

1. For insolence or disobedience to any of the officers; – in a man, whipping, or being knocked down on the spot; in a woman, solitary confinement.

2. Never to gratify our appetites, which is in fact impossible, as the fare will not admit of it.

3. Never to converse from the windows of the building with those outside.

4. To sleep upon sackcloth and pipestems, in imitation of certain saints.

5. A perfect absence of every comfort.

6. Never to get any thing to eat between meal times.

7. If a prisoner persist in disobeying the sheriff, or officers, he or she is to be punished precisely as the said officers may think proper. Smiling is not forbidden, but is absolutely impossible.

8. No recreation at all allowed till work is over, when the prisoners are too much fatigued to think of such a thing.

Add to this, that we were not allowed any sugar, or coffee, or other little luxuries such as we were all accustomed to enjoy, and it does not convey a very favorable idea of the hospitality of the state toward the poor. Certainly, though we were together all day, we played the parts of saints and hermits, as perfectly as if we had lived each apart in a cave or a desert. I trust it will be remembered in my case, that if I have for a time been a backslider from the faith, I have had a goodly portion of my punishment already. To be sure I deserved it all; not for the crime for which I suffered, but for my apostasy.

· ·

As several of my friends desire to learn something concerning the House of Correction, I will relate what little I know. I never had permission to go into any of the cells or other apartments, except on such occasions as I have already mentioned, and the jailer and turnkey were present. During the whole term, the young ladies imprisoned were not permitted to visit their friends in the city, though they were allowed to receive presents of food and clothing from them.*

Complaints were often made to the jailer of loud talking and naughty words, which were frequently repeated aloud. Such things were esteemed violations of the rules, and were punished with bread and water, and sometimes with solitary confinement. We were exhorted to say our prayers, which I take

---

*Though such things were sent, we were not allowed to eat any thing unwholesome.

to be a very tyrannical interference with the freedom of conscience. We were told, too, to search the Scriptures, and those who could read were furnished with them; also with a great many tracts, which were brought by private persons. Those who could write were allowed to send letters to their friends, but open; and were allowed pens and paper if they had money to pay for them. The jailer tore one letter to pieces, and would not suffer it to be carried out. Another person was severely reprimanded because she had written to her friends that the discipline of the prison was too strict for her, and the provisions unwholesome, &c. The jailer scolded her severely, obliged her to admit that she had not spoken the truth, and made her ask pardon for it. She dropped a courtesy down to the floor, and saying that she was very sorry she had offended the jailer, said she would not do the like again.

Some of the ladies were much greater favorites with the sheriff and jailer than others. They sometimes spoke kindly to them, and granted them small indulgences. One young lady, who was commonly rude and impudent, was treated very ill. I often saw her in tears, and once heard her tell the jailer she was tired of the House of Correction, and did not admire hard labor. She was committed, as I learned, for being a common scold, and was in for three months. A number of young ladies were unhappy, whose names I have forgotten. I have learned that they disliked the discipline.

After this the jailer was sick of a bad cold, and I did not see him for two or three days. I attended to my labors in the kitchen, as usual, such as sweeping, boiling, baking, frying, &c. One day, however, I forgot to rise at the usual hour; but waking up and recollecting it, and fearing the jailer would be offended if he did not get his breakfast in due season, I asked permission to remain in my cell all day, telling the turnkey that I was sick, and felt sure his superior would excuse my attendance. He replied, "O yes, Dorah, you can sleep till noon." I went immediately into my cell, and employed the morning in darning stockings, which I had got from the other prisoners. While thus industriously occupied, I heard the outer door open, and the sheriff's voice very distinctly. Being conscious that I had told a fib, I kept as still as possible, lest I should be discovered. While thus employed, I overheard the following conversation between the sheriff and jailer. The former, after taking a pinch of snuff in his usual manner, began by saying, "Well, what is Dorah Mahony about? how does she appear?" I heard *distinctly* from the jailer in reply, that, "According to all appearances, she is either sick or pretends to be so; she has a great command of falsehood." The sheriff then walked about the arch, seemingly much displeased with Mr. B., and cast many severe and improper reflections upon his manner of treating me with injudicious indulgence, which he said made me lazy and presuming; all which his Honor will well remember. He then told the jailer that the discipline of the House of Correction was in its infancy, and that it would not do to have reports go abroad as such long-tongued persons as I would carry out; that I must be taken care of; and then

I heard some words concerning the doctor, and the difficulty of procuring subjects for dissection, from which I inferred that he thought the prisoners, and my own self in particular, were fit for nothing but the surgeon's knife; and that the bloody-minded cannibal, perhaps, intended to kill and eat me. He added by way of repetition that it would not do to treat the prisoners with too much lenity, or make too much "fuss" about them, as prisons were not considered palaces, but places of punishment. He then gave the jailer instructions how to manage me, and entice me to do my work cheerfully; and they soon both left the arch, and I saw no more of them.

The reader will well judge of my feelings at this moment: a young and inexperienced female, shut up from the world, and entirely beyond the reach of friends; threatened with severity, doses of apothecary's stuff, and perhaps dissection itself, with no power to resist the immediate fulfilment of the horrible conspiracy I had just overheard. It was with much difficulty that I controlled my feelings, but being aware that it would do no good to get into a passion, I kept my temper, and succeeded in getting leave to go back to the kitchen without exciting any farther suspicion. I now come to the conclusion that, unless I could contrive to break away from the House of Correction soon, I should have to stay three months longer, and perhaps never get out, unless to change my cell for a glass case in some of the infirmaries, and that every day I remained would render my escape more difficult.

[Dorah eventually makes her escape, by feeding beef to the yard dogs and walking out the back door, then concludes her narrative as follows.]

The next day the Priest called with a chaise to take me to Lowell, and brought with him a pair of iron-shod brogues and a veil, to hide my beautiful countenance; for said he, "If your face is seen, and known, you will be taken back to the House of Correction, and you may rely upon it you will shed tears of blood for the feat you have achieved." Then he entertained me with a most beautiful discoursement upon transubstantiation all the way to Lowell, where I was cordially received by Mr. M., and reinstated in my former duties of dry nurse and servant of all work. I have since been informed that I am reproached for carrying away from prison a chemise that was given me, but if the sheriff will pay me for putting a new seat to his breeches, I will cheerfully refund the value of the said chemise.

And now I have endeavored, to the best of my ability, to give a true and faithful account of what fell under my observation during my sojourn in the House of Correction, and especially during my servitude in the jailer's kitchen. And I leave it to the reader to judge of my motives for becoming a member of the incarcerated community, and for renouncing my bondage.

If, in consequence of my having for a time strayed from the true religion, I am enabled to become a humble instrument in the hands of the Priest to warn others of the dangers of consorting with heretics, and preventing even one from falling into prison, and from being inclosed within its gloomy walls, I shall feel greatly comforted.

Letter to Irish Catholics

Condensed from an Irish Paper

I AM not sure that it is of any use to write letters to you, my dear counthrymen, because very few of you can read. But there are also a few of you who can read. I write to them, and they can read to you. I have already explained to you that it is highly dangerous, if not very foolish and absurd, to learn to read at all. It makes men cantankerous and wise in their own hearts, which is one of the seven deadly sins, and can never be pardoned. Have you not your Priest, and especially your editor, (that's I myself), who is greatly distinguished as a poet, dramatist, historian and grammarian, to read and write for you? Have I not utterly discomfited Miss R. and the Rev. Mr. C., and put them to rout, horse, foot and dragoons? Have I not entirely demolished the editor of the Antimason, killed him dead, and knocked him to smithereens with the thunders of my eloquence? Have I not bespattered all your enemies in most iligant style, and was I not like to get into the stone jug for it, if I had not circumvinted them? Then of what use is it for you to learn to read at all? Your fathers never thought of such a thing. You can have your cabin, and the wife, and the childer, and the pig, and the pratee without taking any such trouble. Besides, it is a great trouble and expense to build schools and maintain them, and a great botheration to the brains to pore over books. The Catholic Sentinel and the Jesuit, those two admirably conducted reciptacles of knowledge, contain all that ever was known since the creation of the world.

If people had not known how to read, do you think they would ever have burned down our Convent? (for which they will roast forever and ever and a day after). Would they have basely stolen the gold and silver ornaments, and pulled the dead out of their graves? Would they have driven women and children from their beds into the fields at midnight? They could read the newspapers, and their brains were turned. "A little learning is a dangerous thing," as one of the fathers iligantly observes.

But especially I warn you to avoid the company of heretics. Think of Dorah Mahony, who was in danger of losing her immortal soul by reason of frequenting the company of heretics. Then coming to Boston to be married to one, she ran full speed into the House of Correction. I have now said all I had to say, and more, and am satisfied with myself entirely.

The Priest's Turf-Cutting Day, A Historical Romance

by Thomas C. Mack (New York: Printed for the Author, 1841)

Set in the dismal village of "Ballywhooloquin" in County Kerry, this very accomplished short novel satirizes many aspects of pre-Famine Irish life, mainly by deft parody of familiar rhetorical conventions. Nearly all of the main events are speeches, in which transparently hypocritical orators reveal their selfishness and corruption. These include Father Mick Murphy, the lazy, avaricious parish priest, Schoolmaster Whiggy, a garrulous armchair nationalist full of platitudinous patriotism, and Captain Robert Saxonboor, the loutish local Ascendancy landlord and commander of the Loyal Tierbread Infantry. Only the Catholic peasantry (who suffer most from the unremitting barrage of self-serving verbiage) are largely exempt from Mack's critical eye. However, the gala "turf-cutting day" does feature the public reading of an "American letter" from New Orleans, which makes fun of the immigrant's ingenuous optimism about life in the New World. An over-arching satiric frame is provided in The Priest's Turf-Cutting Day *by the narrator's voice, which parodies the tone and jargon of travel writing by collectors of folklore from England or America. Though very much a comic creation, the book also contains several passages of serious, even eloquent, indictment of British misrule in Ireland.*

Excerpts from the book include the Sunday sermon in which Father Mick Murphy exhorts his parishioners to prepare for his "day," the narrator's erstwhile observations of an Irish wake and of the customs and ceremonies of the turf-cutting day itself, an example of Mr. Whiggy's fiery nationalist oratory, and the reading of the American letter. Unknown except for this single fascinating novel, Thomas C. Mack belongs in the tradition of Irish irreverent satirists that stretches from Jonathan Swift to Brian Merriman to Flann O'Brien and beyond.

I will here place myself in the situation of the weary traveller, and having rested and had some whiskey and eggs, mixed by as laughing a landlady as ever filled a glass of poteen. It being on the Sabbath, my attention was arrested by the crowds from all parts, moving in that direction of the town. On inquiry, I was informed that Father Mick Murphy would be there in person, to preach a sermon that day at two o'clock. The house soon filled, and many were the gallons of raw barley dew drank previous to the hour appointed for service.

Father Mick was the most pious man, as well as the greatest orator, in all Munster, and thirty years parish priest of Aughwhooloquin; his eloquence was heard of both far and near, and what made the occasion of more importance, it was twelve months since he condescended to preach himself, and that was on the occasion of his last turf-cutting. You must know that the reverend father intended to appoint his turf-cutting day on this occasion also, which considerably increased the excitement. At length the hour arrived, and, with the assistance of the landlady, (through her interest with the clerk), I obtained a seat at a respectable distance from the altar, where I saw every mysterious movement, and heard distinctly the whole performance, one word of which, up to this time, I did not understand: when, at length, Father Murphy came forward to the front of the platform and delivered the following address:

"Shut that door, that the Word of God be not polluted by heretics. Is that Thyge Murphy at the door? Oh, Thyge, I'll have you now, you devil, but I won't vex myself wed you now; I'll preach the Word of God. I take my text from the Holy Book of St. Genesis – never mind the verse as it is a book yees can't read. 'God said to Cain, You shall be a vagabone on the face of the earth.' Now, as I am the representative of the pope, so is the pope a representative of Peter, and Peter is the representative of God; so Peter does the will of God, the pope does Peter's will, and I does the will of the pope, and use his language: thin all of yees, my flock, must do my will: (Oh! oh! oh! shouted all the people; what eloquence:) now, God the Father, God the Son, and God the Spirit is one; thin Peter, the pope, and me is one. (Oh! oh! oh! roared the people.) Thin, according to the word of my text, yees is a set of vagabones on the face of the earth. Thyge Murphy, come forward. (Thyge appears.) Thyge, you are a vagabone on the face of the earth; didn't I bid you to bring butther on last turf-cutting day, and if you had no bacon, to bring eggs? So go from my presence, you vagabone you, and if you don't pull up next time, you will be sorry. Paddy Golaher come forward. (Paddy comes.) Paddy, the words of my text is, that yees is all vagabones on the face of the earth. You, Paddy, is that self same vagabone. Didn't I bid you to send bacon to my last turf-cutting? but wasn't it a mane can of butthermilk what yees sint? Do betther next time, or I'll pronounce the words of my text. Judy Hagerthy, Kit Lynch, Biddy Rearerdhy, Poll Shaughnessy, Peg Dougherty, all of yees vext me at my last turf-cutting: if yees don't pull up this time, I will send you from me as God did Cain. Now, I give out that on the thirty-first of June, that is, next Thursday, will be the parish priest's turf-cutting day. All of yees what hasn't mate, send men; and all of yees what hasn't men, must send mate; and all of yees women that hasn't eggs, send butther; and all yees that hasn't butther, send eggs – and when you are done, walk in order to Conehure's, till ye get your whiskey. And I now pronounce that the first of yee's a vagabone what raises a Botha – I will curse you, bell, book, and candle light. I'll hold a station at your house next Friday; Jack Welch and I hope you won't let your poor priest starve; kill two chickens and after my holy labour is over, I'll try if I can make 'em into fish for myself. Get me a bottle of wine – go to Lowistial for it; a pint of whiskey, if it's ould, will do. And if the colleens of that neighborhood has not something betther to tell me than they had last time, they will be sorry when it's too late; for it will be a bad day for them they saw me, as I will pronounce my text on them; they will be vagabones on the face of the earth. Moll Murtoch; come here. Moll: this is a purty talking I hear about yees; go into that confession box, you scout."

After some time private with Moll, the priest returned and inquired if Paddy Brian was there. "No, your riverance," responded the hearers. "Send over to Conehure's for him. (Accordingly Paddy was brought in drunk.) Paddy, you Bosthoon, isn't it purty pranks you was playing with Moll Murtoch on my last turf-cutting day. You and Moll come home through the breenouch together, and there is purty talk made uf it. Now, Paddy, you must marry Moll; she is as good a father's and mother's child as you are, and an honest colleen till you put your unlucky foot under her. If you don't marry her, I will say as God and the Blessed Virgin said to Cain: 'You're a vagabone on the face of the earth,' and I will shut the book, and put out the light in your face. (Paddy, as a matter of course, consented.) Well, I'll give out that, on next Sunday Moll Murtoch and Paddy Brian will be married. And you, old Paddy Brian, make a decent wedding for your son, and, with the help of the Blessed Virgin, I will be there at four o'clock. Paddy, you're a rich man; kill six pigs, and git a barrel of whiskey, invite the gauger, and the apothecary; and I will now give it out for the parish to be there. Bile a dozen of hams for the gauger, the apothecary, and me; and have plenty of pork, bacon and whiskey for the people, and don't forget my wine. And yees knows that the heretic ministers is paid wid the tithes, but your poor starved priest has nothing but what he gits at christenings, confessions, and weddings. Then you parishioners have no blind excuse, but be prepared for the collection, or I will pronounce the words of my text on you, 'yees is vagabones on the face of the earth.' And if any of yees forget the holy discourse of this day, I will put the mark of Cain on yees from the altar, and blot your names from the book of the Purgatorian Society. I will ring the black bell; and all the bells in hell will ring – the twelve lights of the apostles will be quenched on your seed, breed, and generation – so be it."

The sermon being now over, which entertained me considerably, I postponed other engagements to witness, not only the wedding, but also the turf-cutting, and concluded to spend a few days longer in Ballywhooloquin.

[Moll Murtoch's wedding is disrupted when the gauger (tax collector) toasts the memory of "King William, who freed us from pope and popery, brass money and wooden shoes." The resulting brawl is subdued by the Loyal Tierbread Infantry and the com-

munity is further insulted when the new bride and groom are mistakenly jailed. Thyge the piper suffers an injury and his pipes are trampled.]

The accident that happened to the piper at the wedding, although not mortal, confined him to his bed; and the injury done to his bagpipes preyed so much on his spirits, besides changing so suddenly from an active to sedentary life, produced such an effect on his constitution, that he died after three days' illness; which melancholy event had such a thrilling effect on his neighbours, that the only way to compensate was, to give him a decent wake and burial.

As I had yet a few days to wait for the turf-cutting, I embraced this opportunity to see an Irish wake. I went early in the evening, and beheld the unfortunate defunct laid on an old door, in the middle of the floor, on his back. His bagpipes were at his head; the fragments of the fatal quart bottle carefully collected together, and broke up in small pieces, as they were to be distributed to the mourning friends of Thyge as a lasting relic of the well-beloved piper. There was twelve candles, six at each side; these were to represent the twelve tribes of Israel, and also as typical of the twelve shining stones on Aaron's breast-plate. But above all, they were to show the deceased light across the bridge which separates purgatory from Abraham's bosom; and the bridge, having received some injury from the ravages of time, required repairing. Therefore there was a plate put on the feet of the corpse to receive the half-pennies, to be placed at the disposal of the Purgatorian Society for this purpose. The centre being well lighted, there was no necessity for candles in the corners, where the country boys sat with their sweethearts on their knees, whispering soft sounds in their ears, sounds that are only known to those who have initiated themselves in the sublime secrets of the Court of Venus. After I had been seated some time, a mysterious looking woman rushed into the cabin; her frantic looking features twisted into wicked, curious forms, she threw herself on the corpse and chanted this medley:

"Yerra wisha, Thyge, my darlint, is it yourself that is there? Och, hone! och, hone! och, hone! I remember you since you were only the height of my knee. Och, hone! och, own and your poor pipes at your head. Och, own! och, hone! och, hone! It's a great loss the whole country will have after my own, own Thyge. Och, hone! Wisha, who will play up the 'Grinder' now you are gone? augh, augh, gulla gone! God Almighty rest you and your mother's soul! and may Matthew, Mark, Luke, an' John, bless the bed that you lay on! Och, hone! och, hone! 'twas yourself at last turf-cutting played Patrick's Day, and garryoun ohon! och, hone!"

Her exclamations became so violent and her voice so loud that I could note down no more, and even that much very imperfectly. When she was done, the bottle went round, and the boys and girls played push the brogue and the game of forfeits; when, after a few rounds of whiskey, the singing commenced; but the noise and laughter nearly struck me deaf, so that I could collect no more than Darby Muldoin's, the piper's cousin-german, song and a verse from Kitty Flannagan, who was the lion of the night, and sat on Darby's knee.

["Darby's Song" is a nationalist rendering of events from the 1798 Rising. "Kitty's Song" exhorts wives to follow their husbands into battle.]

There were here such a large collection of contending factions, who evidently appeared disposed to quarrel, that I thought it prudent to retire; but I subsequently heard that they decided their points by a general fight the next fair, where the Calhoons were completely vanquished, the Mulvills having been joined by that strong faction, the O'Shaughnessys. The turf-cutting day has arrived, which left me no farther leisure to visit the country parts.

The thirty-first of June having been appointed by mistake, that month containing only thirty days, the cutting day fell on the first of July; and it being the anniversary of the battle of the Boyne, caused very bad feeling on both sides. Early in the morning of that day I took my station on a hill near the turf-bog, where I was well repaid for my loss of time by beholding the whole country in motion, moving from all quarters to the common centre of the bog patch. The men carrying turf-slanes, pitch-forks, shovels, and various other working tools, on their shoulders; and above all, every man and boy had a cudgel slung to a large button which is sewed on the left breast, which they called the stick button; some of these sticks are heavily ferruled with iron, others studded with heavy nails. The women with provisions of all kinds moving leisurely along, the whole presenting as ludicrous a sight as the imagination could fancy. The work of turf-cutting immediately commenced, which, from the immense number of help present, did not occupy more than one hour; in the meantime the women lighted fires up and down through the fir-bushes for cooking purposes. I having prepared myself with a large horn of snuff, which operated as a passport through the crowds of squatted groops, whose characters for open-heartedness, cheerfulness, rustic manliness, witticism, and rude glee of all denominations were fairly developed. All party fudes appeared to be forgotten; fun and frolic was the order of the day. Nor were the Olympic games unknown to those striplings; the wrestling was superb – leaping, vaulting, kicking foot-ball; and besides the game of hunt the buck, there was leap-frog, which, when under full way, extended at least three miles. My delight was boundless to behold twelve or fifteen hundred men bare-foot and bare-legged bounding through the air. It was at length announced by the sound of cows' horns that dinner was ready. The blooming full-moon faces of the girls with delight witnessing the gambols of the athletic and ruder sex, whose breasts panted for the hour to come for bush court-ing. But, reader, I am here bound to observe that the general modesty of these children of nature would be much calculated to cause a blush in the cheeks of some of those who move in better circles, who may boast of superior refine-ment and education – they were a noble specimen of Erin's virtuous daugh-ters and of her sturdy sons.

When I gazed round and beheld the fertility of hill and dale, the salubri-ousness of climate and grotesque appearance of the face of the country, with materials before my eyes of a fine race of men, who are naked and hungry through the oppression of their task-masters, I must say that their piratical oppressors, when blustering about freedom in the wilds of Africa, much resemble the hollow roaring of the ocean when bellowing through the cav-erns of Ballyheigh, searching its crevices for victims to swallow up in the common gulf.

Here is scope wherewith to exercise the deepest and at once the most contemplative reflections of a profound philosopher, while at the same time it is a lesson from nature's sublime volume to the despot on his gilded throne. See with what joyful countenance both men and women fly to respond to the meek call of their Christian instructor, while the monarch of tyranny is neces-sitated to enforce his arbitrary laws by force of arms.

England's councils are in perpetual session, adding force to force in the vain attempt to ride down the growth of just indignation, which oppression nourishes in the indignant breasts of this free-hearted, but trampled-on, peo-ple of nature's finest model.

Haughty man, think not that yonder stupendous mountain has been reared up by fickle chance. No; methinks in it I see a vast filter, in which the elements are distilled into the crystal stream which steals by curious route down the sloping chasm, watering those spontaneous shrubs in its descent, and spreading its influence to diffuse nutriment to the vale beneath, thereby to refresh and give new vigour to the toil of man. How merrily the lambkin frisks with its placid dam, who gently licks its fleece, then bleats to the famil-iar bark of the shepherd's dog.

How stately the Daffo dilly basks on the rivulet's brink, flirting in the sun-beams, vying with the tulip, whose modesty nature teaches to close its silken leaves as the hillock changes sides to give its flowery burden on the opposite ledge an opportunity to salute the morning sun. And not less chaste are those rural damsels of the mount and glen, whose simple and fluttering hearts cheer up the lovers of future bliss.

No hissing serpent with poisonous fang lurks beneath the banks. But fel-low-man, who may be nicknamed sire, deals death by fire and sword to all who dare assert their right to that produced by their own sweat.

Call not this cruel monster pirate, if you be his friend, who will enter by force and pillage your house of all, and then expect the wretched inmates to exclaim, "God save the king."

> I hope they may be great, glorious, and free,
> The first flower of the earth, the first gem of the sea.

There was a report through the country that a letter of great importance had been received, containing interesting information from America, and it was rumoured that it would be read at the turf-cutting; the anxiety became so general to hear it that Mr. Whiggy was unanimously called, who addressed the people as follows:

"I am now your schoolmaster these thirty years, and it is with great sorrow that I witness the night meetings that were caused by them Tearbread Sasanigs; they put you all in jail for nothing, and you would be no men if you did not resent it; you quarrel with each other, and the common enemy of you all in your sight. Thin, as I have a word to speak to you all, I propose to retire into the high meadow, and let Murty Dhun stand at the gap and get the password from all who enters; then I'll know who I am talking to; an' let all the women go home – then I say to you, Quisseper a bit; I wrote it down for fear I would make them blunders I sometimes make when I am speaking ex tempore."

This measure having been carried into effect, Mr. Whiggy took his stand on a rock in the centre of the field, and commenced his harangue. I gained admission through the parish clerk vouching for me.

Mr. Whiggy. "My countrymen, perhaps this may be the last time I shall ever deliver my sentiments to you; therefore, hear me for my cause, and be silent that You may hear! Probonopublico, you all remember the story I told you at Moll Murtock's wedding – look back at the fiery zeal of our fathers in defence of their native soil! Look back at the slow degrees by which we have been despoiled of our inheritance! Look at our holy church, levelled to the earth and polluted by accursed heretics, and our holy fathers persecuted for obeying their divine calling. They take the pig from your door to feed a bloated, drunken, debauched parson. They make servants of your sons, to carry burdens, and of your maidens, to draw water. Then, if you have any of the spirit of him who went inpropria persona, and conquered – but he died on the field – remember the words of the liberator, 'He who would be free himself, must strike the blow!'* My countrymen, you have no right to pay tydes nor taxes; and there are many of you who are here now assembled, who are absolute legitimate owners of the soil Guredevino: but as it is so lately since our plans proved abortive, the time has not again arrived to attempt any formidable measure. But be preparing, and let all of you, old and young, learn the use of arms, and, above all things, take all the guns you can from the protestant parsons. Have your meetings cautiously, and at night. When it is necessary to hide your guns, put them in coffins, and bury them in the

---

*["The liberator" is Irish political leader Daniel O'Connell (1775-1847).]

churchyards. Oh, I am so full I can't speak – if your old schoolmaster could only live to see your country free, durantevita, he would die in peace. Let no stranger live in your neighbourhood; they are all Peel's spies.* When you want to do a little necessary act, such as to burn a house, the fewer of you who will do it, the better – and whoever the lot falls on, let him do it conamore. The insult you received from the Saxonboors is such as requires immediate action: don't leave a stone of it but you will level; and if they are all burnt up in it, so much the better. Ye can have all done before the yeomen would be out, and the soldiers are all gone back to Limerick. But it would be a good way to burn the minister's house first; it is two miles from Tierbread; and when the yeomen run to that point, you can easily have satisfaction on the Saxonboors. Now, above all things, don't let that gauger know your plans – keep in your mind the toast he drank at the wedding, when he was drunk. He is only a spy. If any of you are suspected or caught, why, you can try to set off for America, where you will all be gentlemen. And if they hang one, what signifies that out of seven million and a half. I expect to hear a good account to-morrow; and that you may know the fine place you will be going to if any of you should be caught, I will read Jerry McCarthy's letter for you. Memento mori."

MY DEER ILLEEN:

"I take this favorble opportunity of riting a fue lyns to darlin Illeen, an' who do you think is ritin' it ? why, then, it's paddy sullivan; you know paddy sullivan – eye, an' him, an' you, wint to scool tiegither; do you mind him, now? Well, as i was sayin', we al wint to scool tiegither, and comin' home thru the bog i alwys bate him al out in the standin' lep; i, a span: an' you no fhin you wood be lookin' i alwys bate him out in hop-step-an'-jump: but, if the win' was in my back, ide bate him a mile; fait, it is meself, Illeen, jewel, is ritin' it: an' he lies, it's i bate him in the standin' lep, you no; but fhin he had the win', he is so lite that he would run like ould – don't balk it – mister cragin's fox-hound. Don't read what I am afther ritin' only to my cussin jarmon, Darby piper; an' Illeen ma cushlamachree, this is a grate place intirely; there is pepel here as yaller as the mud of the cabin, wat in ireland we cals yaller molats, but they cals um here cry ouls; fath, it's a quare name, but that's wat they cals um. But the pepel is very civel to us, an' cal's us greeks, an' you know that's a grate name. Mister wiggy, the scoolmasther, wus, always boastin' about that name; an there grate mag-ishuns, here, intirely; fhat do yu think i saw um do wid me own ise? fait, then, my hand an' word for you, i sau um move a hole hous, to mile of ground, an' it wus cows they puld wid; the cows was al in a ro, like the way the wild gees fli to the logh, and fhat made me wundher more, was, me

*[Sir Robert Peel was British Prime Minister twice, 1834-35 and 1841-46.]

jewel, to se the riges of praties walkin' afther it; for fhat good wud be to muve the hous', you se, widout the praties. 'Twas a grand site, intirely, an' they're makin' fhat they cals a kinel, and the name of it is the estran kinel; an' it's so long, intirely, that the sayin' here wid us is, that they will send it to ireland; an' if they do, we all ar movein' so fast, that i'll soon be workin' on that ind of it; and then my own Illeen can bile my praties an' wash my shirt. An', blessed be the holy vergin, nothin' happinid me, hunny, comin' over, but a bit of a fite we had here, an' it happinid asey; ned scanlon axd me to take a glass of rum – O, rum is very chape, here – an' as I wus sayin', he axd me to take a glass of rum, an' fhin we wint in, divil a bit, God forgive me for cursin', but i had to pay four cents fur it meself; the cents here is as big as the happeny in ireland; an' as I had a sup in, i up wid my stick an' nocked him down, and tim dolan run at me, and tade laverly crosd sticks wid him over my hed, an', my jewil, down runs all the boys, and 'twas as fine a fight as ever you sau at a fair: all i got in it was a few little cuts in the hed, but the docther says mi hare 'ill grow on it agin: and for fear i wud forgit, an thare is a talk wid us to deside it in the crismus holydays, send me the black thorn i left driin' in the chimbly; as thare is no postage now in ireland, you can ty it to your letther, as the ship is so big there will be room anuff, an' besides the pepel here are all fond of firearms. Nails here are very deer, so dhrive in the ful of the ind of it; but civer up the ind of the nails, feer they wud charge duty: an', hunny, there is a scool here we go to here of sundays, an' i am very fur in the gografy. You know that all i wint in ireland was to O; an' 'tisn't that i say it myself – i cud say it as loud as e're a boy in scool: but i was as big that time, you know, as tade cavanagh; an' fhen i come to the next leson i cud say it asey be shuttin' me mouth; fate i say it now for you: the way yud see how fur i wint. Did you put that down, paddy – i can say the name of the nixt purty well – you know the one like the ould hoop wid the tail to it; an' i can say R – did you put that down, paddy? I cud smatter the rest uv 'em down, if they minded me uv 'em, till i cumd to the one like the ould winmil, an' they calls it in this counthry, egs; an' fhen i calls it egs, they all lafs, an' fate if they lafs again fhen i call it egs, for that's the very name they calls it, i won't go there any more; an' don't forgit the stick, for if they lafs any more i 'ill want it. I forgot to tell you fhat great pepel we ar here; fhen fhat they calls the pols, comes, we are grate men as the king himself, an' betther to, for little bisnes he'd have heer then. We alwys elect our prisidint, but this time, eroune – fhen the english sint over a ship ful o' munny, an' bot the situaton for a englishmun, an' put out the one we had becase he was an irishman; but the next time you'd see fhat you hear, they won't do that agin, becase we here in this plase that they hanged thre of the spies in Nue York, an' mabe that won't be a warnin' to em'; an' flen the kinel is dun yees can all cum, an' if yees cud coax misther o'connell, mabe he'd come to, an' thin i beleve we cud have him prisidint. Give my love to biddy haggerty, an' ax hur dos she remember fhen i an' hur futted the turf for parson stot; wasn't it a fine crismus we had intirely un the beacon he gave us: write to me sune, an' as i furgot to say any more, i finish me letther from your own, own jerry mccarty: but let me no if mr. wiggy is alive, an' tim conner, an' we hear that moll murtock is married to paddy brion; well, there was quare talke about them at the turf-cutin'; an' if mr. wiggy is alive, but if he is ded never mine axin' him; let him reed this letther to all the pepel at the next cutin'; mabe nobody else in the country cud reed it, for paddy sullivan is the lernedest a boy at our scool; he bid me tell you, so the way his father hears it. No more at present. A cushla from your own jerry mccarty. Bluranounthers, tell me, had the calhoon's an' the mulvill's any kind of a little fite at the last fair; an' who strud the coat? an' who hit fust? was the peelers there, bad look to um? Illeen, your own −

JERRY MCCARTY

"TO ILLEEN MCCARTY:
    "Ballywhooloquin, parish of
        "Aughwhooloquin, barony of
            "Iroeityfhyn, County of Kerry,
                "IRELAND."

Evening now drawing to a close, with a beautiful June sun setting behind the western hills, its shooting rays added new lustre to the scenery; the variegated semi-circle bid defiance to the most scientific painter's brush, under which men, formed in God's own image, were drove, by cruel necessity, to plan measures hostile to the laws − laws they do not recognise as their own, but those of foreigners, devised for purposes of oppression, which they feel no remorse of conscience to break by every indirect means − open rupture being impracticable, owing to their peculiar position on the terrestrial globe, and having been weakened by various conquests; − then suppose even that this people will sometimes commit rash acts of desperation, look at the provocation which they receive, and your conclusion will be that they are unquestionably driven to such acts. Here are large tracts of country devoted to the sport and voluptuousness of a few descendants of mere mushroom adventurers; while, on the other hand, the bulk of the people are almost in a starving condition. The poor, wretched, small farmer, digging from year to year on a small patch, in some remote corner of the rich man's sporting grounds, where he dare not kill the wild bird or quadruped, which were formed by the Great Ruler for the use of all men: no, no; that would spoil his lordship's day's sport, and thereby disarrange his organs of digestion, by which he would lose his appetite for the dinner which was provided from the sweat of the poor man's brow; while he and his family are sometimes necessitated to eat the herbage which grow round the landlord's fence. Oh, man! the great day of retribution will come. Mr. Whiggy's harangue elated those men to commit acts which were cruel and unnecessary. The committee-men retired to a corner of the field, and had a consultation, which was, of course, secret from me; but you can easily conclude what the subject of their deliberation was, when you hear the sequel.

They all marched in single file, with the weapons of husbandry shouldered, and a very formidable appearance they made, I assure you. When they arrived at the Sheebeen house, I was astonished at the peace, good order, and harmony, with which they conducted themselves. Little did I think that it was only that calm which will sometimes come before a storm. Next morning, the first news I heard was, that Parson Eagerfund's house was burnt down by the white boys; and also Captain Saxonboor's town mansion, the families having narrowly escaped.

When I inquired into the particulars, it appeared that, at twelve o'clock, news came into Tierbread that the parson's house was on fire; the yeomen having been celebrating the battle of the Boyne, were all primed and ready to march, which they did, but they were too late; the midnight marauders had fled. Our loyal troops to show their bravery, amused themselves firing at all the domestic cocks and hens they could see; in the meantime, the Tierbread house was also fired, and burnt to the ground. There was no trace of the offenders to be found, except Murty Dhun, who came into town half drunk, early in the morning. The mud on his brogues, and other evidences, proving he had not been in bed that night, he was of course seized, and put in prison on suspicion. The people flocked to see the ruins, and curiosity led me there also; the general conversation turned on the turf-cutting; and it was the opinion, in Tierbread, that the plot was hatched there. I fell in company with a decent looking man, and, after some commonplace conversation, I had the misfortune to remark that I saw nothing indicative of such a plot. The decent looking man asked me, "Was I at the meeting which took place after the turf-cutting?" I answered in the affirmative, but soon saw my imprudence; for in my life I shall never erase from my memory the cadaverous grin the decent man gave, when he put his left hand on my shoulder, with a loaded pistol to my head; his eyes flashed like a volcano, and pronounced, "you are my prisoner, sir." I was handcuffed, and brought through crowds in this unenviable condition before a magistrate, who examined me in private; but, with great difficulty, I made it clear to him that I was only a traveller. But I was sent under a strong guard, in company with Murty, to Tralee jail, there to finish my stay in Kerry until the trial, as I was held as a witness. At the examination, I had, in self-defence, to tell any names I knew; but all I could describe were the priest's clerk and Mr. Whiggy. A company of mounted peelers departed for their arrest; but the arrest of Murty and I put them on their guard in time to start for the United States, to diffuse knowledge in that republic.

The Adventures of Tom Stapleton

by John McDermott Moore, *Brother Jonathan*
(New York, January 1, 1842 – May 14, 1842)

Immigrant journalist John McDermott Moore came to New York City from Ireland sometime before 1830. An ambitious and versatile writer, he worked for literary periodicals such as Brother Jonathan, *edited at least two newspapers (*The Irishman and Foreigners' Advocate *and* The European, *both in the 1830s), and wrote poetry, fiction, and burlesque drama. His first book was* Lord Nial: A Romance *(1834), which contains several short poems, the long title poem about the legendary Irish hero, and an introductory story, also called "Lord Nial."*

John M. Moore's second book, The Adventures of Tom Stapleton, *was serialized in Brother Jonathan and had three editions in book form, including one in London, where its title was* Life in America. *It is a good-humored, satiric presentation of several aspects of New York life in the 1830s: the frivolity of bachelor boardinghouse life at "202 Broadway," the summer social whirl among "the fashionable set" at Rockaway Beach, the city's grimy underside in a "dock-loafers' den," and the lively, ingenuously dishonest political scene at Tammany Hall. The presiding "universal genius" of the boardinghouse is an Irishman, Philip O'Hara from Donnaraile, County Cork, a likeable, kindly hustler, who is trying to get along with wit and grace. Tom Stapleton, the narrator, is a quieter and less idiosyncratic young man, who embodies Moore's sensitivity to language and consciousness of its uses and abuses for social and political ends. Tom has an ear for dialects, and his ramblings around New York feature comic renderings, in the service of undercutting pretension and hypocrisy, of many voices – a pseudo-aristocratic Frenchman, a Cockney pretender to British nobility, phlegmatic Hudson River Dutch villagers, and the shady and jaded dock loafers. There are also several examples of Irish brogue, the relative thickness of which dictates social and occupational distinctions. Also running through the novel is a parody of the conventions of popular sentimental romance, in the form of a wild and woolly subplot of intrigue, kidnapping, and attempted murder, and a series of sentimental soliloquies by Tom on the subject of his uncertain love life. These are in effective counterpoint to the realistic main plot, which contains much valuable information about New York Irish-American life in the 1830s.*

The bulk of Moore's novel is given over to the campaign for New York City alderman of WASP aristocrat Anthony Livingston, the father of Tom's great love, Lucy.

69

*When Livingston enlists the aid of Tammany stalwart Barney Murphy, the race is on.
The election-day climax is described in this selection. John Moore's original songs punc-
tuate and enliven the text throughout.*

The second day of the election we were hard at it from early dawn till midnight; and even then not a few of the independent voters declined going to
bed, and slept on door stoops and in channels all night, partially because they
were in a state to make all places alike to them, and partially to the end of
being early at business on the following morning.

Mighty were the efforts of genius and valor performed by the belligerents
on this, the second day. At the commencement, the Stubbsites, who flattered
themselves into the notion that the demonstration of the Livingstonians was
a mere flash in the pan, took it easy enough; but by and by, perceiving that
the shilelah of Lawlor the Rattler – the generalship of Barney – and more
than all, the melting of the fifty dollar bill on the previous night, had softened
the hearts of a large number of the "Betwixt and betweens," in favor of the
enemy, they had a general meeting – warmed up their patriotism, with no
step-mother's allowance of *eau de vie* – and went at it like devils.

It was but "Greek to Greek," however, so that they obtained no advantage over us. For every Livingstonian knocked down by a Stubbsite, a
Stubbsite also bit the ground; – for every defamatory handbill issued by the
enemy, we posted a flaming placard setting forth to the effect, that if Stubbs
was elected, the Republic of North America would never recover the shock!

Subjoined I publish a couple of these thunder guns in illustration of the
manner in which we carried on this paper war. The first is from the Stubbs's.

"REPUBLICANS TO THE RESCUE. The honor of the *ward!* – the
advancement of *free principles*!! and your own escape from the *yoke of British
influence* depend on the result!!!

The ARISTOCRAT LIVINGSTON is soliciting your votes. Democrats, this
Livingston was *opposed* to the last war! Democrats, this Livingston lives in a
big house with *marble* steps to the door!! Democrats, this Livingston is in favor
of putting *poor* men in jail for *debt*. Democrats, this Livingston issues *twenty
landlord's warrants* every quarter day!!!! Democrats, this Livingston ought to
be *hanged* instead of elected to the *Common Council!!!!* And therefore
Democrats of the glorious –th Ward, down with him and his British masters
in the dust! and vote for Stubbs – Stubbs the patriot! Stubbs the orator!
Stubbs the *poor* man's *friend!* In a word, our own Alderman Stubbs, who is an
ornament to his race, and a bulwark to the cause of Liberty. Again we cry, to
the rescue!!! and nine cheers for ALDERMAN STUBBS."

The next specimen of our wall literature hailed from the Livingstonians, and was written with more tact and judgment than the above, inasmuch as it did not admit the possibility of defeat, and was therefore better calculated to catch those weather-cock patriots, who don't care a fig which way they vote, so as they are in at the winning side. It was manufactured by Murphy, Stapleton, and company; Barney, by the way, suggesting all the most flagrant falsehoods, and furnishing two-thirds of the brightest of the ideas. I remonstrated with Barney about the absurdity, to say nothing of the wickedness, of stringing so many lies together, as they could be so easily refuted; but his answer was, that the enemy would not have time to refute them before the election was over; and that then it would be too late, as a good character would be of no further use to us. But to the last grand card of the Livingstons, which read thus: –

"HUZZA! HUZZA!! HUZZA!!! – Glory! Glory!! Glory!!! – We have met the enemy and they are ours!!!

Democrats of the – th – you have done your duty nobly! The ward is redeemed! – the dog in office, Stubbs, lies howling in the mud! – and that pure patriot, Livingston, must be elected by an overwhelming majority!

BEHOLD THE ACTIONS OF THE TRAITOR STUBBS!!!

He hires houses and lets them out to under tenants at rack rents! – He voted to double the license for selling liquor! He seized a poor widow woman's furniture, and turned herself and her six small children out of her little room in Mott Street, last Monday, because she was in arrears to him for a month's rent! He testified under oath before Recorder Riker, a few days since, that to the best of his opinion, at least a third of the Irishmen in this country were escaped convicts from Botany Bay! He never bailed a man out of a hobble yet, but endeavored to send that staunch democrat, Thomas Lawler, to prison for seven years, for standing up for the honors of the ward! He is a regular skinflint, and cuts mechanics and laborers down to *nothing* a day, for he never pays them the trifle he promises! He cheated Mary Rooney out of a month's washing, and then sent her up for six months to Blackwell's Island for making a noise about it! And to crown all, Oh, ye virtuous citizens of the –th Ward, he don't live with his lawful wife, but keeps two women, so that his christening of his son by the honored name of Patrick, is a downright insult to Irishmen! But, fellow-citizens, by your glorious exertions, we have this day demolished Stubbs! Yes, the dog in office has been hurled from his throne, and another pull at the ballot box will hide the traitor from our sight for ever! Then huzza! friends of freedom. Come along and let every man who wishes well to the Star Spangled Banner, and loves to see the Eagle of Liberty floating in triumph over his head, deposit a vote for that unflinching patriot – that honest man – that best friend of the poor, and pride of republicanism, Anthony Livingston!

The people's ticket is already about four hundred ahead! Boys, do you hear that?"

———————

The second night was a great night for both sides, and of course an immense one for the glory of liberty and the purity of the ballot-box. It began with meetings in various patriotic houses; – was kept up with any quantity of liquor, "free gratis for nothing," at the expense of the various candidates for office; then branched out into innumerable street fights; and finally settled down into repose made hideous, by dozens of the worn out belligerents lying hither and thither on door stoops, and in channels, making the highways and byways of the city melodious with their snores.

And then might be seen the captains, subalterns, and non-commissioned officers of either host, at work among the sleepers. For instance, an agent of the Stubbsites would come along, and having shaken one of the prostrate independent electors into the possession of one or more of his seven senses, exclaim, "Hallo, friend, who do you vote for, Stubbs or Livingston?" To which, if the response happened to be "Stubbs forever – Livingston be d–d!" the patriot was thence led away in the most affectionate manner possible, and provided with comfortable quarters till morning. But if, on the contrary, he turned out to be a Livingstonian, a bottle of fourth proof was immediately attached to his lips, until he had drank himself into a state of such utter stupefaction, as would be likely to keep him quiet enough for the ensuing twenty-four hours; and then to make assurance doubly sure, a charley would be called, and the inebriate trundled off to the watch-house, there to be kept out of harm's way until the election was over.

The agents of the opposition acted differently in one respect. If the party picked up was a Livingstonian, he was led away, and provided with comfortable quarters, as in parallel cases with the Stubbsites; but if he chanced to be an enemy, he was immediately well liquored, lifted into a cart, and deposited in the hold of a schooner provided for the job, and lying in the East River, which schooner, by the way, pushed off about an hour after midnight, with upwards of fifty staunch Stubbsites on board, whom it landed some twenty miles from New York, from whence they had to return on foot, so that but five of them reached the city that day; and none of them at all in time to help their party, either with a vote or a blow.

Of course this was Murphy's arrangement.

"I don't understand the philosophy of it, Barney," said Starkey, when he heard it proposed, or rather decided on, for Mr. Murphy was a second Bonaparte – as with him to plan and execute were about one and the same thing.

"The divil a wan suspected you ov understanding much ov any thing barrin' drawing up latitats and the like, bad luck to thim!" returned Barney. "But for all that if we don't do it, Stubbs will be more nor even with us."

"How, Barney?"

"Aisy enough; an' sure if your head wasn't too full of book larnin' to give it a chance for howlding any common sense, you'd see through it at a glance! Isn't Stubbs an aldherman, an' be vartue of that same a magistrate. Well, if we put any ov his min in the watch-house, begorra he'll release thim agin in the mornin' before cock crow with a lecture on his tendherness that will make them fight and vote for him more ferociously nor ever; but if he catches any ov ours lyin' about after nightfall, an' not able to get out ov his way, me hand to you if wan of thim will see daylight again until the election's over. An' sure he'd be a great fool if they did!"

"Why, Barney, that's rank injustice."

"No, but it's great soldiering asself; an' he wouldn't be worth his salt as a politician if he done any thing else. But divil a matter, the boat will make us even with him, an' plaise God the watch-house will be in our hands next year!"

"But, Barney, if any of our friends are put in confinement, can't we have them released in the morning?"

"Faix thin ov coorse you can't, the divil a wan ov thim, barrin' you burn down the watch-house or get betune Stubbs an' the Mayor, which might be difficult an' he the Regular Nomination. You see here's the way it is: – The watchmin an' keepers that's in, *is in*! but if any change takes effect in the boord, them that's *in* may be put *out*, an' so ov coorse they'll fight like divils against the People's Ticket in defince ov their places. But as I said, it will go hard with us if we don't man thim fairly; an' with the blessing uv the saints we'll get two for the wan we lose."

Well, the day of days at length arrived – the great day which was to decide whether a Livingston or a Stubbs should be alderman for the next year. And truly it would seem from the anxious faces – the uproar – the little groups gathered at various corners in eager or fierce debate – the hurrying of men to and fro, and other symptoms of revolution, as if the fate of nations hung on the result.

The three belligerent hosts – that is, the Livingstonians – the Stubbsites, and the Federal party (otherwise called the silk-stocking gentry), took the field early; but the two former commenced operations by joining hand and whipping the other out of it, so that long before the sun was in his meridian, they had the battle-ground all to themselves. It is true an odd one of the silk stockings would occasionally snatch a timid peep round a corner, to speculation on what chance he might have of enjoying the *freedom* of the ballot-box; but when any such demonstration was made, a sham-fight was instantly got up among the "Regulars" and the "People's ticket," which generally had the effect of sending the intruder in an opposite direction after his nose, as fast as his legs could carry him. However, these intrusions were few and far between, for a smart shower of rain had fallen, which so damped the ardor of the Federals as almost to keep them away in to-to, after their first drubbing, and thus rescued them from the risk of a second, – for this class of our politicians, be it remarked, were, in those days, so peculiar in their patriotism, that they rarely ventured abroad to vote, only in fine weather!

Well, everything went on smoothly enough through the better part of the day; and as well as it could be calculated, the Stubbsites and us polled about an equal number of votes. This, however, was a result the Regular Nominations were by no means prepared for, and accordingly they began to grow a little wolfish by dinner time, and to talk about a fight, which was no sooner proposed than agreed to all round; and sure enough at it we went, hammer and tongs, and that, too, so indiscriminately, that Stubbsite pitched into Stubbsite, and Livingstonian into Livingstonian, with as hearty good will, as if they had been sworn enemies from their cradles upwards.

However, there was no mistakes made as regarded the shining marks of either host; so that these poor devils, including Tom Stapleton, had to take it with a vengeance, they being considered fair game to every warrior of the opposing party, who could get a rap at them. And let me here observe, that there is certainly a great deal of pleasurable excitement in a general shilelah scuffle, and I don't wonder some people are so fond of them, for it is a down-right luxury when a man has got a whack on the side of the head, from an unseen cudgel, to give vent to his indignation by letting drive like a thunder-bolt at the first devoted head he can come across!

But my enjoyment of the fight was tame and insipid in comparison with that of Lawlor the Rattler, and a hundred others of the leading belligerent spirits. Those heroes seemed to glory and revel in it; and to look at them, one would suppose that they felt as though they were in a perfect whirl of beatti-tude. The rascals actually made their shilelahs sing again, and danced Irish jigs to their music! In fact, it was evident that the fight was regarded as one of the funniest things in the world, and the broken heads, et cetera, that were given and taken on all sides, as mere matters of course, which were necessary to the full development and enjoyment of the scene!

As a general thing it would be invidious to call upon fame, in imitation of Homer, to name the warriors who particularly distinguished themselves on this memorable occasion; but justice compels us to state that high above those of all the others shone the matchless exploits of Lawlor the Rattler, who, there and then, indisputably proved his claim to that title; for he was here, there, and everywhere, in a minute, while the sturdiest Stubbsites gave way before his staff, as though they took him for Goliah armed with a weaver's beam.

The battle continued with unabated fury for nearly half an hour, when Murphy suddenly put an end to it, by proposing, in Mr. Livingston's name, to treat all hands, friends and enemies, with the view of showing his respect for their courage and putting more power in their elbows!

"An' it isn't even brandy he commissioned me to give yees," exclaimed Barney, when the heterogeneous mass had followed him into a large debating room, "but whiskey punches; for whin Alderman Livingston, that is to be, does the thing at all, 'tis himself that does the daicent thing, like all his ancestors from Brian Boru downwards!"

"He'll never live to see the day when he'll be Alderman of this ward," exclaimed a voice; and to my great surprise I immediately ascertained it to be that of my friend, Lawyer Starkey, who had heretofore went it so strong for the Livingstonians.

"D–n politics, bring in the punch," shouted Lawlor the Rattler.

"Amen," "amen," "amen," added a dozen of voices.

And in the punch came by the gallon – for it was already prepared – and then the belligerents fell to and hob-nobbed with each other, as if they were the best and most affectionate friends in the world.

However, Starkey did not give up his point; but mounting the rostrum, when the attack on the punch jugs began to calm off, he thus delivered himself:

"Yes, fellow republicans, and glorious defenders of the liberties of our country, Anthony Livingston must not and shall not be elected! No, fellow citizens, the sun may float in the azure heavens – and the clouds may gather about the golden chamber of the setting sun – but Anthony Livingston must not be elected Alderman of this ward! What has he done for his country? – Treated you to punch! Fellow-citizens will you barter away your liberties for a tumbler of punch? When I gaze around me and behold the keels of our conquering navy riding on a thousand seas! when I behold the Star Spangled Banner floating triumphantly in the glorious breeze of freedom, and when I behold a myriad of other things – which remind me of the marvellous destiny of this proud union, I think of Stubbs – of honest, honest Stubbs – whom we are going this day to re-elect to the station which he fills with such credit to himself and such profit to his native city! But look to your tickets, fellow citizens! Look well to your tickets; for as the principles of republicanism must yet govern the world, and as the blood of the revolutionary patriots washed out the stain of slavery from the proud banner of freedom, so also are there traitors in the camp! But let me not waste your precious time, fellow-citizens and independent electors of this invulnerable ward, for the enemy has brought us in here to endeavor to ensnare us to our ruin! Yes, I see British gold is at the bottom of this trick, and that it pays for the punch you have been drinking! The stumpticket men are delaying us, to give an impression to doubtful voters that our strength is exhausted! – So come along at once! Come to the ballot-box, proud champions of liberty; and in half an hour from this time the Regular Nominations will be triumphant, and the enemy in the dust! (Great applause from the Stubbsites, interspersed with groans and hisses from Murphy and the Livingstonians.) A few words more, fellow-democrats," continued Starkey, "for fear of fraud take your tickets from me, for in the desperation and villany of their hearts, the enemy have issued spurious ones to entrap us!"

And as he concluded, Starkey jumped from the chair on which he had been speaking, and having distributed a number of tickets among the crowd, rushed into the street followed by a long tail of Stubbsites, all cheering the orator, and denouncing the Livingstonians for attempting to impose on them, at the high top-gallant of their voices.

Meanwhile Barney mounted the chair and made a brief speech, which also sent the Livingstonians in headlong career for the ballot-box.

"Barney," I whispered, when we were nearly alone, "what the devil has caused Starkey to turn traitor?"

"Hush!" returned Barney, "It's only a pickpocket fight! He's as true as steel!"

"What, to us?"

"Ov coorse, to us."

"Why man he spoke in favor of Stubbs."

"I know that *avick*; but thin 'twas like the favor of the little boy, that led the blind man into the ditch!"

"I can't see through it, Barney."

"I hope," returned Barney, "that the inimy may have the same story to tell – at least for an hour or so; but if they don't, and can only find Starkey in their way, be the hole ov me coat I wouldn't be in his breeches for the full ov wan ov its pockets ov half aigles!"

"I see," said I, "the mystery lies in the tickets."

"To be sure it does," said Barney, "But if it wasn't for the punch to wash it down with, they'd never have swallowed the bait. However, I don't expect much be it – before it's discovered; but you know, as the owld saying has it 'every little makes a muckle,' to say nothing of the honor ov chaitin' owld Stubbs."

While Murphy was yet speaking, we heard a tremendous uproar without.

"*Turinaunty!*" he exclaimed, "the cat's out ov the bag already – But come till we see the fun."

And out we ran, and were just in time to have our fingers in another fight, for we found the belligerents hard at it; and poor Starkey hanging in rags, and with a countenance which seemed as if it might lately have been playing target for a dozen set of knuckles. We also found – at least such was the rumor – that upward of twenty men had polled the spurious tickets; which, (the votes being so even), was a proud feather in the cap of "our party." Subsequently I was shown one of the Starkey tickets, and the only difference between it and the genuine was, that in the former Stubbs was spelt with a single b, as thus, *Stubs* – while in the latter, it followed the general rule; and here, be it remarked, – certain slanders to the contrary not withstanding – that not only are our aldermen and other functionaries who are voted into office by the people, compelled to understand the proper spelling of their own names, but their patriotic constituents are required to know how to spell them also! At all events, they must all hit on the one way, when they come to the ballot box; for a single letter astray in a name, causes the ticket – so far as the misspelt candidate is concerned – to go for nothing. For instance, in the very year I am writing of, a man named Martin lost the Assessorship of one of the wards because in fourteen of the votes deposited for him, his name was spelt with an e, instead of i; and that, too, notwithstanding it was subsequently shown, and admitted, that it was his immediate opponent (who won the election by four votes,) that had procured the printing and circulating of the spurious ticket. However, as I said before, and as that arch politician, Mayor Noah, said before me again, "all's fair in politics."

The last bold stroke of the Livingstonians was too much for Alderman Stubbs's philosophy. Immediately as he heard it, he run here and there, clasping his hands, turning up his eyes, in pious horror, and giving vent to the indignation of his innocent heart in a series of oaths and imprecations; albeit fame did say, and does say, that he had frequently himself "whipped fortune round the stump" in the same manner; and that even there and then there were tickets in the field, (though I saw none of them), which had emanated from the genius of Stubbs, and in which the g was omitted in the name of his formidable rival.

Waxing still more indignant as he related the story of his wrongs, the worthy Alderman mounted a door stoop, to give outlet to the current – or rather cataract – of his woes, in a speech.

"There, fellow-citizens of my beloved country!" he exclaimed, "In this trick – this atrocious, abominable, and perfidious trick – we may behold us in a looking glass, the treatment that we might expect from our infamous, vile, abominable, and miscreant opponents, if, the wrath of heaven was such, that they chanced to get the ward into their clutches. I will not denounce Anthony Livingston, Esquire – as he calls himself – as a villain, fellow-citizens – No, God forbid that I should call any man a villain! But this I do say, that the getting up of those spurious tickets is his doing, and that any man who would make such an attempt to tarnish the glory of the ballot box, is not only a villain, but a double distilled villain who, if he could, would make a dishcloth of the Star Spangled Banner, and sell his suffering country for a mess of pottage! Fellow-citizens of this glorious Union, if it is your desire, put me out – put me out of office this minute but oh, select some one in my place that is not under the influence of British gold! – some one that in the baseness of his heart would not condescend to rob you of the most glorious of your privileges, the inestimable right of voting according to the dictates of your own consciences! and I will not only cheerfully resign the honors of representing you in the council halls of this great city, but I will kiss the hands that smite me! I do not speak for myself, fellow-citizens – No, I do not speak for myself! In the patriotism and disinterestedness of my heart, I love the freedom and honors of my ward a thousand times better than I love Alderman Stubbs! And if there was one feeling in my bosom that was opposed to the interests of my country, I would not only resist my own return to office, but I would even erase my name from the ticket, before I deposited my vote in the ballot box! Ponder deeply on these things, fellow-citizens! – If you think there is any patriotism, honesty, and virtue, in polluting the ballot box with spurious tickets, let Mr. Livingston – or as he compels people to call him – Anthony Livingston, Esquire – be elected! But if not – if you would perpetuate the inestimable blessings you enjoy – and disperse the black cloud of British influence that hangs over the land, remain faithful, as your fathers have done before you, to the Regular Nominations! – Again, I implore you, fellow-citizens, to let Stubbs go! – Don't mind Alderman Stubbs – Sacrifice me if you will! But oh, in this hour of need, let us rush in a body to the ballot box, and rescue this hitherto uncontaminated ward from the deep infamy with which it is now threatened!"

Here the orator's feelings completely choked him, and he called his handkerchief in requisition, as if to dry up the liquid tribute of his patriotic sufferings. Nor were those sufferings in vain; for the heart of the crowd seemed touched by them; and many an independent elector who came partially determined to vote the Livingston ticket, joined heartily in the three cheers which rent the sky in favor of Alderman Stubbs.

The experienced eye of Barney Murphy at once perceived that this was a moment pregnant with destiny, and that something must be immediately done to counteract the effect of Stubbs' eloquent appeal to the feelings of his constituents. Therefore, having hunted up Mr. Livingston, who now let Barney have every thing his own way, he placed him on a stoop opposite to that which was occupied by Alderman Stubbs, and requested him to make a speech.

"Barney," said Mr. Livingston, "I'm so bewildered that I don't know what to say."

"So much the better, sir," returned Barney, "as it will be easier understood than wan with much larnin' in it! But there's one thing I want you to do, sir – *whatever I say, say afther me*, no matter whether it fits or not; and I think that betune us we'll be an even match for ould Stubbs."

Whereupon Murphy placed himself in the rear of Mr. Livingston with his mouth convenient to his ear, while the latter addressed the audience as follows. The italicised portions of the speech, by the way, were according to Barney's promptings; and odd enough they seemed as emanating from the lips of such a sedate and fastidious old gentleman as Anthony Livingston.

"It is with feelings of deep regret and astonishment, fellow-citizens, that I have been informed that Alderman Stubbs – *turned a widow and her six small children out of their little home on last Monday evening.* And further, fellow-citizens, taking into consideration the position assumed by the present incumbent of the ward in relation to the – *stripes and stars and the eagle of liberty* – (Cheers.) – I have arrived at the conclusion that he is not a man qualified to represent this ward in the legislative halls of the city, and that – *nobody ever saw the froth of his pot yet.* – (Cheers.) – Fellow-citizens, it is with reluctance as you all know, that I have permitted myself to be placed before you as a candidate for office; but still if your choice devolves on me, I here pledge myself to – *vote against all sorts of taxation – to sustain rotation in office, and to see that the independent electors of this ward have their full share of the situations of the city.* – (Great enthusiasm.) – Fellow-citizens, in reference to the tariff question I would say – *three cheers for the eagle of liberty and the true democracy all over the world.* – (Loud applause.) – In following out this idea, fellow-citizens, it seems to me that I am called on to make an exhibition of my principles on certain mooted points, which are – *up with the poor – down with the rich, and to the devil with those that don't like the doctrine.* – (Great cheering.) – Thus, fellow-citizens, incorporating, as we may say, the elements of popularity with true legislation, we perceive there is no human institution so excellent as – *the stripes and stars and the eagle of liberty, not forgetting the harp of green Erin.* – (Tremendous applause.) – And hence, as I should have previously observed, fellow-citizens, the principles of the immortal Jefferson shall be my guide in carrying out my well known views on the subject, in elucidation of which permit me to say – *down with the Bank, and hurra for General Jackson!* – (Great enthusiasm.) – I will briefly expound to you, fellow-citizens, a theory which I have conceived, and, as I think, perfected, whereby it is rendered evident that – *old Stubbs never christened his son Pat, and that he and his tail ought to be put out to make room for better men.* – (A whirlwind of applause, interspersed with groans and hisses.) – Yes, fellow-citizens, your present representative is – *the biggest skinflint that ever seized a poor man's furniture for a week's rent!* In fact, fellow-citizens, philosophically considered, Mr. Stubbs is – *a mere Judy O'Callaghan, and if we don't give him his walking ticket this day, the eagle of liberty may well blush for us – Irishmen are not Irishmen – and the ward's disgraced for another year!*"

A mingled storm of applause and abuse followed Messrs. Livingston's and Murphy's speech, but it was very evident the applause had the best of it, and that the hearts of the bold exiles of Erin were softened by the allusion to the harp, and the fling at the Regular candidate's son Pat. The latter especially carried great weight with it, because Stubbs's love for "the sod" had been long a matter of much doubt and argument; while, as I believe I have heretofore stated, the Irishmen had the ward in their hands – at least they numbered a full third of the votes – and Pat is such an unflinching politician that it is said of him, that he can make one vote go as far as other people can make three. However this may be, the foregoing burst of eloquence had the effect of frightening the Stubbsites out of the majority of their seven senses; and they were on the point of seeking consolation in another fight, when the mantle of genius descended on the shoulders of Stubbs, and his countenance was lit up with an idea that a Barney Murphy might have been proud of. I saw by the clubbing of legislative heads together, and the smiling faces which suddenly pervaded the assembly on the opposite stoop, that some sublime and awful demonstration might be expected; and I was debating in my mind from what point of the compass the storm might blow, that was then brewing for the destruction of the Livingstonians, when Barney exclaimed – "Oh the villain! Murdther, what's this for? – he's going to bring the baby at us!" And at the same moment a servant girl, carrying a fine infant, entered the arena, and surrendered her blooming charge, who was then squalling most lustily, into the out-stretched arms of Alderman Stubbs.

This movement alone produced a powerful sensation in favor of the opposition; but when the devoted parent, holding aloft the miniature edition of himself, made the following appeal to his audience, their enthusiasm knew no bounds, and it was quite apparent that nothing, short of a miracle, could prevent them from carrying all before them:

"My friends – but more especially my Irish friends, the enemy may put me out of office if they please – that I will cheerfully consent to, if it is thought necessary to the good of my beloved country, the honor of the star-spangled banner, and the glory of free principles; but I will not submit to the bleeding wound which they have inflicted on my feelings, in their slanderous statement, that I have not christened this dear pledge of my love by the honored name of Patrick! And, therefore, I now produce him before you, for the double purpose of rebutting their infamous slander; and of making of him an offering on the shrine of my pure Irish feelings, and of the true democracy, for ever and ever."

Barney made a desperate attempt to counteract the influence of this affecting appeal; but it was of no use; for sympathy with the fond father and his offering on the shrine of democracy, ruled the hour; and accordingly the Stubbsites began to poll votes almost as fast as they could hand out tickets. Meanwhile the leading Livingstonians looked on like monuments of despair; for they had played their last trump and lost the trick!

"Murdther, murdther," exclaimed Barney, as he scratched his head in a paroxysm of tribulation, "I'll never forgive myself for not kidnapping the baby! for sure I might have foreseen that he'd be the death ov us."

"Is there no hope at all, Barney?" said I.

"Divil a hope," he answered, "Divil as much as you'd shove in your eye with an awl blade! But, *whew!* let me off!" And on the word he sprang from the stoop and rushed through the street as if he fancied that a legion of fiends were hot foot after him.

Let us follow Barney. It was nearly a quarter of a mile from the place where the poll was held to Mr. Livingston's house, but our political friend covered the ground in about a minute and a half; and such was his hurry, that he almost upset Mrs. Livingston in the hall, as he dashed past her on his way to the drawing room, where he was given to understand that Miss Lucy was entertaining company. Now, Lucy was very fond of her father; and since he became a candidate for civic honors, had been a violent politician. She had made banners for the party; played and sung patriotic songs for them; and danced many a furious Stubbsite into a staunch Livingstonian, at sundry political balls. It is also to be remarked that she was a brave girl – as most girls are, when courage is necessary – and also not averse to a little devilment; which is likewise one of the leading characteristics of the fair sex in general.

When Barney entered, or rather burst into the drawing room, Miss Livingston was in a state of feverish excitement about the election, and consequently but little disposed to entertain a party of ladies who were holding her in conversation.

"What's the matter, Barney?" she exclaimed, starting to her feet, and seemingly unmindful of the presence of her companions.

"We're fairly murthered, Miss!" replied the intruder.

"You don't mean to say that any thing's amiss with my father, Murphy!"

"Nothing, Miss, barrin' that ould Stubbs will get in in spite ov us! But sure that's enough!"

"Oh! Barney, Barney, that's bad news!"

"Divil a worse, Miss. But still there's wan hope for us, and it all lies with yourself!"

"In what way?" said Miss Livingston. "But I see by your eye that you want me to do something desperate!"

"Well, but remember *mavorneen,* that with God's blessing it's the only way to put down ould Stubbs and bring in the masther triumphant! But listen."

And Murphy regaled his fair auditor's ear with a long whisper.

"Oh! Barney! Barney!" she exclaimed, when that individual had brought his mystery to a point – "I dare do nothing of the sort! – That's too much to ask of me!"

"Faix, thin, Miss, the Ward's lost! An' sure you'll be braikin' your heart to-morrow, that you didn't save it!"

"Is there no other hope for us?" said the lady, after a pause of a few moments.

"Honor bright, Miss! Do you think I'd ax you, if there was?"

"Then," said Miss Lucy, "whatever may be the end of it, I'll do as you propose!"

"*Ochone,* but it's yourself that's the jewel an' darlint!" exclaimed Barney, who thereon, to the mingled astonishment, delight and alarm of all present but Lucy, who was habituated to such demonstrations, he threw up his hat, flourished his cudgel, and danced like a madman, about the apartment.

"Immediately, you say, Barney," said Miss Livingston.

"Yes, darlint! An' remimber the green gownd, an' every thing else green that you can find about the house, while I'm getting out the wagon." And Barney, having bowed to the company, whom he then seemed to recognize for the first time, made his exit, exclaiming, "Baby or no baby, the day's ours!"

During the progress of this little scene, the Stubbsites were having every thing their own road at the ballot box. Vote after vote was deposited for them by persons who had previously been in the ranks of the opposition; and to keep up the enthusiasm which had been created in his favor, Alderman Stubbs, who had retired from the stoop, stationed himself at a window in the house in which the balloting was going on, with his conquering son Pat in his arms; so that the poor Livingstonians saw nothing but defeat and humiliation staring them full in the face. As for Anthony, he seemed as if nothing could comfort him; and though a kind-hearted man, it struck me, from the wrathful glances which he threw from time to time at the baby, that he was inwardly wishing that he could look thunder bolts for its sake. And thus matters were proceeding, when suddenly a wild shout at some distance was borne upon the breeze; and then another, and another – each so loud, so long and so enthusiastic, that it might seem as if the whole city had burst forth in a series of general huzzas!

Each party was alike ignorant of the cause or meaning of this new excitement; and we stood on our oars anxiously awaiting its further development, when our drooping hearts were raised, and the ears of the Stubbsites astounded by a tremendous cheer for "*Granuwale,* and Anthony Livingston." And soon afterwards, an immense crowd began to wheel round an adjacent corner; and anon, a horse and a spring wagon, led by Barney Murphy, made their appearance; while in the wagon, to my utter astonishment, stood no less a person than Miss Lucy Livingston, with a harp before her, on which she was performing the soul-thrilling air of the "Exile of Erin."

Miss Livingston had nothing on her head, and her blooming countenance – always lovely – was now magnificent with excitement and animation; and to heighten the effect, she was dressed in a green scarf, green skirt, and green bodice, the former of which, by the way, she had borrowed from one of the ladies, who was along with her when Barney Murphy bolted so unceremoniously into the drawing room.

Arrived opposite the poll-house, Barney stopt the wagon, but Miss Livingston continued to play away, passing from the "Exile of Erin" to "Norra Creena," then to "The Harp that once through Tara's Hall," and so on, from sad to merry, and merry to sad, until her immense audience was in a state of the most perfect enthusiasm; but between two minds as to whether to give vent to it by dancing or crying!

At length the music ceased, and there was a long, deafening, thrice-repeated roar of applause. Then Barney called the attention of all present to the interesting fact that the beautiful creature in the wagon was "Hibernia herself, who was come to vote for the Livingston party." – This produced another tremendous cheer; and then, to strike while the iron was hot, and make capital out of the prevailing enthusiasm, Murphy suggested to all patriots who had the interests of their country at heart, or loved the ladies, the propriety of coming forward and "taking the true tickets out of Hibernia's own beautiful fingers." And this was the sublimest move yet, for instantly a rush was made on the wagon, when a myriad of voices might be heard importuning Hibernia, alias Lucy Livingston, for "tickets, tickets," which that distinguished young lady took especial care to hand out, as fast as her busy little fingers could convey them to those of her anxious votaries.

I was too much bewildered by the scene to notice in detail all the interesting little incidents that occurred in connection with it; but fame does report that during the progress of events, Alderman Stubbs stood at the window attitudinizing, and pinching his son Pat, until he discoursed most eloquent music, but without again being able to find a soft spot in the heart of the multitude below; – that several of the independent electors kissed Hibernia's lily white fingers, as they took the tickets out of them; that not a few carried their enthusiasm so far as to kiss her ruby lips; that she bore all these things in good part, and even considered a vote for a kiss cheaply purchased; and finally, that in their ardor, and gallantry, any number of Stubbsites, (and even persons who belonged to other wards, and consequently were legally disqualified), voted the Livingston ticket, not being able to resist such an appeal to their patriotism as that which was exerted through the lips and eyes of the irresistible Lucy. However all this may be, it was very evident that from the moment of Miss Livingston's appearance in the field, it was all day with the Stubbsites! It is true that they fought manfully to the last, and that little Paddy performed prodigies, in the cause of the "Regular Nominations." But alas! the current had set too strong against them – their hour was come – their "name was Dennis!" – and that night it was announced at Tammany Hall, amid eyes that almost watered the ground with their tears at the intelligence – (and the account was subsequently ratified) – that the Livingston, or more properly, the "People's Ticket," was returned by the overwhelming majority of twenty-seven!

Lest any reader might suppose that the author has over-stepped the modesty of truth at the facts developed in this chapter, the editor thinks it as well to add that he can corroborate from personal knowledge all the particulars so far as they relate to the baby and the lady; and there are doubtless hundreds of persons in the city of New-York, who can do the same thing.*

---

*[An editorial in this issue of Brother Jonathan declares that "the parade of the Harp and of Erin is no fiction, but actually occurred once upon a time during a contested election in this city."]

The Wilderness; or, Braddock's Times, A Tale of the West

by James McHenry (New York: E. Bliss and E. White, 1823)

Through poems, plays, essays, and editorships, as well as novels, James McHenry attempted with some success to make his living and his mark in American letters. Born in 1785 to an Ulster Protestant family in Larne, County Antrim, he trained for medicine and came to America with his wife in 1816. After The Wilderness, *his first novel, he published two volumes of a projected series of historical novels with Irish revolutionary settings* (O'Halloran; or, The Insurgent Chief *in 1824, and* The Hearts of Steel *in 1825), the first play on an Irish legendary theme to be performed on an American stage* (The Usurper, 1827), *a pile of occasional verse, and a virtually unreadable epic poem in ten books based on the Old Testament,* The Antediluvians; or, The World Destroyed *(1839). McHenry spent most of his time in Philadelphia, where he edited the* American Monthly Magazine *in 1824 and became a close friend of one of the best-known Irish Americans of the day, publisher Mathew Carey. Appointed U. S. Consul at Londonderry in 1842, McHenry died in 1845 while on consular duty in his hometown of Larne.*

An avowed aim of McHenry's fiction was the honest depiction of his fellow Ulster Protestant immigrants for the first time in American literature. Fed up with the "low Irish" comic stereotype, already well established in America by 1820, McHenry sets the record straight, and incidentally reveals his own prejudice, in a preface:

It would seem as if no other idea could be entertained of an Irishman than that of a rash, superstitious, although sometime shrewd ignoramus, who can neither speak without making a bull, nor act without making a blunder. It is imagined that the Irish are all Papists and bog-trotters. It is forgot, or rather in most instances it is not known, that in the province of Ulster alone, nearly two millions of people, at least one-fourth of the population of the whole Island, are neither the one or the other.

So it is that the main characters in The Wilderness, *the family of Gilbert Frazier and the novels hero, young Charles Adderly, are sensible, persevering, and courageous Ulster Protestant settlers in western Pennsylvania. To underline his point by contrast,*

McHenry also includes a low Irish figure, Peter M'Fall, the Dublin-bred, Catholic "body servant" of Charles Adderly, who speaks with a pronounced brogue an exasperating prattle of circumlocutions and is congenitally unable to give a straight answer.

The bulk of this novel takes place along the Ohio River during the French and Indian War. It is notable for McHenry's use of Colonel George Washington as a minor character, a failed suitor for the hand of Gilbert Frazier's daughter Maria, and for the detailed description of General Braddock's disastrous western campaign of 1755. A plot tangle of pea-soup consistency culminates in the marriage of Maria Frazier and Charles Adderly in Philadelphia. Colonel Washington takes this defeat gracefully, but with the implication (however unkind to Martha) that his subsequent devotion to his country is a direct result of his rejection by Maria.

The first excerpt here is the novel's opening description of the emigration in April 1723 of Gilbert and Nelly Frazier, who speak with an Ulster burr akin to lowland Scots. Their capture by Indians after ten years of farming is the first of many calamitous plot turns, and it ends this selection.

The second excerpt is McHenry's rendering of the contrasting characters of southern Irish Catholics and Ulster Protestants, enforced by the differing styles of entertainment and song of Peter M'Fall and the Fraziers.

> As slow our ship her foamy track,
>   Against the wind was cleaving,
> Her trembling pendant still look'd back
>   To that dear isle 'twas leaving;
> So loath we part from all we love,
>   From all the links that bind us,
> So turn our hearts where'er we rove,
>   To those we've left behind us!
>
> – Moore

Let melancholy spirits talk as they please concerning the degeneracy and increasing miseries of mankind, I will not believe them. They have been speaking ill of themselves, and predicting worse of their posterity, from time immemorial; and yet, in the present year, 1823, when, if the one hundredth part of their gloomy forebodings had been realized, the earth must have become a Pandemonium, and men something worse than devils, (for devils they have been long ago, in the opinion of these charitable denunciators), I am free to assert, that we have as many honest men, pretty women, healthy children, cultivated fields, convenient houses, elegant kinds of furniture, and comfortable clothes, as any generation of our ancestors ever possessed.

This notion of mine, be it right or wrong, has not resulted from any course of abstract syllogizing upon the nature of things, a mode of discovering truth in which I never had much confidence. It has arisen from that more certain source of acquiring opinions, vulgarly called "ocular demonstration" – having lately had a view of part of that portion of the American hemisphere, which extends from the South Mountain in Pennsylvania, over the Allegheny ridge, to the head of the Ohio river; a country which, in the recollection of many yet living, was long the scene of want, hunger, desolation, terror, and savage warfare, where the traveller had not a path to guide his course, nor, in a journey of many days, could find a hut in which to repose his frame; where the hardy white man, who ventured to make a settlement, had not a neighbor within many a league, and where he seldom retired for the night, without fearing that, before the morning, both his family and himself might become the victims of the tomahawk and the scalping-knife.

As a remedy for the unhappy malady under which the misanthropic believers in the deteriorating condition of mankind labor, I think, that an attentive ramble, at the present day, over this extensive region, making, at the same time, a careful comparison between what it now is, and what it was fifty years ago, would be effectual. Wild and gigantic mountains are, indeed, still there; but beautiful and well cultivated valleys, lying on the bosom of peace, and in the lap of plenty, are spread beside them. At the distance of every two or three hours' ride, a flourishing town or village, inhabited by sober Christians and industrious freemen, salutes the eye of the traveller; while people of all ages, sexes, tastes, and tempers, enliven the road as they pass along, either on foot or on horseback, or in vehicles, which are here to be met with of every description, from the light sulky, which scarcely presses upon its springs, to the heavy, cumbersome wagon, dragged slowly along by six horses. In this region, there is now neither want, nor fear of want; neither enemy, nor fear of enemy; but every man earns his bread in comfort, and eats it in safety, in the midst of his family and friends, without fear of molestation from either civilized tyrants or savage marauders.

Far different was the situation of things in this fair region of the earth, when Gilbert Frazier first erected his log-house on the bank of the Monongahela. Then, indeed, might a misanthropic grumbler have had reason to complain of the condition of men, at least of those men whose fate it was to be planted like Gilbert, in a savage "WILDERNESS." It was fate, indeed, and not choice, as may well be supposed, that had, at first, planted him there; but notwithstanding his residence was exposed to numerous inconveniences, and constant dangers, a stout heart, (for he had a good conscience and feared nothing), combined with a feeling of generosity, the source of which will be hereafter explained, to bind him to it, and Providence had hitherto preserved him in safety. Nay, in process of time, habit had so reconciled him to his situation, that he scarcely looked upon the misfortune that had brought him there as an evil. Years had mellowed its impression upon his mind; and sitting by his winter fireside he would often relate the story to his family with much the same feeling that a sailor, snug on shore, recounts the dangers he has undergone at sea.

He had entered the world nearly about the same time with the century in which he lived, and somewhere between Colerain and Londonderry, in Ireland. Whether his father or mother was forty-second cousin, or no cousin at all, to some nobleman or squire, is of no consequence, merely because he thought it of none, or rather because he never thought anything about it. A far more important matter of recollection with him, was his marriage, which took place in his twenty-first year, with Nelly M'Clean, a pretty rosy cheeked, fair-skinned Irish girl, with dark eyes and black hair, who was about a couple of years younger than himself, and whose heart, although it was as light and as tender as a linnet's, had stood nearly a twelvemonth's seige before it surrendered to his attacks. When it did surrender, however, it was at absolute discretion, and Gilbert ever after found it as faithful and fond as a hearty lover like himself could wish.

As Gilbert wished to make his dear Nelly *a lady*, but was unable, from a cause very prevalent among his countrymen, the want of funds, nothing would now satisfy him but a trip to America, in order to make his fortune. Not that he intended to leave his own country for ever, for with all its poverty, he still thought it was a dear and sweet country, but he supposed that a residence of seven years at the farthest, in a land so far off as America, must make him rich enough to return home, and live the remainder of his days like a gentleman.

"What fine times will it then be for Nelly, (thought he), when dressed in her silks and laces, she visits her poor cousins, the Burrels and the Blairs, and gives each of them every year, on *Hansel Monday*, some handsome presents for a New-year's gift. Faith, it will be happy times for us then!"

To America, therefore, it was settled that he should go; but think not, that he separated from his Nelly – no; he would as soon have thought of separating his head from his shoulders. They set sail together from fair Londonderry one bright morning in April, 1723; and Gilbert felt, as many an Irishman has since felt, on taking the last look of his native country, that it required all his courage to prevent him from betraying his sorrow; for notwithstanding the prosperity that he supposed awaited him abroad, he felt that he was about to purchase it dear by forsaking the land of his nativity. He looked at his wife, as she stood beside him gazing at the fast retiring promontory of Inishowen, which was the last vestige of dear Ireland that she was to see. He perceived that her eyes were swollen with the moisture of grief; and although his own heart was filled from the same cause, he thought it his duty to comfort her, as he tried to comfort himself, by half whispering and half singing in her ear,

"We need not grieve now, our friends to leave now,
For Erin's fields we again shall see;

But first a lady in Pennsylvania,
My dear, remember thou art to be."

Whether this promise of her becoming a Pennsylvania lady, had the consolatory effect upon his wife that Gilbert intended, I cannot say; but it is certain, that except about three weeks, during which she labored under the tortures of seasickness, she endured a boisterous passage of nearly three months with considerable liveliness and good humor. At length, if we may believe Gilbert's own account of the matter, one Sunday morning – (as good luck would have it) – he had the happiness to land on the wharf at Philadelphia, with his Nelly on his arm, and twenty gold guineas in his pocket.

Gilbert was now in the Land of Promise, the bright Eldorado of his imagination, where every thing he did was to be so richly remunerated, that his very scratching of the ground would cause it to teem with wealth, and spreading his hands to heaven would bring down a shower of gold. During the first week after his arrival he was in ecstasy. Although none of the expected riches had yet made their appearance, he very reasonably ascribed this to his not having made any of the exertions necessary to attract them; for he was not such a fool as to suppose that they were to be gained without exertions of some kind. But these exertions he could make when he needed them; and, like a true Irishman, he considered his twenty guineas sufficient for all present purposes. He therefore thought that it could not be wrong to enjoy himself a little in a new country; and, as Nelly, who was rejoiced to have her foot once more on Terra Firma, was unusually cheerful and engaging, he could do no less than spend a couple of weeks in showing the dear girl the novelties of the place.

At length his twenty guineas were reduced to ten; and he began to think, for he had a mixture of Scotch blood in him, that he should do some thing to prevent their farther reduction. He expressed his wishes to several of the natives, expecting that they would make him acquainted with the plan of getting rich which suited their country. They told him to "work."

"Work!" ejaculated Gilbert to himself; for he had the prudence to perceive that it would not do to affront the natives, by expressing audibly any feelings of disappointment respecting their country – "work! an' was it for that, after a, that I left the snug toonlan' o' Maughrygowan, an' cam' owre the ocean, when I thoucht I was become a gentleman on my very landin'! Work! why what waur could I hae done at hame, than to hae labored for my daily bread! But I was nae quite at that need either. Eh! sirs – Nelly, puir lass! is as little likely to become a 'lady in Pennsylvania,' as the sang we used to sing, says, than she was in her ain country!"

However, Gilbert was not of a temper to be cast down by trifles; and, as his eyes were now pretty much opened to the real circumstances of the country, and his funds were every day diminishing, he thought at last of seriously betaking himself to work, as he had been advised. He was healthy, young, and active, and, as far as respected himself, had no other objection to a life of labor, than the slowness with which it brought in that affluence which had been the great object of his emigration. His Nelly, however, was more affected at the thought of his being obliged to earn their sustenance by the sweat of his brow; and her sorrow galled his feelings far more sensibly than the necessity which occasioned them. She became *homesick*, as it is termed, and for several months internally pined after the oat-cakes, the hedge-rows, the genial zephyrs, the warbling groves, the fairy haunts, and the rural sports of her native land. But her mind, naturally cheerful and elastic, soon recovered its tone, and, becoming resigned to her situation, she not only encouraged her husband in his industry, but assisted him by her own.

In a short time Gilbert's diligence and good conduct became noted among his neighbors, and several gentlemen of property were heard to speak in his commendation. It may be here observed, that the manners of the Philadelphians towards strangers on first settling among them, seem, at this day, to be much the same as our friend Gilbert found them to be a hundred years ago, that is, reserved, discouraging, and forbidding, until some species of merit shall appear to justify attention and kindness, which will then be afforded exactly in such proportion as the merit deserves, but in no more. In other words the Philadelphians appear to be the most punctual in rendering justice, but the most backward in displaying generosity, of any people in the world.

Gilbert Frazier's merit was also pretty much of the kind that has always been in highest estimation with the inhabitants of Philadelphia – for *"sobriety and perseverance"* seem to be their characteristics, and might, without much impropriety, be adopted as the motto of the city. It is true, that the warmth of his Irish blood prevented his manners and conduct from being so rigidly regular, tamed, and disciplined in all things, as those of the older citizens, but, for his levities and indiscretions, as they called them, his neighbors had the good nature to make a suitable allowance, on account of his being an Irishman, and also to give him the greater credit for that unexpected degree of steadiness and attention to his employment that he exhibited.

But, although resolute and determined to do what he could to earn a comfortable and honest living, the income of his occupation, which was only that of a common laborer, was by far too inconsiderable to satisfy his wishes. He was also, on account of having received, when he was about five months in the city, from his Nelly, the interesting present of a fine son, to whom, although he was no catholic, he gave the name of Patrick, in honor of his native tutelary saint, the more solicitous to change his employment for one more lucrative. He had been bred to no mechanical trade, and he had neither inclination nor talents for traffic. The management of a farm was, therefore, what best suited him; and it was not long after the interesting event just mentioned, that he agreed with a gentleman, who possessed some land on the Juniata river, a short distance above its junction with the Susquehannah, to remove there, and cultivate a certain number of acres *on the shares.*

On this place Gilbert had resided about ten years, and had thriven so much, that he felt himself able to make to its owner such proposals for purchasing it, as he had every reason to believe would be accepted; when unfortunately, a formidable party of Indians made a furious irruption into the settlement, and after pillaging or destroying whatever articles of value came in their way, they carried off, as prisoners, upwards of twenty families, among whom was that of the unhappy Gilbert. He was at this time, the father of three children, two sons and a daughter, who, with their mother and himself, were carried rapidly for more than two hundred miles, over a pathless and interminable wilderness of thick, lonely, and gloomy forest, corresponding in its state of wild and dismal savageness with the nature of the ferocious and vengeful prowlers, on whose barbarous caprice their very existence now depended.

[As a reward for helping an Indian woman give birth to a child, the Fraziers are eventually freed and return to farming. In the following excerpt, the servant Peter M'Fall acts and sings like the stereotypical stage-Irish-Catholic figure that he is.]

If the French are noted for unthinking frivolity, the Irish are no less so for a fervency of feeling by which they are enabled to suppress the suggestions of care, as effectually as the French can dismiss them. Hence, when opportunity tempts, they are ever ready to yield with their whole heart and soul to the full tide of enjoyment, and swim away on its stream, regardless of consequences. On this occasion, therefore, there was none who entered with more spirit into the humors of the evening than Peter M'Fall.

On a green level sward, by the edge of the rivulet, the party formed a circle: but it was for a very different purpose from that formed the preceding day by the Indian council. Here were no life and death matters to be discussed – here were no serious and vehement calls for the destruction and burning of a fellow-being – no loud and sorrowful manifestations of grief – no fierce and reiterated imprecations of vengeance upon an unfortunate captive. Grief, vengeance, and every other uncomfortable feeling, were banished as unwelcome guests: while good humor, sprightliness, cordiality, and joy, were invited to be present and inspire the revels of the evening by the merry strains of a Frenchman's flute, and the jolly sounds of an Irishman's voice; for, in the intervals of the flute player's performance, Peter, with great spirit, industriously exerted himself, to prevent the company from wanting music, by singing the merry lilts of his native country.

At the commencement of the supple-heeled sport, the Indians had entered the party by exhibiting the various dances of their nation. The war dance, the hunting dance, the courtship dance, the marriage dance, and the birth dance, had each its characteristic gestures and manoeuvres – some of which were, to the eyes of the Europeans, so grotesque, wild, and ludicrous, that they were kept in an almost continued roar of laughter.

Peter was particularly tickled with the romping and capering of the squaws, who were tolerably handsome women, and had been nothing loth to exhibit their personal attractions in the various attitudes of their native dances.

"By the holy Patrick! but it's yourselves can do it in style, my girls!" would Peter every now and then exclaim, while he snapped his fingers and beat time with his feet, in the high glee of admiration at their extraordinary and laughable performance.

His fancy was particularly taken with the gracefulness and agility of the youngest of the squaws, who made really an interesting figure among the groupe; and at every remarkable bound she gave, smack went Peter's fingers in the air, dash went his heel upon the ground, and loud rose his obstreperous cheers of applause.

"Well, done, by the powers of Barnaby! Och! kape it up, you swate little soul, ye! There goes mettle for you!" He thus kept vociferating, while the company kept laughing, almost as much at his extravagancies, as at the singularities of the dancers. At length his heels itched so much to bear a part in the boisterous amusement, that he could keep his seat no longer, but springing up, and with his sound arm, hooking in with the squaw who had pleased him so much, he leaped, and bounded, and capered among the Indians with all his might, imitating as well as he could, their gestures and behavior, to the great admiration and delight of all present.

When the Indians and Peter had finished, the French felt inclined to succeed them in the exhilarating pastime; but as their musician was desirous to join them, and it was impossible for him to both dance and play the flute at the same time, it was determined that Peter should either whistle or sing to them, as he best could, to keep them in time. But he knew none of the airs to which they were accustomed, and after several ineffectual attempts to learn some of them, the French were at last obliged to accommodate themselves to those they did know. They accordingly set off with "Nancy Dawson," to which they tripped airily and nimbly along in measured movements, with great art, sprightliness, and vivacity. Now, (for every ten or fifteen minutes they changed their mood, and Peter had as often to change his tune), the light corant, the gay cotillion, the merry riggadoon, the measured waltz, and the sprightly jig, succeeded to each other, and were rattled off to the successive tunes of the Irish Washerwoman, the Soldier's Joy, the White Cockade, Patrick's Day, and Morgan Rattler. Through these various measures the nimble-toed Frenchmen tript gaily and smilingly without much noise, so that their easy but busy exertions were, in comparison to the violent romping, jumping and tearing which had just preceded them, what the rippling of a gentle river is to the roaring billows of the stormy ocean.

Becoming at length somewhat wearied with this species of pastime, the party sat down to an evening repast, rudely enough served up, no doubt, but plentiful and substantial. This was succeeded by the singing of some jovial songs, of which, only the two following have come into our possession. The first was sung by one of the Frenchmen, and the other by our friend Peter.

. . . .

Peter M'Fall's Song

In Ireland so frisky,
   With girls and with whiskey,
How happy was I when a strapping young lad;
   Every market and fair,
   To be sure I was there,
With my breeches and boots, like a gentleman clad.
   And then as to money,
   Och! sure it was funny,
To hear the dear shillings and sixpences clink,
   And the lasses so sweet,
   Arrah, faith! when we'd meet,
By the powers I could bring them along with a wink!
   Then so snug in the fashion,
   We'd take up our station,
In a tent that was covered with blankets and sheets
   "Arrah, landlord! be quicker,
   And bring us that liquor!"
I would cry – and he'd skip like a cat in the streets.
   So snugly thus fix'd up,
   The punch I soon mix'd up,
Then handed it round so genteely and neat,
   That the girls, the dear creatures,
   With sweet smiling features,
Said – "punch in a tent was an elegant treat!"
   Och! the punch was so cheery,
   That soon we got merry,
And the lass I lov'd best sat so snug in my arms;
   That I courted and kiss'd her,
   And teaz'd her and bless'd her,
Till she blush'd like the moon with a million of charms.
   I was then in my glory; –
   But to cut short my story,

The best thing – och! conscience, I tell you the truth,
   On the girls to be trying,
   To make them complying,
Is a jug of good punch and a neat strapping youth.

[In this last excerpt, the novel's hero Charles Adderly meets the Fraziers and their daughter Maria sings a properly serious and sentimental Ulster Protestant, "Scotch-Irish" song.]

"Alack!" cried Nelly, "bonny Maughrygowan will ne'er be oot o' my head gin a' the Irish in America were to settle beside us. Its bonny green meadows, an' its hawthorn hedges, wi' their sweet smelling blossoms, an' its saft dimplin' burns, wi' the yellow primroses an' speckled daisies on their banks, an' the sweet pretty larks an' the thrushes, an' the lads an' the lasses, an' the sports of a simmer evening, an' the jokes an' mirth o' a lang winter's nicht – ah! I cannot think o' them without a sair heart – for – for I'll ne'er see them again!"

Here Nelly's heart filled, and she was wiping away a tear that annoyed her, when Gilbert addressed her –

"Dinna fret – dinna fret, Nelly, at misfortunes. It micht hae been waur wi' us. God didna forsake us a'tegither. We are aye leevin' examples o' his gudeness, an' hae oor weans aboot us. We hae mony comforts, Nelly, gin we should ne'er see Ireland again. Dinna think o't noo – it maks ye greeve owre muckle."

"Ah, ye may bid me no greeve, gin ye like," replied Nelly – "but dinna Gilbert, dinna bid me no think o't, for I canna obey ye in that. I maun aye think o't, though my heart should bleed for't, as it's sometimes like to do. It would noo please me, Gilbert, to hear Maria sing the sang she learned frae ye, an' which ye're sae fond to hear yeresel, that was made by Tam Beggs, oor neighboor on the Juniata, whom the savages burned on that awfu' day at Catanyan. He made it on leavin' Larne, an' I ne'r hear it but it does my heart gude, it's sae melancholy, an' it shows that there were ither folk that grieved for ither places as muckle as I do for Maughrygowan. An' Maria aye sings it so sweetly that it makes my heart baith pleased and sorrowfu'. Ah it's a warm-hearted, comforting sang!"

"Weel, Nelly," observed Gilbert, "if it will comfort ye ony thing, an' Mr. Adderly has nae objection, I'm sure Maria will please ye. That sang aye pleases me, though it aye mak's me mournfu'."

Charles signified his desire to hear the song, and Maria, knowing that it would yield satisfaction to both her father and mother, required no further solicitation, but sang as follows, with a voice, every tone of which thrilled through Charles's heart, and awakened all his feelings of sympathy, tenderness, and admiration: –

The Haunts of Larne

Oft as I think on other days,
    When with a blithe light heart I rov'd,
Those haunts which lovely Larne surveys,
    Where first I felt, and first I lov'd;
    What sorrows pierce my bosom's core,
        Since I must sigh,
        Farewell to joy!
Ah! lovely Larne! must I ne'er see, ne'er see thee more?

By Curran's shore I often stray'd,
    And scenes of purest rapture knew,
When there I met the sweetest maid
    That ever blest a lover's view;
    But ah those joyful scenes are o'er,
        And I must sigh,
        Farewell to joy!
Ah! lovely Larne! must I ne'er see, ne'er see thee more?

By Inver's banks, so green and gay,
    I join'd each little warbler's song,
And tuned to love the blithesome lay,
    The fragrant hawthorn shades among.
    Fate ne'er can scenes like these restore,
        For I must sigh,
        Farewell to joy!
Ah! lovely Larne! must I ne'er see, ne'er see thee more?

Oh! mem'ry, cease! it gives me pain
    Such recollections dear to wake;
Yet I will think them o'er again,
    Although my tortur'd heart should break.
    Yes, still I'll think, and still deplore,
        How I must sigh,
        Farewell to joy!
Ah! lovely Larne! must I ne'er see, ne'er see thee more?

When Maria had done singing, so deep was the impression which her melodious voice and affecting manner had made upon her auditors, that they all, for a minute or two, sat silent, as if for the purpose of prolonging that luxury of sorrow which she had thus so strongly excited in their bosoms. At length Nelly, whose feelings had become so acute as evidently to require relief from weeping, retired, that she might indulge her grief the more privately.

PART II

The Famine Generation:
Practical Fiction for Immigrants

The Famine generation's fiction reflects and clarifies the complex experiences, ideas, and emotions of this most difficult time in the history of Irish immigration. Life in rural Ireland during and following the Famine, the trials of the crossing, the traumas of settlement in unfriendly cities – in all of these areas the fiction produced by Irish-American witnesses contributes valuable detail and pattern. It is no wonder that these trying circumstances generated three types of utilitarian, practical novels: Catholic-tract fiction to exhort the immigrants to keep the faith on alien soil, immigrant-guide-book fiction to instruct the newly arrived on how to get along in America, and nationalistic-political fiction to aid the cause of freedom from British rule back in Ireland. Often these three aims were addressed by a single author, and occasionally within a single novel.

The writers were so inclined because most were themselves fugitives from the Great Hunger. By my count, between 1845 and 1875 seven people wrote at least three novels each in which being Irish in America is of central concern. All seven were themselves immigrants who had come to America as adults (the youngest was twenty-one), and most of them arrived between 1844 and 1850. Two were priests, Fathers John Boyce and Hugh Quigley. Three were primarily journalists, Peter McCorry, Charles G. Halpine, and Dillon O'Brien. One, David Power Conyngham, was a veteran of both the 1848 Irish rebellion and the American Civil War, and the other, Mary Anne (Madden) Sadlier, was the first important woman in Irish-American publishing. In addition, most of the authors who wrote only one or two novels were also immigrants.

Throughout the nineteenth century, an impressive amount of Irish literature was published in America. Because of the demands of the greatly expanded audience, there was naturally much more of this in the Famine generation than previously. (Although most were unskilled peasants, probably about 75 percent of the Irish immigrants to America in 1850 were literate in English, and by 1910, the number exceeded 90 percent.) Important in the dissemination of literature from the old country, and even more crucial for the development of a new Irish-American literature, was the establishment by 1850 of a number of Catholic publishing houses – all, as it happens, by Irish Americans. These included, in New York, Edward Dunigan and Brother, P. O'Shea, and P. J. Kenedy & Sons; in Boston, Patrick Donahoe, whose weekly newspaper the *Pilot* became the most influential Irish Catholic journal in America at this time; D. and J. Sadlier of New York, Boston, and Montreal; and in Baltimore, John Murphy and Hedian & O'Brien. In the late 1840s and early 1850s, these houses began to publish Irish and Irish-American fiction, in addition to their stock-in-trade: devotional literature, prayer books, and Catholic school readers.[1] Again in response to their new audience, these houses also began publishing collections of Irish music. Patrick Donahoe brought out three such collections very early, including editions of Thomas Moore's *Irish Melodies* and *Songs of Our Land* (divided into "sentimental" and "patriotic" songs) in the 1850s.[2]

There were also, of course, more Irish-American periodicals to fill the needs of the new immigrants, and many of these published fiction. In the already established newspapers there was a shift, with less Irish fiction (by the likes of William Carleton and Gerald Griffin) and more Irish-American fiction being published. Patrick Donahoe's *Pilot,* for example, which had pioneered in the printing of Irish fiction in the 1830s and early 1840s, made the shift by publishing in 1850 Mary Anne Sadlier's first two novels, *The Red Hand of Ulster; or, The Fortunes of Hugh O Neill and Willy Burke; or, The Irish Orphan in America.*[3] These two set the tone for this generation's newspaper fiction, which is mostly in the same vein of Irish nationalist/historical tracts and immigrant guides that dominated in book form. (The *Pilot* was edited from 1848 to 1858 by Father John Roddan, himself a novelist represented in this anthology.) The first issue of the New York *Irish World* (August 12, 1849) carried a front-page serial novel written by its editor, Patrick Lynch. A didactic tale of the rise to success of the son of a fugitive from the Irish Rising of 1798, *Enterprise, A Tale of the Hour* inaugurated a regular fictional feature. (When Lynch died in 1857, his was the most widely read Irish nationalist newspaper in America.) Begun in 1857, the Sadlier-owned New York *Tablet* also published much fiction, including the first, serial versions of most of the novels of the publisher's wife,

---

1. See Patrick J. Blessing, "Irish" entry, *Harvard Encyclopedia of American Ethnic Groups,* 529, and Willard Thorp, "Catholic Novelists in Defense of Their Faith, 1829-1865," Proceedings of the American Antiquarian Society 78 (April 1968), 54-55. The Sadlier Company still publishes Catholic school readers. Edward Dunigan was publishing Christian Brothers readers with an obvious Irish slant by 1855.

2. *Moore's Melodies* appeared in 1852, *Songs of Our Land* also in the 1850s. A third, undated, collection, *The Irish Comic Songster,* seems contemporary with the other two.

3. *The Red Hand of Ulster* appeared in the *Pilot* from January 1 through March 9, 1850, and *Willy Burke,* from June 15 through August 17. Later in the year, another, anonymous story of the trials of an immigrant boy in Boston appeared: Michael Murphy, *A Tale of Real Life,* from October 12 through October 26, 1850.

Mary Anne Sadlier. Irish-American fiction also ran in several other New York City newspapers, and in Buffalo, Louisville, St. Louis, St. Paul, and New Orleans.[4]

Famine generation Irish-American fiction contains a few recurrent themes, often organized into a predictable pattern:

1. A hard life of great suffering in Ireland is presented, marked by landlord exploitation, famine, painful eviction from the old home, and the reluctant decision to emigrate. At the same time, the country of Ireland is often seen as an ideal pastoral home, only temporarily despoiled by the British invaders.

2. The crossing to America is seen as a wrenching rite of passage, the violence of which is often symbolized by a fierce storm at sea.

3. The disorientation of the immigrant's first months in the New World is evoked, with swindles, humiliation, and the most dangerous threats to morality and the faith.

4. Right and wrong ways of meeting these challenges are exemplified in the contrasting careers of Irish Catholics who keep the faith and those who lose it. Failure most often means succumbing to drink, dissolution, and early death. Success means working hard, holding a job, and keeping one's family together and Catholic. There are very few spectacular achievements, economic or otherwise, in this cautious body of fiction. The reality of life for this generation was too harsh to support what would have been cruel fantasy.

5. The moral of the story is pointed with directness and emphasis, often four or five times in the last two pages.

Of course, this pattern is the Irish-American version of a venerable American genre, the rags-to-riches moralizing tale, which loomed large in the imaginations of this generation and its writers. Telling reference to that genre and typical qualification of its promises appear in journalist Thomas D'Arcy McGee's advice to his fellow Famine immigrants in his New York *Nation* for February 10, 1849:

> You may buy in Cork, in Dublin, or in Liverpool, or wherever you sail from, a little shilling book, which I earnestly recommend to you as the best preliminary study for an Emigrant. It is called *The Life of Franklin*, and therein you will read how, by industry, system, and self-denial, a Boston printer's boy rose to be one of the most prosperous, honorable, and important citizens of the Republic. It will teach you that in America no beginning, however humble, can prevent a man from reaching any

---

4. Other newspapers that published Irish-American fiction during the Famine generation (and the years checked by me) are the *American Celt*, Boston and Buffalo (1850-53); the *Catholic Advocate*, Louisville (1869-70); the *Leader*, St. Louis (1855-56); the *Morning Star*, New Orleans (1868-71); the *Northwestern Chronicle*, St. Paul (1867-69); the *Irish News*, New York (1856-61); the *Emerald*, New York (1868-70); the *Irish World*, New York (1870-75). All of these newspapers are available on microfilm at the University of Notre Dame Library.

rank, however exalted; that, though the land does not grow gold, neither does it smother any energy by which fortune is created; that, above all, the genius of the people, and the State, is entirely and radically, *practical*. These are lessons you should have by heart.

In novel after novel, one convention illustrates the points being made: the deathbed scene. The good die peacefully, surrounded by loving family, and not without occasional angelic music and lighting; the bad die horribly, weeping, gnashing their teeth, and calling – too late – for a priest. An important site of feelings for Irish and Irish-American cultures, this convention remained strong through the rest of the nineteenth century. Indeed, it was not fully exorcised until the final page of James Farrell's *Studs Lonigan Trilogy*, published in 1935.

Seven of the eight selections in Part II of this anthology exemplify the didactic, moralizing genre just defined. Although predominantly a fiction of programmatic, sentimental plot and idealized, exemplary characterization, this is a body of work chock full of valuable detail about Irish-American life in the 1850s and 1860s. Some of these novels are transparent propaganda. Often the titles alone convey this orientation; for example, Father Hugh Quigley's *The Cross and the Shamrock; or, How to Defend the Faith* (1853), a novel written for the "special instruction of the Catholic male and female servants of the United States," and Peter McCorry's *The Lost Rosary; or, Our Irish Girls, Their Trials, Temptations, and Triumphs* (1870), a story of Famine immigrants to New York City. Despite its creaking didacticism, John McElgun's *Annie Reilly; or The Fortunes of an Irish Girl in New York* (1873) provides much information about the typical immigrant's journey from Cork to Liverpool to Castle Garden. Similarly, Father John Roddan's *John O'Brien; or, The Orphan of Boston* (1850) explains a lot about what life was like for young Irish clerks and apprentice-boys in Boston in the 1830s and 1840s.

Also excerpted here is *The Blakes and Flanagans* (1855), the first bestseller by the most prolific and influential of the Famine generation's writers, Mary Anne Sadlier. And Charles James Cannon is represented by a piece from his 1855 novel about the rise of anti-Irish-Catholic nativism, *Bickerton; or, The Immigrant's Daughter*. Many of these selections exemplify the heightened religious tension and bigotry on the part of both native Americans and the Irish during this time of dramatically increased immigration.

The watershed experience of Irish-American participation in the Civil War was registered in one of this generation's few humorous literary inventions, Charles G. Halpine's Union soldier, Private Miles O'Reilly, whose *Life and Adventures* (1864) constitutes the one selection in Part II that is wholly free of moralizing. And finally, a unique perspective on the situation of the Famine generation comes from Father John Boyce, who countered Yankee caricatures of the Irish in America by describing the visit to Ireland of a prototypal American tourist in *Mary Lee, or the Yankee in Ireland* (1860).

John O'Brien; or, The Orphan of Boston, A Tale of Real Life

by John T. Roddan (Boston: Patrick Donahoe, 1850)

Born in Boston of Irish immigrant parents in 1819, John T. Roddan entered the priesthood in his twenties and, because of his brilliance, was sent to Rome to study at the College of the Propaganda. Returning home after his ordination in 1848, he became a missionary priest over a wide area south of Boston, including the towns of Hingham, Quincy, Randolph, and Bridgewater. He began contributing to the Boston Pilot *and served as editor of that influential archdiocesan newspaper from about 1851 until his death in 1858 at age thirty-nine.*

Like John O'Brien, the hero of his only novel, Father Roddan was eight or nine when his father died, and he experienced great poverty as an Irish boy in Boston. It is fair to assume that John O'Brien *contains many autobiographical elements.*

The novel is clearly aimed at educating Catholic youth. John O'Brien's trials among the hostile Yankees of Boston and Hartford are presented as warnings that locate the novel firmly at the head of the tradition of "practical fiction for immigrants." Indeed, John O'Brien *is less a novel than a long chat with Father Roddan, full of extensive doctrinal disquisitions that impede the narrative flow. And yet, Roddan's evident wit and the presentation of John as a healthily mischievous boy with a talent for finding trouble make much of the book pleasurable reading. In addition, it contains a wealth of detail about the daily lives of young clerks and apprentice-boys on their own in early nineteenth-century American cities; for example, in the excerpted chapter VIII.*

Roddan explains John O'Brien's youthful denial of his Irishness and Catholicism by presenting many examples of prejudice against the immigrants in Boston, including an assessment of the miscarriage of justice following the burning of the Charlestown convent in 1834. He describes life on the "Hartford mission" in 1832 and the dispersal of the Irish over New England by means of railroad construction projects. He also provides an effective parody of the anti-Catholic horror stories purveyed by the likes of Rebecca Reed:

It seems that sausages are made of Protestant meat in some of the West India Islands. The way it is done is this: The churches and convents have dungeons under them, for the punishment of heretics. One of these is a sausage factory. The

Protestant is tumbled into a kind of hopper, that soon makes mince-meat of him.
He goes in, buttons and all, at one end, and comes out at the other, half a mile of
sausages. These are reserved for the eating of priests and nuns. (201)

John O'Brien *also illustrates an important change in the Irish-American self-image. Before the Famine much of the literature suggests the identification of Irish Americans with Ireland and Irish nationalism. After the Famine, perhaps because the backward look had become too painful, the identification is more often religious. It is not surprising that Irish characters in a novel by a priest should define themselves primarily as Catholics. However, Father Roddan sedulously avoids any mention of the situation in Ireland. It must surely have been an effort of will to keep all news of the Famine out of a novel about the Irish in America published in 1850. Such avoidance is a measure of the cultural trauma.*

Chapter VIII

John Gets Disgusted with His Trade. – Firemen. – Military
Companies. – Tea-Parties. – Apprentices' Library. – Mary Helps
to Make Him Understand the Part Which Nature Meant for Him.

The last chapter is a story of disputes about religion. I have not lugged it in by the head and horns; for every one, who is familiar with the mechanics of Boston, knows that in their shops a stray Catholic has little peace, if he be a silent man or boy. If he *be* disposed to talk, he will have quite enough on his hands. Scarcely a day passes that does not witness a dispute, and it often ends in a noisy quarrel, sometimes in a fight. Protestants are often so foul-mouthed, and almost always so unreasonably ignorant, that an irascible Catholic is in a constant fume. I have given an account of a small part of my experience in the last chapter.

I wish that I had been as fond of going to my duties as I was ready to defend them. But I worked with Protestants, and lived with them, while my Catholic life was confined to an hour or two at church on Sundays. Under these circumstances, I became again careless, I saw and heard little to remind me of my Church, unless when a dispute turned up; and disputes about religion never begat any piety in *me*. I don't believe they ever did in any one else. They are *occasions of sin*.

I began to frequent theatres. That is, I thought that I might treat myself to a play, once a month or so. I have little good to say of them. They are pits dug with the devil's own hands. I do not mean to say that they are necessarily so, for they are not. There is no harm done when a man represents on a stage the person of another, and is helped by dresses, scenery, and music. The theatre *might* be what it is so often falsely called, a school of morals, and of good ones, too. It is very possible that the witnessing certain plays would do no harm. But it is so managed, that it is a school for scandal – deep scandal to souls. A good play will not draw a house unless a worse than naked woman exposes her person in a suggestive dance; unless a lewd song be sung, or an immoral farce be added to the bill. Vile characters are often represented in a way that makes them look quite inviting; and real virtue is not seldom hissed, it is shown in such unfashionable colors. In a word, the little good is so mixed with the bad, and in the ratio of one to ten, that you cannot witness it alone. You must take nine doses of corruption to get one scene of harmless amusement. An innocent representation in a theatre is like an oasis in a great desert – you faint before you reach it. This is especially true in these latter years. There was a time when the so called legitimate drama could draw houses. Now, the public taste has become grossly corrupt. And it is not the least evil of the theatre that it brings you into the very presence of her whose feet lay hold of hell. A man has to risk something who goes after her to her own dwelling. But in a theatre, he can leave his wife or his sister in the box, and go to the galleries, and there is no one to hiss, or to say that he has done a vile deed.

I used to select the plays I wanted to see with some care; but every one who knows any thing about theatres will agree with me that no pains can ward off the evils to which a theatre-goer surely exposes himself. He cannot help seeing and hearing things that are sinful. There is one fact, of which I have thought sometimes, that I cannot understand. More than once I have thought of my prayers in the theatre, and have said them, too. I wonder if it was ever done before? And I wonder what the prayers were worth?

My master set his face against it; and very properly, too. He said that he had no wish whatever to force his religion upon me. But as for theatre-going, my Church discountenanced it as much as his did; so I should not go. He made such a vigorous opposition, that I promised not to go while I remained with him.

By some miracle or other, I escaped a danger that besets almost every young man in a Boston boarding-house. That was the danger of being enrolled in an engine company. The tubs were served in those days by volunteers, and the young men were what would be called choice spirits. They were generally young tradesmen. They were *good fellows,* in the common acceptation of the term. They were well drilled in the work of putting out a fire. They seemed to know precisely where it was, and they would run by the straightest road to it. When they got there, they behaved like salamanders; they acted as if they were born in places where fire was plenty. They would risk their lives to save property or persons from the flames. In a word, they worked at a fire like generous fellows who were fond of the excitement. After they put it out – and it was not their fault if it were not subdued – they would have a good time.

The excitement which attends the duty of a fireman brought many young men to the engine-house; and when they were in it, there was a charm to keep them there. It was a good rendezvous for evenings, and especially for Sundays, which were spent there by many young men. There were target excursions, balls, suppers, and parties. There were always some prime fellows who would tell a story well, and crack a nice joke. It was a pleasant road to ruin, and many a youth has walked therein.

I was often asked to join them; but I never went to fires, and I was not sure that I would always obey the call at night. Besides, I saw young men every day becoming more and more in love with the tub; and, as their liking for its haunt increased, their taste for work grew less. Many an hour was spent there that ought to have been employed in getting bread to eat for soul and body. The examples I had before my eyes seemed to prove that the engine-house was no place for a man who had the least desire of salvation. I was never in the houses more than twice, and each time it was Sunday. There was quite a gathering at both. In one, I heard nothing good; and in the other, a hog was telling a ribald story that would have disgraced a brothel. In fact, I was convinced that going to an engine-house, in practice, meant – going to the devil.

But, in avoiding Scylla, I struck upon Charybdis; and that was a military company. In Boston, a man must do the state some service, even if he ruin himself in doing it. Every one must be a military man, or an engine man, a militia man, or he must pay a small fine. Now, I eschewed engine-houses; but I was not satisfied to let well-enough alone, and pay my fine.

For I had read of battles!

And I longed, not exactly to follow a chief, but to be one, and lead armed men to muster. When I was six years old, I had a nice belt, sword, and feather; and I remember one artillery election day, when I walked guard, – for the soldier let me pass, – and marched up to the place where the governor and his attendants were sitting. After putting my head in the mouth of a cannon to see where the fire came from, and hearing the touch-master-general say that if I did that again I would have my head blown to the top of the State House, I heard the music play a beautiful air slowly. I was then walking towards the governor.

Presently an officer, who was so stiff with gold and tassels that he could hardly move, started from his post, in front of the company, and began to march up to the governor, very slowly, and very grandly. I thought that I could march as well as he did; so I threw out my legs at each step, as if I wanted to fall backwards, held my head up, and balanced my sword as he did his pike. He came straight to the front, and I reached the settee as soon as he did. The governor and his attendants laughed so heartily, that I was afraid something would happen to them. I saw nothing to laugh at, neither did the officer; so we both looked grave.

General, said the governor, is this young officer going to command the company next year?

I don't know, your excellency, said the general – a fine white-haired soldier. He looks as if he would not wait to be asked twice.

What is your name? asked the governor.

John O'Brien.

Do you want to be captain of that company yonder?

I reflected a moment. I'll ask father; and if he won't let me, I'll enlist.

Well, said he, hold this. And I stood near him, holding the pike, until the cannon roared, the band played, and another officer marched up as grandly as the first, and took the weapon.

The common, on public days, was the boys' paradise, of course. I like to go there now, on such days, and see the little fellows capering as I did in bygone times. The only thing that could tempt me to play truant was the sight of a company marching along. It cost a hard struggle to get rid of the temptation; and, to this day, the spectacle has not lost its attraction. I would march after the Brigade Band a mile, and then after the Brass Band another.

Well, I attended the militia training twice, and got heartily tired of what I saw and heard. I told my master that I would be a military man, and walk in the pathway to glory.

It is no place for you, you may depend upon it, said he. You will get into bad company, and perhaps contract bad habits. I was fool enough to join them in my younger days; but, after a while, I saw the folly of it.

Well, I can't help it. I must be a fool, too, and see the folly of it for a year or two. And so I did.

The military school in Boston was no better than the fireman's school. The same sort of boys go to both, and for the same purpose. The main difference is, that one likes the excitement of a fire, while another prefers the excitement of wearing a colored coat, and marching under the admiring eyes of smaller, but not younger boys, after a band of musicians. There is also this difference: the soldiers have fewer meetings; they never assemble on Sundays; and when a meeting takes place on week evenings, it is always for business. So there is one advantage they have over the firemen; the road to ruin is more slowly travelled.

I saw the folly of it in a year or two, but not before I had spent more money than I could afford. A man who can throw away fifty dollars a year, may afford it better than I could. I remember a target excursion, where I came off third best. There were ninety shots fired, and only three hit the board. A tour for *camp duty* was another amusement. Its object was to make us hardy soldiers, ready to endure the fatigues of actual service, if the country should happen to need our strong, protecting arms. Accordingly, we would march a hundred miles or so in the cars, and then endure the privations of a hotel. Sometimes we would sleep a night under our tents. Sleep! no, there was no such thing; only the articles of war *said* that we would sleep. I have often wondered how a drunken soldier could manage to stand in his place, and go through the exercise. It was a mystery to me; and yet it is done. It is like another mystery which I have known to come off at the theatre. An actress would be so drunk that she would have to be *walked* on the stage; but when she faced the audience, she went through her part tolerably well.

At the time of the Rhode Island rebellion, when patriotism there was hissing hot, and when the democratesses there had got up a clam-bake, and had invited distinguished speakers to come and stir them up, – just as if a meeting of women needed any speakers, – our company was detailed for actual service. Several wanted to be discharged; but the adjutant-general swore by his whiskers that they should march. I, for one, made my will, leaving my debts to be paid, and six cents, besides my uniform, to pay them with. We were under orders, but we did not march. The reason was, that Dorr only drew his sword, but his legs didn't give his arm time to use it.* Moreover, the meeting of the democratesses had ended in clams, tea, and talk. I am very glad we didn't go. I should have hated to meet an army of those democratesses, after they had eaten their clams; especially if they were all like one of them I happened to meet afterwards, and whom I told of our intended march. She wished that I was *her* son for a quarter of an hour; just for a quarter of an hour! She'd take me across her knees, and *spank* me until –.

There is a queer kind of evening party that is very much admired, and often got up by the Protestants of that class to which I belonged. I have seldom seen it among Catholics, unless they be Protestant Catholics, as I was. It is generally got up by women. It goes by the name of a tea party; but the young women call it a kissing party. The end of the institution is, that twenty or thirty young men and women, who, perhaps, never saw one another before, may meet together in a private house, and kiss one another from eight or nine in the evening to two or three in the morning. The ceremony begins thus: The ladies who give the party are waiting in the parlor at eight o'clock. The first arrival is a bashful young man. It is the first time he ever went to a party, and he has had his hair curled with hot tongs. He has also taken lessons of a friend concerning his demeanor on entrance, and so he puts his left hand under his vest, and bows profoundly thrice. At the third bow, his pantaloons, which are new, and very tight, give him a hint that he has made one bow too many. So he sits down, and wishes that he were at home, only he is too bashful to ask for his hat. The next arrival dooms him to a ten minutes' agony, for it is a young lady whom he never saw before. The hostess leaves the two to

---

*[In 1842, Thomas Wilson Dorr led an abortive rebellion of disfranchised Rhode Islanders who opposed the anachronistic state constitution that restricted suffrage to land holders. His men attempted to seize the state's arsenal, but were captured easily.]

amuse themselves, which he does by looking alternately at the clock and at the door, and thinking that the young lady has fallen in love with him. She amuses herself with watching his motions, which she can safely do, because he never looks her way. By and by, he begins to think that she knows what he is thinking about, and he glows like a live coal. He screws himself to the point of looking at her; but he is so slow about it, and shows so plainly what he is going to do, that she has time to pretend to be watching a bug crawling across the carpet. At last he is relieved by the arrival of the other guests, who make a very formal entrance always, and then sit down and say nothing. Bashful young man happens to sit in a conspicuous chair; so he shows his ease of mind by drumming a tattoo on his knees, and putting his legs in all sorts of positions, each more ungraceful than the last. It always happens at these parties, that they who arrive first do not know one another; and a general introduction, on entering, does not warrant conversation. So they all sit bolt upright, and look at the carpet, without saying a word. It is singular what stress is laid upon an introduction between two parties. They sit side by side for half an hour without exchanging a word, looking as grim as if they were thinking of the best way to poison one another, feeling very miserable, and wishing that the whole concern were at the Red Sea. The hostess steps forward. Miss Tightlace, shall I make you acquainted with Mr. Bedpost? Then the two enemies become warm friends; they make fifty affectionate inquiries concerning one another; and Mr. Bedpost escorts Miss Tightlace home, promising to call again, and goes away thinking that he has been acquainted with her for a hundred years.

More arrivals, and the girls sit on one side like a bed of marygolds and hollyhocks, while the men occupy the other like a line of onions and pepper-grass. The party is all here, and the silence is painful. Some try to speak in whispers; but every body looks that way, and they stop. This is the first phase of the party, and it is called – waiting for the ice to be broken. Every eye is fixed upon the carpet. At this stage of the proceedings, a serious Christian would suppose that it was a prayer meeting. The mistake was made once or twice, to my knowledge. A church member sat there, looking as grim as the rest, and thinking that they were all so still because they were expecting some one to begin. He waited a reasonable length of time, and, seeing no one preparing to begin, he determined to act as leader himself. So he gave two or three monitory coughs, which made every body look at him. Whereupon he put on his most melancholy look; and, in his "very best double bass tones," he said, Let us pray! The ice was broken, and a roar of laughter ensued, for every body thought it was a joke upon their silence. *He* didn't; for after looking about him as if he were taking a last leave of them before they went to the naughty place, he took his hat and disappeared.

Another serious Christian, who very properly disapproved of these parties, went, nevertheless, to one of them, with the intent to break it up.

Accordingly, when every body was breathing hard and looking at the carpet, he spoke: Brethren and sisters, shall we meet again in heaven? Here every brother and sister stared. Shall we –?

Stop! exclaimed a wag. There is always a wag at these parties, who does nothing but make mischief. Stop! It's out of order to preach before singing. Dear brethren, and especially the sisters, before brother Groan-soul preaches, we'll sing the sixty-eleventh tune, any metre –

> "O, I'm bound for the kingdom! will you go to glory with me?
>   Hallelujah, kingdom come.
> If you get there before I do,
> Look out for me, for I'm coming too!"

The disturber sloped.

But the ice is commonly broken this wise: The hostess enters with the cover of a flour bucket. She gives each person his number, beginning with number one; and then, giving the cover a twist, it spins on its edge while she calls a number – number seven. The number called must jump up and catch the cover before it falls flat. If that is not done, a forfeit is declared, which is paid in kisses. Number seven is the bashful man, and he doesn't understand the game; so he sits still. Inquiry is made, and all eyes are turned upon him, while he thinks the world is afire, and all the doors locked. He is instructed in the game, and number seven is called again. He rushes to catch the cover, and he fails. A forfeit! Go to any lady, and ask her what to do. He asks the lady who came in first and fell in love with him. Kiss all the ladies in the room but *me*. One used to the game would begin with *her*; and she casts a comical look at him, as he goes away without saluting her. He does his work very much as a bear would in hugging a cat on hot irons; but he finishes it without tearing more than ten dollars worth of lace, and then sits down, and wonders which girl he will have.

This is the way, and the fun lasts until past midnight, interrupted only by a little wagging of jaws over nuts, apples, and cake. The most extraordinary ways for promoting forfeits are invented, and most laughable modes of executing them are enforced. After four or five hours spent in this fashion, the young women go away quite satisfied; and why shouldn't they, when each has had kissing enough to last a married woman all her lifetime?

It is hard to cheat the devil in a more cunning fashion than this, admitting that he *is* cheated by it, which is more than doubtful. I would not let my wife run the gantlet so; neither would I a sister, if I had one. And if I were not married, the trotting out of my intended in such a fashion would induce me to leave her in the market. It is not innocent amusement. The serious man asked a very proper question, and he did not ask it out of season, either.

I became a member of the Mechanic Apprentices' Library Association,

shortly after my engagement with Mr. Bowen. I received a great deal of benefit from this institution, and a little damage, all my own fault. At that time the
society occupied humble rooms in Cornhill. It has since removed to splendid
quarters, and seems to be doing well. Its object is, to gather together the
apprentices of Boston, and give them opportunities for mental improvement.
They would obtain it better by assembling together only apprentices, because
there would be no rivalry excepting that of talent; no difference of condition
would enable one to overawe another, or to push him aside. Each apprentice,
feeling himself among equals, would gain far more than he would in any
other society, where a certain distinction of rank was tacitly acknowledged
and maintained. No one could remain a member after the age of twenty-one.

It owned a library of about a thousand volumes. It was not a select
library, for books had slowly accumulated by way of donations. Yet there was
enough good reading to employ the spare hours of a boy from his fourteenth
to his twenty-first year. There was a large shelf for novels, and this shelf was
the most visited, and its contents the best thumbed. There were several books
of a very bad character; but they were dry reading, and they were seldom
consulted. One of them was the Age of Reason. It was not called for once in
a year, and an incautious librarian removed it without saying any thing. As ill
luck would have it, a young infidel asked for it; but it was not forthcoming.
He complained to the society, and there was a long debate, in which the mer-
its of Tom Paine were discussed. The consequence was, that the book was
read by half the members before three months went by.

The publishers of the Boston papers furnished the society with newspaper reading in abundance.

We had lectures in the winter season: The beginning was an humble one.
For a few years our past members, and a few of the eldest active ones, did the
work. Occasionally, some distinguished friend would volunteer his services.
By and by, the talent enlisted in our behalf increased; and now the course is
scarcely second to any in the city.

An elocution class met regularly, and sometimes gave exhibitions before
the society at large. The audience was made up of the members, their mothers, sisters, and female friends. But the debates gave more instruction and
amusement than any thing else.

A subject would be proposed at a previous meeting, and a committee
appointed to manage the debate at the next gathering. I have heard some
poor discussions on these occasions, but I have also heard some good ones.
It seldom happened that something was not said worth hearing. I have heard
worse debates in the assemblies of bearded men. The questions discussed
were generally useful ones. But once in a while a queer demand would be
proposed for debate – Ought a man to get married when he was young?
When this question was proposed for the next wrangle, one got up and
moved that the ladies be excluded. This motion was lost, to the satisfaction of

every one; and we listened to the funniest debate I ever heard. For there were twelve speakers, some under seventeen, and none over twenty-one.

The society was a very good school for us all. That is, it was the best one then offered to a Boston apprentice. The good done by such associations, when they are well managed, is not to be estimated. It is true that they take little of the boy's time, for two or three evenings in the week are not much. But they absorb a great part of his thoughts, and a boy has a *great many* to spare. If he happens to be an officer of such a society, so much the better; for he will be sure to devote himself to it faithfully, and more than faithfully. He has the meeting twice a week. He has his book at home to read in the evening. He perhaps has his piece to learn for the elocution class, his part to sustain in the next debate, or some committee business to attend to before the next meeting. In one way or another, the society will engross a fair share of his spare time and thoughts. This helps to keep him from the engine-house, and out of barrooms or other vile haunts. A boy of seventeen has a world of curious fancies in his brain; and, if his thoughts do not get a safe direction, he *will* be likely to go astray. He will seek excitement somewhere. If he gets it from a tolerably innocent source, so much the better for his soul and body. Of course, the confessional is the best and safest of all schools. No other can be entirely safe. But, in speaking of merely human means, which may be used by God in keeping a boy from bad company, I rank these societies very high. I am satisfied, in most cases, that a boy's tastes run in a tolerably good direction, when he takes particular pleasure in going to these societies, or in seeking the company of honest females. The boy that does both, as a great many do, is in a pretty fair way, humanly speaking. It is remarkable what a hold these societies get upon the mind of a boy. I have belonged to several; and I was an active member of a musical society for some years. We only met once a week; but I believe that I thought of little else from Sunday morning to Sunday morning. It is a little laughable, too, when I think of it now, what *great* importance a boy attaches to the affairs of his society. The government think, and talk, and look as if they had upon their minds the affairs of an empire. The President thinks that if a procession were got up, he ought to walk by the side of the president of the nation. A breach of the constitution is an enormity only to be equalled by the violation of our American instrument. The members always respect the assemblies too much to appear in them unless dressed in their best, and shaved, if they have beards, which seldom happens. They call one another gentlemen, and they behave in a way that gives them an undoubted right to the name. The courtesy and good feeling always manifest at their meetings might be copied, with great advantage to themselves, by many who have had superior means of self-culture. They might be copied by grave legislative assemblies; yea, by the senate of the nation. The senators are potent fathers; but they are not so grave and reverend as a meeting of Boston apprentices, assembled to debate whether Jackson did well in removing the deposits. Master mechanics and parents would do well in encouraging their boys to take an active part in such societies; and they ought not to grudge the time and money expended in them. They should only ask whether the society be a good one. They should take it as a starting-point that the boy *will* have excitement, at one rate or another. Then comes the question, Shall he go after it to the engine-house, the grog-shop, and the theatre; or shall he seek it in the halls of these societies? Besides, they make a *man* of a member. To be sure, this is an evil. A boy ought to be a *boy*. The *man* is a man, not so much on account of his stature, his beard, his bass voice, and his wife, as on account of the nature of his thoughts. The sum of these make the *man.* Well, the boyish member of these societies has very big thoughts, as I said just now. I remember that this thing caused some astonishment to my master. I was an officer in two or three societies, and I fancied that I and Daniel Webster were two great men. Sometimes, when my good master would give an order, or ask a question, I would be abstracted, and often downright saucy. He never got angry, – I never saw him angry; but one day he asked after the health of my eldest child, and advised me to give him a flogging, if he were saucy. Well, this evil is almost inseparable from active membership in these societies. God forgive me! I have shown it in a far more august presence than that of my master. But I would prefer that my boy be a *man* than an imp of darkness. When I *must* suffer one of two evils, I choose the least.

I was a member of this society about the years 1834, '35. Of my associates who are living, the greater part are master mechanics and tradesmen; at least two are in the legislature; several have entered learned professions. No one has repented of the time spent in our little hall.

The Blakes and Flanagans

by Mary Anne (Madden) Sadlier (New York: P. J. Kenedy, 1855)

Mary Anne Madden was raised by her father, a wealthy merchant, at Cootehill, County Cavan, Ireland. When his death left her orphaned, she emigrated in 1844 at age twenty-four to Montreal. There she met and married James Sadlier, the branch manager for his family's Catholic publishing house, D. and J. Sadlier, which had been founded in 1837 in New York City. Immediately, Mrs. Sadlier began writing fiction, essays, and translations, and by 1860, when the family returned to New York to live, she had established herself as the most insistent and prolific Irish Catholic voice in American letters. Widely serialized in periodicals such as the Pilot, Thomas D'Arcy McGee's *American Celt, and the Sadlier Company's New York* Tablet, *Mrs. Sadlier's works ultimately filled some sixty volumes. She died in 1903.*

The aim of her fiction was set in the preface to her first Irish-American novel, Willy Burke; or, The Irish Orphan in America *(1850):*

> *This little work was written for the express purpose of being useful to the young sons of my native land, in their arduous struggle with the tempter, whose nefarious design of bearing them from the faith of their fathers, is so artfully concealed under every possible disguise.*

Mrs. Sadlier tended to deal with one sort of tempting "disguise" per novel: for example, the business world in Willy Burke, *the life of servant girls in* Bessy Conway *(1861), the plight of Irish children in public orphanages in* Aunt Honor's Keepsake *(1866), the dangers of making it into the upper classes in* Old and New; or, Taste vs. Fashion *(1862), and the generally pernicious effects of the urban environment (overcome by the protagonists' moving to near-idyllic Iowa) in* Con O'Regan; or Immigrant Life in the New World *(1864). She also wrote ten novels with Irish historical settings, from* The Red Hand of Ulster *(1850) to* Maureen Dhu *(1870). Mrs. Sadlier's "American" novels remain her most valuable contribution to literary and social history: they document lavishly many aspects of nineteenth-century immigrant life.*

The novel excerpted here, The Blakes and Flanagans *of 1855, was one of the most popular. The only Sadlier novel to be translated, it was published in German in*

1857 as Alt-Ireland und Amerika. *The catalyst for composition was the controversy in the late 1840s and 1850s about sending Catholic children to the public schools. Amid reports of Protestant proselytizing through classroom use of the King James Bible, American Catholics at this time were establishing their separate parochial school system. Reprinted here in full is chapter I, in which, in typical Sadlier style, contrasting Irish-American families are presented – the faithful Flanagans and the backsliding Blakes. Repudiating their Blake cousins' intellectual, social, and economic ambitions (encouraged by the public schools), the Flanagan children remain Irish, Catholic, and in the leather business (encouraged by St. Peter's School).*

Also included here is Mrs. Sadlier's crushingly judgmental summary of the fate of Henry Blake, who goes from bad to worse, from the public school to Columbia University, and gains material success while losing his soul.

Five and twenty years ago, when our story opens, even the great city of New York was more staid and sober than it now is. It was simply a thriving commercial city, "well to do in the world," and not much ahead of its sister cities. Its ways were quiet and old-fashioned compared with what they are now. But times are changed since then; the age of progress is hurrying all things onward with a rapidity that makes one's head dizzy. It is unfashionable now to speak of the past with regret, and any one who has the hardihood to do so is set down as "behind the age." For my part I am quite willing to be "behind the age," for "the age" goes much too fast for my liking, and my sympathies are more with the past than the present. But this is not the question; I was going to tell a story of New York, twenty-five years ago, and here I am, making comparisons which many of my younger readers may deem invidious. And yet the digression, if it be one, is very natural, and perhaps necessary, as the times to which I refer are precisely those of which I mean to write.

About twenty-five years ago, then, before Nativism had developed itself into Know Nothingism, there lived in Chapel street (now West Broadway), New York, a worthy Irishman of the name of Flanagan, a real homespun Tipperary man, hot-blooded, blustering, and loud spoken, yet kind and generous and true-hearted. A real unmistakeable Milesian, reminding one of poor Wolfe's description of his "own friend – "

"So bold and frank his bearing, boy,
Should you meet him onward faring, boy,
   In Lapland's snow,
   Or Chili's glow,
You'd say, what news from Erin, boy?"*

---

*[A Milesian would be an authentic Irishman, descended from the legendary old Celtic group, the Sons of Mil. Charles Wolfe (1791-1823) was a Dublin poet and the cousin of Irish patriot Wolfe Tone.]

He had left his native land immediately after his marriage, and the young bride, who then for the first time quitted her father's home by the silvery Suir, had since become a wise and prudent matron, the mother of three sons and two daughters – all "natives" – ay! every one of them. Timothy – or as he was more generally called – Tim Flanagan, followed the trade of a leather-dresser, and had gained, by his persevering industry, a position of ease and comfort. His wife was a quiet, home-loving woman, a neat, tidy housewife, a careful and affectionate mother, and, to crown all, a simple, sincere Christian – an Irishwoman of the good old times. Neither Tim nor his wife was much versed in controversy; they knew little, and cared less, about the various newfangled systems of religion; they were good, old fashioned Catholics, as their fathers were before them, and their chief ambition was to bring up their children in the same faith. As for the children themselves, they were just what might be expected from such parents; healthy and blooming as mountain flowers, cheerful, docile, and obedient. Various shades of character were, of course, discernible amongst them, but these were, more or less, common to all. There was Edward, or Ned, a fine boy of twelve, Thomas and John, aged ten and eight, and two little girls, Ellen and Susan, the one between five and six, and the other four. Susy was, as might be expected, the pet of the family; and as there seemed no likelihood of any further increase, her dominion became every day more confirmed, a fact of which the little damsel seemed fully cognizant. Take them altogether, there was not in New York city a happier family, or one more free from guile. Religion was the sun of their solar system, giving life and warmth to themselves and all around them. If either Tim or Nelly had their failings – and who has not? – they were so few, and so little obtruded on their neighbors, that they were both respected and beloved by all who knew them.

Timothy Flanagan had a sister some years older than himself, the wife of a Galway man, named Miles Blake, who kept a provision store in the next block. The Blakes were a good sort of people in their way, but not by any means so good as the Flanagans. Both husband and wife were more anxious for making money than anything else; and though they professed to be good Catholics, and were so considered by many people, yet religion was, with them, only a secondary object – all very well in its place, so that it did not engross too much time or attention. "Business! business!" was the grand affair with the Blake family – at least the elders of the house. Otherwise, they were, as I have said, a worthy couple, strictly honest in their dealings, kind and affectionate between themselves, and, with all their closeness in money matters, still ready and willing to spare something to those who really stood in need of it. Miles Blake was never behind any of his neighbors when a collection was taken up, especially if it were for the building or repairing of a church, for Miles thought that churches ought to be built and repaired, ay, and the priest decently supported. But further than that Miles did not care to

go. Schools, or convents, or the like, were, in his opinion, by no means necessary: people could get on without the convents, "though he didn't deny but
they did a great deal of good," and as for Catholic schools, he did not see
what the people wanted with them, when the State had provided good schooling for their children, free of all expense. Yet still, Miles was always on pretty good terms with his priest, and complied, once a year or so, with his religious duties, deeming that quite sufficient. Of several children who had been
born to them, Miles Blake and his wife had but two remaining; one a boy, of
fourteen or fifteen, and the other a girl, of twelve. The latter was so pale and
delicate looking that it seemed as though she were destined to follow her
brothers and sisters to an early grave. Perhaps it were better she had, but such
an idea never occurred to her doting parents, who loved their children "not
wisely, but too well."

The two families of Blake and Flanagan lived on the most friendly and
familiar footing, and if a cloud did at times overshadow the brightness of their
intercourse, as clouds *will* overshadow all things human – it was soon dis-
pelled, either by some little dextrous manoeuvre on the part of good Mrs.
Flanagan, or, perhaps, an act of contrition from Tim or Miles, or whoever
might be the offending party. Thus had things gone on for years and years,
ever since Tim brought out his pretty young wife, on the special advice and
invitation of Mrs. Blake and her husband, who had made the grand voyage
some ten years before. So now that I have brought forward the leading characters of my story, and given the reader an idea of their distinctive features, I
will leave them to speak and act for themselves.

The children of the two families had been brought up together, as one
might say, and were almost like brothers and sisters all round. Eliza Blake,
being, from her infancy, of a frail and delicate constitution, was regarded alike
by brothers and cousins, with a sort of pitying tenderness; her little whims
were all humored, and her wishes, in most cases, anticipated; her faults were
not many, and, such as they were, might be chiefly ascribed to the over-indul-
gence of all around her. She was, by nature, mild, gentle and affectionate, but
sickness had made her somewhat querulous, and the extreme fondness of parents and friends made her over-exacting; still she was a very good little girl,
and as for prudence and discretion, they seemed to have been born with her,
or, at least, developed themselves in her much earlier than they usually do in
children. She was what is called "an old fashioned little girl," and was, moreover, the oracle of the family, as a petted child too often is. Harry, the brother, was a fine healthy boy, full of fun and frolic; talented beyond most boys
of his age, but exceedingly averse to study. Generous and high-spirited to a
fault, he was easily offended, and just as easily pacified, so that, though constantly engaged in some boyish quarrel, he was still a general favorite
amongst his companions. Harry was a particular favorite with his uncle
Flanagan, probably because he was an exact counterpart of himself. The

neighbors used to say that Tim Flanagan hadn't a child of his own so like him as Harry Blake – "and he's no disgrace to him, either; for he's a fine likely boy, and a good-hearted fellow, with all his wildness."

This "wildness" was considered the more excusable, as it generally manifested itself in quarrels with his school-mates on the score of religion. There was scarcely a day that Harry Blake did not get into some "scrape," defending his religion. His father was well pleased to hear of these tilting matches, in which Harry was almost sure to come off victorious; he gloried in his son's "mettle," and proudly prognosticated that he would sooner or later "cram the truth down their throats – that he would; he'd teach them to vilify his religion, and blacken poor old Ireland!"

And why was it that Tim Flanagan's boys, sturdy and robust as they were, and brought up by a mother so good and pious, were never seen or heard fighting for their religion? Simply because they were not exposed to hear it reviled or calumniated. True to his character and principles, honest Tim Flanagan never sent one of his children to a Ward school. His motto was: "Shun danger wherever you see it," and, in pursuance of that prudent precept, he always declared that a child of his should never set foot in a Protestant school, with *his* consent. "At least, while *I'm* over them," he would add. "If they choose to run the risk, any of them, when I'm gone, they may do it, of course, but not till then." His wife smiled and said nothing, but it was well known that, with all her mildness, she was, on this point, to the full as inflexible as her husband.

Many and many a time did Miles and Tim discuss the question; sometimes they talked very loud, and grew very hot upon it, but still matters remained as they were: Miles sent his boy and girl to the Ward School, and the young Flanagans daily went their way to the Catholic Schools attached to St. Peter's Church.

St. Peter's School had two departments, one for boys, the other for girls – the former taught by a certain Mr. Lanigan, a fine specimen of the good old Catholic teacher; the latter under the direction of the Sisters of Charity, and a flourishing school they had of it. There were but few Catholic schools in the city, perhaps not more than two or three, and St. Peter's was about the largest. And a very good school it was. Many and many a valued citizen did it bring up for the State, and not a few of the boys who "sat at the feet" of worthy Mr. Lanigan have since attained a good position in society by their industry and good conduct, not to speak of the sound business education there received.

The school question was always a bone of contention between Tim and Miles, but, as I have already observed, neither could succeed in convincing the other, although Miles had been known to admit, after some of these debates, that, "sure enough, Tim came pretty hard on him."

Sometimes these discussions took place in presence of the children, and though, at first, they seemed to pay but little attention to the matter, it gradually sank into their minds, and was often discussed amongst themselves when their parents were not present. Eliza Blake was the first to adopt her uncle's views, as far as a girl of her age could adopt them, but when she ventured, for the first time, to tell her father that she would much rather go to the Sisters' School with her little cousins, he cut her short at once, and told her, with unusual sternness, not to think of such a thing. "The school you're at is a very good one, Eliza, and as long as your mother and myself are pleased with it, *you* need not object. You would not have been as far on as you are now, take my word for it, if you had been at the Sisters' School. Keep quiet now, Lizzy, and don't be getting your uncle Tim's notions into your head. Let me hear no more of it, or I'll not be pleased with you."

For some years Mrs. Blake did not much care where the children were sent to school, so long as they *were* sent, but she had no fancy for seeing Harry come home day after day with some unsightly bruise on his face, a black eye, a swelled lip, or a bloody nose. She had a womanly dislike for "fighting," and would have been better pleased to see her boy less of a pugilist, and more of a scholar.

"Now Miles, what on earth is the use of all this squabbling and fighting?" she said one day to her husband, after laying some sticking-plaster on a cut over Harry's eye-brow. "It's a mercy that the boy isn't killed long ago – that's what it is, and I wonder at a sensible man like you to encourage him in these wild pranks."

"Why, man alive, woman, what would you have me do?" retorted Miles. "You wouldn't have me tell Harry to run away from the young vagabonds – would you? Isn't it all on account of his religion that they're down on him, and I'm sure you wouldn't wish a son of yours or mine to give in to a parcel of young scamps like them, when they get a-running down his religion?"

"Well, no, Miles, I would not, " said Mary hesitatingly, "but see – see how the Flanagan boys don't get black eyes or bloody noses, as Harry does?"

"Humph!" said Miles, "to be sure they don't, and why would they? haven't they it all their own way there? They haven't to stand up for their religion, like poor Harry."

"And maybe they're better off, after all. I'm sure it saves their mother many a fright that *my* lad gives *me*."

"Ay, but then, Mary, you must own that it's worth some trouble to have Harry learn to defend his faith. The Flanagans will grow up regular nincompoops – not a word in their heads, and no more spunk in them than so many kittens. I like to see a fellow ready with a word or a blow to keep up his religion, and I tell you once for all that there's no place so good as a Protestant school, for a Catholic boy to learn *pluck*."

"Well, well, Miles, you know best," was the submissive answer. "What pleases you, pleases me. Come here, and empty this bag of potatoes – I want the bag for something else."

Before the potatoes were all turned out, in came Tim Flanagan, his fine open countenance brimful of sly humor, though he thought proper to affect a grave demeanor. "Good luck to the work," said he, "for I see you're handling the murphies, there – and fine specimens they are, too, considering that they didn't grow in Ireland. What's gone wrong with Harry this morning?"

"Oh! not much, Tim, not much," said Miles, rubbing the dust leisurely off his hands; "he's been at his old trade, that's all, cramming the lies down some of the Yankee boys' throats, and, as there was three or four of them on him at once, he got a little scratch of a cut over his eye. But it's not worth a pin."

"Poh! poh! and is that all?" cried Tim, "why, the Johnson boys and the Herricks, and all of them, are making a great brag of how they gave Harry Blake a good trouncing this morning, and one, they think, that he'll not get over for a while."

"They lie, the young scoundrels – they lie," cried Miles in a towering passion. "They did their best, the cowardly set – they did their best, but that wasn't much. Harry was more than a match for the whole half-dozen. "

"Well! that same's a comfort, anyhow," put in Tim, with his roguish smile. "He'll be a first-rate buffer one of these days – ay, faith! Neither Dan Donelly nor Deaf Burke could hold a candle to him, if he goes on at this rate."

"Ay! you're making your game of me now," said Miles, somewhat cooled down, "but so long as the boy fights for his religion and the honor of old Ireland, he may fight away and welcome. He wouldn't be *my* son if he didn't."

"Ay, there's the rub," said Tim, earnestly, "it's all very well while he fights for his religion, but, just keep him at the same school for three or four years longer, and you'll see he'll be readier to fight *against* it."

This raised Miles's ire again. "Why, then, by this and by that, Tim Flanagan, but you're enough to set a man crazy. It's well come up with you to talk of *my* son turning Protestant – did you ever know a turn-coat in the family – tell me that now?"

"What matter whether I did or not," retorted Tim, "I tell you pat and plain, as I often told you before, that you're thrusting your two fine children – and that's what they are, God knows! into the very jaws of perdition. I don't want any argument about it, for I know it's no use arguing with you, but I appeal to Mary, there, if I'm not right."

"Well, as you put the question to me," replied his sister, "I can't deny but I'd twice rather see Harry and Eliza going to St. Peter's School with your youngsters. It seems unnatural-like to be sending them to a Protestant school."

"Why, bad manners to you, Mary, sure there's no Protestant schools here – they're" –

"Ay! what *are* they, Miles? – do tell us!" said Tim, coaxingly.

"What are they, is it?" said Miles, somewhat puzzled by this home-thrust;

"why, they're not for any religion in particular – they're for all religions, and you both know that as well as I do."

"Begging your pardon," returned Tim, very coolly, "they're for *no religion* – that's what they're for."

"Why, what do you mean by that?"

"I just mean what I say – a school that's for *all* religions, as you say, is, in fact, for no religion, because no particular religion can be taught without giving offence to some parties concerned."

"Well, and that's just what I want," said Miles, exultingly, "school is not the place to learn religion; let the parents teach that at home, and the priest in church."

"Well, that does seem right enough, Tim, after all," said Mary, "there, you see, Harry and Eliza go to catechism every Sunday morning, and I'm sure *I* do all I can, and their father in like manner, to make them good Catholics."

"All right, Mary, all right, as far as it goes, but do all Catholic parents do the same? Do you think all the Catholic children attending Ward Schools are sent regularly to catechism on Sunday? or do they all get as good teachings at home, and see as good example before them as yours do? and" –

"Now, Tim," said Miles, suddenly breaking in, "the short and the long of it is, my children are as far advanced in their learning as any other boy and girl we know of the same age, and as for religion, they're not a whit behind anybody else's children. If it goes to that, there's not a boy in the city readier to stand up for his religion than my Harry, and he'd never have been so courageous, or so staunch, if he had been at a school where there was no Protestants."

"Then how did you and I get to love our religion so well? I'm sure we didn't either of us go to a Protestant or an infidel school. Poor old Master Finigan that taught me all I know, was as strict a Catholic as any in the parish, and, for the matter of that, it's few Protestants we had in the same parish."

"And we hadn't one – not one," said Miles, "there wasn't one within miles of us."

"Very good, and yet you see you're not a bit colder or more careless about your religion than if you had been fighting for it every day of your life."

"Well, now, Tim, there's no use in talking – things are different here, as I often told you before, and as long as I see the children getting on well with their education, and still remaining good Catholics, I'm willing to send them to the Ward School, because I'd be very ungrateful if I didn't, when the State is so good and so kind as to educate our children without meddling with their religion. What do you say, Mary?" But Mary was busily engaged, preparing some Indian corn for the pot, and had no mind to "bother herself" with such debates. "Just talk it out, yourselves," said she, "you're the best judges; as for me, I don't know much about it. You've been arguing about schools these five years, and I don't see that it makes any difference. If I were ye, I'd give it up, for it only makes dissensions between you." So she went on with her cooking, compared with which the school-question sank into nothing in her eyes.

"Well, good-bye," said Tim, rising and taking his hat, "I wish you both a good appetite for your dinner, and a better knowledge of what is good for your children. I hope you'll never have reason to regret your blindness. "

When he got home, he could not help expressing his indignation: "I declare, Nelly, them people below are enough to vex a saint. Only think, if Miles isn't as proud as a peacock, because Harry gets the better of the Yankee boys."

"Well, Tim dear, I wouldn't be bothering my brains arguing with him – he'll find out his mistake some of these days."

"Yes, but isn't it provoking to see a sensible man, like him, acting so foolishly? By my word, I think he's bewitched. And then, Mary too. I know she's at bottom, as much against sending the children to the Ward School as you or I, but she hasn't the pluck in her to say so. She's so submissive, and so willing to leave it all in Miles's hands, just as if she hadn't as good a right to the children as he has! They're a temptation to me – I vow to God they are!"

"Well! well! Tim, the worst will be their own; as for Miles, you often say yourself that you can make nothing of him," and, she added with an arch smile, "I'm sure you're not the man to blame a wife for being submissive, eh, Tim? Sit over, now, and take your dinner."

[The Blake children, Harry and Eliza, grow up to become Henry T. Blake and Mrs. Thomson. Both marry non-Catholics, and the dire consequences are recorded in the novel's conclusion, as follows.]

. . . New York has now its Jesuit colleges, its Christian schools, its Mount St. Vincent, and its Sacred Heart, watchwords of hope and joy to generations yet unborn.

And Henry T. Blake and his sister, Mrs. Thomson, saw all these Catholic institutions rising and flourishing around them, but no child of theirs ever entered such sacred walls. The dark spell was upon them – the cold indifference of their youth – their year-long neglect of the means of grace – their contempt for Catholic customs and Catholic devotions had grown into a hard callous crust, impervious to the genial rays of faith, hope, or charity. Religion was dead within them, and the world – the fashionable world, was the god of their worship. They sent their children to the same schools where their own faith had been shipwrecked, and the consequences were the same, only more decided. Henry T. Blake came from Columbia College a very bad Catholic, his sons went into it without religion of any kind, saving a sort of predilection in favor of the Baptist sect – what they came out may well be guessed. Ebenezer and Samuel were trained up by their mother and her family in a wholesome horror of Catholicity, and a great contempt for everything Irish;

it is, therefore, quite probable that they are now to be found in the front ranks of the Know-Nothings, urging on the godless fanaticism of the age, in a crusade against the religion of their fathers and the children of their own race. As for their father, he gloried in his freedom from all prejudice, as he was pleased to call piety and religious influence. He was a staunch opponent of the Catholic party in all their struggles for freedom of education, and by his eminent talents did good service to the opposition. Many a worthy son of Ireland was put to the blush by Henry T. Blake's example, cited for their imitation by those who hated their race and their creed, and many a time was the fervent exclamation heard: "I wish to God he hadn't a drop of Irish blood in him, for he's a disgrace to his name."

But still the world smiled on Henry T. Blake; he attained to a prominent position at the American bar, and after some time got into the legislature. Outwardly, all went right with him, but inwardly, all went wrong. A fine intellect, a noble nature, were going rapidly to ruin for want of the pruning hand, and the salutary restraint of religion. The mocking demon of doubt and incredulity was gradually taking possession of that soul whence faith had been so early expelled. Henry T. Blake was fast becoming a scoffer – a declaimer against all religion.

Still it must not be supposed that Henry T. Blake ever formally left the Catholic Church. On the contrary, he always called himself a Catholic, and would never listen to any suggestions recommending change. Many a time he was besieged with all the reasoning and vituperative powers of Tomkins, Pearson and Company, but he had still a way of getting out, and generally contrived to evade the discussion. He used to spike the enemy's guns, as he laughingly boasted to Joe Smith.

· ·

And now that I have brought my story to a close, I would beg all Catholic parents to "look on this picture, and on *this.*" It is for themselves to choose whether they will have such sons as Tom Reilly, and Mike Sheridan, and Edward Flanagan, or Henry T. Blake and Hugh Dillon – daughters like Ellie Flanagan, or like Hannah and Celia Dillon. Under God, it depends entirely on themselves. I have carefully avoided all exaggeration or undue coloring in this simple tale. I have merely strung together a number of such incidents as we see occurring every day in the world around us, growing out of the effects of good or bad education. If it be true – and I fear it is – that a large proportion of the children of Catholic parents are lost to the Church in America, it is altogether owing to the unaccountable folly of the parents themselves in exposing their children to perish. Catholic parents who so act are more inhuman than the heathens of China and of Madagascar who destroy their helpless infants. They throw them to be eaten by dogs or swine, or expose them to the savage denizens of the forest, but what is the destruction of the body in comparison to that of the soul? Ah! it would be well if Catholic parents would think more of these things than they do. If they would only consider that they are accountable to God and his Church for the precious gift of faith, and are bound, under pain of deadly sin, to transmit it to their children pure and undefiled, they would not dare to send those children to godless schools, where they are almost sure to lose that precious inheritance, or to have it so shorn of its splendor, so poor and so feeble, that it is no longer worth having. The faith of a young man or a young woman, brought up under un-Catholic training, is no more the faith of their fathers or mothers, than the vile brass-ware displayed on street stalls is the pure gold of the jeweller.

In conclusion, I will lay before the reader some appropriate remarks on this subject, from the pen of an American prelate: "Though the Catholic Church in this country has increased much more largely by conversions than is generally supposed, yet, for the most part, its rapid development has been owing to the emigration of Catholics from foreign countries; and, if we desire to make this increase permanent, and to keep the children in the faith of their fathers, we must, above all things, take measures to imbue the minds of the rising generation of Catholics with sound religious principles. This can only be done by giving them a good Catholic education. In our present position, the school-house has become second in importance only to the House of God itself. We have abundant cause for thankfulness to God on account of the many blessings which he has conferred on us; but we will show ourselves unworthy of these blessings if we do not do all that is in our power to pro-mote every good work by which they may be increased and confirmed to those who shall come after us."*

*Right Rev. Dr. Bayley's History of the Catholic Church in New York.

The Cross and the Shamrock; or, How to Defend the Faith, An Irish-American Catholic Tale of Real Life

by Hugh Quigley (Boston: Patrick Donahoe, 1853)

A much-traveled immigrant priest, Father Hugh Quigley was born in County Clare in 1819. Trained for the priesthood by five years in Rome, he was appointed curate to his native parish of Tulla. He then served at Killaloe, spent several years on the English and Scottish missions, returned to Ireland to join the Young Ireland movement, and migrated to New York shortly after the failed rising of 1848. During his first years in America, in a diocese near Troy, New York, he wrote The Cross and the Shamrock. *Also a wanderer in America, Father Quigley was a missionary priest in upstate New York, Milwaukee and La Crosse, Wisconsin, and Eureka, California. He wrote three other books: a history of* The Irish Race in California and on the Pacific Coast *(1878), and two more novels,* The Prophet of the Ruined Abbey *(1855), a nationalist tale set in Ireland, and* Profit and Loss: A Story of the Life of a Genteel Irish-American *(1873), a cautionary novel about the perils of respectability. He died in Troy in 1883.*

The Cross and the Shamrock *is an early, classic example of practical immigrant fiction, "Descriptive of the Temptations, Sufferings, Trials and Triumphs of the Children of St. Patrick," as its subtitle proclaims, and written "For the Entertainment and Special Instruction of the Catholic Male and Female Servants of the United States." For his setting, Quigley drew upon his first American parish, the small New York and Vermont farming communities northeast of Troy. The excerpted chapter, "Mass in a Shanty," is typical. After delineating and criticizing examples of Yankee discrimination against Catholics in the area, Quigley describes the sort of mass that he must have celebrated often as a missionary priest. Here it is complete with a sermon of exhortation to the faithful to become missionaries themselves on America's "virgin soil." The chapter ends with a Yankee farmer's grudging recognition of Catholicism's sway over "the ungovernable Irish race." Quigley's irascible anti-Protestantism may have been a factor in his peripatetic missionary career. This novel must have met a need among the Famine immigrants, for it is reported to have sold over 250,000 copies.*

Mass in a Shanty

There was great bustle and preparation in the valley of R— Creek, on Ascension Thursday. Hired men were up at *three* o'clock that morning to do "chores," and hired girls were busy the night before in arranging the household, so that the female *bosses* of the several farm houses would be able to find all things in order. Many and violent also were the arguments that passed between Catholic servants and their heretical masters and mistresses, on one hand to ignore, and on the other to assert, the right to worship according to one's conscience. Yes, to their shame be it told, the Protestant sects in America, as they do in all countries where they have sway or are tolerated, practically deny that article of the federal constitution that guarantees the right to every citizen to worship God according to the dictates of conscience or individual judgment. With the word *liberty* ever on their lips, like the lion's skin on the ass, to deceive, the sects, great and small, from the church of England down, down, down to the Mormons or Transcendentalists, through the grades of Presbyterian, Methodist, Baptist, all play the tyrant in their own way. All act the despot, and would exercise spiritual tyranny, if in their power. For proof of this, the history of the "Blue Laws" in the land of the Pilgrims is only to be consulted, on this side of the Atlantic; and at the other side, modern as well as by-gone records show, that, wherever Protestantism had the power, *there* the few were oppressed by the many. Every sovereign from Elizabeth down to Victoria, acted the tyrant over the Catholics; and in Sweden, Denmark, Prussia, and the Protestant Swiss cantons, persecution is now a part of the laws of these several states. Persecution is not sanctioned by the laws of the United States, if we except the proscriptive code of New Hampshire, which comes under that genus; but if it be not legalized, we are not to thank Protestantism for that. Wherever it has sway in the family, in the town council, or the assembly, there the cloven foot of intolerance and persecution is seen from under the sanctimonious gown it puts on. Indeed, although the compulsion of the conscience is not enforced by state laws, it is attempted, as far as practicable, where its effects are more galling, and its existence more intolerable – namely, in the family at home, or in the camp or barrack abroad. Catholic servants are not only denied the right to attend their duties in many families, but actually forced to hear the disgusting ranting or ludicrous prayer of any imposter who may take on himself the office of preacher. And Catholic soldiers are punished by fine and severe corporal chastisements for refusing to attend the service of an heretical chaplain. And no senator, zealous for liberty, raises his voice on behalf of the Catholic soldier, and of the Catholic servant girl, while they are exposed to a persecution such as no Catholic government, king, or despot ever attempted to force on the consciences of their dissenting subjects, not even Queen Mary of

England, excepted; for the so called persecution by Catholic princes has never been to compel men to adopt a new religion. Protestants in Europe and here attempt to compel the adoption of their false tenets by those who are neither desirous nor willing to adopt them, and who already profess a true religion. This is what makes a vast difference between the persecution your "Madiai" suffer, and this ten times worse persecution which many an otherwise honest and kindhearted American farmer allows to take place in his family. The day of judgment alone will reveal to light what trials, crosses, and real persecution Catholic servant men and women have to endure in remote and country places from the bigotry, hypocrisy, and cruelty of ignorant, unfeeling farmers and their wives, goaded on, no doubt, and urged, by low, base, and brutal parsons, who have scarcely enough to eat, and who envy the priest the comparative independence which the liberality and true Catholic charity of his flock enable him to maintain.

By these remarks I am not to be understood as saying that good nature, justice, and even generosity, do not govern the conduct of the American people. I am aware of their kindness, hospitality, and philanthropy; but these fine traits of character are obscured, perverted, and rendered prostrate, whenever the demon of sectarian influence touches them with her black rod. And, like the Jews, while they are persecuting the Holy One of God in his humble members, they think they are doing a service to God. Such is the effect of the poison, in the shape of religious instruction, infused into the minds of this noble people by the lying and ignorant teachers that they allow to instruct them. The American people are generally so busy, so intent in making a fortune or a livelihood, that they have not time, as they cannot have the inclination, to pay much attention to religious training. Hence it is in the science of the soul and salvation, as in that of medical science, the number of impostors and quacks is infinite.

The following dialogue between an Irish Catholic servant and her *evangelical* mistress will serve faintly to illustrate what is the weekly, if not daily, recurrence in tens of thousands of families all over this "free country:" –

"You can't go, that's the amount of it, Anne," said Mrs. Warren to an Irish Catholic servant maid of hers, who heard of the priest's being at the shanties on this morning.

"Why so, ma'am?" said Anne. "All the girls of the country around are allowed to go; but I never get a Sunday or holyday to myself. It is too bad."

"Why don't you come with us to our meeting, where all the decent folks go, and none of your Irish are present?"

"Many decent folks go to 'Old Harry'!" cried Anne, in anger. "Is that the reason I must go too?"

"Anne, your obstinacy in refusing to join our family worship has made me resolve not to let you go to hear the old priest. And your refusal to attend to the sermon of our preacher, Mr. Scullion, has also displeased me much. I mean to punish you according."

"Why should I go hear the old sinner's stuff," said Anne, "when your own sons laugh at him and say he is a fool? Besides, I am told he is ever abusing the Catholics, and I heartily despise his nonsensical, lying cant."

"Well, Anne, I am determined to punish you for it," calmly replied the mistress. "So you can't see the priest to-day. That settles it."

"I beg your pardon, ma'am; the priest I will see, please God, let what will happen."

"You must leave this house, then."

"Small loss, madam. America is wide, thank God," answered Anne.

"Don't you know Mr. Scullion is a brother of mine?"

"I don't care, ma'am, if he was your father. I know he is ignorant or malicious, either one or the other, or may be both, or he would not speak of the Catholic church as he does. O, dear," she cried, bursting into tears of anger, "what a 'free country' it is! The Protestants in Ireland were decent. They came, attended by the peelers, to their tenants, telling them they must conform to the will of the landlord, or quit their homes; but here ye say all religions are equal, and yet ye try to compel us to go to listen to low, ignorant preachers, who know they are lying about the church of Christ. Ye want us to change the religion of St. Patrick and of the martyrs for such ridiculous churches as ye have here. O, dear! O, dear" said the poor girl, as she contrasted her present situation with what it was when she was at home at her father's, where she heard mass daily, and knew not what it was to suffer persecution for conscience' sake.

While scenes such as we have here described were taking place in the farmers' houses, and such scenes are not occasional nor unusual, all was busy preparation at the shanties. The largest shanty in the "patch" was cleared of all sorts of lumber. Forms, chairs, tables, pots, flour and beef barrels, molasses casks, and other necessary stores were all put outside doors. The walls, if so we can call them, of the shanty, were then hung round with newspapers, white linen tablecloths, and other choice tapestry, while a good large shawl, spread in front of the altar, served as a carpet on which his reverence was to kneel and stand while officiating. Green boughs were cut in a neighboring wood lot and planted around the entrance by the men, while around the altar and over it were wreaths of wild flowers and blossoms, gathered by the little girls of the "patch" in the adjacent meadows, in order to prepare a decent place for the holy mass. At an early hour the priest made his appearance, and was very much pleased to see the transformation which the piety of these poor, hard-working people wrought in the appearance of the humble shanty. For fifteen miles along the line the crowds were gathering, and the works were suspended for the day. The over-seers and contractors, to do them justice, had no objection to this occasional interruption of their profits. At all events, they knew it was a holyday; and even they, with all their irresponsible control over their men, had ample proof that, even in the wild deserts and savage woods of America, the Irish Catholic "remembers" the Sabbaths and festivals of his God or his church.

Long before the hour of mass, the shanty was crowded, and many were the comments and remarks made on the physical powers and other external accomplishments of the new priest.

Some remarked that his reverence – God bless him! – need not be afraid of travelling alone through these lonesome glens, for it would require "a good man to handle him; that it would."

"That's thrue," said another; "he would be able to 'settle bread' on a half dozen Yankees any day; that is, provided they did not use any weapon but the arm that God gave 'em."

"But you know," said a third, "these Yankees always carry a *rewolwer* or two in their pockets, the treacherous rogues. Look how they killed that Irish peddler, and robbed him, and fired six shots into Michael Gasty's house the other night, and he in bed quietly sleeping."

This and other such narratives and comments were the order of the day outside the door only, where those who were careless or not preparing for their duties were congregated. Inside, a large crowd of women and rough-fist-ed men gathered around the door of the temporary confessional; and it was near noon before the priest ascended the temporary altar to offer up the "vic-tim of peace" for the assembled sons of toil. Upon his reverence asking if there was any body to answer or serve mass, several presented themselves; but he accepted the services of Paul, because he had been accustomed from his childhood to wait round the altar, and he was the most intelligent of those who offered to assist the priest while celebrating.

The substance of the priest's discourse was, that they should not forget that it was God's will that the holy sacrifice should be offered in "every place, from the rising to the setting of the sun," and that probably they were made the instruments which he made use of for the *literal* fulfilment of that famous prophecy; for if they were not here employed on these public works, proba-bly the holy sacrifice would not be, for years and years to come, offered up in such places as this. That they should all regard themselves as missionaries engaged in God's service to spread the knowledge of the true religion in this virgin soil among a people who had lost the true mode of God's worship, though a generous and successful race of men. That they should guard against drunkenness and faction fights, for these crimes brought their proper punish-ment both here and hereafter; and that they should, by pure morals and fidelity to their religion, rather than by controversy or disputation, make a favorable impression on, and confute the errors of, those opponents of their faith among whom their lot was cast. In fine, that they should lose no oppor-tunity of receiving the sacraments, for, without their use, salvation was very difficult, if not absolutely impossible. Let them not regret the loss of this day, or think it too much to dedicate it to God's service: that was the chief end for which they were created. When population was small, and a livelihood easily obtained, and men had to work but little, God had appointed one day in the week to rest and service. Now, when the cares, distractions, and labors of life had increased a thousand fold, it seemed not too much if, instead of one day, two or more days were devoted to rest and worship. And if the Church had her way unrestricted, she, by her festivals and holydays, would do a great deal towards alleviating the present hardships of labor, and men would be taught to be content with a competency, and employers would treat their men with kindness and justice combined.

"You, poor fellows, have to work hard, frequently for years, without having a chance to frequent the sacraments. Thank God, then, and be grateful for this opportunity, and spend this day as becometh Christians. You are exposed to dangers from accidents, and frequently from the influence of evil-advising men. In Religion and her resources alone you can find the only safeguard against the effects of the former, and the best security against the wiles of your enemies: keep the commandments, and hear the church."

On this day no less than ninety-five received, and the effects of this one visit even were felt by the overseers and employers of these men for months to come. Even Anne Connell, the girl whom we introduced as disputing with her ignorant mistress about "the freedom of worship," – and which dispute was then decided in Anne's favor by the interference of the boss, who remonstrated with his wife on her imprudence in resolving to discharge her maid in the midst of their hurry, while there was no chance of having her place supplied, – even Anne, brought to a better sense by the advice of the priest administered in confession, when she came home asked her saucy mistress' pardon for speaking back to her this morning.

"I forgive you, Anne," she said; "though I am sure there is not a *lady* in the hollow that would put up with your impudence but myself."

"I know I am hot," answered Anne, smothering her anger at this second provocation in being called *impudent*. "The priest told us to be obedient to those even who are not amiable nor kind; to serve them for God's sake, as a punishment for our sins."

"Now," said Mr. Warren to his wife, "you see Anne has rather improved by her visit to the priest which you thought to prevent. Were you and I to be *at her* for six months, we could not get her to acknowledge as much as she now has. The fact is, I am certain those much-abused priests are far ahead of our dominies in knowledge of religion and human nature. It is impossible otherwise to account for the influence they exercise over the ungovernable Irish race, and over those millions whom they instruct and rule."

"It's all priestcraft," said his wife.

"I don't know, Sarah, what craft it is, but I wish our ministers learned a little of the same craft; for they are fast losing all influence over the minds of the people, and especially over that of the youth. That we can all see."

"That's because people are daily getting worse," said this female philosopher.

"Worse! Then whose fault is it that they are? What have we ministers for, but to prevent this state of things? There are six of them in the small village of S—, and it can't be beat in the Union for blacklegs and rowdies. Would we have so many wild, irreligious young men, and women, too, if instead of six preachers, we had six Catholic priests? I would like to see one of your young ones show such signs of a superior mind and training, such manliness and fortitude, as that Irish Catholic lad, Paul, down at Prying's. They have had all the ministers within fifty miles of you to convert him, but they could no more move him than they could Mount Antoine. In fact, he beat them all to pieces in Scripture and argument. Take no more pains about religion, wife," said the honest Yankee; "let Anne alone. I won't have her disturbed any more on the subject. If there be any religion on earth, those very people have it whom you want to bring round to the exact pattern of your favorite minister's manner of doubting. It's ridiculous, wife," said he, rising, and calling his men to the fields; "it's ridiculous to try to convert these Catholics, who appear to have some religion, to the countless systems of NO RELIGION that are so numerous on all sides around us. I say it's ridiculous," said he, departing.

Bickerton; or, The Immigrant's Daughter

by Charles James Cannon (New York: P. O'Shea, 1855)

The son of Irish Catholic immigrants, Charles Cannon was born in New York City in 1800. He made his living as a customs-house clerk and as a part-time advisor to Catholic publisher Edward Dunigan, for whose house he compiled school readers and a spelling book. Devoted to literature, he had a fascinating but unsuccessful career, producing four volumes of verse, several plays, and eight novels, from Oran the Outcast *in 1833 to* Tighe Lyfford *in 1859, one year before his death. The persistence and variety of Cannon's fictional grapplings with Irishness in America both before and after the Famine make him an important and transitional figure in the development of Irish-American literary self-expression.*

"The Beal Fire," from Cannon's 1835 collection of stories and poems reveals the nostalgic and nationalistic cast of the pre-Famine mind. Set on the Ulster coast at the time of the Rebellion of 1798, it contains a number of major Irish themes, including a lost legendary hero, the "Cathleen ni Houlihan" figure of an ardently patriotic old woman, and a familiar set of conflicts – Catholics vs. Protestants, the upper class vs. the peasantry, and, as in Yeats's play, Cathleen ni Houlihan *(1902), love for a woman vs. devotion to "the Cause." Cannon also introduces the American context in the form of references to George Washington and the American Revolution as exhorting models for Irish nationalism.*

Published twenty years later in 1855, Bickerton; or, The Immigrant's Daughter *exemplifies the emergence after the Famine of an Irish-American fictional identity defined in terms of religion. This is Cannon's best novel because it is his most direct, realistic examination of the problems of being Irish and Catholic in America. In* Bickerton *his penchant for sentimental digression is held in check by the validity and urgency of the novel's historical context – the rise of nativism and the Know-Nothing Party in the wake of the first wave of Famine immigrants.*

The novel's first two chapters describe the hard landing in America of Manus O'Hanlon, his infant daughter, and ailing wife. Their shipload of immigrants is swindled from the start – dumped on a New Jersey sand-spit so the ship's agents can avoid paying New York's taxes. Two of Cannon's chapters are excerpted here. In the first, O'Hanlon gets work as a canal laborer after his wife's death on the beach. His attitude toward his rough and bibulous compatriots reflects Cannon's position as a member of the transitional generation of established American Irishmen who observed the Famine

130

influx with mixed feelings.

The second excerpt is a detailed description of "Little Dublin," the Irish working-class neighborhood of Bickerton, the eastern port city where Manus O'Hanlon's daughter Aileen ultimately ends up. Cannon astutely praises the parish priest for allowing the immigrants to retain their native customs, notably the celebration of All Saints' Eve, the Celtic "Samhain," on October 31. Bickerton has an active branch of the nativist, anti-Catholic secret society, the "Thugs of Hindostan" (obviously modeled on the Know-Nothings), who mount an anti-Catholic demonstration on All Saints' Eve and march into Little Dublin behind a brass band playing the Irish Protestant anthem, "Boyne Water." The beginning of the bloody riot that ensues is described in the concluding pages of this chapter, which ends with the crazed Thugs making a rush for the Catholic church. Houses are burned, the church is severely damaged, and several people are killed. Thus, Cannon's rendering of nativist violence is a vivid indictment of the climate of hatred faced by immigrants in the 1850s.

A Struggle for Existence

"**F**arewell, my dearest Moya, and God rest you!" said O'Hanlon, as next morning he rose from the grave of his wife. "Loving and kind were you to me always, and ever ready to excuse the faults that others were only just, perhaps, in condemning, and may the good God now, with all His love and kindness, reward you for your unwavering truth and charity. I may never again have even the poor consolation of looking upon your grave; but, wherever my feet may wander, my heart will never travel so far from this poor spot, but that, until we meet in eternity, it will turn here daily, as to an alter, to offer up its prayers to Heaven. And now, once more, farewell, and God rest you, Moya!" Then with a bundle over his shoulder of such things as were absolutely necessary, he took his little daughter by the hand, and set out in search of some employment, that would afford temporary support for himself and his child, for in his present impoverished state, he was not willing to present himself to his friends in the city.

But his search was a weary one; for though it was continued until the poor child became so footsore that she could walk no further, it was wholly unavailing, the farmers, who perhaps had good reason for what they said, declaring they had already had too much of "Greeks" and "Greenhorns," and would have nothing more to do with them; and it was not until he had changed his last shilling that he met with a countryman of his own, who offered him, what seemed to him, very handsome wages, to join a gang of labourers on a canal; an offer that was readily and most gratefully accepted.

This gang was made up entirely of men of his own country, and – as far as profession went – of his own faith; but unhappily of a class that reflected no credit either upon creed or country. Ignorant as the iniquitous laws under which they were born could make them; unrestrained in their vices by the presence of a priesthood who had exercised over them a salutary authority, based upon the truest kindness, and almost brutified by the constant use of alcoholic poisons, supplied to them without stint at the store of the contractor, who cared not how they spent their earnings, provided they were spent to his profit, they were fast sinking into a state of savageness, which, as De Maistre says, is not an original condition of the human race, but one to which tribes and nations have been reduced by their wilful forgetfulness of their duty to God. Times, thank Heaven, are greatly changed since then, and the labours of the missionary priest, and of the true disciples of Father Mathew,* who have sought no unhallowed union of Temperance with Politics, have not been without their reward, in the vast moral improvement of our canal labourers; yet the nightly brawls of such as those O'Hanlon was then associated with, and their miserable "Faction fights," upon their only day of rest, have left a stain upon the Irish name in that part of the country which will not soon, if ever, be effaced.

With people like these, however much at first his heart might have warmed towards them, because they were from his own land, O'Hanlon could find no companionship; for though "among them, he was not of them," and, to separate himself as much as possible from them, he spent his Sundays, because there was no place of worship to which they could go, in wandering through the woods and fields with his little daughter, upon whose young mind he sought to impress the simple truths of Christianity, by relating in language suited to the capacity of a child of seven, the history of the meek and loving Saviour, who, stripping himself of the power and glory which had been his from eternity, became man, and suffered and died, to save his creatures from the ruin their sins had brought upon them; and of men and women, and even young boys and girls, who, by taking Him for their great exemplar, had, by their holy lives on earth, obtained the indescribable happiness of becoming saints in Heaven. Or, he would talk to her of her mother – and then his tongue became truly eloquent, for it gave utterance to the promptings of his heart – and tell her how good, how patient, how loving, how forgetful of self she had always been; and, to keep alive within her the memory of this dear and excellent parent, he composed a little prayer, which he taught her morning and evening to repeat, in which she asked the "BLESSED AMONG WOMEN" to supply to her the place of the mother whom God had taken unto himself. For he hoped by means like these to prepare her, in some degree, for the difficulties she would have to encounter, in case of his death, among a people who were neither of her blood nor of her faith.

. . . .

*[Rev. Theobald Mathew (1790-1856) was a highly successful temperance crusader in Ireland, England, and America in the late 1840s.]

Little Dublin

"Little Dublin," was among the oldest parts of Bickerton, comprising within itself indeed at one time almost the whole of the city, and, notwithstanding the changes every where going on around it, still retained much of its original appearance, being narrow and ill-paved, with walks that would hardly admit two abreast, and houses, mostly of wood, of two stories in height, with small windows, and doors formed of an upper and lower part, and broad wooden stoops with comfortable seats. But if the houses were not large, the families that now occupied them certainly were. It has been said that the command, or whatever it may be called, that was given to our first parents, "Increase and multiply," has been obeyed by no people so fully as by the Irish, and one had only to pass through "Little Dublin" any fine evening, to be satisfied of the truth of the saying, for not only would he see the windows, doors, and *stoops* of its old-fashioned tenements filled with a goodly proportion of the future men and women of America, but the walks, sometimes the street itself, swarming with them.

The Irish, without the clannishness of their Scottish relatives, are a peculiarly gregarious race. Where one takes up his abode another is sure to follow, and so on, until in the cities where they dwell, they form whole districts by themselves. "Little Dublin" was one of these. One family from the "old country" coming into it had necessarily brought others, until the original settlers of the place were obliged to look out for new habitations, their old ones having been taken possession of by these strangers, who soon turned the quiet Dutch street into a noisy Irish one, where there was plenty of fun, and no little fighting, almost every day and night in the year, as was to be expected among a people whose natural gayety whole ages of suffering have been unable to "crush out" of the national heart, and whose gunpowder tempers it required only the merest spark at any time to set in a blaze.

"Little Dublin" was in the parish of St. Mary's, and among the first, and not the least, of the undertakings of its excellent pastor, was to introduce into this portion of his charge, something of the decorum more becoming a Christian people than had hitherto marked the conduct of the dwellers in "Little Dublin," whose lives had unfortunately been but little in accordance with the principles of the religion they professed, and had only too often given just grounds for reproach from their more circumspect neighbors. To do this he began with the young, whom he gathered into schools, where manners and morals were attended to with no less care than reading and writing, and through their influence he extended his refining process to the parents, for however indifferent men and women may appear to the opinions of the world, they are generally anxious to retain their superiority in the eyes of their children.

Yet little comparatively could be done in the way of reform, while the evil

of intemperance was permitted to go unchecked, and where every other cellar was turned into a dram shop; this evil had become an epidemic that could
only be arrested by the most vigorous measures on the part of him who
attempted to deal with it. But the strength of Mr. Eldridge did not waste itself
in wordy declamation, or denunciations from the pulpit, of the vice he wished
to correct, but, taking with him some of the medals that have been so blessed
in the hands of Father Mathew, he went with them from house to house, and
to every family in each house, and by earnest appeals to their religious feelings, and, what was even more powerful in most, their national pride, prevailed upon whole families to join with him in the temperance pledge; and
the example of these was not lost upon their neighbours, who, if they did not
become teetotallers, strove thenceforth to use without abusing that which is
unlawful only in its excess.

But while labouring for the moral and social elevation of this people,
Father Eldridge did not, as a less judicious reformer would have done, seek
the destruction of habits, not evil in themselves, which had become a second
nature, or the abrogation of customs to which, because they had come from
"home," they now clung with the tenacity of the heart to a first love. "Let
them dance," said the good and wise Fenelon to an over-zealous curé, who
complained that the peasants would dance on Sunday afternoons, and "Let
them enjoy themselves in their own way," said the priest of St. Mary's, "since
they will not enjoy themselves in ours. Let them have their set days and seasons, and their social gatherings, where the aged meet to smoke and talk over
old times, and the young for 'a bit of innocent diversion,' when it matters not
how much they 'welt the flure,' as long as they do not welt one another. There
is no more sin in a jig or a song than there is religion in a long face." So they
still adhered to many of the customs of their native land, and enjoyed, without fear of the priest, their frequent gatherings.

Now among their set times and seasons, there was one day, or rather
night, that was considered hardly less sacred to mirth in "Little Dublin," than
it had ever been in the beautiful island from which the great majority of the
people of "Little Dublin" had come, the observance of which, though a custom of heathen times, when, after the gathering in of the fruits of the earth, a
feast was held to Beal, or the sun, the God of the Irish, as it had its origin in
human gratitude for the favour of heaven, if not positively sanctioned, was
never, we believe, formally prohibited by the Church, the clergy generally
contenting themselves by inveighing – to very little purpose, we are afraid –
against the superstitious practices that too often attended it, practices that, in
spite of her rigid Calvinism, so greatly prevail in Scotland. This was All-
Saints'-eve, the "Halloween" of the Scotch, and universally called "Holi-eve"
by the Irish and their descendants.

And Holi-eve, to which the young had looked forward for months with
such anticipation of pleasure, and which was no less welcome to the old than

to the young, with its nuts and its apples, its tricks and conjurations, was near at hand, for it was already the afternoon of the last day of October; and that was a poor family indeed in which something beyond the ordinary fare was not prepared for supper, or a few apples and nuts, those to be ducked for and these to be eaten or burned, according to the inclinations or fancies of the parties present, were not provided, and throughout "Little Dublin,"

"All went merry as a marriage bell."

But there was one family in particular who had looked forward with more than ordinary pleasure to the coming of this Holi-eve. Patrick Scanlon had come to this country some years before, leaving behind him a young wife, an aged father and mother, and three sisters. Out of his earnings, as a mere labourer, he first paid the passage of his wife, and then of his oldest sister, with whose assistance, in little more than a year after, he was able to pay the passages of the other two, when, by clubbing the slender means of all four, they, in little more than two years from that time, were enabled to bring out the old people, towards whose support they had in the meantime liberally contributed. They were now only little more than a week in the country, and their arrival was to be celebrated this evening by a grand gathering of relations and friends, who were to keep their Holi-eve under the roof of Patrick Scanlon.

Old Scanlon was sitting with his youngest grandchild on his knee, when the pageant turned into "Little Dublin."

"Moosic, moosic," said the little one, jumping down, and toddling towards the door.

The grandfather followed, and took him up in his arms, that he might have a better view of the sight. But when aware of the air to which that gay procession was marching, an air, to judge from the heart-burnings and bloodshed to which it has so often been the prelude, must have had for its composer the devil – the real "Sam" – himself, he turned away with a feeling of bitterness that did not often find place in his kind old heart.

At this moment, a pistol – whether by accident or design we cannot say – was discharged by some one in the procession, when immediately a cry was raised, that the Irish were firing upon them from their houses, a cry that was followed by an instantaneous discharge of firearms to the right and left, and a pistol ball entering the breast of the old man, he fell heavily forward, crushing out in his fall the young life he would have died a thousand deaths to save.

It would not be easy to describe the confusion that ensued. There were but few men at home at this time, and these were either the aged, or those who were unable by sickness to have gone to work, and the whole place seemed given up to women and children, who had crowded every window, door, and stoop, from which a sight could be had of the approaching pageant, and who, upon the firing of the first volley, shrieking, disappeared within their houses. But as the majority of the pious processionists had come armed with revolvers, which they now discharged in rapid succession, these poor women, made desperate by their fears, although many of them were covered with their own blood, or that of their children, rallied in defence of their lives and homes, and returned the fire of their assailants with stones and brickbats, and every missile they could most easily command, until scores of the aggressors were made, in poetic language, "to bite the dust," or, in plain prose, were knocked down in the street, and trodden almost to death by their companions. In the meantime, the driver of the Bible-car, putting his horses to their speed, was soon out of danger, and the riders in the barouches, "the Black Guards," as, on account of their "customary suits of solemn black," they were called, turned tail on the first appearance of disturbance, and drove back to the general rendezvous by a different route.

The news of this rencontre was – without the expence of an "Extra" – spread rapidly through the city, and while the Thugs were constantly receiving reinforcements from the crowds in the streets, the women of "Little Dublin" were not long left to act on the defensive alone, but were soon joined by husbands and fathers, and lovers and brothers, who, the moment the rumour reached them, quitted their work, and bearing with them shovels and hoes, and hods, and picks, and crows, and whatever else they were using at the time, now to be turned into implements of war, hurried to the scene of conflict, and threw themselves into the thickest of the fight, where they did men's duty, until finding their homes in a flame, in the vain hope of saving their little property, and the lives of the dear ones shut up within them, they unwillingly turned from one enemy to encounter another hardly more cruel or unsparing. And then as many of the Thugs as were still uninjured rushed forward to a new object of attack, crying one to another, "To the Church! to the Church!"

Mary Lee, or the Yankee in Ireland

by John Boyce (Boston: Patrick Donahoe, 1860)

Born to a middle-class family in County Donegal in 1810, Father John Boyce was ordained a priest at Maynooth in 1837 and came to America in 1845. Following an initial pastorate at Eastport, Maine, he served on a number of mission stations in central Massachusetts and eventually became pastor of St. John's Church in Worcester. A friend of Father John T. Roddan, Boyce had his first novel serialized in the Pilot. *This was* Shandy McGuire; or, Tricks upon Travelers, *set in Donegal in the 1820s, and published as a book in 1848 under the pseudonym "Paul Peppergrass." A second novel,* The Spaewife; or, The Queen's Secret *(1853), was a clumsy period piece, in which Boyce worked out his spleen against conservative Catholic intellectual Orestes Brownson, who is portrayed in the novel as a rigid, pompous nobleman in the reign of Queen Elizabeth I.*

Excerpted here is Boyce's third and last novel, Mary Lee, *which was published in 1860, four years before his death. Set on the northern coast of Donegal in "185-,"* Mary Lee *features a fascinating protagonist, the garrulous Yankee huckster, Mr. Ephraim C. B. Weeks. In Ireland "speculating" in matrimony ("and how could he possibly fail in a land of such ignorance and beggary"), Weeks is a type of the arrogant American abroad. Boyce uses him to criticize New Englanders for their main-chance hustling and their contemptuous treatment of Irish Famine immigrants. The main tenets of Weeks's faith are blind acceptance of the American ideal of success through constant activity (contrasted with the easier, less driven ways of Ireland), embrace of Unitarianism and intolerance of Catholics, and acquiescence in anti-Irish discrimination in Boston. Says the narrator, "He was, in short, a Yankee." Not surprisingly, Weeks's suit for the hand of Mary Lee, the lighthouse-keeper's daughter, is rejected, and he leaves Ireland and the Irish in a huff, swearing that you couldn't find such "a tarnation set of varmints in all almighty creation." In one scene, a meditation in a Donegal churchyard, Boyce drops his narrator's stance and speaks with passionate directness of the sufferings of his fellow immigrants.*

There are three excerpts from Mary Lee *here. First is the novel's introductory chapter, in which Boyce enumerates the false American stereotypes of the Irish that prompted his own fiction. Second is the portrait of Weeks as the essential Yankee. (At the end of the novel we find that his interest in Mary Lee stems from his secret knowledge that she is really an heiress.) Third is the powerful churchyard scene, which comes*

137

in the middle of the novel during Weeks's Irish visit.

Dear reader, have the goodness to run your finger down the map of Ireland to its northernmost point, or, if that be inconvenient, let your imagination run down without it to the easternmost promontory of the County Donegal; you shall then have transported yourself without trouble or expense, and in a manner suitable enough for our purpose, to the spot where our story commences.

It may happen, however, in this rambling age, that one day or other you would grow tired of travelling by the map and hand-book, and make up your mind to quit the fireside and see the world for yourself – preferring your own eyes to your neighbors' spectacles. After a long tour through Europe you may yet, some fine evening in August or September, find yourself standing on the pier of Leith or Dunbarton heights, looking across the channel, and wishing you were in Ireland. Don't resist the temptation, we pray thee, but leaving your national prejudices behind you with your Scotch landlord, book yourself for Dublin, in the first packet, and with a good conscience and an honest heart take a trip over the water, and visit, were it only for a week, the land of poverty, gallantry, and song.

If, however, you happen to be one of those very respectable young gentlemen who go over to make pictures of Irish-life, with the view of being stared at and lionized in village drawing rooms on their return – one of those extremely talented and promising young men, who voyage in crowds every year, for a supply of Irish barbarisms and Romish superstitions, – if you happen, we say, to be of that class, let us remind you, dear reader, that the Mull of Cantyre is a dangerous sea, worse by all odds than the Bay of Biscay. Don't venture through it by any means, but like a prudent young man, finish your tour with Ben-Lomond and the Trossachs, and return home to the States with as little delay as possible. As for the Irish peculiarities you would go in quest of, they are now very scarce and difficult to procure – we mean fresh ones, of course, for the old sets are bruised so much in the handling as to be entirely valueless; even the manufacturers of the article, who made so jolly a living on the simplicity of stripling tourists twenty years ago, are no longer in existence. They have passed away as an effete race, and are now dead, gone, and forgotten. Pictures of Irish life are indeed very difficult to dispose of, at present, either to the pulpit, the Sunday newspapers, or even the Foreign Benevolent Societies; unless they happen to be drawn by master hands. Such pictures, for instance, as the "Priest and the Bottle," the "Fiddler and the Beggars," the "Confessor and the Nun," have lost all point, since Mr. Thackeray's visit to that country, and are now grown as stale and flat as small beer drippings off a pot-house counter. Twenty years ago, however, the case was very different. An Irishman then, in certain sections of the United States, was as great a wonder as a Bengal tiger, or an Abyssinian elephant; and he felt so far below the ordinary standard of humanity in those days, as to be considered unaccountable to human laws. We have ourselves been assured on most excellent authority, that certain ladies of Maine, even within the time mentioned, actually went as a delegation to an unfortunate Irishman, who strayed into their neighborhood, and set about manipulating his head all over, in order to ascertain, by personal inspection, whether his horns grew on the fore or hind part of his cranium. The manner of their reception, by the courteous and gallant barbarian, is still related by some of the actors in the little melo-drama, and though quite characteristic of his race, would hardly be accounted edifying in this simple narrative. This much, however, we may venture to affirm, that since the event took place, there has been but one opinion on the subject in that locality – that the Irish wear no horns of any description whatever, either behind or before – are endowed with the ordinary feelings and senses peculiar to the human family – and exhibit arms and legs, hands and hair, precisely like their Norman and Anglo-Saxon neighbors.

But whilst they assimilate thus in all their physical developments, there are still certain national peculiarities, which distinguish them from the people of all other nations. In the first place, the *brogue* is very peculiar. It differs from that of the Scotch Highlander, the Vermonter, and the German in what is called intensity of accentuation – and it is very remarkable that this peculiar intensity of accentuation is most striking when they speak on the subjects in any way connected with religion – the broad sound of the vowels, which they have still retained since their old classic days, exhibiting a striking contrast with the reformed method of pronunciation. The collocation of their words, too, sounding so strange to unclassic ears, (though admirable in the Italian and French), contributes perhaps in some degree to aggravate the barbarism. But we must not venture on details, or we should never have done; suffice it to say, that according to all accounts, and particularly the accounts of American tourists, the Irish are, one and all, the strangest people on the face of the earth. They never do any thing, we are told, like other people. Whatever they put their hands to, from peeling a potato to shooting a landlord, they have their own peculiar way of doing it. Whether they eat or drink, walk or sleep, tie their shoes or pick their teeth, they are noted for their wonderful originality. And it is not the people only, but, strange to say, the very cows and horses in that remarkable country, bellow and neigh quite differently from those of other nations – the tone and style being quite unique, or, in other words, "peculiarly Irish." It's but a few weeks ago since a certain Mr. Gustavus Theodore Simpkings, of Boston, returned from Ireland with the startling discovery that hens laid their eggs there in a manner quite different from that adopted by the hens of other countries. We may be allowed also to add, by way of appendix to the fact, that in consequence of the important nature of the discovery, a board of commissioners will shortly be sent over to investigate the matter, in order that the poultry fanciers of New England may take measures accordingly to promote the interests of their excellent associations. Whether the country at large, however, will approve this new method is still a disputed question. Our own opinion is, the New Englanders will reject it, not solely because it's Irish, though that indeed would seem reason sufficient, but rather on account of the danger of propagating Popery in that peculiar way. We have heard of "treason" eggs, (Mr. O'Connell and Marcus Costello were arrested over two pair of them in Horne's Coffee Room, Dublin, five and twenty years ago avowing their guilt), and if treason could be propagated in that fashion, we ask, why not Popery?*

Now, after all this nicety to which certain things are carried, simply because they are Irish, it is quite needless to say that the national peculiarities of that people are all but exhausted, and consequently the young tourist fresh from the counting-room can expect little there to requite him for the fatigue and expense of such a journey.

But, dear reader mine, if your heart be in the right place and above the reach of paltry prejudice, if you be man enough to think for yourself, and instead of viewing Ireland in printshop and pantomime, look at her face to face with your own honest eyes, – if you be determined to see things in their true colors and to avoid the vulgar blunder of mistaking the Irish *brogue* for inveterate barbarism, and gold watch chains for genuine civilization – if you be one of that stamp – then in Heaven's name step aboard as soon as possible, for a crime it would be against your conscience to turn back within sight of the green old Isle where Moore and Griffin "wept and sang."**

[A portrait of Ephraim Weeks: an American Yankee's views of Ireland and the Irish]

Mr. Ephraim Weeks, as the reader may have already suspected, came to Ireland to speculate in matrimony. He left home with a cigar in his mouth, and stepped aboard the packet as she moved past the wharf, with as careless and indifferent an air as if he were dropping down to Sandy Hook to visit a friend. As to meeting with any serious obstacle, in a country whose inhabitants, to take them in the lump, were no better than South Sea Islanders, he never dreamed of it for a moment: why should he? He knew what the Irish were, every soul of them, and could read them through as he could the alphabet. He met them on the wharves, on the railroads, on the steamboats, in the police offices, saw them dramatized on the stage, tried at the bar, and dissected in the pulpit. In a word, he knew what they were at home in Ireland, just as well as if he had been living with them there all his lifetime. What had he to fear? He had succeeded so far in various speculations in New England, and how could he possibly fail in a land of such ignorance and beggary as Ireland! To be sure, there must necessarily be some intelligent men in the

---

*[The Irish political leader Daniel O'Connell was arrested for conspiracy in 1831.]
**[Irish poet Thomas Moore (1779-1852) and novelist Gerald Griffin (1803-40).]

country – it could not well be otherwise – but what of that? There were no smart men amongst them. *Smartness* to him was every thing. It was the embodiment of all the virtues, moral and intellectual – the only quality for which man deserved admiration or respect. The estimate he formed of his neighbor's moral worth was not in proportion to his integrity of character, but to his ability for speculating and driving hard bargains. The man who contented himself with a competence and a quiet life at home he despised; but the jobber in stocks, who was smart enough to make a lucky hit on 'change, though he risked half a dozen men's fortunes on the chance, was the man after his heart. Such were Mr. Weeks's sentiments. Nor was he much to blame for them either; for he was bred and born in the midst of speculators. Every man he met in the street, from the newsboy to the judge, from the policeman to the governor, was a speculator in something. He began himself, in his very infancy, to speculate in marbles and hobby-horses; and if he made but a cent a week, his father patted him on the head, and prophesied his future greatness. When arrived at man's estate, he found himself in the company of young men, whose sole study was to make money in the easiest manner and shortest time. He saw them every where engaged in some kind of traffic, – no matter what, if it only happened to be profitable. Whilst in other countries each grade in the community had its own legitimate trades and occupations, it was the very reverse in the States. There it was a universal scramble, in which every body snatched at what came handiest. The tailor dropped his needle and mounted the stump; the lawyer burned his briefs to trade in molasses; the shoemaker stuck his awl in the bench and ascended the pulpit; and the shopboy flung his yardstick on the counter and went off to edit a Sunday newspaper. Surrounded on all sides by such influences, what could Mr. Weeks have possibly been but what he was – a speculator in chances – a man of one idea – one object – one aspiration – money? Learning was nothing in his estimation, if it failed to realize money; nay, the highest mental accomplishment was not only valueless, but contemptible without money. In this respect Mr. Weeks represented a large class of his countrymen of New England; – we say a class, for it would be unjust to say more. He was not an American gentleman, by any means, either in habits or education. That was plain the instant he spoke a word or moved a muscle, and those of his fellow-citizens who could rightfully claim that distinction would never have recognized him as one of their number. He was, in short, a Yankee, – a man to be met with every day and every where – on the sidewalks – at the banks – in the theatre – in the cars – standing at hotel doors picking his teeth – selling soap at cattle shows – or lobbying for a patent right behind his agent's back in the Senate House. But to return.

With such views and sentiments as we have here ascribed to Mr. Weeks, it may be easily conceived with what assurance of success he landed in Ireland, and with what confidence he entered on his plans and speculations.

The possession of Mary Lee as his lawful wedded wife was the great secret of his journey. Why it was so the sequel must tell. It appears, however, he had but a limited time to accomplish his designs; for hardly had he reached Crohan, when he called to see Else Curley. The reputation she had acquired, all the country round, and the wonderful stories told of her power over the spirits of the nether world, led him to think he could win her to his interest by tempting her cupidity, and that she, as a secret agent, might do what it would otherwise require a long courtship to effect. How his expectations were met, in this respect, will be seen in due course of the story.

[Composition of place: meditation in a Donegal churchyard]

Over the tops of the trees which skirted the demesne below, and through the vistas which time or the axe had made, appeared patches of Mulroy Bay, shining as calm and bright as a mirror. On its southern shore a little white-washed building, showing a gilded cross on its gable, stood facing the sea, and round about among the fern and hawthorns, with which it was surrounded, a number of white headstones peeped out here and there to mark it for a bur-ial place of the dead. This was Massmount, where our foreign friend first saw Mary Lee, as she knelt at the altar. It was a solitary spot, and as pleasant for the dead to rest in as could be found in the whole world. No house within a mile of it, and no noise to disturb its repose but the twitter of the swallow about the eaves of the little church, or the gentle wash of the waves amongst the sea shells at its base. And if, on the Sunday morning, the silence which reigned there through the week was broken, it only seemed to make the still-ness which succeeded the more solemn and profound. To the eastward of the chapel, and surrounded by a belt of trees, stood the modest residence of Mr. Guirkie – its white chimneys just visible from the windows of Crohan House; and trending away to the westward lay a long tongue of meadow land called Morass Ridge, on the tip or extreme point of which rose up the still majestic ruins of *Shannagh*, once a stronghold of the far-famed O'Dougherty of Innishowen. Midway between these two prominent features in the landscape appeared the old churchyard of Massmount, with its little white chapel facing the sea.

Mr. Weeks, touched by the simple beauty of the scene, laid himself down half unconsciously on the greensward to enjoy it at his leisure.

Dear Irish reader, let us sit down beside him for a moment, and view the picture also. There is nothing in it new to your eyes – nothing you haven't seen a thousand times before. It was only an old churchyard, and old church-yards in Ireland, you know, are always the same. The same old beaten foot-paths through the rank grass – the same old hawthorn trees which in early summer shed their white blossoms on the green graves – the same old ivy walls overshadowing the moss-covered tombs of the monk and the nun. No, there was nothing strange or new in the picture – on the contrary, every thing there was as familiar to you as your own thoughts. But tell us, dear reader, – now that we can converse quietly together, – does not the sight of such a spot sometimes awaken old memories? Do you still remember the place in the old ruins where the prior's ghost was seen so often after sunset, or the fairy tree beside the holy well which no axe could cut down, nor human hand break a branch off with impunity? But, above all, do you remember the shady little corner where the dear ones lie buried – the grassy mound where you knelt to drop the last tear on bidding farewell to the land you will never see again? O, dear reader, do your thoughts ever wander back to these blessed scenes of your youth? When in the long summer evenings, after the toil of the day is over, you sit by the porch of the stranger enjoying the cool night air, and gazing up at the sparkling heavens, does your eye ever roam in search of that star you should know better than all the rest, the bright one that shines on your own "native isle of the ocean"? When your heart feels sad under a sense of its isolation, – nay, when it turns with disgust from the treacherous and the cold-hearted, who, having wiled you to their shores, now deny you even a foothold on their soil, – does memory then ever carry you back to the old homestead among the hills, where in bygone years you have met so many generous souls round the humble hearthstone? Alas, alas! when you look at those once stalwart limbs you gave your adopted country as a recompense for the freedom she promised you – now wasted away in her service – when you think of the blood you shed in her battles, the prayers you offered for her prosperity, the pride with which you heard her name spoken of in other lands, and the glorious hopes you once entertained of seeing her the greatest and the best of the nations of the earth – and yet to think, O, to think that the only return she makes for all this is to hate and spurn you, – when thoughts like these weigh down your heart, dear reader, do you not sometimes long to see the old land again, and lay your shattered frame down to rest in that shady corner you remember so well in the old churchyard?

But they tell you here you must not indulge such thoughts as these. On the contrary, you must forget the past; you must renounce your love for the country that gave you birth; you must sever every tie that knits you to her bosom; you must abjure and repudiate her forevermore: the songs you sang and the stories you told so often by the light of the peat fire, must never be sung or told again; all the associations of home and friends, all the pleasant recollections of your boyhood, all the traditions of your warriors and sainted ancestors, must be blotted from your memory, as so many treasons against the land of your adoption. Or, if you do venture to speak of old times and old places when you meet with long, absent friends round the social board, it must be in whispers and with closed doors, lest the strangers should hear you as they pass by. And behold the return they make you for these sacrifices! They give you freedom! What! freedom to live like helots in the land they promised to make your own – freedom to worship your Creator under a roof which a godless mob may, at any moment, fire with impunity – freedom to shed your blood in defence of a flag that would gladly wave in triumph over the extinction of your race. Speak, exile! are you willing to renounce your fatherland for such recompense as this? O, if you be, may no ray of sunlight ever visit your grave – no friend or relation, wife or child, ever shed a tear to hallow it. If you've fallen so low as to kiss the foot that spurns you, and grown so mean as to fawn upon a nation that flings you from her with disgust, then go and live the degraded, soulless thing thou art, fit only to batten on garbage and rot in a potter's field. Go! quit this place, for the sight of an old Irish churchyard has no charms for you.

The Life and Adventures of
Private Miles O'Reilly

by Charles G. Halpine (New York: Carleton, 1864)

Born in 1829, the son of a Church of Ireland clergyman in County Meath, Charles G. Halpine had a typical Ascendancy upbringing. He dabbled at Trinity College, Dublin, read for the law in London, married his childhood sweetheart, and came to America in 1850 to make his fortune. His career in journalism and light verse began in Boston, where he contributed to B. P. Shillaber's Carpet-Bag, *the short-lived (1851-53) but influential humorous periodical in which Mark Twain's first published story appeared. After moving on to New York City, Halpine worked all through the fifties as a journalist on several different newspapers, and when the Civil War erupted, he joined New York's Irish Sixty-ninth Regiment.*

While stationed at Morris Island, South Carolina, in August of 1863, Halpine drew up the first "dispatches" which featured Private Miles O'Reilly, "a youthful warrior of Italian extraction." Immediately popular and widely reprinted in newspapers, these pieces were collected early in 1864 into a wartime best-seller, The Life and Adventures of Private Miles O'Reilly. *Even President Lincoln is said to have been amused. Perhaps this book helped to counter the bad publicity that had been garnered by the Irish as a result of the violent anti-black, anti-draft riots in New York City in July 1863. At any rate, the popularity of* Private Miles *certainly contributed to the visibility of Irish soldiers for whom the Civil War provided an opportunity to demonstrate the seriousness of their commitment to America. One of the excerpts here, a speech at the White House by the famous leader of the Irish Brigade, General Thomas Francis Meagher, makes this point: "the race that were heretofore only exiles . . . are now proud peers of the proudest and brave brothers of the best." The war effort was a significant watershed in Irish assimilation into American life.*

After the war, Charles Halpine had a frenetic three years of life left to him. He worked as a journalist, edited his own anti-corruption newspaper, supported the Fenian movement for Irish freedom, and, in 1867, he was elected to the lucrative position of New York City Register of Deeds. In August of the following year, he died of an accidental overdose of chloroform, taken to combat chronic insomnia. He was thirty-eight years old.

Excerpted here are two of the most popular of the Miles O'Reilly dispatches of

1863. Pardoned by the President after his arrest for the "crime" of song writing, Miles pens his most famous ballad, "Sambo's Right to Be Kilt." Widely reprinted and anthologized, the song argues for the acceptance of black soldiers as cannon fodder with a bald cruelty that was an undeniable part of its appeal to prejudiced northern whites who had opposed the recruitment of blacks on the grounds of Negro inferiority. After his release from prison, Miles goes on to a triumphant reception at the White House at which General Meagher speaks. In his combination of humor and seriousness partially rendered in Irish dialect, Halpine's creation paves the way for Finley Peter Dunne's "Mr. Dooley" columns of the 1890s.

Miles O'Reilly Pardoned

WASHINGTON DISPATCH, *N.Y. Herald,* Oct. 1863.

We are gratified to be able to announce that the President, always attentive to the cry of suffering and deserving soldiers, has granted a free pardon to Private Miles O'Reilly, Forty-seventh regiment New York Volunteers, now a prisoner on Morris Island, South Carolina. The President takes the view that O'Reilly's original offence was but "an innocent joke" in his own eyes, however contrary to the letter or spirit of the Revised Regulations for the Army. O'Reilly has been ordered North, and is expected here by the next steamer. Mr. Lincoln, in giving instructions to Colonel E. D. Townsend, Assistant Adjutant-General, for issuing the order of pardon, referred to the old proverb about "making the ballads of a nation, and allowing any one else to make the laws." It is believed that Miles will be confidentially employed at the White House in rendering into popular verse the stories and traditions of the great Northwest; and no doubt such a volume – the materials and anecdotes furnished by Mr. Lincoln, and the verses by the Bard of Green Erin – will be quite equal to anything in the same line since the days of Æsop's Fables, translated by the poet Gay.

It is said that the immediate impelling cause of this step on the part of the President – a very strong one in view of the stand taken with regard to Private O'Reilly by certain high authorities in the Navy Department – was a song brought to the notice of His Excellency by Captain Arthur M. Kinzie, of the Illinois Cavalry, a very deserving young officer, who, in the "halcyon days long ago," collected, drilled, and disciplined the first regiment of Colored Troops that had been raised in the United States since the days of General Andrew Jackson, who was of the opinion – concurring therein with General George Washington – that colored men could stop a ball or fill a pit as well as better; and that the exclusive privilege of being killed or maimed in battle, or worked to death in the trenches, was not that kind of privilege for the exclusive right of which any great number of earnest and sensible white men could long contend. Capt. Kinzie, in the letter transmitting the following

verses to the President, declared that they had been of the utmost value in rec-
onciling the minds of the soldiery of the old 10th Army Corps to the experiment of the 1st South Carolina Volunteers. The verses were as follows; and
although the author never declared himself, they were universally attributed
through the Department of the South to Private Miles O'Reilly: –

Sambo's Right To Be Kilt

Air – "*The Low-backed Car*"

Some tell us 'tis a burnin' shame
    To make the naygers fight;
And that the thrade of bein' kilt
    Belongs but to the white:
But as for me, upon my sowl!
    So liberal are we here,
I'll let Sambo be murthered instead of myself,
    On every day in the year.
        On every day in the year, boys,
            And in every hour of the day;
        The right to be kilt I'll divide wid him,
            And divil a word I'll say.

In battle's wild commotion
    I shouldn't at all object
If Sambo's body should stop a ball
    That was comin' for me direct;
And the prod of a Southern bagnet,
    So ginerous are we here,
I'll resign, and let Sambo take it
    On every day in the year.
        On every day in the year, boys,
            And wid none o' your nasty pride,
        All my right in a Southern bagnet prod,
            Wid Sambo I'll divide!

The men who object to Sambo
    Should take his place and fight;
And it's betther to have a nayger's hue
    Than a liver that's wake and white.
Though Sambo's black as the ace of spades,
        His finger a thrigger can pull,
And his eye runs sthraight on the barrel-sights

From undher its thatch of wool.
So hear me all, boys darlin',
Don't think I'm tippin you chaff,
The right to be kilt we'll divide wid him,
And give him the largest half!

Whatever may be thought of the spirit animating this ditty – which certainly is extremely devoid of any philanthropic or humanitarian cant – the practical results of its popular diffusion redounded undoubtedly to the best interests of the service, "with a view to soup." The white soldiers of the Department began singing it round their camp-fires at night, and humming it to themselves on their sentry-beats. It made them regard the enlistment of the despised sons of Ham as rather a good joke at first; and next, as a joke containing some advantages to themselves. Very quickly they became reconciled to the experiment; and it was not long before they commenced to take in the movements and doings of their humble colored allies, that sort of half-ludicrous, half-pathetic interest which a jolly-hearted, full-grown elder brother takes in the first awkward attempts at manly usefulness that are made by "little Bub," who is some score of years his junior. This was General Hunter's object in all his orders and other measures relative to the organization of colored regiments. He urged the matter forward purely as a military measure, and without one syllable or thought of any "humanitarian proletarianism." Every black regiment in garrison would relieve a white regiment for service in the field. Every ball stopped by a black man would save the life of a white soldier. Besides, if the blacks are to have liberty, the strictness of military discipline is the best school in which their elevation to the plane of freedom can be conducted. It was Hunter's chief misfortune, and the greatest curse of his Department, that this purely military experiment was interfered with by a swarm of black-coated, white-chokered, cotton-speculating, long-faced, philanthropy-preaching fanatics – the grand hierarch of whom appeared of opinion that "a white man, by severe moral restraint and constant attendance upon his (the grand hierarch's) preaching, might in time elevate himself to something very like an equality with an average buck-nigger just fresh from the plantations." For the presence of these civilians in the Department, General Hunter was not responsible; nor for the evil effects of their mischievous, and only mischievous, interference should he be blamed.*

"That song," said the President, on hearing it read by Colonel Hay, "reminds me of what Deacon Stoddard, away down in Menard County, said one day, when a woman that was of suspected repute dropped a half eagle into the collection plate, after one of his charity sermons: 'I don't know where she gets it, nor how she earns it; but the money's good, and will do good. I

*[Union General David Hunter was an early advocate of the use of black troops. During part of the war, Halpine was his chief of staff.]

wish she had some better way of getting it than she is thought to have; and that those who do get their money better, could be persuaded to make half as good a use of it.' I have no doubt, Hay, that O'Reilly, in whom you seem to take such an interest, might be a great deal better man than he is. But that song of his is both good and will do good. Let McManus step over to Colonel Townsend, and say that I want to see him." It was under these circumstances that Private Miles O'Reilly obtained his pardon.

Miles O'Reilly at the White House

[From the *N. Y. Herald.*]

WASHINGTON, Nov. 26, 1863.

Let to-day be chronicled as a great day for Ireland, and let it live as the greatest of Thanksgiving Days in American history! This afternoon took place the interesting ceremonial of presenting Private Miles O'Reilly, Forty-seventh Regiment New York Volunteers, to his Excellency the President of the United States, by whom, in turn, the young Milesian warrior and bard of the Tenth army corps was presented to several members of the Cabinet and foreign diplomatic corps, who were paying a Thanksgiving Day call to the President when the cards of General T. F. Meagher and Father Murphy were handed in by Colonel Hay – these gentlemen having kindly consented to act as the *chaperons,* or social godfathers and godmothers of Private O'Reilly, who was accompanied by Major Kavanagh and Captain Breslin, of the old Sixty-ninth New York, and by Mr. Luke Clark, of the Fifth Ward of your City, as his own "special friends." The details of this interview will hereafter form an instructive episode in the grand drama of our national history. It was in a manner the apotheosis of democratic principles – an acknowledgment of our indebtedness to the men who carry muskets in our armies. It had its political significance, also, and may prove another link between our soldiers in the field and the present lengthy occupant of the White House, who is understood to be not averse to the prospect of a lengthier lease of that "desirable country residence," which has none of the modern improvements.

Picture of Private O'Reilly

Private O'Reilly is a brawny, large-boned, rather good-looking young Milesian, with curly reddish hair, grey eyes, one of which has a blemish upon it, high cheek bones, a cocked nose, square lower jaws, and the usual strong type of Irish forehead – the perceptive bumps, immediately above the eyes, being extremely prominent. A more good-humored or radiantly expressive face it is impossible to conceive. The whole countenance beams with a candor and unreserve equal to that of a mealy potato which has burst its skin or jacket by too rapid boiling. He stands about six feet three inches, is broad-chested, barrel-bodied, firm on his pins, and with sinewy, knotted fists of a hardness and heaviness seldom equalled. On the whole, he reminds one very much of Ensign O'Doherty's ideal picture of the Milesian hero: –

> One of his eyes was bottle green,
>   And the other eye was out, my dear;
> And the calves of his wicked looking legs
>   Were more than two feet about, my dear
>   O, the lump of an Irishman,
>   The nasty, ugly Irishman,
> The great he-rogue, with his wonderful brogue,
> The leathering swash of an Irishman.

What He and His Cousins Think About England

Private O'Reilly says that he was born at a place they call Ouldcastle; that he picked up what little of the humanities and rudiments he possesses under one Father Thomas Maguire, of Cavan – "him that was O'Connell's frind, rest their sowls"; and he is emphatic in declaring that he and seventeen of his O'Reilly cousins, sixty-four Murphy cousins, thirty-seven Kelly cousins, twenty-three Lanigan cousins, together with a small army of Raffertys, Caffertys, Fogartys, Flanigans, Ryans, O'Rourkes, Dooligans, Oulahans, Quinns, Flynns, Kellys, Murphys, O'Connors, O'Connells, O'Driscolls, O'Mearas, O'Tooles, McCartys, McConkeys, and McConnells – all his own blood relations, many of them now in the service, and all decent boys – would be both proud and happy to enlist or re-enlist for twenty years or the war, if his Reverence's Excellency the President would only oblige them "the laste mite in life" by declaring war against England. He is of opinion that no excuse is ever needed for going to war; but adds that if any were, it might be found in the recent Canadian-rebel conspiracy to release the prisoners in camp on Johnson's Island.

"If we let this pass," he says, "divil resayve the so illigant an excuse the dirty spalpeens may ever give us again! They gripped us whin we wor wake, an' med us give up them two rapparees, Shlidell and Mason. We've now got five iron-clads to their one, boys dear; and Mr. Lincoln," he adds, "won't be the jockey we bought him for, if he don't give John Bull his bellyful of 'neuthrality' before he gets through his term." Mr. Luke Clark, of the Fifth ward, is understood to be very strong in the same view.*

Arrival at the White House – Scenes at the Door

On the arrival of the party at the White House there was a great scene of handshaking at the door between Private O'Reilly and Edward McManus, the chatty old greyhaired gentleman from Italy – where O'Reilly knew him – who has kept watch at the gate through five administrations; and who is now assisted by Mr. Thomas Burns, also from Italy, who has outlived the storms of two reigns. It was "God bless you, Miles," and "God bless you kindly, Edward," for as many as ten minutes, the handshaking being fast and furious all the time.

General Meagher's Speech

General Meagher, in presenting Private O'Reilly to the President, made some remarks to the effect that he was happy to have the honor of introducing to one who was regarded as the Father of the Army this *enfant* perdu, or lost boy of the Irish race. His friend, Colonel John Hay, the President's Secretary, who had served as a volunteer in the Department of the South, was acquainted with O'Reilly's character in his regiment, and knew that it was good, though chequered with certain amiable indiscretions, having their origin in the fount of Castaly, or some other fountain – of which he had forgotten the particulars. (Laughter.) He wished to assure Mr. Lincoln that the bone and sinew of the army – his own countrymen in it not least – had eyes to see, and hearts to feel, and memories to treasure up the many acts of hearty, homely, honest kindliness, by which the Chief Magistrate of the nation had evinced his interest in their welfare. In the golden hours of sunrise, under the silver watches of the stars; through many a damp, dark night on picket duty, or in the red flame and heady fury of the battle, the thought that lay next the heart of the Irish soldier – only dividing its glow with that of the revered relic from the altar, which piety and affection had annexed, as an amulet against harm, around his neck – was the thought that he was thus earning a title, which hereafter no foul tongue or niggard heart would dare dispute, to the full equality and fraternity of an American citizen. ("Hear, hear," from the President.) Ugly and venomous as was the toad of civil strife, it yet carried in its head for the Irish race in America this precious, this inestimable jewel. By adoption of the banner, and by the communion of bloody grave-trenches on every field, from Bull Run to where the Chickamauga rolls down its waters of

---

*[In late 1863 there had been a "Canada plot" to free Confederates from the Union prison at Johnson's Island in Lake Erie. James Mason and John Slidell were the newly appointed Confederate ministers to England and France when their seizure at sea by the American Navy in 1861 caused an international incident. To avoid forcing England into the war on the Confederate side, President Lincoln released the two. "Rapparee" is an Irish term for a member of a nationalist secret society given to guerrilla warfare.]

death, the race that were heretofore only exiles, receiving generous hospitality in the land, are now proud peers of the proudest and brave brothers of the
best. (Deep emotion, Secretary Seward tapping the table with his fingers, and
Mr. Chase gravely bowing his head in approval.) On behalf of Private
O'Reilly, he desired to thank Mr. Lincoln for the clemency which had failed
to see crime in an innocent song. Although the verses of Private O'Reilly had
become conspicuous, they were far from being the only or the best efforts of
the lyric muse to which the fast frolic and effervescing life of camps had given
birth. Whenever Clio shall aspire to write the history of this war, that sagest
sister of the sacred Nine will be obliged to draw largely on the rough, but
always heartfelt, often droll, still oftener tenderly pathetic verses, with which
Euterpe will be found to have inspired the rough writers and fighters of the
rank and file. ("Hear, hear," from the President, the Baron Gerolte and
General Cullum.) Seeing that Lord Lyons was present, General Meagher
would not now refer to the Fenian Brotherhood, of which the Chevalier John
O'Mahony was the Head Centre.* He thanked the President, Mr. Seward, Mr.
Chase, Mr. Stanton, General Halleck, the Baron Stoeckl, the Baron Gerolte,
the Count Mercier, Colonels Townsend and Kelton, Assistant Secretary of the
Navy Fox, and the others who were present, for their interest in this interview,
of which accident had made them witnesses. Had he had the slightest inkling
how his Excellency had been engaged, he should most certainly have post-
poned the visit – a wish for which had been conveyed to him through
Secretary Stanton. He would now briefly introduce to the President Private
Miles O'Reilly, the bard of Morris Island, whose self and family – snug farmers and very decent people – he had well known many years ago in the Green
Isle, which was their common birthplace.

. . . .

How Private O'Reilly Shakes Hands

All this time Private Miles O'Reilly, Forty-seventh regiment New York
Volunteers, had been standing in the first position of a soldier – heels in, toes
out, body rigid and perpendicular as a ramrod, and the little fingers of his
open hands resting behind the side seams of his sky-blue inexpressibles. He
had a twenty-five cent bouquet in the breast of his blue coat, and in his eyes
that stolid expression or total want of expression which is imparted by the
order – "eyes front." No sooner, however, did the President extend his hand
than the sinews relaxed, and his countenance brightened up as if some crazy

---

*[General Thomas Francis Meagher ("Meagher of the Sword") was one of the most admired
Irishmen in the Union Army. He had come to America by way of transportation to Tasmania as a
political felon. In 1858, Irish immigrant John O'Mahony founded the Fenian Brotherhood, the
American branch of the Irish Republican Brotherhood. Both Meagher and O'Mahony had been
supporters of "Young Ireland" in the 1840s.]

millionaire had suddenly offered to give him its face in gold for a twenty dollar greenback. Instantly he made the sound of spitting into the palm of his right hand, then raised the arm to its full height, and brought down his open palm against the Presidential palm with a report that rang through the council chamber as if one of the "torpedo devils" of Chief Engineer Stimers had been exploded by the concussion.

The Lost Rosary; or, Our Irish Girls, Their Trials, Temptations, and Triumphs

by Peter McCorry (Boston: Patrick Donahoe, 1870)

An ardent nationalist, Peter McCorry edited the Irish People, *"A Weekly Journal of News, Politics, and Literature," that served as the official organ of the Fenian Brotherhood in New York City during the late 1860s and early 1870s. Using the pseudonym "Con O'Leary," McCorry also wrote three novels, all of which were published by Patrick Donahoe in Boston.* The Irish Widow's Son *(1869) was a tale of the 1798 Rising that focused on British atrocities against the Irish people.* Mount Benedict, or The Violated Tomb *(1871) was a shrill, outraged retelling of the burning of the Charlestown convent. (Comparing this novel with the controlled satire of* Six Months in a House of Correction, *the immediate response to the 1834 events excerpted in Part I, reveals much about the differing emotional climates of pre- and post-Famine Irish America.) Dedicated to "the ever faithful Irish girls in America," McCorry's middle novel,* The Lost Rosary *of 1870, is excerpted here.*

In a preface, McCorry says that the need for such a novel was suggested to him by Patrick Donahoe, "the eminent Irish and Catholic publisher of America." It is the author's "hope that our IRISH GIRLS will profit by every line of what is written specially for their benefit," and the result is a classic novel of instruction in the pitfalls of America and exhortation toward keeping the Catholic faith. The plot traces two pairs of emigrants from County Donegal, Barney McAuley and Tim Heggarty and the girls who love them, the cousins Mary and Ailey O'Donnell. The men go to America first, in 1845, and the women come over a few years later, in flight from the worst of the Famine.

The first excerpt describes the shipboard experience of Barney and Tim, and features the archetypal storm at sea, which symbolizes the disturbing immigrant transition in so many of these novels. The second contains the book's didactic center – a list of the virtues necessary to the spiritual survival of Irish girls in America.

At Sea – Old and New Acquaintances

"Build me straight, O worthy Master,
  Staunch and strong, a goodly vessel,

154

That shall laugh at all disaster,
And with wave and whirlwind wrestle."

On the first of June, 1845, the good ship "St. Patrick" sailed from Liverpool for New York, with a human cargo of six hundred souls. On board this ship were Bernard McAuley and Timothy Heggarty – two young men who "kept themselves by themselves," as an old Irish woman remarked. There were also from the same place, Farmer Clarkson, his wife, and Jenny and Nelly Clarkson.

What a strange assemblage of people were gathered together in the steerage of that ship. The large majority of the passengers were Irish, and of these there was every description of every class of people, old and young, good and bad; some comfortable, others poor; some with cash in their possession, others without a penny; some well provisioned, others without a bite to eat other than the ship's allowance; some, and they were the fewest number, with some prospects before them on landing; others going out on speculation, ready to face and to dare hardships of any kind, rather than submit to those at home, without even a chance throughout life to better their miserable condition. As a rule, all were lighthearted. They had passed the bitter ordeal of leave-taking with friends and relations; they had looked for the last time on the graves of parents and children, gazed tenderly and affectionately on the well-remembered spots of their childhood, with feelings which no pen has ever yet or ever shall be able to describe. Some had left fathers and mothers, and sisters and brothers; some had left wives and young families, dependent on the mercies of a cold and callous world, who sustained themselves with the thought that, with God's help, before long, they would be able to send the first remittance to cheer the desolate homes they had left forever. Others again were there, whose families were indirectly the cause of their expatriation. Parents, whose want of forethought and foolish notions about their children, had permitted themselves to be wrecked in the middle passage of life, relying solely on the strength of the ship's hull, rather than on the proper management of the ship's sails, that were carrying them and theirs over life's billows.

That ship, the "St. Patrick," was a miniature of the world's life. Two passions were predominant in the minds of the emigrants: pure and unalloyed love; open and undisguised hatred. How strange that such mental antitheses could live and flourish at the same time in one human breast. Both passions were absorbing, and yet they were co-existent. Love asserted its supremacy and filled their whole being. Hatred, the opposite, most antagonistic and repugnant to love, was welcomed and fostered with as much assiduity as love itself.

There are lessons here for the statesman, if he will condescend to learn them at such an humble source. These lessons are worth a world full of statistics, for they precede them, and are the cause, the other being but the effect.

This hatred extended to those who were the authors of the desolation that afflicted the people who were driven from their homes. The spirit of religion battled strongly for possession of the minds of those so afflicted, and whatever result followed, was the change of hatred from persons to principles of government. The love owed much of its intensity to the hatred that we speak of, for the sufferings of those left behind induced the one and helped the other.

. . . .

A Storm at Sea – Reflections Thereon

"Then fell her straining topmasts
Hanging tangled in the shrouds;
And her sails were loosened and lifted,
And blown away like clouds."

Fourteen days at sea, and everything had gone well. Every lonely heart was beginning to raise itself. The passengers had nearly all become acquainted, one with the other, and song and dance, and jest enlivened the monotony of ship life. The heart-wrung pangs of separation were, if not forgotten, fast yielding to the gentle wooings of inspiring Hope. The merry laugh, with its silvery tones, displaced the smothered moan. The rosy cheeks of youthful maidens, so long bedewed with tears of sorrow, now beamed in all their guileless beauty, showing the gladness that reigned within, and tinged their thoughts with the light of a happy future.

The moon rose from the ocean depths, like a globe of fire. The dull red beams she sent athwart the waste of waters, showed the rising billows of the sea, cold and angry looking, and sending forth a deadened hollow murmur. A few clouds sped quickly overhead, followed by a sharp and broken whistling of the wind. The rigging of the ship began to creak uneasily, and a weird-like music played among the shrouds. The glass gave indications of unsettled weather, and the ship rolled uneasily. In a little she began to heave, and rose and fell in obedience to the whitening waves on which she rode. Suddenly a sea dashed across her bows, and the noble craft staggered with the force of the blow. That was the indication of a storm which the skipper had foreseen for hours before, and did his best to guard against.

The passengers had gone below, but were soon awakened by the unusual motion of the vessel. They looked uneasily at one another, and not a few were flung back into the full horror of the sickness they had but lately passed. In a couple of hours the storm had fairly broken over the gallant bark. At one moment she was lifted by a giant wave, to be plunged in the next down, down into the gulf below. Anon, she lay on her beam ends, as if unable to right herself again. It was during these struggles the people suffered most. They held their breath in painful suspense, and a dead silence prevailed, save when some exclamation reached the ear, such as, "O God, we're lost!" and the stoutest heart quailed at the despairing tone of the sufferer.

"Double reef every inch of sail," shouted the skipper, overhead, "and keep her head close to the wind – mind, there!"

"Aye, aye, sir," was the response; but the voices seemed to proceed from treble their distance.

"Fasten down the hatchways."

"They're down, sir," was the reply.

Yes! they were nailed down; there was no alternative on that dreadful night. It was death without, and death within. The storm raged with ruthless fury, and the bright hopes experienced only a few hours previous, blended with the sunshine of promise, were driven back upon the heart, black, and despairing. The berths of the ship became stifling with an imprisoned miasma, – while seas washed overhead, and swept the deck of every movable article.

Louder and fiercer, was the war of the elements; crash followed crash, as the stout ship tried, like a thing of life, to face the power that beset her. A moment, and every timber strained and shook, like the nerves of a full-blooded steed, suddenly reigned in by the hands of its rider.

"Heavens! did you feel that shiver?" asked Barney of his companion. "Feel it, aye: who could miss feeling it," replied Tim.

A report, like the boom of a cannon, was heard overhead – then another – and another!

"God an' His blessed Mother presarve us," exclaimed poor Moll Hanley, "what is that?"

Then there arose a long and piteous wail among the females, old and young. They had tried to suppress their fears, but the awful noises overhead seemed created to banish hope from their hearts.

The mainsail was rent in a thousand pieces and the mast that gallantly bore it was snapped in twain, as if a cannon ball had struck it. The ship lay on her side disabled, and as if frightened to rise from the trough of the sea. Every hand was at work to clear away the wreck, and these indications of life formed the only consolation to those distressed hearts below.

Hundreds of young women were engaged in what they believed were the last prayers they would ever offer to God in this life; others were speechless with silent horror; while the strong beatings of many hearts proved the terror of the men.

Hour after hour passed away. It seemed the reflex of eternity. Not a few were pitched here and there throughout the compartments allotted them – while others, again, overcome by the sickness engendered by foul air, lay stretched like corpses on the floor.

How like to the voyage of life was that passage of the "St. Patrick!" Its first days out, were the spring of life – everything happy and cheerful; then came the summer – joyous and short-lived; and the winter, with its storms and wrecks, sufferings and privations, fears and tribulations. But not a soul was lost! And there was a communion of prayer, too, in the noble ship, unknown, for the most part, to those who participated in it, and joined in by those thousands of miles removed!

So it is with those who have the happiness of being born in the Catholic Church: storms and tempests assail her children: the blackness of despair surrounds the tortured soul and destruction seems inevitable. Bear up, brave soul, thou art overwhelmed with darkness and suffering, but prayers ascend in thy behalf. See! a light beaming in the young East – fresh and holy as the first dawn in Eden. The goodly mast is gone, that bore thee gallantly through the storm, but Heaven has still a smile for thee. The first soft streaks of day are blushing at the work of night. The storm is passed, and gladdened hearts are busy repairing the good ship's loss. Profound thankfulness now stirs the souls of all who were endangered. No purer, holier offering ever ascended to God, than the humble tribute of those lonely girls, those pure daughters of Erin, who had risked the storms of the sea, and those of the world, to prove their devoted affection to those who had cared for them when unable to care for themselves.

Storms and trials you will meet, brave hearts, – but remember your night of storms upon the sea. Temptations will surround you; sin will encompass you; aye, as the dark waters surround you now. Then remember your only hope. Call back the Faith that saved you when Hope was trembling at your hearts. That will be your anchor, brave Irish girls, when alone and battling against every storm. Cling to it, like the tempest-tossed mariner who feels his heart grow stout and warm within him, as he gazes on the anchor of his ship. Varied the forms and designs of the quicksands and shoals that will beset thee. Thy virgin modesty will be shocked, and thy ears assailed betimes with language unknown to thee before. Fear not. Vice will cunningly allure you, with its deformities hidden beneath the garb of wealth. Be on thy guard. Soft words and honeyed speech will rain upon thy hearing in order to reach the purity of thy hearts to destruction. Be as those who are deaf. Foul words and practices will cross thy paths; curses will fall around thee, but remember the waves against the sides of the ship. If thy souls be troubled, remember the roseate dawn that followed the Night of Storms! Be true to the old father, and the old mother. Let the music of their voices be always in your ears, to guide and guard you. Remember their gray hairs, and their faltering voice. Mind the Old Chapel and its humble Cross. Think often of the hours you spent within its walls; of the evenings spent at the "four roads." Think of the old hearthstone, and the bush before the door of the cabin. But, before and above all, think of God! . . . Be cheerful, too; enjoy life heartily and well. Let thy temper be as sweet as the dews of May. Laugh till you're tired; work with a will; get married; but mind – aye, there's the rub girls – mind the choice. Never let your hands be sullied by a RING THAT THE CHURCH CANNOT BLESS. Your own, and the salvation of others, aye, of generations, depend on that one act of your lives. Choose poverty, rather than run the risk of marriage with one that professes not your faith. You need not wait to examine the advice here tendered. It admits of no examination. Under any circumstances, a mixed marriage is an unmixed evil. The trials and cares of life are numerous enough, under the best circumstances. Add not to these the never ending strife of union with one who differs from you in religion. Not even if your intended partner be of easy mind, and careless of his own belief. This often aggravates such unions, for indifference in one partner often begets the same in the other. Above all, a mixed marriage in America, where you will be removed from the holy influences of home, and the care of those who are dear to you, and you to them, is worse, a thousand-fold, than under other circumstances. Fly the very thought of such unions, as you would the vilest snare. Heed not the example of others, whose pride and passion lead them to look on such things as quite common, and of no consequence. Beware even of association with those who might lead you into such a state.

. . . .

[McCorry's list of exemplary virtues]

Brave Irish girls! it is seldom by such standards as these ye are judged. The hidden virtue passes lightly among those of the world. The sneer of the ignorant is reserved for some awkward act, and the gentle titter of senseless dandies are the estimates too often formed of our Irish girls. Self-abnegation is unknown by your betters – your betters, quotha!

Your CHASTITY, sweet maidens, is the butt for the coarse and brutal joke.

Your MODESTY sometimes wins upon the world; at other times it is valued below the vulgar display of obscenity and vice.

Your HONESTY – Well, those who make money succeed in the world – "but success at the cost of conscience!" whispers some Irish beauty at my elbow.

Yes, my girl, success in the acquirement of anything at that expense, is, after all, a miserable failure. We may try to hide it from ourselves, but, if we ever possessed that genuine article – a true conscience – we must at least acknowledge so much.

SELF-ABNEGATION – better practise it, than bear the thought for one hour, that we have been remiss in our duty to our neighbor.

CHASTITY – A flower that out-rivals all glories of earth, that commands the admiration of archangels, and blossoms most when hidden.

MODESTY – Sweetest of virtues, that can well afford the taunts of the brazen-faced and worldly. Lovely violet that sheds sweet incense among the rankest weeds of life.

HONESTY – in principle and act, the guardian of society. The pride that flows from such is a noble pride, and well befits a queen.

SUCCESS – a badly understood term; when applied to our condition in life; always best when moderate and unaccompanied with too strong a desire, lest its companions in virtue should suffer by its exaltation.

SUFFERING – The lot of all, and not without its finer advantages.

See poor Mary O'Donnell, now indeed an orphan! She has stood by the grave of her mother, surrounded by strangers, without even one kindly heart to comprehend her sorrow. She hastens from the grave to the bedside of the sick. Ailey demands her care, and the heart of the poor girl is thankful that she has at last obtained leave to nurse her cousin through her sickness. Weary days passed on, and Ailey O'Donnell's life hung trembling in the balance. Doubly watchful, now that her care devolved on only one, Mary sat at that post of duty, and carefully tended the sick one until all danger was past.

Illustration for the lively election-day scene in John M. Moore's *Adventures of Tom Stapleton.*

Prolific Irish-born novelist Mary Anne Sadlier (1820-1903) and the title page of her 1853 work, with its conventional death-bed scene.

NEW LIGHTS:
OR,

LIFE IN GALWAY.

"TELL YOUR FATHER," SAID SHE SLOWLY AND WITH DIFFICULTY, "TELL HIM HONORA O'DALY FORGIVES HIM."—SEE PAGE 158.

BY MRS. J. SADLIER.

NEW YORK:
D. & J. SADLIER & CO. 164 WILLIAM STREET.
Boston: 128 Federal Street.
MONTREAL: COR. OF NOTRE DAME AND ST. FRANCIS XAVIER STS.
1853.

"*When she sat down to her work again, her hands went about it mechanically under the fixed mask of her face.*" Thomas Fogarty's illustration for "The Exiles" by Harvey J. O'Higgins which appeared in *McClure's Magazine* in March 1906.

Finley Peter Dunne as a young Chicago journalist.

Annie Reilly; or, The Fortunes of an Irish Girl in New York. A Tale Founded on Fact

by John McElgun (New York: J. A. McGee, 1873)

All that is known about John McElgun is that he wrote this novel. He was prob-
ably an Irish immigrant to New York City, because, amid the welter of familiar spasms
of sentimentality and didacticism, his book provides the fullest description available of
the Queenstown (Cork) to Liverpool to Castle Garden immigrant journey of the
Famine generation. Annie Reilly's family is evicted from their small Munster holding
through the machinations of a despicable middleman, Ryan, the town pork butcher;
Annie's beau, James O'Rourke, is accused of planning to rob a police barracks of arms.
Both young people flee to America at different times, hoping to meet again in New York;
both trips are rendered in valuable detail by McElgun.

The relevant sections of James O'Rourke's journey are here reprinted. We learn of
the squalor of the lodging houses and the danger of "mancatchers" in Liverpool, and of
the gauntlet of hustlers and sharpers at Castle Garden. James ultimately finds a crowd-
ed boarding house (fifty people in fifteen rooms over a saloon) and a job as a long-
shoreman. Although she is harassed by a loutish Scotsman, Annie's crossing is easier,
and she finds on the other side the exhorting example of her relatives, the Sweeneys, who
have, through "industry and good habits," achieved middle-class respectability, com-
plete with a brass plate on their front door. Needless to say, James and Annie find each
other and marry near the end of the novel.

Liverpool Man-Catchers and Lodging Houses

We shall now return to James O'Rourke, whom we left in the rather unpleasant position of bidding a hasty good-by to his sweetheart, while he dreaded every moment the faithful upholders of justice and fair play in Ireland would be upon him. After parting from Annie, he turned his steps northward, hoping to reach Dublin before the authorities there could be apprised of his flight. He deemed it better to take this direction, as the police would be certain to warn their brothers at Queenstown to look out for him. Neither did he think it prudent to travel by the main roads, but kept to the by-lanes and open country.

The short night passed quickly away, but, when morning came, James had left his home a long way behind, and found himself in a part of the country totally unknown to him. By making enquiries of some laborers who were going to their toil at that early hour, he found the road to Dublin; and, as his apprehensions had calmed considerably since he left his native county, he struck boldly into the road, and that evening, tired and footsore, reached the city. The Liverpool boat was about to leave in a few minutes after he reached the dock, and, as he did not care to delay in the capital, he took passage, and was soon out on the Irish Sea.

James and his fellow-passengers had a pleasant voyage. The night was calm and fine on their departure, and continued so till morning; when, just as tall wreaths of smoke began to curl up from the houses along the Mersey, they reached Liverpool. A motley crowd of ship-runners and lodging-house keepers met the passengers on their landing, and surrounded them like a pack of hungry wolves; some crying out they represented such a ship – "the very best on the ocean" – and beseeching all sensible passengers who valued their health and future prosperity to take no other; some frantically roaring out the numerous striking qualities of their boardinghouse: what attention – we don't doubt that – what good meals, what cleanliness was to be found there. It would be much better for those man-catchers, as they are called, not to mention cleanliness, lest some inquisitive emigrant should look at their faces and hands, and begin to reflect, till, seeing they told one lie, probably doubt all they had to say. But shout, and yell, and declaim they will, and always give their voices a little higher pitch at the word cleanliness. James, not being encumbered with much baggage, escaped pretty well till he reached the dock, where he stood looking at the scramble, and din, and noise going on on the gangway and around him. It looked like a fierce charge on a well-fought field, only more terrible; for, when a man fell here, no companion in swind – in arms, bore him to the rear.

The man-catchers bore down on the passengers as they left the boat, the latter slowly but steadily driving them back. Old scoundrels, who had made emigrant-swindling a lifelong business, and were very much attached to it now, were knocked down and walked over every day by their stronger competitors; but, nothing daunted, they would be at their posts the following morning as determined as ever.

At length, when the strife subsided, and the assailants began to carry off their spoils, in the shape of innocent men, women, and children who had probably never seen a city before, James, seeing a man standing with his back towards him, clad in very shiny black, looking out on the river, made up his mind to ask him the way to the ticket-office. Thinking he must be some distinguished personage, James approached respectfully, and said, "Please, sir, will you be kind enough to direct me to the shipping-office? I am going to America."

The man turned towards him, and, if James O'Rourke had been a keen observer, he would have seen at once that a front view of the gentleman was hardly in keeping with the appearance he presented from behind. His face was very long and irregular, his mouth very wide – much wider than nature had intended it should be, as a deep, bluish scar on one side added considerably to its proportions. His eyes were very small and round, and seemed determined, through time, on making their way through his brain to the other side. His nose seemed to have met the same adverse fate as his mouth. It hung down in a heavy red bunch in front, owing, we think, to the part nearest the eyes being completely flattened, probably by some blunt instrument, as the doctors say. His forehead – well, that very important part of his head was concealed from view by an immense wide-brimmed hat, which had once been as shiny as his coat, but was now assuming an auburn hue. He wore his coat buttoned up close, a yellowish necktie, but no collar.

"My dear young fellow, hi shall be 'appy to direct you," said he, turning to James, on hearing his question. "Step this 'ere way a little." And he led him a few yards further away from the boat. "Hof course, you want to sail by the best line?"

"Certainly I do, sir," said James, after a little hesitation, "if it does not cost any more; for, to tell you the truth – "

"Not ha penny more than the leakiest hold tub as crosses the Atlantic. 'Ere his the name hof the ship; she sails to-morrow morning."

"Thank God!" thought James, delighted at the prospect of spending so little time in Liverpool.

Now, it so happened that the gentleman, in showing the notice to James, flaunted it a little too much, so that it caught the eyes of a number of disappointed man-catchers, who were standing here and there, looking very rapacious and sullen. In a moment they were upon them, pushing bills into James's hand, and each begging of him to put no trust in the others, but be guided by him. The old gentleman was pushed to the outside of the crowd in a moment, but his frantic warnings could be heard above all. One in his desperation caught him by the hand, and tried to pull it open, that he might leave his card there.

"Let me speak, for heaven's sake," said James.

"Yes, sir; yes, sir; say whatever you have to say, and come on with me," exclaimed half a dozen voices.

"I am going with none of you, blast you!" shouted James, dashing from their midst. "This gentleman," pointing to the man he had first spoken to, "has kindly consented to do all I want for me."

"All right, go with him; I wish you luck. You'll not get skinned. Oh! no," said the same voices.

"What do they mean by attacking a person in that way?" asked James of the other, who had taken his arm to lead him off.

"Ho! that's the way as they do things haround 'ere hin general," replied the other, pulling down his tie, which in the scuffle had got up around his ears. "You're ha fort'nate man to miss 'em."

"Please direct me to the office," said James, looking back at the crowd. "I'll leave Liverpool as soon as I can."

"Ho! you must not judge Liverpool by what you see 'ere this mornin'," said his companion. "When you see the place as I'll take ye to, your hopinion of the Hinglish 'ill change; but we'll go to the hoffice first."

They walked a long way along the docks, his companion still holding James by the arm, and pointing out all the places of interest to strangers – which, by the way, were chiefly high, old, dirty-looking stores, with broken doors and windows, outside of which sat groups of ill-clad, ill-favored looking men, black with smoke and grease; and an occasional large dray, pulled by huge, lazy horses – so lazy that you would want to be close by before knowing whether they were moving or not – was also an object of curiosity to James. At length they turned up a side street, walking over heaps of half-naked women and children at every step, till they reached a somewhat neat-looking building – neat only when contrasted with its neighbors – and entered an office on the ground floor. The only furniture of any kind it contained was a triangular desk of very doubtful material, and a fat, dull-eyed, middle-aged man of undoubted Saxon nationality. He was eating a lump of cheese, which he held in the palm of his hand, and did not seem to notice them as they entered.

"The best-'arted man in the world," whispered the guide.

James thought, if that were so, it had very little control over his manner; but he said nothing.

"How d'ye do, Mr. Bluffy?" said the other, approaching the desk. "I 'opes as yer well, sir."

"Well enough," was the reply. "Have you done anything to-day? I am afraid you're going in the back of the books here, Lantern."

"Why, 'ow is that, Mr. Bluffy?" said that gentleman, with a rueful look, which was his best look. "Han't hi hout hearly and late a watchin' and a strivin' for this 'ere company?"

"That may all be," said Bluffy, reaching for a pint of ale which a boy had just entered with, "but you an't doing anything."

Mr. Bluffy put the measure to his mouth and drained it to the last drop, smacked his lips, handed it back to the boy, and added: "There's where the mistake comes in."

"Do you call this 'ere nothin'?" said Mr. Lantern, pointing to James. "Hi took 'im from thirty on 'em; hi did that, Mr. Bluffy."

"Well, well," said the other, "a bob, and no more about it."

"Ho Mr. Bluffy, Mr. Bluffy!" And he put an old, torn red handkerchief, which came out of his pocket like a rope, to his eyes. "Hi earns it 'ard as hany man, hand why not" – a sob – "give me the same has hanother man?"

"You know the rules," said the other: "one bob for one, three bob for two, and so forth."

"Them 'ere rules is 'ard on a poor man," blubbered Lantern.

But looking towards James, and noticing he was not so shabbily clad as the majority of emigrants, he brightened up a little, and, approaching near to his patron, whispered a word in his ear. The latter let his heavy eyes fall on James, and said:

"All right, if it can be done."

"Come 'ere now, my young friend," said Lantern, "hand get yer ticket. "

James walked up to the desk.

"Give me the money," said the man behind it.

"How much is it, sir?" asked James anxiously.

"£5 15s." was the reply.

O'Rourke's face flushed a little. "I thought, sir," he said, "£5 10s. was the highest rate of passage?"

Bluffy looked at Lantern, and the latter quickly said:

"The hextra vive bob his for hextra accommodation. Mr. Bluffy, the best-'arted man in Hingland, says as 'ow you'll not be treated like hanother pas-senger."

"Oh! but I am satisfied to rough it with the rest," said James. "My funds are very low."

"All right," grunted Bluffy, "if you want to sleep up by the engine, and have the smoke and dirt blowing over you every night." And he began to make out the ticket.

"Young man, you're ha destroyin' of yourself. You may get blinded," whispered Lantern, clutching James by the arm. "Let me hadvise you, has a honest man as does fair by 'is fellow-man, to change your mind."

"I'll pay it, then," said James; "but it seems strange to charge more than the advertised rate."

"Your wisdom 'ill make yer fortin', young man," said Lantern, not heed-ing the latter part of the other's remark.

James paid the money, and turned away; but, as he did so, the corner of his eye caught Mr. Lantern picking up two of the very half-crowns he had paid, and thrusting them hurriedly into his pocket. He was about to make some remark, but, thinking it might be some money due him by the other, he merely sighed and wished himself out of Liverpool.

. . . .

If the streets presented a wretched appearance in daytime, they looked doubly so at night. They were literally filled with poverty and vice of the very worst kind. Beggars with awful-looking sores stood or lay in knots around the lamp-posts, frantically telling the wretched passers-by of their sufferings and pain. A blind or disabled musician of some kind, clad in rags, scraped or thumbed a miserable instrument before nearly every door. Drunken men and women rushed into the streets with yells, curses, and shouts of obscenity, occasionally stopping for a moment to dance to the wretched music, then hurrying on, trampling over the children and helpless.

Bad as his lodging-house was within, it was some relief to James to escape from such a scene. None of the other boarders had returned, and he requested to be shown to his bed. Mrs. Witles handed him a candle, and, pointing up the dingy old stairs, told him to push open the door of the first room he met, and lie down on any bed he chose. Of beds he had a noble choice. The room, which, by the way, was the entire floor, was so closely packed with beds that no one might attempt to walk from one side of the apartment to the other, except he stepped from bed to bed. James held the candle down between two beds, that he might see the floor; this was no easy task either, for it was covered to the depth of a couple of inches with dust and other dirt, all of which did not belong to the inanimate kingdom. He raised the candle and looked around the room, on the green and black walls, down which the rain had poured for years and years; and from the quantity of cobwebs which covered the ceiling – what of it remained – and the angles of the room, it was evident Mrs. Witles made very little use of her broom.

James, being very much exhausted from hardship and long want of sleep, selected a bed on the outer row, which looked as if it had not been occupied for some time, lay down on its edge, and soon fell asleep. How long he slept he knew not, till he was aroused by the noise of voices around him – loud, coarse voices – and, looking up, saw the same group he had met at dinner; some walking over the beds to reach their own on the far side, others crowding in at the door, and one and all in an advanced stage of intoxication.

Some were pale, sick, and sad; others were sentimental, who wept to themselves over past attachments in their own and other lands; a few were belligerent, and, assuming numerous fighting attitudes, boasted they were afraid of no man in "Hingland, without reference to the present company"; and the old soldier from whom Mrs. Witles snatched the lump of fat stood up on his bed, and screamed in a dismal, broken voice a verse of "Rule, Britannia!" By-and-by, all fell here and there on the beds, in different positions, and went to sleep. But so stifling was the atmosphere from the fumes of bad whisky that James went out on the landing, where he remained till daylight.

As soon as Mrs. Witles appeared, he paid her the amount of his bill, and went down to the docks to wait till the time for going aboard would arrive. Soon other emigrants, with packages and bundles of all kinds, began to assemble at the quay, and James went amongst such of them as he knew were from Ireland, and talked with them till the hour for starting came.

About mid-day, the ship weighed anchor, and steamed down the Mersey. James O'Rourke was not much of a philosopher; but, as he stood on deck, looking at the noble buildings which rose here and there on the Cheshire coast, and thought of what he had witnessed in Liverpool, he could not help thinking that a nation composed of two such extremes must one day break in the centre.

The passage down the Irish Sea was beautiful. James waited with great anxiety for their arrival at Queenstown, that he might, probably for the last time, feast his eyes on the hills and valleys of his native land. But to his great mortification, it was almost dark night when they entered the harbor. The day, even at sea, had been very warm, and with evening came lowering clouds and other signs of a storm. For a time, he stood on deck looking at the row of lights along the harbor, thinking of home and the base villany that had driven him thence; of Annie – what was she doing now? This was about the time they used to meet on the river's bank. Did she go there alone now, and sit and think of him, and remember him in her prayers, as she had promised to do? Was it beyond hope that they would ever meet again?

This thought sickened his heart so much that he leaned against the cabin-door, and turned his eyes away from the coast. A gruff officer, carrying a light, passed down the deck, and ordered him "to stand some place else." He went down to his berth, and, throwing himself on his face, wept til the ship was far out to sea.

James O'Rourke's First Day in New York – A Fraud and a Friend

After a comparatively safe and speedy passage, James O'Rourke reached New York. It was one of those mellow days in the early fall when everything looks so serene and calm that the anxious passengers were landed. How beautiful New York Harbor looked! The waters seemed asleep on the bosom of the bay, save where disturbed by the lively ferry-boats ploughing their way backwards and forwards in every direction, and the little snorting tugs, puffing in and out here and there, busy as bees of a June morning. A number of large, majestic-looking ships, that had just come in from all ports of the world, lay out in the stream, looking weary after their long voyage.

It being early day, the passengers were not delayed at Castle Garden overnight, except such as chose to wait for friends who were expecting them. James had no friends, and he walked into the streets and up along Broadway, wondering at the size, and beauty, and cheerful look of the buildings along that noble thoroughfare. It was at the time of day when Broadway is at its liveliest, lined with wagons, carriages, carts, and drays, and the sidewalk so crowded with people hurrying along that it is impossible for any of them to make much speed. James walked on – he knew not where – looking on himself as the most lonely and friendless of the great throng. At length he came to what seemed to him a neglected waste of ground, which, having mortally offended the city in some way, was left behind, forgotten, haggard, and cheerless. Near the centre of this waste stood a large building in a half-finished state, looking so dreary that the ill fate of the neighborhood seemed to have visited it at last.

A number of men were standing around the doors or sitting on the steps of the building, and all looking so much like men that had nothing to do, that James thought it might not inconvenience any of them much to tell him where he might find work. So approaching a gentleman with a wide-leafed straw hat, a tight-fitting coat, much too short for him, and very long, wide pantaloons, who stood on the end of a row picking his teeth, James asked:

"Please, sir, can you tell me where I may find employment? I am a stranger here."

"Most undoubtedly, sir; follow me," said the gentleman, putting his tooth-pick in his vest pocket. "Come along, sir."

James, delighted beyond measure at this sudden good luck, hurried after his new friend, but found it no very easy task to keep up with him. He had such a happy method of diving past crowds which jostled against the other that he had once or twice to wait for him on the corner. At length the gentleman swept into a low, narrow door in one of the side streets, and when James rushed in after him, he found him seated behind a neat little desk, looking as composed as if he had been sitting there since morning.

"So you want employment, do you?" said he, surveying James from head to foot.

"Yes, sir," replied the latter.

"What kind do you prefer?" said he, opening a book which lay on the desk before him. "We have a variety."

"Well, sir," replied James with a smile, "I am not afraid of any kind of work, but would of course prefer whichever pays best."

"Let me see," said the other, closing his eyes and resting his chin on his hand, "let me see. You are strong enough to work in a dry-goods store?"

"You mean, sir – "

"I mean what you call a cloth-shop in the Old Country."

"Oh yes; I beg your pardon, sir," said James, greatly elated. "Certainly I am, sir."

"You landed this morning, eh?" said the gentleman.

"This morning, sir."

"Any friends in New York?"

"No, sir."

"All alone, eh?"

"Quite so, sir."

"Well, now, sir, I'll tell you what I'll do. You give me three dollars, and I'll send you right up to the establishment."

James felt greatly surprised at this, for he really thought the gentleman was an extensive employer himself. He had never heard of an "intelligence office," and was quite at a loss what to think. He couldn't be a swindler, having such a handsome place.

"No; he *must* be an employer, and probably wants this money as security for a day or two, till he sees how I get on," thought James.

And looking at the gentleman again, and seeing him busy writing, and apparently utterly oblivious of his presence, he was confirmed in this latter idea.

"I'll pay the money, sir," said he, taking from his pocket a few shillings and one half-crown, which was his entire store.

The gentleman thought it most remarkable, but nevertheless it was true, that the coins when changed into dollars amounted to just the required number and ten cents over. So he swept it into a drawer, and, throwing a ten-cent stamp on the desk, drew a piece of paper to him, and, having written a few words on it with violet ink, handed it to James. The latter glanced at it and said:

"What way am I to go there, sir?"

"You see I am so busy, or I would take you up myself. But, anyway, all you have to do is to cross over five blocks to your right, then down a long street you'll see with a marble building on the up-town corner, then one block to your right, then take the cars – you know the street-cars – and ride eleven blocks more, and any one can point out Van Sleuthers & Duckey's dry-goods store to you. Go inside, and show them that address, and you're all right."

James thanked him, left the office, and went in search of Van Sleuthers & Duckey's.

That he did not find it, and that there was no such firm in the city, it is needless to say. He had been swindled out of the last penny by an "intelligence agent"; and after travelling up and down the streets, looking at every sign, stopping to make enquiries at every clothing establishment, he found himself at nightfall close by the East River, footsore, weary, and dejected. He sat down on a log on one of the docks, and, covering his eyes with his hands, began to think over his forlorn, desolate state.

In a large city, without a friend, without one face he had ever known, without a single penny in his pocket. Where to spend the night or get a morsel to eat he knew not; he had spent the ten cents riding up and down in search of Van Sleuthers & Duckey's. He sat a prey to these thoughts for some time, till, raising his head, he saw coming leisurely towards him, from the direction of the street, a man in his shirt-sleeves, smoking a large briar-wood pipe.

As he approached, James could see he was of his own race, and made up his mind to speak to him. This was no difficult matter, for the stranger came on, puffing like an engine, and, sitting down beside him, remarked it was a fine night.

O'Rourke saw at once, from his large, rough hands, that he belonged to the working-class, and, observing his neat white shirt and black tie, and everything he wore so clean, thought of the miserable appearance of the English working-men.

"You're not long out from the ould counthry, I think," said he kindly.

"No, indeed," said James. "I came ashore this morning."

"Well, well," said the man, moving close to him, "I am glad to see any one so late from the ould dart. How is things there now; anything better?"

"Oh much the same as usual," replied James. "Improvements come very slowly in Ireland."

"That's so, that's so, me friend," said the other, with a sigh. "But the people an't starving as they wor when I left there?"

"Not so bad as that now," said James.

"Do you live around here?" asked the stranger, after a pause.

"I have no home," said James, drawing back his head a little.

"No home," said the other, "and a greenhorn; why, that's rough. I suppose be that ye mane you haven't got any money neither."

"Not a penny," was the reply.

Then James told him how he had been cheated by the intelligence agent.

"You're not the first who has been fleeced by thim robbers," said the other in a rage. "They swindle dozens of poor innocent people every day, and you'll niver hear of one of thim bein' arristed. But," added he, checking himself, "it can't be helped now, and I'll niver see one of my countrymen that desarves it out in the streets at night while I have a room; so you must come wid me to-night. The ould woman 'ill find some place for you to sleep."

James thanked him again and again, and, after enjoying a smoke from his pipe, they walked up the dock and along the street a little way, till they came to a somewhat neat-looking brick house with a wooden stoop. The man entered, and both went up a flight of very clean but carpetless stairs to the third story, and, turning the knob of the door, entered a tidily furnished room of comfortable dimensions. Over the wooden mantel-piece hung a handsome engraving of Archbishop Hughes, side by side with another of St. Patrick, and on the opposite wall hung a picture of Killarney Lakes. Several other pictures, some of Irish clergy, some of American, were fastened round the walls, all very tastefully arranged.

There was no person in the room on their entrance, and the man, seeing James look closely at the archbishop's likeness, began to tell numerous stories of his kindness and benevolence. After some time, a woman came in, carrying a basket on her arm; and from the appearance of her face, and the trim, cleanly way in which she was clad, James knew at once whose taste had arranged the room.

"Well, well, Terence, and what a man you are," said she, laying down the basket, and looking at her husband with a smile, "to leave housekeeping."

"Oh! in troth, I was afraid she'd begin to screech whin ye'd be gone, Bridget, so I left her inside with Mrs. Kearney. She stays as quiet wid her as wid yourself," said her husband.

"Oh! just so; anything to get rid of the job. But keep quiet now; she's asleep in Mrs. Kearney's arms, and I'll bring her in and put her in the cradle."

The woman left the room, and soon returned, carrying in her arms a little babe of a few months old, and, shaking her hand at her husband to say nothing, lest he should rouse the infant, went through the passageway into another room.

The man conversed with James for awhile, then, telling him he'd be back in a moment, followed his wife. Both soon returned, and James could see from the kind, sympathetic look the woman gave him that her husband had been telling his story.

"Excuse me," said the man, "but ye haven't tould me yer name."

James told him.

"In troth, and a good name it is. My own is Terence McManus, and this is Mrs. McManus, and that sleepy youngster ye seen a minute ago is Mary McManus. So we know each other all roun' now, and are quite at our aise."

The agreeable, honest, good-natured manner of the man did make James feel much easier in mind than he had felt for some time. Mrs. McManus prepared a good meal, of which all three partook. This over, they sat together, and talked over matters in the old and new country. One important point to James came out from this conversation, and that was he learned that his host, who worked along the docks, being what is commonly called a 'longshoreman, would find him employment at the same business the following day.

. . . .

James O'Rourke's Experiences in a New York Menagerie

James O'Rourke continued to work along shore for several months, saving up all the money he could, and sending it to his father. He had written to Annie the day after his arrival, but, receiving word from Francis that she had gone to New York, tried by every possible means to learn her whereabouts in the city. He went to Castle Garden, hoping to receive some information in that very correct establishment; but no such name had been entered on the books about the time he mentioned. This he gleaned from a clerk after a day's delay – the very clerk to whom Annie had given her name. He even advertised in some of the daily papers, but without effect. When his hard day's work would be over, he went around to the houses of such as he had learned were from that part of Ireland, and requested them to make every enquiry; but months went by, and he heard nothing of Annie. The only conclusion he could arrive at was that she had gone on to some distant city.

This bitter disappointment weighed heavily on his mind. If she were in Ireland, where he might hear from her now and then, he would not have felt so heart-broken; but to know she had been and probably was in New York, that perhaps he saw the ship that carried her over coming into the harbor, and that every effort of his to see her or hear of her proved in vain, was painfully distressing.

Meanwhile, the class of people amongst whom he was thrown were not calculated much to improve his spirits. We do not mean by this his fellow-laborers, who were for the most part honest, hard-working men like Terence McManus. The latter had told James, when he first went to work, that he could board with him if he chose; but O'Rourke knowing, from the limited accommodation he possessed, that this offer was prompted only by goodness of heart, sought out another boarding-place – an act which he very soon after regretted.

This establishment stood in one of the side streets, directly over a beer-saloon. It consisted of three floors, divided into five or six rooms each, and served no fewer than fifty boarders. That these rooms were of small compass need not be told. Those which looked out on the street or into the yard in the rear were the largest, and contained two and three beds each. The middle bedrooms were of such small dimensions, and the doors leading into them were so narrow, that the beds they contained must have been built there. These were sometimes called the dark bedrooms – a most appropriate name; for, except the door is open or broken down, as sometimes happens, not a ray of light can enter them. We defy any man, even the most unimaginative, to sleep there one night without thinking of dungeons, skeletons, and ghosts.

All the floors were bare but clean, except where covered with tobacco-juice or the ashes of pipes. The beds – well, one of them would not be the most soothing place in the world for an ill-tempered man with the toothache. The straw or hay, or whatever it might be, had an obstinate habit of getting into hard, round lumps, which, if you tried to smooth down in one spot, instantly burst up in another. The first night a person sleeps on one of those beds he is sure to start up with the impression that some one is beating him about the ribs; and, to complete the comfort of the thing, the pillows are hard enough for the head and neck of any patriarch.

The kitchen was on the lowest floor in the rear, and so hot and fierce did it look from the front room that the most stout-hearted boarder never ventured to enter it during the warm weather.

The first evening James came to the establishment, the boarders were assembled at supper, and the lamp on the table burned very dimly. A first glance along the row of faces, and his heart sank as he thought of Liverpool; but when he was seated, and surveyed them more closely, he saw that every man had his hands and face washed. This must have taken considerable time; for James saw but one wash-stand in the hall, and one towel sewed together at the ends, which turned on a round piece of wood like a weaver's reeling-stick.

The boarding-mistress, Mrs. Grady, stood at a small, narrow table by the window, on which were placed two such large dishes of corned beef and soup that James wondered how they maintained their balance, busily engaged serving out their contents. On the table were pickles, radishes, tomatoes, onions, cheese, butter, and baker's bread in every variety of shape, but all in very small quantities, and so close together in the centre of the table that it must have required extraordinary exertions on the part of those at the ends to reach them at all.

Mrs. Grady's object in thus placing them may probably have been a very laudable one. Her husband, a small, weazen, crabbed-looking fellow, who was what is commonly called a "curbstone broker," or vagabond real-estate agent, always sat at the middle of the table, and she may have been determined to give him sufficient, no matter who wanted.

The swarm of flies on and around the table was something awful. Bread, butter, boarders' hands and arms, meat, soup, eyes, noses, and sometimes mouths were infested with them; and the increased hum they kept up seemed to prevent Mrs. Grady hearing any boarder who happened to want his plate replenished.

James felt nearly as much disgusted as he had been in Liverpool, and ate very little supper, hurried outside, and went down to the docks to catch a little fresh air from the river.

When he returned, the boarders were about to go to bed, and Mrs. Grady pointed out to James his bedfellow while he remained in the house: "A very nice, clean man," she explained. O'Rourke looked at his hollow, drunken eyes, and old, torn red shirt, and gravely doubted the good lady's recommendation.

James sat for some time at the window, looking at a wrangling crowd of Dutchmen outside the saloon, one of whom kept continually shouting, "Vat for you do mit das, ha? Vat for you do, ha? Vat for you, oder any man, in the city of Ni Yorik, dare exult me oder mine olt voomans?"

When he had roared himself hoarse, and no one appeared to show cause why himself or his wife should be insulted, he muttered a few drunken curses at a crowd of boys who had gathered around himself and his comrades, and staggered into the saloon again.

James left the window and went up-stairs to his room, which, by the way, was one of the dark bedrooms. As he approached the door, a faint light, dimly visible through the keyhole, attracted his attention. He pushed open the door, and there, lying on his back in the middle of the bed, with all his clothing, shoes included, on, was his new comrade, quietly smoking a long white pipe. James thought this a novel place to smoke in, but he merely threw the door open; for, from the close heat of the room and the fumes of the tobacco, the apartment was well-nigh suffocating.

He sat down on his trunk – the only seat, except the bed, in the room – and began taking off his shoes, hoping the smoker would leave the bed, that he might lie down. But, no; he lay there, lamenting the high price of liquor, and predicting the consequent ruin of the country, till his pipe was smoked down, when he turned over on his side, and, pulling a paper of tobacco from underneath the bolster, began to refill it, which having done, he dived after a match in his old, torn vest, lighted it on his thigh, and went on smoking as before.

James's patience was exhausted, and he said: "Do you intend smoking all night? If you do, you had better sit outside here, and let me lie down."

"Augh! the divil a bit hurry I am in to go to bed," said he. "Me and a couple more got a little bit tight around noon-time, and the boss sacked every man of us; so I am not goin' to work in the mornin'.".

"Well, I am not so," said James. "I want to go to bed. It wasn't on your account I spoke, I assure you."

The other kept silent, and smoked away.

"Stand up and leave that pipe away! I wonder how you can tolerate the smell of it yourself; I am sick half an hour ago."

"Arrah! take it aisy, can't ye?" said he. "I'll be through now in twenty minutes."

"Up with you to your feet!" exclaimed O'Rourke, losing all patience; and, catching him by the shoulder, he lifted him to his feet, and left him standing on the floor. "If I have the misfortune to be in the same room with you any more, I'd recommend you to quit smoking in bed."

"All right, I'll get square one of these days, me lad. I'm the ouldest boorther in this house, and ought to have the same privilege as any other man; but I'll get *square*. And he sat down so heavily on the other's trunk as almost to crack the lid.

"If you break my trunk, I'll *flatten* you," said James, as he searched for a peg to hang his clothes on.

"I want me rights," said the other, with a drunken leer, and raising his left shoulder to his ear.

"What rights?" asked James.

"The same as other men," he shouted, waving his hand toward the other rooms.

James looked out and saw at least a dozen boarders, some outside, some inside the bedclothes, while the smoke from their pipes was struggling desperately to escape through a broken pane.

He threw himself on the bed, and, having worked very hard that day, was soon asleep. Happening to wake up during the night, the first object that met his eyes was the red glare of his companion's pipe close by his face.

The next day he made enquiries after a new boarding-house; but, being told by his fellow-laborers that they were all alike, he made up his mind, in case every effort to find Annie failed, to leave New York.

Every effort in that direction did fail, as our readers know. So when the demand for workmen at the oil-fields in Pennsylvania came, James and a few others set out there.

PART III

The Third Generation:
Literature for a New Middle Class

The American literary world after 1875 was a battleground between advocates of idealizing, romantic fiction and those of the "new realism." Basically a New World version of British Victorianism, the "genteel tradition" in American letters called for the inculcation through literature of Christian morality, piety, and respectability. Its supporters argued that art ought to provide ideal models for conduct, and that certain themes, character types, and situations were potentially corrupting and thus improper. To a large extent, popular taste echoed these values. Toward the end of the century, adult best-sellers included a number of moralizing historical romances (*Ben Hur, Quo Vadis, The Prisoner of Zenda*) and books now considered children's classics (*Heidi, Treasure Island, Black Beauty*).

On the other hand, the realists argued, in the words of their champion, William Dean Howells, for "the simple, the natural, and the honest" as literary criteria. They indicted the Victorian values of the genteel tradition as distorted, hypocritical, constricting, and tyrannical, merely the expression of a worn-out romanticism and wholly unresponsive to the realities of American life – especially urban life. Fiction produced in the service of such values, it was argued, was crippled by clumsy didacticism and cloying sentimentality. Furthermore, the supporters of realism saw as undemocratic (and hence un-American) the preference for and deference to characters of wealth and high social standing in much genteel fiction, and they called for fiction about common people leading ordinary lives. Rooted in the honest provinciality of so-called "local color" writing (Sarah Orne Jewett's coastal Maine, George Washington Cable's Louisiana), realism became the province of most of the better writers in the last quarter of the century, including Howells, Henry James, Edith Wharton, and Kate Chopin. Subsequently, the realistic movement was extended in another direction by the naturalists, among them Stephen Crane, Frank Norris, and Theodore Dreiser, who aimed for scientific objectivity in rendering a deterministic vision of humanity – often in bleak, urban settings – as the powerless victim of instinct and environment.

Irish-American writers after 1875, the third literary generation, were actually second-generation Irish, because they were, in fact, the children of the Famine immigrants. Not surprisingly, many followed the dictates of the genteel tradition. After all, this new literary generation coincided with the emergence of an Irish-American middle class. Themselves charter members, many novelists consciously wrote for the audience of new Irish bourgeoisie and promulgated genteel values through their fiction. In addition, as we have seen, Irish-American fiction of the previous, Famine generation had been predominantly romantic, didactic, and sentimental, thereby providing precedents and models. Thus, the new romantic writers were the true heirs of Mrs. Sadlier, Father Quigley, and Peter McCorry, and the result of their labors was a second volley of propagandist fiction. There were quite a number of these writers. In the interests of space and compassion toward the reader, none of their fiction appears in this anthology. However, for anyone who wishes to explore further this ample and dreary vein, the essential figure is Maurice Francis Egan (1852-1924), whose dozen works of fiction mirror perfectly the Irish-American genteel mind in its nascent state.[1]

Also bolstering the romantic camp was Irish-American interest in the end-of-the-century cultural revival in Ireland, which was reinforced by the lecture tours of W. B. Yeats and Douglas Hyde. American editions of recently collected or translated folk tales, myths, and legends were published swiftly and sold well. Between 1889 and 1892, Yeats published a number of original literary essays in the Boston *Pilot* and the *Providence* (Rhode Island) *Journal.* Furthermore, some Irish Americans contributed directly to the revival. Dr. Robert Dwyer Joyce, an immigrant to Boston, wrote poetic versions of the legends of Deirdre and Blanid in the 1870s, and Wisconsin native Jeremiah Curtin visited Ireland, collected, and published three respected anthologies of Irish folklore in the nineties.[2] Also, as early as 1880, the New York Society for the Preservation of the Irish Language was sponsoring Gaelic concerts and language study, and after its Irish foundation in 1893, the Gaelic League began to sprout American branches almost immediately. To be sure, there were significant contributions here, and American support of these various projects was sincere. But it is also clear that the popularity of a misty,

1. See especially Maurice Francis Egan, *The Disappearance of John Longworthy* (Notre Dame: Office of the Ave Maria, 1890); *The Success of Patrick Desmond* (Notre Dame: Office of the Ave Maria, 1893); *The Vocation of Edward Conway* (New York: Benziger, 1896). An insightful study of these and other, better works is Paul Messbarger, *Fiction with a Parochial Purpose: Social Uses of American Catholic Literature,* 1884-1900 (Boston: Boston University Press, 1971). See also Fanning, *The Irish Voice in America,* 198-214.

2. Curtin's seminal works were *Myth and Folk-Lore of Ireland* (1890), *Hero Tales of Ireland* (1894), and *Tales of the Fairies and of the Ghost World* (1895). See Maureen Murphy, "Jeremiah Curtin: An American Pioneer in Irish Folklore," *Eire-Ireland* 13: 2 (1978), 93-103. Robert Dwyer Joyce, *Deirdre* (Boston: Roberts Brothers, 1876); *Blanid* (Boston: Roberts Brothers, 1879). William Butler Yeats, *Letters to the New Island* (Cambridge: Harvard University Press, 1970). See Philip L. Marcus, *Yeats and the Beginning of the Irish Renaissance* (Ithaca: Cornell University Press, 1970), 231-32, 257.

romantic "Celtic Twilight" vision of Irishness discouraged a realistic approach to Irish-American letters. Why read about the often unattractive situations of urban Irish Americans next door when one could dwell on picturesque tales of the fairy folk and mythic heroes from the old country, 3,000 miles and several centuries away?

Still and all, a significant number of Irish-American writers embraced the tenets of the realistic movement in various ways. These pioneers took the first hard look at the Irish immigrant and ethnic experience in America. By 1880 over a third of America's Irish-born citizens were living beyond the East Coast, and that significant dispersal is reflected in this generation's fiction. Notable writers began to appear as far afield as the Adirondacks, Chicago, Nebraska, and San Francisco.

A further measure of support for Irish-American realism came from the stage. Despite the prevalence of slapstick and stereotyping, the musical comedies of Edward Harrigan contained recognizable scenes from Irish urban life, as did the plays of second-generation-Irish dramatists Augustin Daly and James A. Herne. Especially influential here were the eight plays about the rise to respectability of the Mulligan family of New York City that Harrigan and his partner Tony Hart produced in the 1870s and 1880s.[3]

Finally, additional reinforcement for realism came from the example in the 1890s of several realistic works about Irish-American life by writers from the American literary mainstream. These included Brander Matthews (*Vignettes of Manhattan*, 1894), Sarah Orne Jewett (*A Native of Winby and Other Stories*, 1893), Harold Frederic (*The Return of the O'Mahony*, 1892, and *The Damnation of Theron Ware*, 1896), and Stephen Crane (*Maggie: A Girl of the Streets*, 1893, and his unfinished novel, *The O'Ruddy*, 1903).[4]

Part III of this anthology is a selection from the works of the realists, the most promising writers of the third nineteenth-century Irish-American literary generation. Henry Keenan's novel *The Aliens* (1886) describes the privations and prejudice endured by Famine immigrants to Rochester, New York. George H. Jessop's "The Rise and Fall of the 'Irish Aigle'" (1888) provides a rare perspective – Irish-American nationalism in San Francisco, observed humorously by the jaundiced eye of an Anglo-Irish Protestant. One of James W. Sullivan's *Tenement Tales of New York*, "Slob Murphy" (1895), details with stark power the short, disadvantaged life of a child of the slums. The ruthless advance in American urban politics of a canny young immigrant is concisely portrayed in a chapter from *Père Monnier's Ward* (1898) by William A. McDermott, who wrote under the pseudonym Walter Lecky. The classic

---

3. E. J. Kahn, Jr., *The Merry Partners: The Age and Stage of Harrigan and Hart* (New York: Harper & Row, 1955). Edward Harrigan's *The Mulligans* (New York: Dillingham, 1901) is a novel loosely fashioned of incidents from the Mulligan plays.

4. Of particular interest is a recent collection, Jack Morgan and Louis Renza, eds., *The Irish Stories of Sarah Orne Jewett* (Carbondale: Southern Illinois University Press, 1996).

opposition of Catholicism and Irish nationalism is dramatized in the climax to John Talbot Smith's *The Art of Disappearing* (1899). Kate McPhelim Cleary's "The Stepmother" (1901) is a moving story of a woman's painful experience in an Irish immigrant family on the bleak and lonely prairies of Nebraska. An Irish-American *Silas Lapham*, Katherine Conway's novel *Lalor's Maples* (1901) charts the material rise and moral fall of a Rochester builder's family by focusing on the house that symbolizes their success. *"The Exiles"* (1906) by Harvey J. O'Higgins describes the psychological cost of the difficult life of a New York Irish servant girl.

This book's final examples come from the first Irish voice of genius in American literature, that of Chicago journalist Finley Peter Dunne. Evoked vividly in weekly newspaper columns through the decade of the 1890s, Dunne's saloonkeeper/philosopher Martin J. Dooley made a lasting contribution to social history and literary realism.[5] The depiction here of the Chicago Irish working-class community was a pioneering example of the potential for serious fiction of common speech and the common life of immigrants. Mr. Dooley's clientele of millworkers and teamsters, streetcar drivers and firemen, have memorable depth and dignity. Dunne's body of work constitutes the coming of age of Irish-American fiction. He has given us the great nineteenth-century ethnic novel – in weekly installments.

5. See Charles Fanning, "Mr. Dooley Reconsidered: Community Memory, Journalism, and the Oral Tradition," in Ellen Skerrett, ed., *At the Crossroads: Old St. Patrick's and the Chicago Irish* (Chicago: Loyola University Press, 1997), 69-83; Finley Peter Dunne, *Mr. Dooley and the Chicago Irish: The Autobiography of an American Ethnic Neighborhood*, edited by Charles Fanning (Washington, D.C.: The Catholic University of America Press, 1987); and Charles Fanning, *Finley Peter Dunne and Mr. Dooley: The Chicago Years* (Lexington: University Press of Kentucky, 1978).

The Aliens. A Novel

by Henry F. Keenan (New York: Appleton, 1886)

Henry Francis Keenan was born into a poor Irish family in Rochester, New York, in 1849. He grew up there, went off to the Civil War as a private, and returned to become a journalist on the Rochester Chronicle. *Around 1870 he moved to New York City to pursue his career on the* New York Tribune. *Between 1883 and 1888, Keenan worked full-time as a novelist, producing four books, of which* The Aliens *was the third, and the only one that drew directly on his own family's immigrant background. None of these novels made money, and Keenan returned to newspaper work. Subsequently, he wrote one more novel,* The Iron Game *(1891), based on his own Civil War experiences, and a popularized history,* The Conflict with Spain *(1898). A few of his letters survive, and they reveal him to have been bitterly disappointed in his failure to succeed as a writer. Keenan died, virtually forgotten, in Washington, D.C., in 1928.*

Based on the experience of the generations of Rochester Irish represented by Keenan's parents and grandparents, The Aliens *tells the story of the Boyne family, who arrive in "Warchester" from Belfast sometime in the 1830s. At the outset, Hugh Boyne distinguishes himself before the dockside crowd by rescuing his son Denny and the son of Mayor Warchester from drowning. At the mayor's home that evening, a discussion of the immigration "problem" ensues. Prevalent Irish and German stereotypes emerge and most of the guests favor immigration restriction, although Governor Darcy, himself of Irish descent, refutes them: "If our ancestors had been of your mind, I should have been toiling in the bogs of Kerry to-day."*

Keenan himself is guilty of stereotyping in his presentation of the opposing fates of the German Ritters and Irish Boynes. Blessed with "a servility born in the bone and bred in the long life of emphasized class distinction," the Ritters settle stolidly into the American scene. On the other hand, because he is a Celt ("None so faithful when trust is given them; none so rancorous when doubt is instilled"), Hugh Boyne drinks up his stake and disappears. His wife Kate ruins her health under the strain of trying to keep the family together. Northern Irish religious discord also plays a part in the tragedy. Recalling that Kate had brought the contamination of Catholicism into the Protestant Boyne family, Hugh's brother James, well-settled in Warchester, heartlessly evicts his sister-in-law and her children. They end up in the almshouse, where Kate goes mad and dies at the age of thirty.

181

In the two excerpts printed here, the orphaned Denny Boyne and his sister Norah are being brought up by the kindly Dr. Marbury. The presentation of Denny's school days reveals the trials of being a "Paddy-boy" in the public schools of the late 1830s and 1840s. Mitigated somewhat by the friendship of Dilly Dane, the fair-minded daughter of a rich Yankee farmer, Denny's sufferings nonetheless result in his acceptance of "alien" status at an end-of-term party in the schoolhouse.

There is no dearth of additional incident in this novel's tangled narrative. Denny Boyne enlists for the Mexican War, and goes through the Vera Cruz campaign with General Scott. Then, in a preposterous dénouement, Hugh Boyne returns to Warchester as a wealthy adventurer, thus clearing the way for his penniless son to marry Dilly Dane. The one strength of The Aliens, *though, is its presentation of the anti-Irish climate in upstate New York in the period before 1850.*

[Denny Boyne's school days, as told by himself]

"Then the dear home life! The gardens, gay with holly-hocks, dahlias, and a hundred other simple blossoms; the groups of nodding sunflowers behind the dairy windows, whose heads turning to the sun we watched with solemn wonder; the four-o'clocks, whose regularly closing petals excited our awe; the lustrous currant-hedges, where, like young Bacchuses, we gorged the luscious berries; the wonder of wonders, the 'Jack and Jill' brook, that comes from ever so far off in the West, and was lost in the Alleghany Mountains. Who shall count the joys of these fairy realities to us, at a time when the mind was plastic and the habit of doubt was not known? I learned that brook by heart – miles of it, I mean – from the great pond over beyond the school-house, where the black snakes lay coiled in the sun, to the cavernous gap far below, where it branched off southeastward. I knew every sylvan secret of the Marbury meadows before the year was out, though I never shirked my chores, nor missed the school tasks. I haven't spoken of my little bedfellow, the grandson of Dr. Marbury. He was one year older than I. His mother had died the year before, and his father had left him with his grandmother. The boy was an affectionate little fellow, and we got on with but few wrangles, and these, I think, were generally my fault, though I didn't think so in those days. Sometimes he would return from a visit to his cousins, who lived in the city, and so soon after these as he happened to fall out with me he would run off a safe distance and call me 'Paddy!'

"Now, I had been tortured by this nickname at school; whenever the boys had a quarrel with me, they poured wormwood on my sensitive wounds by calling me this ignominious term, indicating Irish: and in those days to say that meant to embody the race most contemned of all the aliens settling the country. I couldn't understand the reproach, or why Irish was so repulsive or intolerable, but it became my horror by day and my torture by night. Once, hearing Mrs. Marbury alluding to some one who had offended her in the neighborhood as a 'good-for-nothing Irishman!' I grew quite white with suf-focation as I turned and asked her:

"'Aunt Selina, why is it low and wicked to be Irish?' She was sitting in her high-backed arm-chair knitting, the sunlight falling over her shoulder, and framing her kind old wrinkled face in such peace as you may see in some Flemish portraits. She dropped her knitting on her knees and looked down at me below her spectacles. Norah was standing in the pantry-door, and Byron – Aunt Selina's grandson – stopped spinning a top, with which he had been disturbing the afternoon dreams of a lion-like cat that remonstrated with him from time to time by a sharp gruff noise like a growl, and a slap with the flat of her paw, very like a human stroke.

"'Why, Denis, child, come here.' As I sank at her knees, hiding my face, she patted me on the head, and said gently:

"'My child, I was wrong to make use of that word in that way. It is not low and wicked to be Irish, but people have come to look on all who are low and wicked as Irish. It is wrong, no doubt. Indeed, it must be wrong, for my grandfather was an Irishman, and my son's wife was Irish. But generally, since the canal came through the country, people have associated ignorance and lawlessness with the gangs that dug the canal, and most of them were Irish. When your comrades call you Irish, you mustn't mind it; they don't know themselves what they mean, and, if it were not that, it would be some-thing else.'

"I was soothed, but not satisfied, with this specious explanation; and the next time I was called Paddy I gave my tormentor such a thrashing that the affair came up in the class-room. The teacher heard the story, and, when it was ended, said grimly:

"'Well, Denis, I don't see why you object so fiercely to being called Irish: you are Irish. Of course you can't help it, nor can any one help calling you what you are, especially when you act so like an Irishman as to black the eyes and bruise the body of one of your playmates.'

"It was thus officially proclaimed that my race was a disgrace. During the years that I remained in Marbury, 'Paddy' was the name I was known by, and I found it better to answer good-naturedly than resent it. I should not have been so easily reconciled, had it not been for a scene that happened one day at the end of the third summer term, when I was in my eleventh year. The whole family had attended the closing exercises, when Denis Boyne was called up to receive two prizes in scholarship and one prize for conduct, and was loudly applauded for a recitation by the visitors. Norah was very proud, and talked of her brother all the way home, and you may be sure that young fellow didn't suffer much on finding everybody praising him. At supper-table my dear Doctor, looking kindly at me through his great round goggles, that at first made me laugh when I looked at him, said, in his cheery, benignant tone:

"'Who knows, mother, perhaps our little Paddy may be a great man some day – President or Governor: Jackson is an Irishman.'

"It was too much to have the hateful name and reproach brought against me in the glory of my triumph. It was more than my excited mind could bear. I choked over the mouthful I was swallowing, and, with a bursting heart, bolted from the table, and, flying madly to the spot where the plantains were high and thick, I flung myself prone on the ground in a passionate outburst of misery. Norah came out presently and called me, but I never answered. It was nearly time for my evening work, and I was thinking miserably of facing the rest, when Aunt Selina came upon me from the currant-bushes. She patted me gently on the head, and rather made me ashamed of my foolish griefs. That night, when I was sneaking off to bed – (in those days we all went to bed by twilight; I never remember a candle lighted in summer, and I never had a light to go to bed with even in winter; such indulgence being regarded as an effeminizing luxury) – as I was sneaking off to bed, the kind Doctor came out after me, and said, with something very like sternness:

"'My boy, you must get over this silly shame about your origin. It is not what a man is called, or what he is born, or what his fathers were, that make him either good, or useful, or to be admired or hated. You must learn to look upon men just as though they were all cut from the same piece, and were worth just what they made themselves worth; or, like your figures in arithmetic, of value only as they take place in a column. It doesn't make you one bit better or worse to be Irish, German, or French. In the days of the Romans, all the world, not born in Rome, were barbarians. But we aren't people of their lordly ways. When I was a college boy in Baltimore, I was made miserable by being pointed out as a Yankee, while the most arrogant spirits in the town were the descendants of the Irish, who had been great families when the English ruled the province.'

"I can't say that the Doctor's philosophizing eased my anguish, or that I bore the taunt with equanimity until many a year after, when I came to comprehend and estimate at its just value the vulgar prejudice against the Celt as a citizen in the New World. But I redoubled my work, determined to employ all my faculties to make such a man of myself that my race should be no reproach to me. Events soon came to pass that changed the current of my existence, and altered the shaping factors in my career; and, please God, though I have endured sorrows since, it has never been for any act of mine that could be justly called disgraceful or unworthy. But, as I look back upon those years, I sometimes wonder that my heart wasn't wholly hardened, and that I didn't become the outcast and reprobate that the harsh and thoughtless, who had much to do with me, prophesied. For I think now that, though I was an affectionate and tractable child, I was difficult to govern, for mischief was as natural to me as the brogue to Donnegal. That I didn't fulfill those dark predictions was, under the good God, the wondrous chance that gave me the friendship and, finally, love of a being so rare and pure and perfect that I shrink from even naming her at this miserable epoch of my life.

"My first days at school were marked by the trials and anguish inseparable to an introduction to companions of one's own age. Shy, and, when not shy, reckless to the utmost limits of impudence, the Irish in me was a wellspring of malicious pranks and tests on the part of my comrades. One day, when they had exhausted every other artifice to worry me, it was proposed that I should kiss all the girls when the school closed, under penalty of being dragged in the mill-pond. Now, this pond, which spread to limits of fascinating terror to me, far away among the gloomy swamps, was filled on warm afternoons with monstrous water-snakes – the very sight of which to this day turns the marrow in my bones to ice. It was agreed that the boys should hold certain girls near the gate and that 'Paddy' should 'smack' each one loud enough to be heard by the whole band. Sure enough, when the teacher had disappeared, as the girls came trooping out a dozen of them were caught, and I was ordered to do my duty. To tell the truth, I didn't mind the matter very much, as most of the girls had shown me profound disdain and contempt. But, as I was thrust forward by two stalwart young ruffians, and the girls, who had made but little objection to the other lads seizing them, began to rain down blows on my bare head for my presumption, the fun was too good for the leaders to give up at once, and they kept me at it, blinded, scratched, and now angrily struggling to be released. But the more I was buffeted the more in earnest the rest became, and it was resolved that, as I had not succeeded in kissing one girl, I should be flung into the pond at the roots of the willows, where the snakes were biggest and always sure to be found. I was bleeding and helpless, and unable to kick at my tormentors as they dragged me over the sand and sod to the water's edge. Some of the girls became compassionate at this, and cried out against it.

"'Pshaw! it'll do him good; they don't have snakes in Ireland,' cried the leader of the merry-makers, Arthur Kennel.

"The pond was across a wide field from the school-ground, and they dragged me along, shrieking. Once I must have fainted, for, when I became conscious, I was lying quite unmolested on the ground, the boys staring at me in a sort of fright. As I opened my eyes slowly, Arthur exclaimed:

"'Oh, fudge, he's only shamming: these Irish are coons for tricks. Heave him along. I can see the snakes uncoiling to welcome him.'

"O my God! the horror of that moment. I sprang at the nearest boy and buried my teeth deep in his cheek; a hand came near me: I think I must have bitten a finger quite to the bone. I was mad with fear and rage – principally fear – and, before they bore me down by force of numbers, three of them were howling with pain and quite bloody. I was blinded with blood, and I never knew how they got to the edge of the water. Here I had regained strength, and made another fight; but Arthur, by a sharp welt across my eyes with his satchel-strap, quite blinded me, and I lay on the ground kicking and striking out in an agony of horror. They were too tired to resume for the moment, and I had just time to catch a glimpse of great monstrous coils of scaly serpents wound around the limbs of the willows that grew perhaps ten feet from the water's edge. Then I yelled, 'Murder!' but Kennel and another boy, throwing themselves on me, stuffed a handkerchief in my mouth. My terror now gave zest to the purpose, and they seized me again by the shoulders and feet, a boy holding each arm. Then, as we reached the water's edge, Kennel said suddenly:

"'Paddy, can you swim?'

"I thought they were going to relent, and I clutched at the chance of escape. I told a lie.

"'No, I can't.'

"'So much the better. But you're too foxy, Paddy. I saw you swim down at the Devil's Pool. You can't fool me, Irishy!'

"Then, before I realized his purpose, my arms were strapped under me, and the rest halted to take breath before flinging me in. I held them at bay with my legs, kicking viciously, and squirming around in the soft soil until I could feel even my skin, through the clothes, wet and muddy. They threw themselves on me, however, and were lifting me for the plunge, when a terrified voice said:

"'Why, boys, what are you doing?'

"They turned, and some of them relinquished their hold. I looked eagerly. It was Cordelia Dane, the daughter of the Deacon, one of the rich farmers of the country.

"'Ah, Dilly, you're just in time for the fun. We're going to throw Paddy in among the snakes; he never saw any in Ireland, and we want him to see what we've got in this country.'

"'But what has he done to you? It is very cruel. He is bleeding and hurt,' and she came nearer to me and shuddered as she saw the plight I was in.

"'It's all perfectly fair, Dilly,' Arthur Kennel said, 'We'll leave it to you. We gave him his choice: kiss the girls or be ducked. He wouldn't, or couldn't, and we must keep our word. If he had kissed one girl we would have let him off. Wouldn't we, boys?' asked Arthur, winking at the others.

"'Oh, of course,' they chimed in.

"'You are wicked and dreadful boys, and I shall tell the teacher of you,' she said hotly. 'You're cowards: all of you against one. Go away; let the poor boy go home.'

"She came quite close to me now, where I sat on the ground, all sense of danger quite gone, and lost in wonder at the interposition of this, the most timid and shrinking girl in the classes; for, though I had seen and sat near her on the benches, she had never noticed me nor did I dare speak to her. She bent down and tried to loosen the strap, but it was tied with a cord.

"'Come, come, Dilly, we're bound to have our way. This is no place for girls; go home and tell the teacher that we've given the Irishman a bath. He needs it, doesn't he?' and Arthur pushed her roughly from me, while the rest laughed.

"'You say you'll let him go if he – he – kisses one girl?' She blushed scarlet. The boys gathered near with grinning curiosity.

"'Yes, if he'll kiss a girl we'll let him scoot. What do you say, boys?' and Arthur looked at the rest.

"'Agreed!'

"She came to where I sat, and bent down until her rosy cheek was quite at my lips, and said:

"'Denis, kiss me.'

"I touched the soft flesh timidly as Aladdin the hand of the princess.

"'But the bargain was that it was to be a "smack" that we all could hear. No one heard that.'

"'Yes, that's so, a smack, a smack, or no fair,' was the unanimous shout.

"Dilly looked from one to the other in gentle entreaty; but the young cannibals were remorseless. She came close to me again, and as she did so I saw the handle of a short case-knife in her dinner-basket. Though my arms were tied, my hands were free, and I seized this quick as a flash. In a second I had cut the strap and was free.

"'God bless you, Dilly!' I said; 'but I won't let you do that again for me, to please vagabonds like these. – Now,' I said, 'if you want to throw me into the water, come on!'

"They saw the knife; it had been ground down, and came to a sharp point; it would have been a dangerous weapon in determined hands. Then they slunk away, and we were left alone. They kept up jeers and taunts until they were out of sight. I was afraid to go near the water to wash myself, for I thought the great limbs were snakes. I was too shy to speak to the little maid; I walked along behind her. She never said a word, but once, as I caught up with her, she silently handed me her handkerchief to wipe the blood from my face. I was too abashed to take it, and shook my head. We walked to the forks of the road together, nearly half-way to the Doctor's, and never a word was spoken. The bobolinks were singing on the rail-fences, the red kingbirds fluttering in the elders, and she seemed to be intent only in watching and listening to the pleasant summer sounds. I knew a spot by the brook that crossed the road where violets and yellow cowslips grew, and I noticed that the girls had little bunches of these on their desks, and sometimes gathered them for the teacher. As she walked on ahead of me, I furtively plucked a pretty handful of these, and, as we reached the parting where she turned to the right, trembling with shame, I came silently to her side and held them out. She blushed prettily as she took them, and said:

"'Thank you, Denis Boyne; I think you're a very good boy.'

"I stood rooted to the spot as she walked away, and glowing with wonder and admiration, as she turned, after she had gone a little way, and looked back. All the way home the bobolinks kept saying:

"'Good boy, Denis Boyne; good boy, Denis Boyne,' until I thought that the birds knew me, and knew what was in my heart."

[At the end of the academic term, a party is being held in the schoolhouse.]

Watchful eyes were upon him, and if he but raised his trembling glance to the tender little maid there were buzzing comments and tattling to the Deacon's family. Too proud to complain, and too mindful of Dilly's comfort to resent this, he never made known to her by word of mouth the conduct he was pursuing. But he knew that she understood it, for once, when the boys were formed in two ranks and the girls had to "pass the gauntlet," as it was called, she gave him an adorable smile as he fell out of line and refused to claim his right to kiss her, as the game provided. Poor Denny was so cowed by the persistent malevolence of his companions, boy and girl, that he never supposed for a moment that Dilly had any other feeling for him than pity. How could it be different?

How could she care for one whom all her associates reviled? How could a native care for an alien — an Irish alien at that? Wasn't the burden of it in his ears every play-hour? If he were admitted to the boyish sports, wasn't there always a sort of contemptuous toleration? When the play-houses were made among the recesses of the "huckleberry" swamp behind the school, where the blackbirds kept up such a saucy protesting chatter, wasn't he always excluded, after he had torn his flesh and frayed his garments in climbing the birch-trees for the fragant limbs to adorn these sylvan bowers? None of the girls would admit to him as a member of the little households, and he was left alone in the triumph of his elfin edifice.

Childish woes, you say! I doubt if the Napoleons felt half as bitterly the refusal of the royal families to bestow their daughters on the parvenu empire, as Denny when the Marbury boys and girls declined to take part with him in those youthful travesties of housekeeping. But persistent as this deconsideration was, it didn't sour his temper. He was the merriest of the group. His wit was quick, his temper hot, his diligence untiring, his purpose unconquerable. He meant to lead all his classes, and he did it. He meant to lead in all games of skill, and he did. He was the swiftest runner in all the township. He could climb trees that made the other boys dizzy. In the water he was fearless as a duck — if there were no snakes about. Nature he read in all her varying pages by a sort of intuition. He knew where all manner of birds were to be found. He could point out the storehouses of half the squirrels that scampered over the Marbury fences. He could supply wild honey at an hour's notice for the school picnics. He wasn't fond of gunning or fishing, and was well hated by the others for that. Poor lad! he needed all these compensations to counter-poise the burdens of his daily life. He was a tall boy now in his last teens, but his mind was as simple as when he trudged over the hills with Kate.

Darcy Warchester was but a year or two older than Denny, but his min-gling with the world, his repose and self-confidence, made him appear three or four years older. It was the last term Denny was to attend the Marbury School. There was nothing more for him to learn. Indeed, he had long ago exhausted the simple course of the curriculum, and this last winter, in return for desultory glimpses of French, he had relieved the teacher of all the ele-mentary classes. Oswald, in return for hints in woodcraft, had lent him German text-books, and helped him in the acquirement of his soft Saxon pro-nunciation. The term, which ended in April, wound up with an evening party at the school-house. The event was very gay. All the families of the township came in cutters, for in those days winter lingered in severity far into May.

There were to be games, and a modest feast was to be set on the desks, which had been made into long tables running through the middle of the school-house. The windows were festooned with spruce-branches and holly-berries, and the rostrum was turned into a fairy bower. Some of the young men brought fiddles and a flute, and there was an attempt at dancing, which was but feebly supported, and collapsed with a very dispirited Virginia reel. The diversions of the evening tended to games in which there was a good deal of kissing. Norah and Denny sat in the background, taking no part. They did not feel at all neglected, for they had come to regard themselves very much as the colored aliens of the South. They were set apart by the crime of their birth, and were quite content to be permitted to see the gayeties of their bet-ters, without being part of them. Once during the evening Dilly Dane, who had been behind the green bushes on the rostrum, found herself without a partner, or "beau," as it was the simple fashion to call the masculine play-mates in those days. All the rest of the girls were seated in rows, with the indispensable "beau," and, as Dilly's name was called, she came down to select her partner. But all were taken. She looked about, and, seeing Denny, hesitated and blushed.

"Oh, take Paddy, Dil; he'll do for the game, and I'll do the kissing," said young Orlando Gates, a neighbor's son.

A general titter followed this, and everybody looked curiously at the blushing girl. She raised her head with a flash of defiance in her kindly, seri-ous eye, and, walking down the aisle made by the boys and girls, stopped before Denny and held out her hand. Denny was quaking like a leaf in a March wind. His head fairly reeled, and he sat quite immovable.

"Come, come, Paddy. It's bad manners to keep a lady waiting," called out one of the boys maliciously; and then everybody tittered, the elders grinning discreetly.

"Go, Denny," whispered Norah.

He got up trembling and walked very much abashed to the vacant place reserved for the two, and never opened his lips to his partner. When the kissing came he turned his head away, and when the game was ended led Dilly back to her seat, under a merciless fusilade of jeers and cat-calls. The elders did not remain for the last of the frolics, and most of the young people were left in charge of neighbors who lived near the school. It was midnight when the lights were put out and the revelers packed themselves into the sleighs. Norah drove off with a neighbor from the farm-house next below the Doctor's, and Denny trudged off on foot.

The Rise and Fall of "The Irish Aigle"

by George H. Jessop, *Century Magazine* 15 (December 1888)

This story provides new ideological and geographical perspectives on the later nine-teenth-century Irish-American mind. It was written by a member of the Irish Protestant Ascendancy who made his way to the American West – to San Francisco. Born in the manor house at Dury Hall, County Longford, George Jessop studied law and letters at Trinity College, Dublin, and began a literary career by contributing to the London mag-azines. In 1872 he arrived in California, where he soon got work writing for the Overland Monthly, *which had been founded in 1868 by Bret Harte. He then edited a newspaper called* The National, *probably the model for* The Irish Eagle *in this story, and he went on to become editor of the humorous periodical* Judge *in the mid-1880s. Published in the* Century *in 1888 and 1889, Jessop's Gerald Ffrench stories were popular enough to be collected as* Gerald Ffrench's Friends *in 1889. His pref-ace explains that "all the incidents related in this book are based on fact, and several of them are mere transcripts from actual life. . . . The purpose is to depict a few of the most characteristic types of the native Celt of the original stock, as yet unmixed in blood, but modified by new surroundings and a different civilization."*

Jessop also wrote plays and two novels, Where the Shamrock Grows *(1911), and* Desmond O'Connor *(1914). He died in England in 1915.*

Set in San Francisco in 1874, "The Irish Aigle" is typical of the stories involving Gerald Ffrench, a young Protestant Irish journalist obviously modeled on Jessop him-self. Down on his luck, Ffrench agrees to edit The Irish Eagle, *a nationalist newspa-per founded by a group of garrulous Irish-American "patriots." Jessop uses the story to satirize their ignorance, pompous and windy rhetoric, obsession with the past, excessive drinking, and facile support of violence – as long as it takes place six thousand miles away. The succeeding Gerald Ffrench stories are similarly critical of the Irish Catholic immigrants in San Francisco, but on lesser grounds than those apparent in this tale. The Boston* Pilot *roundly condemned Jessop's stories as presenting a distorted view of the American Irish.*

Mr. Martin Doyle, Mr. Andrew Cummiskey, Mr. Peter O'Rourke, Mr. Frank Brady, and Mr. James Foley were seated in the private snuggery behind Mr. Matthew McKeon's sample room on Washington street, San Francisco. It was late in the evening of Thanksgiving Day, 1874, and these gentlemen had met by appointment to discuss a very serious and important matter of business. The apartment was small and its atmosphere was changing into a pale blue haze. This was due to Mr. McKeon's cigars, one of which was wielded by each of the party. From the saloon outside muffled sounds of holiday revelry stole in, swelling into positive uproar when the host opened the door, which he did every ten or fifteen minutes, to put in his head to inquire if "the jintlemen wanted anything." To each of these appeals Mr. Martin Doyle made the same reply: "Nothin', Mat, nothin'; we're here for business, not for dhrink." And the door was closed again.

The truth was that all five were patriots of the most advanced type, and had met to determine upon the best means of freeing old Ireland from the bloody and tyrannical yoke of the Saxon oppressor. It is true that "opprissor" was the word used in their frequent repetition of this formula, but the meaning was the same.

In spite of the periodical refusal of McKeon's offers of refreshment the table round which they were seated was fairly furnished with drinkables: perhaps this circumstance emboldened them to decline further supplies. Messrs. Cummiskey, Brady, O'Rourke, and Foley paid attention to a portly bottle of Kinnahan's L. L., the contents of which they qualified in varying proportions with hot water, lemon, and sugar. Mr. Doyle's tastes had become so vitiated by long residence in America as to lead him to prefer simple Bourbon whisky; but, this detail apart, he was as true an Irishman still as on the day, now some twenty-five years ago, when, a lank, ungainly boy, he had entered Tapscott's office in Liverpool and engaged passage for the land of promise. Indeed, it was Mr. Doyle who had called the present meeting together.

By 10 o'clock the bottles were almost empty and the cigar smoke had grown so dense that the mild features of Robert Emmet, who stood in all the glory of green uniform and waved a feathered hat exultantly from an engraving above Mr. Foley's head, could scarcely be distinguished. Mr. Martin Doyle's notable scheme had been thoroughly discussed in all its details, and the proud projector arose somewhat unsteadily.

"Fri'nds and fellow-countrymen," he began, "the death knell of Saxon opprission has nearly sthruck. Ye can come in, Mat," – this to Mr. McKeon, whose head appeared in the doorway, – "ye can come in; we've most finished, an' we 'll be havin' a dock a dorrish prisintly. Well, as I was sayin', the Saxon opprissor –"

"To —wid him!" broke in Foley impulsively, and the rest of the company contributed a deep voiced "Amin!"

"Misther Foley, and jintlemen," expostulated the speaker, "I have the flure. We're agreed, I belave, that the pin is mightier nor the sword. All in favor of that proposition will signify their assint by sayin' 'Aye.' Contrary minded, 'No.' The ayes have it, and it is so orthered. Therefore, jintlemen, we bein' prisint here this night do agree each to conthribute the sum of wan hunthred dollars, bein' five hunthred dollars in all, to defray the immejit expinses of startin' a wakely journal, the same to be called 'The Irish Aigle.'"

Enthusiastic cheers drowned the speaker's voice. He smiled, answered a pantomimic suggestion of McKeon's with a nod, and, draining the glass which the host handed to him, proceeded.

"We five jintlemen here prisint, havin' the cause of an opprissed people at heart, do hereby resolve ourselves into a thryumvirate to solicit further conthributions from local pathriots, an' such aid in the way of advertisements an' subscriptions as we may be able to secure. All in favor of this plan will signify the same by sayin' 'Aye.' Contrary minded, 'No.' The ayes have it, and it is so orthered. Mr. Foley, Mr. O'Rourke, Mr. Brady, Mr. Cummiskey and me unworthy silf, as members of the Thryumvirate, will git to work. Long life and success to 'The Irish Aigle'!"

As soon as the toast had been duly honored, Mr. Cummiskey took McKeon aside and pointed out to him the immense advantage he would reap from advertising his saloon in the new organ. The representation which appeared to have most weight with the liquor dealer lay in these words:

"Ye see, Mike, the offices of 'The Aigle' will be only three dures from you and sivin from Jerry McManus. Now, ye know yersilf pathriotism is dhry work, and McManus knows it too."

On the strength of this argument the astute Mr. Cummiskey booked a ten-dollar "ad" on the spot, and laid the foundation of that generous rivalry between the two saloon keepers which afterwards became such an important factor in the well-being of "The Irish Eagle."

The preliminary work of engaging a suitable office and hiring type was undertaken by Mr. Doyle and was executed, as the legend in his own shoestore set forth, "with promptness and dispatch." Two weeks afterwards the first number of the new paper was for sale on the newsstands, glorious with a rampant eagle flaunting a Celtic motto from its beak. The reading matter was largely made up of patriotic poems and clippings from other journals of the same way of thinking, but the editorial page was original – thoroughly, unquestionably original. The united wisdom of the Thryumvirate had been expended on that effort. There breathed the fiery utterances of Cummiskey, the butter-seller; there sparkled the neat epigram of O'Rourke, the truckman; there were set forth the lucid arguments of Foley, the tanner; there the reader might trace the sportive fancies of Brady, the bookbinder; and the whole bore witness to the massive genius of Martin Doyle, the shoemaker. It was a great number, and its appearance was duly celebrated at McKeon's by the Thryumvirate, resolved for the moment into a mutual admiration society.

At this meeting a new arrangement was made. The paper should be edited, not by the whole committee acting as a body, but by the individual members holding office in rotation. The five issues succeeding the first came out in this way, and lost nothing in originality even if they suffered in variety.

Peter O'Rourke began the series and Frank Brady brought up the rear. Each recurrent editor was thoroughly satisfied with himself, but felt hurt to see the line of policy he had projected during his week of office ruthlessly abandoned by his successor. It became evident that something must be done in the interests of uniformity. The paper was pulling five ways at once, and, doubtless for that reason, had so far failed to deal any really fatal blow at British institutions. Every one felt this, and the eyes of the nation were upon Mr. Martin Doyle. That gentleman rose to the occasion, and called an extraordinary meeting of the Committee of Stockholders. The enterprise had been duly incorporated according to the laws of California, under the name of "The Eagle Publishing Company." The session took place in McKeon's saloon, and Mr. Doyle laid the matter before his colleagues in a neat impromptu speech.

"Ireland," he remarked, "has groaned for six hundred years beneath the yoke of the Saxon opprissor." Mr. Doyle's oratory had the merit of taking up his subject at the very beginning. Having briefly called attention to the principal groans which had been uttered by the suffering island during the centuries referred to, the speaker proceeded.

"At a pravious meetin' of this honorable body it was determined that the best and most immejitly practical way of rightin' the wrongs of our sufferin' counthry was to dissiminate them broadly through the world; to call on all Irishmen in ivery climate under heaven to organize an' be free, an' to paint the black behavior of the Saxon tyrant in the brightest colors. Wid this object we started 'The Irish Aigle,' the first couple of numbers of which have already reached England and sthruck terror to the sowls of a bloody and sowlless aristocracy. But, jintlemen, we cannot disguise from ourselves the fact that no tangible result has yet been perjuced, and this I atthribute to the followin' rason, namely, to wit: while we are all alike animated by the same burnin' love of freedom, we differ in matters of daytail. While wan advycates the sword, another is of opinyun that an open risin' would at prisint be primature. We all belave in organization, but no two of us has the wan notion as to the manes and maning of organization. Therefore the paper sez wan wake wan thing, and another wake another, which is confusin' to the ignorant pathriot; an' that many of our best pathriots is ignorant, it is not you, me fri'nds, nor me will deny. The ignorance of the masses is another crime on the bloody beadroll of Saxon opprission. Therefore, jintlemen, what I propose is as follows, namely, to wit: that we do ingage a jintleman of scientific attainments an' practised litherary vocations, to idit this journal an' say for us what we have to say betther nor we can say it for ourselves, an' such a jintleman I have been fortunate enough to discover an' unearth. He is an Irishman, av coorse; a native of the county Westmeath, an', what is more to our purpose, a graduate of Thrinity College, Dublin. He is young, but sure Robert Emmet was young, an' he 'll come all the ch'aper on that account; an' he is racently from the ould counthry, an' therefore posted in all the latest daytails of its sufferin's. His name is Ffrench, wherefore we may assume that he is a near relative of the immortal liberathor, Daniel O'Connell.* Now, jintlemin, we can arrange the business part later; all I want to do now is to take the sinse of this Thryumvirate in the ingagin' of an iditor for 'The Irish Aigle.' All in favor of that proposition will signify the same by sayin' 'Aye.' Conthrary minded, 'No.' The ayes have it, an' it is so orthered."

There could be no doubt as to the approval with which this speech was received. "A great idea intirely," "Could n't be betther," "A sthroke of janius," were a few of the phrases in which the Thryumvirate indorsed the proposal of its spokesman. Mr. Doyle, with a brief "Ye 'll excuse me, jintlemen," and a modest consciousness of having deserved well of his country, withdrew.

"Ye done grand work wid your issue of the paper, Andy," remarked Mr. Foley; "it was really great."

"I thought it was n't bad, Jim, till I seen yours," responded Mr. Cummiskey, "an' thin I seen what a man of native originality c'u'd do wid the subject"; and so, like hand and glove patriots as they were, each proceeded to exalt his neighbor and complacently to drink in such dews of applause as descended on himself, till Mr. Doyle returned and introduced Gerald Ffrench.

"Mr. Ffrench, jintlemen," he said; "a man of rare scientific attainments and university eddication." All rose, and one after another grasped Mr. Ffrench's hand. This operation was conducted silently, and reminded Gerald of a chorus of conspirators in opera-bouffe. As Mr. Foley, the last to advance, dropped the young man's fingers, he remarked in a husky whisper, and with a suggestion of emotion in his voice:

"This is a great day for Ireland."

"Ye 're right, it is," said Mr. O'Rourke. Then he stepped to the door and called: "Mountain dew, Mat, and bug juice for Mr. Doyle. Ye can drink the ould stuff?" he added, turning to Gerald. Gerald admitted that he could, and then the conversation languished. All resumed their seats, and the ten eyes of the Thryumvirate were leveled at the young man. He bore the scrutiny uneasily, and his color rose. They were "taking stock" of him.

Gerald Ffrench was about twenty-three, and a fair specimen of a class of young men of which the Silent Sister turns out several hundred every year.** At this time he had been in America some eight months; in San Francisco less than two. He came of a good old Irish family and had received the younger son's portion of two thousand pounds immediately after his twenty-first birthday. He had read a little for the bar and did not like it; he had thought of entering the army but did not quite fancy it; on the whole, it occurred to him that he could not do better than to try his fortune in the United States. He left

---

*[Daniel O'Connell's uncle, General Count Daniel O'Connell, had been an officer in the Irish Brigade in France under the Bourbons. Daniel the younger had also been sent to secondary school in France.]

**[The "Silent Sister" of England is Ireland, specifically the Anglo-Irish Protestant subculture that Jessop means to differentiate from the Irish Catholic majority.]

Ireland for New York, but did not travel direct. He first visited London and thence passed over to Paris. He found the latter city very fascinating and remained there some time. Then, as it was so close at hand, he thought it a pity not to see the Vienna Exhibition, and he went to Vienna and saw it. The young fellow, accustomed to deny himself nothing, and with more money in his pocket than he had ever possessed before, did not exercise a becoming frugality. When he had had enough of Europe he sailed for America, and New York was scarcely less to his taste than the Old World capitals. He lingered there for several months, but finding himself unappreciated he started for California. He selected the route by Panama, and treated the voyage over tropic seas as a veritable pleasure trip. In San Francisco he remained, possibly because he had not money enough left to go farther. It was not till he had changed his last twenty-dollar piece, however, that he realized his position. He had received all he was entitled to and had spent it. That twenty dollars, represented by a fast-diminishing pile of silver, must be replaced by his own exertions. For what was he fitted, this young man endowed with nothing but health, a good education, and a certain amount of superficial experience? He did not know. He wandered about the streets and envied the blacksmiths and the bricklayers. He would willingly have bartered his education for a good trade. Then he began to write for the papers, but speedily found that the qualifications which had won him an occasional medal for composition at Trinity College were of no value at all in the city department of a newspaper. Again and again were his contributions rejected with the curt remark, "We've no room to print essays." He offered to write editorials, but was laughed at, though he felt he could have amended the halting English of many of those oracular utterances. His rounds of the journals entailed much wear of heart and of shoe-leather, and but little of silver solace. Still he made a few acquaintances, and it was one of these, an Irishman, and the city editor of an evening paper, who introduced him to Doyle as the very man for "The Irish Eagle." Gerald had jumped at the idea eagerly, and had succeeded in impressing Mr. Doyle with a due sense of his attainments. His eyes sank before those of the Thryumvirate, however. A single question from any one of these shrewd-looking, middle-aged Irishmen might prick the bubble and display him in his true colors – as a man who knew no more of the routine work necessary for a paper than he did of casting its type. He might have reassured himself. Not one was there who did not regard him as an incarnate battering-ram, built expressly to level the battlemented tyranny of England in the dust.

McKeon entered with the refreshments. "Will ye oblige us wid the last number of 'The Irish Aigle'? said Mr. Doyle, solemnly. Mr. Cummiskey on the right, Mr. Foley on the left, Mr. O'Rourke in front, and Mr. Brady from the rear simultaneously and solemnly proffered one to their chairman.

Gerald, who had been led to study the paper by the first hint of the honor in store for him, saw this and hurriedly restored his own copy to his pocket.

The action, however, had not passed unnoticed, and called forth an approving smile from the Thryumvirate. Mr. Doyle took a paper from the man nearest him and waved it in the air. He was evidently loaded and primed for a speech.

"By the unanimous vote of mesilf an' colleagues," he began, "you, Mr. Ffrench, are called to the iditorial chair of this journal. The stipind will be seventeen dollars and a half a wake." He paused, to let his words have their due effect. Gerald leaned back with a sigh of relief. It would go hard but he could retain his position for one week at least, and $17.50 looked to him like boundless wealth. The Thryumvirate was watching him. He felt that he was called on to say something.

"Very liberal, most happy," he muttered; and then, as no one spoke and the silence became embarrassing, he ventured to add, "By the bye – 'Irish Eagle,' you know. Is n't it rather an odd name?"

"Why?" asked Mr. Doyle, severely; and Mr. Brady, who had not suggested it, hastened to add: "Maybe Mr. Ffrench could think of a betther?"

Thus appealed to, Mr. Ffrench, after some hesitation, thought that a more personal name – something like the "Fenian," or the – He was interrupted by a very tempest of opposition, and sat appalled at the fury of the storm he had called forth.

"Fenian!" "The dhirty rats!" "The cowardly time-servers!" "They 're the curse of Ireland!" Such were the exclamations that broke from the group; but presently Mr. Doyle's voice rose in connected statement, dominating the confusion.

"Misther Ffrench," he said, "I'd have ye to know that this organization is thorough! We are no advycates of half-measures, and we propose to free Ireland, if we have to swim in blood to do it. We are advanced Nationalists; we 're far beyant the Fenians! We say, 'Burn London,' 'Burn Liverpool,' 'Import cholera germs into Dublin Castle,' 'Blow up Windsor Castle!' 'Put to the sword the Houses of Parleymint' – ay, Irish mimbers an' all, for they 're no betther nor the rest, keepin' terms with the bloody Saxon opprissor. An' if an army of thim half-hearted Fenians was in it I'd say blow thim up too; for they 're no use, an' they 're only palterin' wid the liberty of their counthry. The day of Vinegar Hill is over. It's not in the open field we 'll honor thim by burnin' powdther, but undher their houses, undher their bridges, undher their public buildin's, an' that's the mission of 'The Irish Aigle'."

Gerald's astonishment that any class of Irishmen should be, as Mr. Doyle phrased it, more "advanced" than the Fenians was swallowed up in amazement at this vigorous denunciation. Like most young Irishmen of family and education he had no sympathy whatever with the discontent of the peasantry, and indeed he had only vaguely heard of its existence before he came to America. There, however, he had soon found, to his surprise, that from the mere fact of his being an Irishman it was accepted as inevitable that he must hate England and everything English. To the brother of the Conservative member, Edward Ffrench of Ballyvore Park, all this had seemed absurd enough, but he had let it pass without comment. Now he found himself the central figure of a knot of men who talked bloodshed and savored the word as they uttered it as though it were pleasant of taste – men who condemned war and battlefields as not murderous enough, and who scouted as insufficiently villainous the most reckless organization he had ever heard of. However, brief as had been his newspaper experience, he had learned that in journalism it is not seldom necessary to support one side openly while secretly holding the opposite tenets. This he had come quite prepared to do, and this explosion, murder, and sudden death horrified him for a moment, till the very extravagance of the language brought its own comfort. It was something to laugh at, not to revolt from, this little group of Irishmen proposing to wreck Great Britain from the back-room of a San Francisco saloon; and then there was the $17.50 to think of. He could not afford the luxury of high principles. He would humor the joke and write an article on blowing up the Thames, if they wanted it. It would put money in his pocket and would not affect the Thames.

"With regard to the title of this journal," proceeded Doyle, waving the sheet, "it was silicted by me wid the approval of me colleagues here for the followin' raisons, namely, to wit: In the first place, the aigle is the emblem of America; for we are all American citizens, an' the counthry of our adoption is sicond in our affections only to that of our birth. In the nixt place, the aigle is universally regarded as the burrud of freedom: I niver seen wan free mesilf, nor any other way than in a cage at Woodward's Garden beyant, but it is so rigarded. This is 'The Irish Aigle'; high may she soar an' long may she wave, an' deep be her talents in the black heart of the Saxon opprissor!"

As soon as the wild applause which this sentiment evoked had subsided Mr. O'Rourke rose. "I propose," said he, "that we do now adjourn to the office and install Mr. Ffrench in the iditorial chair, afther havin' inthrojuiced him to our foreman. All in favor of this proposition will signify the same by –"

But as all rose at once, it was not considered necessary to press the question to a vote.

The editorial offices of "The Irish Eagle" occupied a single room at the top of a neighboring building. The apartment was divided into two unequal portions by a board partition which did not reach to the ceiling. In the outer room was the "plant" of the paper, consisting of a few cases of type, a roller for "pulling proofs," and half a dozen galleys. There was an imposing-stone in the center on which lay the forms just as they had come back from the printer. A shaky old man was distributing type at one of the cases. To him Gerald was duly presented. "Mr. Ffrench, this is our foreman, Mr. Mike Carney. Mike, this is the new iditor. Come inside now, an' take charge"; and the whole party trooped into the sanctum.

It was a small place and seemed crowded when all had entered. The furniture was scanty, consisting of a large table, a few office stools, and an arrangement of shelves against the partition for the accommodation of the unsold copies of the paper. The table was littered with exchanges, and a volume of the poems of Thomas Davis lay on the floor.

Mr. Doyle at once proceeded to business. "The paper goes to priss Fridays," he said; "so ye see, this bein' Monday, ye have no time to lose. How are ye off for copy, Mike!"

"Bad," answered the old printer. "I've a little reprint, but no original matter at all."

"We 'll soon remedy that," said Gerald cheerfully, with all the ready complaisance of a new hand. "How many editorials do you generally have?"

"The more the merrier," said Mr. Cummiskey. "Now here 's a good subject – 'The Duty of the Day.' I started it mesilf." Gerald took a slip of manuscript from his hand. It was written in pencil and showed many corrections and interlineations. It was not easy to read, but the new editor was in no position to neglect a hint.

"Since MacMurragh flourished and died a traitor's death," so Mr. Cummiskey's contribution began, "there has been only the one duty for Irishmen, and that is vengeance." Gerald paused in thought. Who was MacMurragh, when had he flourished, and for what had he been hanged? He wished that his new employers would not deal so much with obscure history. He ventured an observation.

"Undoubtedly the judicial murder of the unfortunate MacMurragh calls for exemplary vengeance," he began. A howl of execration interrupted him. "The vilyan! The thraitor! The bloody agint of Saxon opprission!" Evidently he was on the wrong track and MacMurragh was anything but popular. Gerald read the paragraph again, but it furnished no new light. "Let me see," he said tentatively; "what was the exact date of MacMurragh's – ah – ahem – death?"

"Elivin hundhred an' sivinty-sivin," shouted the Thryumvirate as one man. Evidently MacMurragh belonged to a familiar historical epoch. Gerald swallowed his surprise and merely remarked, "Ah, yes; I had a dispute with Professor Galbraith once on that very point. He maintained that it was 1188, but I knew I was right."

"Av coorse ye were," said Cummiskey, triumphantly. "Sivinty-sivin, an' I 'll maintain it agin the wurruld."

"But," ventured Gerald, "as your article is on the duty of the day, don't you think we are going back rather far for an illustration?"

"Who the divil wants an illusthration! It's an apoch: since Dermot MacMurragh – bad cess to him for that same – invited the English into Ireland, the counthry has niver been quit of them. Our duty began that day, an' it has n't changed since. It 's to kill ivery Englishman."

"But to do that we must organize!" broke in Foley, springing on his favorite hobby at a bound; "organize an' be free! That 's the lesson to tach Irishmen to-day. Make yer first article on organization, Mr. Ffrench."

"With pleasure," said Gerald. "Do you advocate any particular plan of organization?"

"Niver heed the plan. Jist organize. Whin Irishmen the wurruld over are wilded into a solid new clayus, thin the death knell of Saxon opprission will be flashed abroad visible as the firmymint. Thim 's the very wurruds I stated in me own iditorial on the subject."

"And a noble sintiment it is," said Mr. Doyle.

"Nobly expressed," added Gerald with a bow to Mr. Foley, thereby making that gentleman a friend for life.

"Without wishin' to dictate to ye, Mr. Ffrench," said Doyle after a brief pause, "I 'll ax if ye know anything about dynamite."

"I know it is a very powerful explosive," said Gerald, somewhat surprised, "and that it bids fair to take the place of all other preparations of nitroglycerine; but why?"

"Why?" repeated Mr. Doyle, in a deep voice. "Because what Ireland needs is a powerful explosive; what England will get is a powerful explosive; that 's the why, an' the chief mission of "The Irish Aigle" is to bear powerful explosives to the sufferin' children of Erin, whether they cower beneath the glass-ears of the North or hide their woes under the thropics. Come, jintlemin, that 's all that 's to be said. We won't waste Mr. Ffrench's time any longer. If ye want any information as to daytails, Mike Carney's the boy to give 'em ye. Good day to ye, sir." And the Thryumvirate filed out, leaving Gerald to collect such meaning as he might from the suggestions offered and to condense them into an article which should teach the Irish race that the duty of the day was to organize dynamite.

As time wore on, Gerald found himself face to face with a difficult task. Having entered upon his duties with a tacit assumption of qualification, he felt obliged to live up to the character he had brought with him. This prevented him from asking questions, at least directly, and he was constantly on the watch to pick up any unconsidered crumbs of knowledge that might fall in his way. Being engaged as an expert, he could not learn as an apprentice, and yet the trivial details of even such an office as that of "The Irish Eagle" were all new to him. Mike Carney quickly fathomed his ignorance; but the old printer was good-natured, and not only kept the young man's secret, but made an elaborate pretense of belief in him. This, of course, did not impose on Gerald, who reciprocated by always observing the fiction of Carney's sobriety, and the two got on very well together. The editor learned something every day. He soon came to distinguish between brevier and nonpareil, and he corrected his proofs without marking errors in the middle of the line as they happened to occur. The Thryumvirate never suspected that an editor was being educated in the office, and the tangible results, as shown in the paper, were on the whole satisfactory. Gerald always wrote at least three articles – one on organization, one on the manifest duty of Irishmen, and one on the theory and practice of dynamite. These essays – for they were nothing less – abounded in long words and involved sentences, and in so far as they were incomprehensible to the patriots gave eminent satisfaction. There could be no doubt of the new editor's ability and scholarly attainments. But Doyle, who had all his life been accustomed to call a spade a spade, and an Englishman a bloody, brutalized robber, detected a certain weakness in the academic phrases of the young collegian. "Our hereditary enemies," "the despoilers of our land," etc., were to the Irishman far less direct and forcible than "spawn of the Saxon thraitor," or "red and pitiless monster," and Gerald's incapacity to realize the fact that an Englishman of moral life or good intentions is as much a creature of fancy as the unicorn was at first rather trying to the patriot. "But he 's young," Doyle would remark by way of consolation, "and he has n't been ground under the heel of the Saxon for over forty years as I have"; which, as the speaker had been a resident in the United States for a quarter of a century or thereabout, was quite likely to be the truth.

But, all in all, Gerald suited them very well. His editorial utterances took on more of the tone of his surroundings, and while still marshaling his verbal three-deckers for weekly action he contrived now and then to throw a hot shot into the enemy's stronghold which delighted Doyle himself. As for Foley, he had sworn by the young man from the first, and committed to memory long passages from the paper and recited them as opportunity offered either in the bosom of his family or in McKeon's saloon. Gerald soon began to enter with spirit into the game of vilifying the Saxon. His common sense told him that no harm could result from the frothy nonsense, and he even took a mischievous pleasure in sending his brother a copy of the paper each week. These, however, were addressed by the boy who wrote the wrappers. He would not have identified himself with the sheet for twice his weekly salary.

This same salary was the principal thorn in young Ffrench's bed of roses. It was never paid. He received money, to be sure, when his necessities urged him to press for it; but it was five dollars at one time, two at another – sometimes only fifty cents. "When the paper gets upon its legs" – that was the only answer he received when he asked for a settlement. There was no regular paymaster. A request addressed to Mr. Doyle, who seemed the moving spirit, would call forth some such answer as, "Money? Av coorse; why not? Can ye get along wid three dollars till tomorrow?" But to-morrow, in the sense that Gerald looked for it, never came, and the Eagle Publishing Company sank deeper and deeper into his debt.

Indeed, the paper was not prosperous. Subscriptions fell into arrears; advertisers did not pay up. McManus withdrew the card of his saloon altogether, on the ground that McKeon received all the office patronage. Carney was forthwith provided with a dollar and instructed to go out and invest it over McManus's bar. This he did with scrupulous exactitude, but without result, unless his incapacity for work during the remainder of the day can be regarded as such. The change of whisky did n't agree with him, he said. The following week McKeon reduced his advertisement. "As long as McManus don't put his card in the paper," argued McKeon, "there 's no sinse in my carryin' such a big 'ad.'" Truly the "Eagle" had fallen on evil days.

The fact was that, though all five of the original promoters were enthusiastic in their self-sought mission, they had not calculated upon, nor could they afford, the constant drain which the paper made upon them. The office rent had to be paid; also the paper bill, and the weekly account for presswork. Gerald and Carney were less imperative items in the expense account, and they had to wait accordingly. The latter was not exacting: as long as he had a few "bits" to spend for liquor he seemed satisfied, and Gerald was at least making a living, such as it was, which was more than he had been able to do before. His receipts may have averaged twelve dollars a week, and he paid the balance willingly as the price of experience, confessing to himself that he was only an apprentice.

An appeal to the wealthy Irishmen of the State, drawn up by Gerald and signed by the Thryumvirate, did not meet with conspicuous success. There were few responses. Mr. Patrick Byrne, the millionaire vine-grower of San Antonio County, sent a full-page advertisement of his "Golden Wine" marked for one insertion, and inclosed his check for two hundred and fifty dollars. But this was only a sop to Cerberus. The paper bill took most of it; Gerald and Carney got ten dollars apiece. Evidently things could not go on in this way. "The Irish Eagle" was falling after a brief flight of some six months; it was slowly starving to death, and the first pound of dynamite was still unbought – the lowest step of Queen Victoria's throne was still unshattered.

The end was not long deferred. Gerald had just finished a handsome obituary notice of Mr. Phelim O'Gorman, a wealthy and prominent Irish resident who had died the day before, and Mike Carney was engaged in embalming the virtues of the deceased in cold type, when the Thryumvirate filed slowly into the editorial sanctum. There was gloom on the brows of the patriots and sorrow in their tones. Mr. Martin Doyle flung a small sheaf of advertising bills on the table. "I can't collect the first cint," he said with a groan. The groan was echoed by his colleagues, and the editor looked serious and sympathetic. He felt that this was not a moment to urge the question of his arrears, though during the last few weeks the sum had rolled up with startling rapidity.

"They would n't organize," remarked Mr. Foley, despondently. "They might have been free by this time if they 'd only have organized."

"They've neglected the clare duty of the day," said Mr. Cummiskey; "an' this is what it 's brought us to."

Mr. Doyle cleared his throat and rose, but evidently he did not feel equal to a rhetorical flight. He only said:

"At a meetin' of the stockholders of the Aigle Publishing Company, duly called an' convaned, it has been decided to discontinue the publication of 'The Irish Aigle' for the prisint."

The announcement did not take Gerald wholly by surprise. He had been looking for something of the sort.

"And what about me?" he asked.

"This issue will be printed an' published as usual," said Mr. Doyle. "It 's all med up, anyhow, an' goes to priss to-night. Afther that, Mr. Ffrench, the company will have no further call for yer services."

"You owe me, as I suppose you are aware," began Gerald, but a storm of indignant protests drowned his voice.

"Bad cess to the dhirty money!" "Is it yer arrairs ye 're thinkin' of whin the last hope of Irish indipindance is shattered in the dust?" "Are n't we all losers together?" and much more to the same effect. Gerald waited till silence was restored, and then attempted to renew his appeal, but Mr. Doyle turned on him with oppressive dignity.

"Ye 're an Irishman, Mr. Ffrench, I belave?"

Gerald admitted his nationality.

"Very well, thin; it 's proud an' thankful ye ought to be to make a thriflin' sacrifice for the land of yer burruth." In moments of excitement or emotion Mr. Doyle's native Doric took on a richer tone. "We've all med our sacrifices for the good cause. Let this wan be yours."

It was impossible for Gerald to explain to these perfervid patriots that their cause was not his – that all his sympathies, all his habits, bound him to the class they were aiming to overthrow. Out of his own mouth, or rather out of his own editorials, they would have convicted him as something more advanced than a Fenian; weak, indeed, in details of Irish history, but sound to the core on the great question of Irish liberty. As he sat silent, vainly seeking some reply to this appeal to his patriotism, the Thryumvirate rose as one man and stalked from the room.

From the case outside Mike Carney could be heard in a flood of song:

> Oh, how she swum the wathers,
>   The good ship Castletown,
> The day she flung our banner forth,
>   The Harp without the Crown.

The old printer was occasionally patriotic in his cups. Gerald likened "The Irish Eagle" to the dying swan, and realized that the end was near.

The following week was one of anxious inaction. Ffrench vibrated between the office and McKeon's saloon; Carney confined himself strictly to the latter. The Thryumvirate was seldom visible; and had it not been for a lucky accident, the editor of "The Irish Eagle" would have left that paper penniless. A son of the late Mr. Phelim O'Gorman, pleased with the prominence given to his father's virtues and ignorant of the suspension of the paper, entered the office one day and found Gerald seated, like Marius, alone among the ruins. The greater part of the edition was still unsold on the shelves, and when Mr. O'Gorman, Jr., asked for a few copies of the issue containing the notice of his father's death the editor was prompt to accommodate him. How many would he have?

"How many can you spare me?"

"All you want," answered Gerald, briskly; and young O'Gorman purchased two hundred "Irish Eagles" at their regular retail price of ten cents apiece, and departed leaving Gerald with a glow of gratitude in his heart and a twenty-dollar-piece in his pocket. He gave the defunct publishing company credit for this amount in his account for arrears.

So fell "The Irish Eagle."

Gerald Ffrench turned his back on Washington street and patriotism, and took himself, his talents, and his new experience to more sordid and business-like journals. He began to meet with more success. He had learned habits of thrift and industrious routine, and he had imbibed a hearty hatred for Irish Nationalists and all their ways. This last fact, however, was long unsuspected by Foley, Cummiskey, and the others. Mr. Martin Doyle, in particular, followed the career of the dethroned editor with deep interest, and considered him the shining light of the San Francisco press. He used to point out Gerald with pride as one who "had worked hard and med his sacrifices for the cause." He even invited the young man to attend a banquet of the Red Cross Knights on St. Patrick's Day. This invitation was declined, Gerald keenly recalling that immortal anniversary the year before and his mortification when the Thryumvirate had insisted on having "The Irish Aigle" printed in green ink in honor of the day. But that was all over now. Mr. Ffrench had resumed his ancestral role as a "Saxon opprissor," though the scattered members of the Thryumvirate were slow to believe it.

Conviction came on them at last, and with crushing force. A certain noble earl was murdered in Ireland under circumstances of peculiar barbarity. The victim was an old man, but he was also a large land-holder, and a howl of exultation at his death and execration of his memory went up from all the Irish societies. An important election was at hand, and the city papers, willing to cater to the Irish vote, took up the cry. The murdered earl was branded as a tyrant, tales of harrowing evictions were invented and ascribed to him, and it was broadly hinted that he had received no more than his deserts. This was more than Gerald Ffrench could stand. He had known the old gentleman in former days, had dined at his table and been "tipped" by him as a school-boy. He sat down and wrote a letter to "The Golden Fleece," a weekly paper of wide circulation. He took the earl's murder for a text, and told all he knew of the "wild justice of revenge" as executed by a blunderbuss from behind a hedge. His heart guided his pen; he rang out a withering impeachment of the methods of his countrymen, and signed it with his full name.

Mr. Martin Doyle, Mr. Andrew Cummiskey, Mr. Peter O'Rourke, Mr. Frank Brady, and Mr. James Foley met the same evening in the private snuggery behind Mr. Matthew McKeon's sample room on Washington street. Mr. Doyle had a paper in his hand.

"Have ye read it?" he asked.

All admitted that they had.

Mr. Doyle arose. "Fri'nds an' fellow-counthrymen," he said: "this letther, difindin' the memory of a black-hearted landlord; this letther, callin' the noblest atthribute of our common humanity, the atthribute of rivinge, a crime, was written by Gerald Ffrench [groans]. Is he an Irishman? ['No, no.'] I don't care a trauneen if he was born in Westmeath; I don't value it a kippeen if he was eddycated in Thrinity College; it 's nothin' to me if he did idit 'The Irish Aigle' for filthy lukker; I here and now do brand and stiggatize him as a vile spawn of the Saxon opprissor. All in favor thereof will signify the same by saying, 'Aye.' Conthrary minded, 'No.' The ayes have it, and it is so orthered."

All recorded their votes of censure against Gerald, even Mr. Foley, who acquiesced with a shake of the head, adding, "But he had grand ideas intirely about organization." Mr. Cummiskey took the suffrages of the party on the advisability of waylaying the culprit some night and giving him "the bating he had deserved," but this was overruled by Mr. Doyle. "It 's no use, boys," he said; "a diginerate Irishman like that wud think nothin' of app'aling to the police for purtection. L'ave him alone. Vingeance will overtake him, along wid the rest of the accursed Saxon brood."

Slob Murphy

by James W. Sullivan, from *Tenement Tales of New York*
(New York: Henry Holt, 1895)

Born in Carlisle, Pennsylvania, in 1848, James William Sullivan came to New York City and worked first as a proofreader and printer, and subsequently as a journalist and writer. A reforming sociologist, he wrote mostly about labor and the urban poor. His books included Trade Unions' Attitude toward Welfare Work *(1907),* Markets for the People *(1913), and* Socialism as an Incubus on the American Labor Movement *(1918). During and after World War I, Sullivan was an associate of Samuel Gompers and an official in the American Federation of Labor. He died at the age of ninety in 1938.*

Tenement Tales was Sullivan's attempt to fictionalize the lives of the Irish, Jewish, and Italian immigrants whose problems engaged him as a sociologist and labor leader. A second collection, more essay than fiction and more explicit in its proselytizing for relief of the sufferings of the laboring poor, was So the World Goes, *published in 1898. Though obviously a sideline and marred by occasional lapses into sentimentality, Sullivan's fiction is pioneering work in the vein of urban realism that Stephen Crane, Abraham Cahan, and Finley Peter Dunne were also mining in the 1890s. The accuracy of Sullivan's picture of slum life was praised by the New York Times reviewer, who said of* Tenement Tales: *"Each and all of the stories have in them the spirit of truth, and on them is stamped the truth" (June 12, 1895).*

Reprinted here is "Slob Murphy," the story of the life and death of an eight-year-old street urchin, which Sullivan tells in four stark sections: "His Manner of Life, His Death, The Wake, His Funeral." Pat Murphy dies after having been trampled by horses, and the traditional Catholic deathbed scene (perfected by Mrs. Sadlier and her contemporaries) is immediately undercut by a playmate's practical question: "Wot's dey a-goin to do wit' his old cloze?" Moreover, the "bold pantomime" of grief at the wake by Pat's drunken, brutalized father is as chilling as the more famous scene of Mrs. Johnson's histrionic keening at the end of Crane's Maggie: A Girl of the Streets. *And the sordidness of the funeral, where everyone – undertaker, gravediggers, priest – cuts corners and rushes mechanically through, rounds out Sullivan's honest depiction of painful aspects of the life the Irish made for themselves in American cities. Indicting the "poisonous moral atmosphere" that has produced this miniature tragedy, the narrator, a steamboat worker, recognizes that "dirty, ragged, bad Slob had had goodness in him which ought to have had a chance."*

206

I
His Manner of Life

Pat Murphy – a boy of eight years, whose clothes were old and dirty, whose hair was tousled, face smudgy, and hands blackened – was one afternoon in the late autumn swinging on the battered iron area gate of a shabby lodging-house in a busy, narrow, down-town street.

"Hello, Steamboat!" he called out to me, as I passed up the stoop of the house on the way to my room – top floor front, hall. "I hain't had a nickel fur a week. Y'ain't got a little bit o' change about yer cloze?"

"None for you, Pat."

One of Pat's many bad habits was begging from the lodgers. He already knew the art of asking for money. First he would try for a quarter; failing in that he would come down to a dime; if still unsuccessful, he would name a nickel; lastly, he would hang on for a penny, reckoning that it would be given him to get rid of him. But the old lodgers never gave him anything; they had not found Pat a lovable boy. He would fawn, but he had no gratitude. He would smile innocently, but he was sly and deceitful. Cunning enough to play frank and good-humored when wanting anything, he was oftenest sullen or skulking off to avoid the punishment due some underhand trick.

As I mounted the stairway to my narrow room, the unpleasant traits in little Pat's character occurred to my mind. Yet in no wise was it strange that he should be what he was – his mother dead, his father a drunkard, the house filled with rough workingmen, and his only companions those of the street in a miserable neighborhood. The only woman's hand that ever did a turn for him was that of Mrs. Brady, the slattern landlady, and that hand he felt the weight of in a blow oftener than in an act of kindness. Little time had Mrs. Brady to attend to Pat, and her usual reply to his childish importunities was an impatient word. Small wonder, then, that neglected little Pat was growing up bad.

Reaching my room, I hung up my street coat and put on a light house-jacket. In the pockets of this jacket I had the day before left about a dollar in change and my smoking-tobacco. The tobacco was still there, but the money was gone. Pat's doings, I concluded. Useless to say anything about it. If accused of the theft, he would, as he always did, deny it and boohoo. If I told his father, he would be terribly beaten; but that would neither bring back the dollar nor mend Pat's ways. The boy's character was in the mold of surroundings that would undergo no change, bruised and beaten though he be every day of his life.

Seated at the open window with my pipe, I looked down in the street. Pat was at play. He was lazily standing on the lower step of the stoop, a paper of candy in one hand, a whip twirling in the other. My dollar was giving him a bad boy's joy. Pat never ran about at play with the vigor of cheerful young-sters; he was a born loafer. At the present moment his manner suggested at once the child's pleasure in stolen sweets and the thief's dread of retribution. He was perturbed by my arrival, but he had toys and candies!

After a time the cloud passed over with him. As I made no complaint, he supposed his hour of punishment postponed, and the boy in him reasserted itself. A little girl walked by. Pat held out toward her the paper of candy, and when she reached to partake of the proffered goodies, he struck her hand sharply with the whip. She cried, and the boy laughed impishly.

A few moments later a party of boys straggled by. The last was a little fel-low whose bare legs were red with cold. Pat cut him right and left over the calves until his cries brought back his crowd to the rescue. Pat scampered through the area-way into the house. When the indignant urchins were gone, he reappeared, tickled over his fun.

A grocer's boy came lounging down the street, a pitcher of milk in his hand. Pat stole behind him and dropped a bit of coal in the pitcher. When the boy delivered the milk to a woman a few doors away, Pat shouted to her that he had seen the boy fighting, and that a lump of coal thrown at him had gone into the pitcher. The woman poured the milk into a tin pail, found the coal, scolded the boy, and packed him off for another supply. As the boy hulked away, Pat cried out after him: "Yer boss sells milk wid dust in it!"

Presently a cart-horse was led past in the street by a stableman. Pat sneaked up behind the horse and lashed its hind legs with his whip. The frightened animal plunged forward toward the stableman, at which Pat laughed hugely. But in a flash it threw up its heels, knocking off Pat's hat and grazing his head. The boy let his hat lie in the street and ran back on the stoop, where he stood still for a while, white and frightened.

Pat's next bit of fun was safer. A lean cat nosed her way along the gutter and crawled into an ash-barrel that stood, lid up, a few yards from where Pat was lying in wait for mischief. While the cat was inside the barrel, pawing for bones, Pat cautiously drew nigh, and, clapping down the barrel-lid, impris-oned her. Then he sat on top, chuckling, while the cat furiously dashed about inside. When she quieted down, he stuck his whip-handle through a hole and stirred her up, while she spat and plaintively mewed. When tired of this fun, Pat sat still. Two boys came along. Pat asked them to look way down in the barrel; there was a gold ring there. When they opened the lid to look in, the imprisoned cat leaped out in their faces. Pat took refuge in the basement hall-way, the boys in pursuit, bent on getting even with him. A rumpus ensued, but Mrs. Brady quickly threw the strange boys into the street, and with her open hand gave her nephew's face a resounding thwack. The boys picked up stones in the street, called Pat "Slob," and defied the whole house. But find-ing no fight, they went off to a neighboring corner, to hang around and plot revenge.

Pat, driven alike from house and street, sought refuge in the areaway. There he sat on a stone step and chewed candy. Poor, thieving, lying, tricky young rowdy! How his pranks of the past half-hour had told of the devil that mastered him and was developing in him. Whatever dormant intellect he possessed, – what relation to it had our civilization? To him what meaning had refinement or the higher life? That immortal soul of his – what was being done for it by this prosperous and religious world? Of all the institutions which the great heart and conscience of society nurture, can none reach little Pat?

Pat, happening to throw back his head, espied me regarding him from my window's height. He hailed me in his down-town New York Celtic dialect:

"Hello, Steamboat! Wot boat d'ye work on now – de black pipe bo-at or de red pipe bo-at?"

"Black."

"Is ye on de day trick or de night?"

"Night."

"Dat's w'y yer loafin' now, ain't it? Soy, Steamboat! A man bought me dis yer whip."

"All right, Pat. But I'll not give another man a chance to buy you whips with my money."

"'Twuz Cousin Johnny McNaghatally's daddy gi' me it. Hope I may be struck dead if 'twuzn't!"

But at this moment Pat's conciliatory tones to me gave way to a scream. A man had approached him from behind and had blindfolded him with his hands.

"Soy, lemme go! Wot's de matter wit' you?"

The man lifted him up at arm's length in the air.

"I know you. It's you, Tim Foy. You're drunk ag'in. Lemme go!"

"Ay, Pat; I am half shot. But I'm not so full I can't throw you on one of my horses."

Foy had driven his truck to the curb. Swinging the boy back and forth, to get play for his effort, he seated him on the nigh horse. Pat was frightened.

"I'll fall off and hurt meself," he shrieked. "Lemme be!"

"Oh, I kin toss you on the off horse and not miss him," boasted Foy. "Here you go!"

Taking the lad off the nigh horse, Tim prepared to throw him over on the further one.

But Foy's footing was insecure. He slipped as Pat went over the first horse, and the boy fell between the two. The further horse, startled, moved off, and there was Pat's head underneath one of his hoofs, with the boy's body wriggling on the ground like an eel's. The horses walked away. Tim Foy ran to their heads and stopped them. The body of the truck passed above Pat, the wheels not striking him, but he lay in the street apparently lifeless.

I hurried downstairs and carried the boy into the dining-room in the basement. Foy was at my elbow as I put Pat, all limp, on a lounge. Mrs. Brady hustled in from the kitchen. Foy tremulously said:

"Ould woman, I've been skylarkin' wid Pat – and – and Pat – he hurted hisself!"

Pat's condition called for water, quiet, and some examination of his wounds. But Mrs. Brady, so far from meeting the needs of the occasion, acted the ignorant woman with a woman's heart. First she set up a screaming and bemoaning that roused the neighbors; then her turbulence somewhat subsided, her fright and pity turned to anger, and she rained on Tim Foy a tirade of denunciation that made him blanch. I wrapped my handkerchief around Pat's head and left the two to their noise, – Mrs. Brady tongue-lashing and Foy explaining, – and ran to summon a doctor.

I found one. He hastened with me to the house. Pat was still lying on the lounge unconscious. A crowd of neighbors had come in, and chattering tongues were telling how Foy had killed Slob. We put the people out of the room, to have them gather in the hallway and about the dining-room door, talking the matter threadbare there. The doctor set to work on Pat's head, I assisting him.

Suddenly Mrs. Brady emerged from the crowd, pushing her way into the room, and demanded of me, loudly and reproachfully:

"And didn't ye sind fur the praiste?"

Mrs. McNaghatally, with little Margaretta and Johnny McNaghatally after her, ran breathless into the room. The cousins had heard the news of Pat's accident blocks away. Mrs. McNaghatally's first words were:

"Did ye sind fur the praiste?"

Neighbors continued pouring in; the lodgers came home. The one inquiry of the excited newcomers was:

"Did ye sind fur the praiste?"

Pat by and by regained consciousness, and the doctor and I left him to the cackle of the women and the officiousness of volunteer nurses. While passing up to my room I saw Mrs. Brady in the hallway, in conversation with a man in clerical garb. Mrs. Brady was closing the clasp of her pocketbook and putting the pocket-book in the bosom of her dress.

The doctor, after much thumping and punching, had said that Pat's skull was not fractured; and when, after a time, the boy had opened his eyes and answered questions, the neighbors saw they were disappointed of a tragedy. It had turned out to be no more than the everyday matter of a boy getting a hard knock on the head. So they drank off the beer that had been sent for, and in a little while went home, their interest in Pat as the hero of a first-ward event much abated.

Again seated at my window, I presently saw Pat's father, Mick Murphy, coming down the street homeward. He made his way slowly. He was lame, having once, through an accident, been badly injured. The knot of morbid idlers had left the front of the house, and Mick Murphy reached our stoop in ignorance of his son's mishap. He saw me at the window and called up:

"Good-evenin', Kane. That b'y o' mine, I'll break his back some day. I've towld him ivery day fur a month to bring me me grub to the fact'ry at dinner time, and he's nivver showed up wonst. He'd ought to come to the corner to meet me in the evenin', too, and he do-an't. He's no good onyhow."

Complaining thus, he passed into the area-way. In a moment I heard a tumult in the kitchen. Mick Murphy had heard the news. Amid the din of howls was wafted:

"Howly God! did ye sind for the praiste?"

Yes; one institution of the great, good world could be called on to do something for little Pat!

II
His Death

The next day Pat was up early. Mrs. Brady washed his head and bound it up in great white bandages, and he went out and stood about on the stoop, and had the street boys look at him in wonder as "the kid who had been trampled on by a horse and lived."

But the day after that we lodgers were told that Pat was down again. He had been put to bed in a little dark room in the basement, between the dining-room and the kitchen. There, for several days, he lay quietly enough, little said about him – as his skull was not broken. During that time I saw nothing of him. About the third or fourth day, however, at noon, Mrs. Brady's bulky form appeared at my room door. Quite solemnly, in a hoarse whisper, she said:

"Good-mornin', Kane. Pat's goin' to die."

"What makes you think so?"

"Och, he goes on so. He talks queer. You're the only one in the house. Would ye stay a bit wid Pat after yer breakfast, while I go fur Mick Murphy – an' the praiste?" She spoke in awe-stricken tones, as if Death stood at her elbow.

I consented. I ate my breakfast and then went into the kitchen. Mrs. Brady at once put on her shawl and set out on her errand, leaving me alone to look to Pat.

The little room in which Pat lay was entered from the kitchen. A bright gas-jet was burning above Pat's head. I had not seen him since the day of his "accident." I went in silently. I entered prepared to see dying, perhaps miserably, an unkempt, hateful-tempered boy, whose budding character had suffered from a poisonous moral atmosphere, and whose countenance, despite his tender years, had already received the forbidding stamp of vice. Really, would his death differ much from the death of a brute?

Stay!

My friend, you have at some time retired to rest for the night, leaving the wintry landscape, as seen from your chamber window, barren and black and dismal. You have awakened in the morning to witness a miracle. Snow had fallen while you slept, and the face of nature had been changed. You can now bring back the transformed picture to your mind. The earth is wrapped in a dazzling sheet of white; fairies have touched tree and bush with multifarious forms of grace; and over all the sun is shining resplendently. Snow-covered, the dead vegetation, the weather-worn fences, the barren hills, all are now beautiful. At the sight your heart leaped in joy and wonder.

As strange, as surprising, the change I now beheld in little Pat. He was clean to sweetness. His hair, neatly combed back from his forehead, shone in the gaslight glossy and golden. His face, flushed a little with fever, was round and full. His Irish blue eyes were bright with a light new to them. His countenance was composed, his expression placid, and his gaze, now directed straight at me, steady. A gentle smile played about his childish mouth. The old Pat – the dirty, sneaking, suspicious, deceitful rogue – was vanished. Before me lay little Pat, a cherub boy – confiding, honest, open-eyed, innocent.

Pat's recognition of me was a plaintive smile. It seemed to say: "I know you have thought me bad; but the past is all past now."

I spoke. "Pat, you know me, don't you"

"Oh, yes, Mr. Kane!"

How sober he was, and how steady his voice!

"Are you very ill?"

"Not at all ill."

"Are you in pain?"

"No pain."

"What ails you then, Pat"

"I'm waitin' fur to die."

"What makes you think you are going to die?"

Slowly, with both hands, he smoothed the bed-covers about his breast. After a pause he said:

"I seed me mudder this mornin'. She died when I was t'ree year old. She comed to de front door in a open kerridge. She was all dressed in white, the kerridge was white, and dere was hitched on to it four white horses. She said, 'Paddy, my own darlin' little Paddy, I've come to take ye up to heaven.'"

Was his mind wandering? Or was his real spirit shining forth at last?

For a while he lay quiet. The busy hum of the streets was carried faintly to my ear; bringing to me for the moment a wave of the outer world – the harsh, pushing, struggling, selfish, sordid world – the world that had brought hardship, misery, and sin to little Pat, and that, should he live, promised him every chance for life-long shame and degradation.

By and by he spoke again:

"I stoled yer dollar, Mr. Kane."

"Never mind that now, Pat."

"I've did lots o' bad things. I towld me mudder I wusn't fit fur heaven. But she said, 'Darlint, ye did the best ye could. There's a seat in the kerridge beside me fur ye's. I'll take ye wid me shtrait up to heaven, and ye'll never be parted from yer mudder agin.' Mr. Kane, I know every word me mudder said to me."

I remained quiet. I could find nothing to say.

"Mudder's at de front door agin. I t'ink I'm goin' to die quick."

He no longer looked at me, but upward. He spoke slowly:

"Please tell me fader I said he mus'n't git drunk no more. Tell him to give his wages to aunty. Tell him little Pat can't never now take his grub to de fac't'ry no more, but even if dead I'll meet him every evenin' at de corner when he comes home from de shop. Tell everybody good-by an' God bless dem all."

He lay again very quiet, the patient, thoughtful expression gradually merging into one of deep reverence. In a voice barely audible, he said:

"Our Fader —"

A brief pause. Then, in a tone a little louder:

"Who art in heaven — "

Clearly and musically he now spoke.

"Hallowed be T'y name – Wot's hallowed, Mr. Kane?"

"'Holy,' 'sacred,' Pat."

With deeper fervor he repeated:

"Hallowed be T'y name, T'y kingdom come — "

Then, as if to himself:

"Dat means me mudder's to come in de kerridge."

"T'y will be done on eart' as it is in heaven – on eart' wid me fader so he won't git drunk. Give us dis day our daily bread – dat's fur de oders; I don't need none no more. An' furgive us our trespasses – dem's sins – as we furgive dose who trespasses 'ginst us. And lead us not into temptation – dat's fur me fader, too."

Nothing further for a long while. He breathed regularly, but lightly. His eyes had half closed. His air was that of one listening and seeing something afar. Last of all, slowly and distinctly, but in a faint voice, he said:

"But deliver us from evil. Amen."

His head turned over a little against the pillow. A pallor suddenly overspread his face. Little Pat was dead.

A noise at the front door. A sound of bustling feet. In hurried old Mrs. Brady; at her heels Mick Murphy, Mrs. McNaghatally, and others.

I said: "Pat has just died."

Screams from the women. A powerful howl from Mick. A general confusion of sounds.

I left the basement and made my way up toward my room. In the upper hallway stood little Johnny McNaghatally. He said:

"How's Slob?"

"He is dead."

"Wot's dey a-goin to do wit' his old cloze?"

III
The Wake

The morning after Pat's death I was awakened by someone knocking at my room door and calling to me that the coroner wanted me on his jury downstairs. When, in response to the summons, I reached the parlor, Mick Murphy was standing in the middle of the room vowing vengeance on any officer of the law who should dare to lay a finger on Pat's body. The coroner and an assistant, indifferent to Mick's vaporings, were informally putting hurried questions to those present. They had been summoned for jury duty – the German grocer from the corner below, Tim Foy, and three of the lodgers. I had been called as the sixth necessary juror. Directly on my entrance the coroner bunched us together, swore us to our duty, and snapped his fingers at Mrs. Brady to come in from the hall and answer as a witness.

"How did this boy come to his death?"

"Well, sir," with her apron to her eyes, "he was a-playin: an' he tumbled down an' hurted his timple. He thin tuk cowld, an' he was sick abed wit' a fever fur siveral days, an' thin he died."

"No one beat him or kicked him on the head, I suppose?"

"Oh, my! no, indeed."

"Does anyone know to the contrary?"

Silence.

"Gentlemen, it's my opinion that deceased came to his death by meningitis – inflammation of a membrane of the skull. Maybe he fell against something, as boys do, and then took cold. I instruct you to find in accordance with the evidence."

"Yes, sir," said Tim Foy, with a sigh of relief.

"Then sign."

And we all signed.

An ejaculation now from Mick Murphy: "Hold! No mutilatin' knife of the dissectin' surgeon shall touch the fair brow o' me departed son!"

Mick had been watching the proceedings with a scowl, as if seeking a grievance to argue over.

The coroner and his assistant packed away their papers and walked out of the house, bestowing not even a look on Mick. The moment they were out of the door, Mick threw an oratorical hand in the air, and announced:

"Gin-til-min, ye are intoitled, each an' iviry wan uv ye, to a dollar a head, jewry min's salary. An' ye kin foight fur yer rights in the courts o' the land."

I went back to bed and had out my sleep. I was away from the house all that afternoon and half the night, doing duty on the "black-pipe boat." When I returned to my lodgings after work it was nearly three o'clock in the morning. The two lower floors of the house were illuminated. I opened the front door with a latch-key, and was about to pass up to my room when I was intercepted by Tim Foy, who came out of the open parlor door and said:

"Come in an' see Pat. He's a splendid corpse."

Tim would listen to no excuse. I entered. In front of the mantelpiece, resting on two black undertaker's stools, lay Pat in his coffin. At the head stood a tall branched brass bracket, holding a dozen lighted wax candles, which threw a brilliant and steady light over the room. The men and women seated in the parlor left a wide open space about the coffin. Of these wakers, some were conversing in low voices, while others gazed pensively at the floor.

I walked across the room and stood at the foot of the coffin. The only story that the face now told was that the spirit had fled. Its color was ghastly; the mouth was twisted; the eyes were darkened and sunken. Only cold clay now.

Mick Murphy stood beside the coffin, enacting grief in bold pantomime, wringing his hands, mumbling, groaning, and aspirating hard. On the mantelpiece and on a table at the pier-glass, over between the windows, stood tumblers and black bottles.

"Mick's been going on fearful all night," whispered Foy to me. He then suggested that wake etiquette required me to take a seat for a while in the circle of mourners. I found an empty chair near the entry door. Foy moved about the room, picked up a black bottle and a glass, and, handing them to me, asked me to help myself. Foy was master of ceremonies. He performed his duties with a sympathetic face and with an evident desire that no guest should be overlooked. A man sitting next me told me in an undertone that Mick had given Tim precedence over the relatives in order to show that he was forgiven his share of the blame for Pat's accident.

"Oi'm the very best loight-weight man in the whole city of New York!" – Mick broke the silence in a loud voice. He limped into the middle of the room and stood there theatrically. He was a strangely maimed and distorted man. A red scar ran across his neck and chin; another seared his forehead. His head was set askew upon his shoulders. One arm crooked back and spread out his thumb and fingers. One leg was straight, but the foot of the other rested on the floor only at the toes. Mick's air was that of chief mourner – a personage entitled to prominence. He proceeded to deliver himself of a speech, in alternate shouts and hoarse whispers.

"Oi were wance the very bist loight-weight in the Shtate of New York! Oi'm shtill a moighty good mon! Oi'm the bist mon in this room, an' Oi'll bet on it. Oi got more mus'l, an' more boan, an' more sinnoo, an' more strinth than any blacksmith in the war-r-d. Me father lived to be a hunder an' t'ree years owld. Oi'm afther followin' 'im. Oi kin drink more this day than iver I cud. Oi've been daddy to thirteen children – sivin dead an' aight livin. The dirty spalpeens 've all left me an' run away, except Pat, the fourteenth, an' there he lies shtiff in his burial cerements."

Mick's auditors sat regarding him silently and with awe. They respected the agonies of a bereaved father. He limped back and forth across the room, and reassumed his orator's attitude. The man next me whispered: "Now he's goin' to tell about his tumble." Did Mick go through all this performance for every arrival?

"Oi'm not the mon oi wance wuz. Because Oi had a calamitous fall. Oi was a-carryin' hod to the top of a five-story buildin' up in Captain O'Connery's precinct. Up a-top Oi shtarted to take a short cut over the bames, which wos all the flures there wuz, an' Oi wuz limber and sure-futted in thim days, an' the flures were not there yit, only the bames an' the joices, an' Oi made a misshtep, an' the hodful o' brick went shootin' an' showerin' down to the cellar, the hod click-a-de-clack after thim, rattlin' 'ginst the bames, and me suddint-like afther the hod – only Oi shtruck wid me back at the fourth flure on a joice. Oi didn't soon enough git me hands behind me, an' so Oi slid off, the back o' me head cracking the bame, an' in a jiffy Oi was a-straddlin' another joice on the third flure. That Oi hunged to fur a full minute, but Oi wuz dizzy and fell to the flure nixt. There Oi shtruck a shtake wid me chin an' broke it off, an' thin Oi tumbled from that to the nixt flure below, and that wos the cellar. Oi had a hunder an' twenty-one bones broke as counted at the hoshpital. Oi wuz in hoshpital sivin months two days. Oi revived an' was discharged a cripple fur life. Think o' that! Where's nother mon loike me?"

The spectators still regarded Mick solemnly; he was mourning the dead, and they respected his anguish.

Mick limped to the table, turned up a black bottle to his mouth, and walked beside the coffin. Here he ended his act, declaiming over the corpse, his voice a sustained cry:

"Och, me poor b'y! The last of thim all, for they're all dead to me now. Ye have brought me me grub ivery day to the shop – ivery day, an' ye hardly iver missed it wanst. An' ye used to meet me at the corner alwus whin Oi camed home. Ye towld Mr. Kane fur to tell me nivver to dhrink agin; an' Oi nivver wull – afther this night – nivver. But me grief's killin' to me now. Pat, ye ar' a saint. Ye alwus wuz. Oi kin ricollect ivery blissid act o' yer loife, an' now" – here he threw his arms wildly above him, and shook his head violently, his voice rising – "an' now ye are dead, dead, dead! Och! Pat! there ain't no God an' there ain't no divil. If there wuz, he wouldn't take ye from me, an' me a-lovin' ye so. Oi wuz alwus kind to ye, an' ye were a-growin' up stiddy an' honest an' good an' noble. Oi learned from me other failures wid childer what to do wid ye. Here by yer breathless an' inonimate corpse Oi shwear to be a better mon than iver. Oi'll dhrink no more. But Oi'm a desarted father. Oi owe nothin' to none o' me childer. Me offspring's recreant to me. Oh! sharper than a serpent's tooth it is to have a gang o' thankless childer!"

He was now shrieking. Foy whispered to me that perhaps if I went Mick would not feel obliged to "keen" further. Declining a proffered bottle, I left the room. After Mick had sent up two or three more piercing yells, quiet was restored. No one called at the house later, and Mick subsided to the position of a mere watcher.

IV
His Funeral

As soon as I was astir the next noon, Mrs. Brady waited on me, and, saying the funeral would start in an hour, invited me to be a pall-bearer.

A line of carriages, rather paint-worn and with faded trimmings, but yet carriages, soon afterward formed along the curb at our side of the street. A child's hearse, painted white, drove up to the door. Neighbors hung out of the windows, staring. Groups of little girls and bare-headed women gathered on nearby stoops and gazed at the preparations for the funeral.

The parlor could not hold all the mourners who came. The men waited on the sidewalk or in the hallway, in knots. I myself stood in the rear of the hallway. While there, I heard a voice from the kitchen stairs, close to me, saying:

"Mr. Kane!"

I looked down. It was Mrs. McNaghatally. I went down several steps. She came part way up and whispered huskily:

"Mr. Kane, me best respects an' sympathies to Mrs. Brady an' Mr. Murphy in the hour of their bitther beravement, but I can't attend the funeral, owin' to sudden 'disposition since the wake last night."

I observed she had a bad black eye. I answered consolingly that I would deliver her message.

"An' tell thim, wid me compliments, that little Margaretta and Johnny 'll take me place in one o' the kerridges."

I nodded assent, and she retired into the sympathetic obscurity of the back stairs, where she could peep through the banister rails without being seen.

As I got back to the landing at the head of the stairs, a man in clerical garb was there, speaking with Mrs. Brady. She was closing the snap of her pocket-book and putting the pocket-book in the bosom of her dress.

There were no religious services at the house. It was understood they were to take place at the cemetery.

"Hurry up!" said the business-like undertaker. "We're half an hour late now. We'll have to take the short cut when across the river."

All took a farewell look at Pat. It was with some difficulty that Mick Murphy could be led away from the coffin. He kissed the dead boy's face and moaned and cried aloud. It looked as if the scene of the previous night was to be repeated, but Mrs. Brady took him by the shoulder and said gruffly:

"Come along here. There's enough o' this nonsense."

The drivers went off at a trot. As the carriage I was in turned a street corner I mentally noted that the hire of the vehicles in line represented two or three months' wages for Mick. I was thinking of this extravagance when one of the three other men with me said:

"Well, gentlemen, suppose we ante up."

"Eh?"

"I engaged this here kerridge for a dollar a head, anticipating that no individual occupant would back out of his social obligations."

We other three each gave him a dollar, Johnny McNaghatally, a fifth among us, not counting. The money safe in his pocket, the collector was amicable. He informed us that he was an old friend of the Murphy family. He would not see them go down in social standing by sending a small and shabby funeral from their door, so he had hired a carriage, relying on the generosity of those sharing it with him to get his money back. He observed that other intimates of the family had done likewise, and it was a most creditable funeral. Altogether, it was comforting to the relatives of the deceased. He then politely passed around a small black flask.

After crossing the river, the short cut was taken. Instead of following paved streets, the undertaker took us diagonally across open lots, at places hilly, at others marshy. Through our hack window I caught occasional glimpses of the hearse. At times it was halfway to the hubs in puddles, the horses splashing the water at a trot. Again, in going up a steep incline, it seemed as if the coffin might slide out behind. The coaches fell out of line. Each driver chose his own best short cuts. At one place, one of the drivers from the rear brought his hack up abreast of ours. Little Margaretta McNaghatally, leaning out of its nearer window, piped up:

"Hello, Johnny! We's goin' faster'n yous."

"We'll beat you to de winnin'-post," was the reply. "But de hearse has de best team uv all."

The sun was going down when we reached the cemetery. The scene was gloomy, – its more striking features chilly white headstones, leafless old forest trees, relics of the time when the graveyard was a wood, and moist and mournful evergreens. Other city funerals, homeward bound, seemed bent on swift runs and short cuts. Our hacks drawing up in front of a chapel, the men quickly alighted, throwing away their cigars. Pat's coffin had already been carried inside the building by graveyard employees. We straggled inside hastily in a bad procession. Two other funeral parties were already in the chapel. In front of the chancel was a huge black table, with castors set in it like those of a hearse bed. On it three coffins were ranged side by side. There were fixtures for six. At the altar two men in black robes were beginning to say prayers. Their work proceeded speedily, mechanically, the impressiveness of the ceremony lost to them in repetition. During their rapid and indifferent utterances, our group of lodgers in adjoining pews maintained silence, though uncertain as to when to kneel and when to stand. Suddenly, after sprinkling the coffins with water, the prayer-makers passed out of a side door. Not a word had been said of the dead or to the mourning families.

Mrs. Brady followed the black-robed men to the sacristy. In a moment she returned, closing the snap of her pocket-book and putting the pocket-book in the bosom of her dress.

Our undertaker's men had taken Pat's coffin and were walking off rapidly. Again our procession hurried along, and when I caught up to the undertaker he had reached Pat's grave and was having an altercation with two gravediggers.

"I was tole he was a three-year-old," said a digger, "an' the grave's not big enough."

He stooped, placed a hand at each side of the grave, and swung himself down into it. With a short shovel he scooped the earth from the head end without enlarging the top, threw the loosened dirt out, climbed up, and proceeded, with another digger, to lower Pat to his last resting-place. The coffin being too long to go down level, Pat was almost stood on his head as he descended. Then the smaller gravedigger got down in the grave, astride the coffin, and wedged the head of it up into place.

Meantime the funeral party stood in a circle about the grave, looking on. The evening shadows were gathering; the air was chilly. Good-by, little Pat! You lived your brief day; bent to the rough winds that blew upon you; suffered, body and soul, from what was beyond your understanding; lighted up for a brief moment with a miracle of spirit, and died. Good-by!

The gravediggers began filling the grave.

Mrs. Brady turned toward me and said in a low voice:

"There's four in that grave of ours now. We bought it wid de privilege of six. Mick Murphy 'll be buried there next, and me last, a-top."

The grave filled with earth, we turned away, entered the hacks, and at a rapid pace were driven homeward. I sat up on the box beside a driver. I had nothing to say, evidently to his disappointment, as he was inclined to be sociable.

In the block next the ferry-house he drew up his horses to the curb. The other drivers had done the same. I asked what it meant. He replied, somewhat aggressively:

"Well, at respectable funerals it's customary to treat the drivers."

The ground floor of every house in the block was a saloon fitted up for funeral trade. Our entire party, drivers and all, entered one. Bartenders busied themselves arranging drinking-tables, greeting the drivers as everyday friends, and taking orders. In a brief while all were enjoying drinks and cigars and the spirit of chumminess. I slipped away.

All that night's trick on the steamboat I saw little Pat beneath the gaslight in the little basement room, praying with his heavenly smile, just before he died. Dirty, ragged, bad Slob had had goodness in him which ought to have had a chance. I wondered if his dying wishes would inspire Mick Murphy to keep the oath of sobriety he had taken at his dead boy's coffin.

My trips done, I quitted my post and repaired to my lodgings. In the silence after midnight I passed up the narrow street, opened the door with a latch-key, and made my way upstairs in the dark. On the second-story landing I stumbled over something stretched on the floor. I struck a light to see what it was.

It was Mick Murphy – dead drunk.

Père Monnier's Ward. A Novel

by William A. McDermott (New York, Cincinnati: Benziger Brothers, 1898)

Born in Ireland in 1863, William A. McDermott came to America as a child and grew up in Lawrence, Massachusetts. As a young man, he traveled widely. His first job was as a reporter in Chicago at age seventeen, and he spent the next five years as a journalist in the tenement districts of Chicago and New York. He also went to New Orleans, Mexico, and Europe, where he met Cardinal Newman and Pope Leo XIII. He taught at Villanova University, studied for the priesthood later in life, and spent his last years as pastor of a parish in the Adirondacks. There, he found leisure to write most of his books, which include two critical studies of American Catholic literature, Down at Caxton's *(1895) and* Impressions and Opinions *(1898), several short stories, and two novels set in New York City and the Adirondacks,* Mr. Billy Buttons *(1896) and* Père Monnier's Ward *(1898). Father McDermott always wrote using the pseudonym, "Walter Lecky." He died at the age of fifty in 1913.*

The chapter from McDermott's second novel reprinted here is an archetypal immigrant tale in capsule form, rendered sketchily, but with real satiric and admonitory bite. James Fortune is a Catholic orphan who has been raised as a servant by Mr. Brown, a Protestant Poor Law Guardian in their native Stranorlar, County Donegal. The boy flees to America on the immigrant ship "Blackbird," and is befriended by a generous fellow Donegal man, Jamie McDade, a ward boss and tavern keeper in New York. Bright and opportunistic, James Fortune marries McDade's pretentious daughter and vaults up the New York political ladder, from alderman to Congress to a mansion on Fifth Avenue. He begins his rise by praising Ireland and those who are proud of their heritage, and by founding an Irish nationalist club. Upon reaching the top, he resigns his Irish memberships, joins the "St. Andrew's Society," and declares himself to be "Scotch-Irish." (This was a common ploy used by newly middle-class Irish in the later nineteenth century to distance themselves from later waves of working-class immigrants.) In a final stroke of hypocrisy, James Fortune allows his fourth child to be baptized "Chichester Hartley Fortune" – in the Episcopal Church.

The excerpt opens as young James Fortune gets his first opportunity to make a political speech – in support of congressional candidate Clancy at New York City's Concordia Hall.

"**W**hy not give Fortune a chance?" suggested one of the bartenders. "He's always spouting around here. I have often heard him say that he could do as well as half the fellows he heard shooting off on platforms. It would do no harm to give him a chance. If he can't help, sure he can't hurt. One thing I can tell you, boys, he won't falter for want of gab. If you want him, as soon as he comes from his supper I'll send him down to the hall; that is, if you say so."

"Well, just as John says, he can't hurt us a bit – that's sure; so why not give the youngster a chance? If you don't try these young fellows you will never know what's in them. I vouch that he won't break down; he's not of the soft brand. Let him take my place. What's your opinion?"

There was a hearty yes to McDade's question, and the bartender was told to hunt up James Fortune.

Concordia Hall was filled to overflowing with followers of both candidates. They had come to hear the Hon. James Hunter, to enjoy his latest witty sayings. They had heard the other speakers and were growing tired and impatient. Some were leaving the hall. At this juncture Mr. McDade shouted: "Fortune! Fortune!" The crowd took up the shout and yelled itself hoarse, and kept on yelling until a handsome, finely dressed young man at the rear end of the platform arose, advanced towards his audience, and began talking with the utmost confidence and coolness, silencing the audience in a moment. As he warmed up in his speech he became fiery and cutting. He painted Clancy as a man born on Irish soil, bred in the fairest land the sun shines upon, loving that land, becoming a member of a society vowed to free that land, and banished – his only crime. He would not sell that land. The leaving his native land, the cruel partings, the voyage on the fever-ships, the landing and the rise of Clancy from a 'longshoreman, his simplicity that no honors could destroy, his generosity – all were held up to the audience with a fire and earnestness that spell-bound them.

"You should vote for Clancy," said the young orator, "because Clancy is an exile from his country, and for a reason that does honor to the man. He loved Ireland and he hated England. Will you, exiles of Erin, blame Clancy for following not only in your footsteps, but in those of every Irishman who is not a craven or a coward? Clancy is proud of being an Irishman; he does not deny it. He has not changed his name, nor vowed that his ancestors came over in the *Mayflower*. He admits that he is Irish, and Irish to the backbone. I have heard them say, these Yankees, on the streets that they will vote for Gilligan, because Gilligan, at any rate, was born over here, while Clancy is but a greenhorn. They think they could make a tool of Gilligan; they know that they can never touch Clancy. Irishmen! exiles! what answer will you give these politicians who loathe you because you are Irish? I know an answer that will humble them in the dust. I hold in my hand here a telegram from the Hon. James Hunter to the friend of all of you, honest James McDade. Hunter says he is sick, and he says it at the eleventh hour; but it's not the first time the Irish made the Sassenach sick.* We can do without him. We will thank him for his kindness by voting for Clancy."

As Fortune finished his audience went wild, shouting for Clancy and booing for Hunter and everything he was supposed to represent. On all sides it was said that young Fortune was a coming man, a saying emphasized the next morning with half a column in *The Morning Democrat.*

"The unexpected is always happening," said Disraeli. It is an aphorism that one may hold with no little security. Gilligan and his friends were so confident of success that they had ordered a banquet to celebrate the victory. They had also, as they boldly avowed, steeped a rod in vinegar for McDade. When, then, contrary to all expectation, the news came that Clancy was elected by a large majority, the word sped rapidly through the district that young Fortune and his speech were the making of the Hon. Mike Clancy. From that moment he was no longer the obscure bartender of James McDade, but a man of "pull" and power. Clancy was of that type of politicians who hold that a friend in need is a friend indeed, and at any rate he had learned that young Fortune could be a dangerous enemy. It was but the work of a wise man to bind him to his standard.

The Hon. Mike Clancy was a cellar-digger: few things in those days paid better. His triumphant election meant more contracts than he could well fulfil; besides most of his time would now be spent in making laws. Supervision by some one interested in his business was necessary. After a talk with McDade the firm of Clancy & Fortune was founded. At the suggestion of the junior member the firm branched out in various directions. James Fortune, who had won his hold by politics, had no intention of abandoning that which so speedily put him on the road to success. He founded the "Shamrock Club," which met weekly at McDade's to discuss the best means of freeing Ireland – and at the same time of holding a grip on New York. This club in a few months became so large that a hall was rented, and despite the protests of James Fortune, their president, who wished to call the hall "The Sarsfield," was named Fortune Hall. The president graciously submitted, claiming as his privilege the right to decorate the interior in a suitable manner, which was done to their taste. The decorations consisted of green flags, green ribbons, framed pictures of Saint Patrick banishing snakes, Brian Boru in his tent, Sarsfield in battle array, Emmet in a reverie, O'Connell on Tara's hill, framed sentiments, mostly warnings to "cruel England," that the day of retribution was near at hand, and if she valued her safety she would relax her grip on green Erin.

At the end of the hall was a streamer on which was sewed in large golden letters: "We Come From The Thirty-Two Counties Of Ireland! We Are The Kindly Irish!"

About this time the death of Peter Quigley made a vacancy in the board

---

*["Sassenach" is Gaelic for an English person.]

of aldermen, and the news being discussed at the Shamrock Club, one of the members, pointing to the motto on the streamer, said: "Let us show how kindly we can be by electing our president in Quigley's place. I don't want to say much against the dead – I guess they had better rest – but you all know what I'm going to say just as well as I do, that Quigley, before he got office, talked nothing but 'Ireland, Ireland', and what he would do for the Irish, but as soon as he had his fat job he forgot all his promises, and he and his family became so proud that they would as lief meet the devil as one of us. I tell you, he is not the first that has risen through us, and, when up, despised us, and forgot the shoulders on which he mounted. What do you think, boys, of my suggestion? It's as good as they make them."

That evening a committee waited on James Fortune, tendered him the nomination and their support, which was later ratified by the regular organization, making, as it did, the best of a bad matter. To oppose the Shamrock Club would have been poor and foolish policy, and from politics we expect the wisdom found in the vulgar phrase, "Save your own bacon every time."

A few weeks later Alderman Fortune, fresh from his glory, at the age of twenty-eight, and much to the mind of Mrs. McDade, whose ideas were high and whose mourning was constant over what she called "the slackness of her husband for honors," called at the McDade residence on a pleasant errand. He was met by Mrs. McDade, a short, stout woman, resplendently clad.

He was led into the spacious parlor and seated himself at the wave of her bejewelled hand.

Mrs. McDade, in her own way, was gracious and talkative, and the alderman was full of pleasantry.

"I knew you would be elected," said Mrs. McDade. "I told the governor so. How your people, if they were alive, would rejoice! Mr. Mac told me that your family was one of the best, if not the very best, in the county he comes from, but that they sacrificed all for Ireland. That Irish business is wearying, but you dare not say a word about it when the governor is around. I see he has you in it. You are a young man, and, if you take a woman's advice, you will leave the Irish severely alone. Mr. Mac makes his living out of them, but you're now where you can afford to ignore them, and you can do it easily; besides you have such a name that nobody would put an Irish construction upon it. What can you make out of McDade, even if the governor wanted to give it a twist? No matter how you roll it, 'tis Irish and nothing else. Of course, if the governor was around I would lose my head for less than I've said to you. You know he lives on his imagination. According to his story, he will free Ireland, and then he and I and Miss Molly, so he says, will own Daffadowndilly Castle and have nothing to do but give orders and have them obeyed. I tell him that he had better attend to his business and leave the Daffadowndillys alone, for if they ever catch him over there they'll give him a life-sentence.

"Then it is enough to drive me wild, the kind of characters he's in with in this Irish business – hod-carriers, carpenters, bricklayers, and that set, with their thick tongues, and their thick brogans, wandering over the brussels, and in danger of breaking my brickety-brack. Poor Molly, she dare not say 'boo.' No; the governor will have nothing here but Irish, and so I and his poor girl must suffer. The other night the poor, dear child went with the Flammers to the Episcopals, and maybe she will never hear the last of that! The governor was like a wild man; cried like a child, said it was the first disgrace in his family, and if she ever went there again she should never darken his door. When the row was over I stole into her bedroom and told her to go when she felt like it, and not mind her father's bad tongue. I suppose she won't be long with us. Mr. Mac told me to-day at dinner that you were coming to-night to see me on a little business. I can easily guess what it is. Molly herself has given me an inkling of it. Well, when I married McDade I took my own advice and pleased myself, so it's for Molly to do the same. She has taken a fancy to you, and I will not, indeed, gainsay it. If she burns her fingers she cannot blame me. Molly is the finest girl in the city, the only thing we have to make us happy, and whoever gets her will have to live with us for a spell. We couldn't see her leaving us."

Mrs. McDade sobbed violently, and Miss Molly, hearing her mother, was soon by her side.

The lovers had long agreed. The consent of the mother, now given, was all that was needed.

The day after the marriage the generous McDade presented his daughter a fine residence, boasting, as he signed the transfer papers, that the first male of the line of Fortune and McDade should have a similar present.

This honestly meant boast was never to be put into effect. It was a spiritual writer with much foresight who said that in the midst of life we are in death. Happy in his daughter's marriage and in his new son's schemes and speculations, McDade planned away into the future, promising himself in the not distant time that sweetest of pleasures, children's loving prattle.

Merry are the bird-songs in the crisp spring morn, merry are the voices of the loitering brooks, but merrier far the babbling speech from children whose chubby little hands toy with your face, whose laughing little eyes tell the old, old story of love!

A cold, laughed at at first, then doctored, off and on, at the request of friends, finally settled into pneumonia. Medical skill was useless. The big, brave, generous Irishman, who had watched so many ships come into port, who had welcomed so many immigrants to his home and helped them with his purse, lay cold and dead in the handsome house where he had dreamed of romping with his grandchildren.

It is said that the dreams of our early life press upon us closer as death comes. "Poor Mac," as they called him – those who made his district, and they were of every nationality – in his last illness sang of his native Donegal, wept for his Erin, gave the command to his soldiers to charge Daffadowndilly Castle and hoist the standard of the dauntless McDades. A few minutes before he died, the battle was over. He had conquered; the Daffadowndillys were in flight; he was lord and master of his ancestral estates; the dream of his life had been fulfilled. Those who surrounded his bedside heard him say, as a momentary consciousness came to him: "Read over me from Malachy McCrudden's prayer-book." But that gleam of reason faded, and as lord and chief of his clan, in full possession of his dream, passed away what bluff old Captain Campbell, with honest tears in his eyes, called "the tenderest heart that I ever brought over the sea."

At his death his property passed into the hands of James Fortune, whose business capacity and power of amassing wealth were well understood.

It was the opinion of those who were keen judges that the income of the property would increase in the new hands, and the thought was right as evidenced in the succeeding years.

With Fortune as alderman and Clancy in Congress, the contracts for work grew yearly, until ten years after the company's inception its founders were reckoned worth a quarter of a million dollars each. It was then that Clancy sold out his interest to his partner, resigned his seat in Congress, and withdrew to spend the remainder of his life in his fine country mansion at New Rochelle. Before he resigned he so arranged it that his old business associate found no difficulty in occupying his long-coveted seat in Congress.

This new honor brought the Fortunes to Washington, and with them came the jubilant mother-in-law, now Mrs. Dade. She was filled with the ambition to dazzle, and her word in the household was law. Daily in her barouche the young Fortunes, gayly dressed, clustered around her. She drove on Pennsylvania Avenue, her quick eyes seeing the latest fads of fashion, and noting them for consultation with her daughter. The fourth child, Chichester Hartley Fortune, was born in Washington, and at the request of the Chichesters, for whom it was named, was baptized in St. John's Episcopal Church, one of the presents on this occasion coming from the President, with a little note which Mrs. Dade treasured to her dying day and showed to all her friends as evidence of the high standing of the Fortunes. When Mr. Fortune's time in Congress expired he returned to New York and purchased the Wormley residence on Fifth Avenue, from which date his former political friends noted a change. At the request of Mrs. Dade, but very willingly complied with, the Hon. Mr. Fortune resigned the presidency of the Shamrock Club, and sent brief letters of resignation to the various Irish organizations to which he belonged and through which he had received his rise and fortune. When these notes were read, they brought to his associates the old story of the result of mounting a beggar on horseback. There were two listeners who had other thoughts – the bartender who first launched him into political life and the man who first pressed his name as the genuine Irishman who should take Quigley's place. One said to himself: "This patriotism is a humbug, and the quicker we learn that those professing Irish patriots are in the thing for a living the better." The other: "Whom can you trust these days? It was Father James Cahill that knew them when he said: 'John, have nothing to do with them. I am thirty-two years as a priest in New York, and have some experience, and in all that time I have not met one of those political chaps who talked Ireland, and, thanks to the foolish Irish, rose to big positions, who did not, as soon as his purse was fat enough, turn on them, insult them, and know them no more; keep away from them, John.' I wished I had taken his advice, but it's not too late yet to warn my children. This is only the beginning. We won't have long to wait for the end."

"Coming events," sang the poet, "cast their shadows before," and the burden of his song was right.

To an invitation of the Shamrock Club to dine with them on St. Patrick's Day and respond to the toast "The Irish in America," the Hon. James Fortune sent a curt note saying that he no longer believed in fostering the spirit of nationality in free America – that there should be neither Irish, French, nor German in America, but Americans; and that those who did not like to be Americans should go where they could be Irish, French, or German.

The reading of this note brought curses and threats, but there were those of the club who were sad and silent, blaming themselves for putting him into a position to ignore their threats and curses, and through that position to amass enough wealth to make the position secure.

At the St. Andrew's Society dinner, which Mr. Fortune later attended, he boasted of his ancestors, strong of limb and sparing of speech, who had come to Ireland from that land of lands, the home of Walter Scott and Bobby Burns. He was proud of being Scotch-Irish, and with pride he referred to what those of that race had done in the upbuilding of the great American people. Some of them, he continued, had like himself been born in Ireland – a mere accident; but their love of Scotland was, if he might say so, strengthened instead of weakened by that accident.

One part of his speech was loudly applauded:

"Gentlemen, while I pride myself in being a scion of that wonderful race, the Scotch-Irish, and while I pride myself on the battles of my ancestors for holding aloft the banner of Presbyterianism amid a hostile race, I at the same time put my Americanism above all things. I hold that America is the greatest land under high heaven, and to be a citizen of this land is the highest honor a mortal can enjoy. It behooves us who are here tonight to vow that this land shall never become the prey of any potentate whatsoever, temporal or spiritual, king or pontiff. It behooves us to maintain, even with our lives, the little red schoolhouse which has done so much for the commonwealth; it behooves us to keep the State and Church apart, and to blend all people into the American people – a people destined to be the liberators of humanity!"

This speech as reported in the morning journals was the last straw to break the camel's back. It severed the last tie with his old friends. Even Clancy, a few weeks after, shut the door in his face and spoke of him as a renegade and a scoundrel.

The loss of these old associates worried not the Hon. James Fortune. New associates of high standing, as the world counts, were at his beck. Mrs. Dade was glad that her distinguished son-in-law had cut loose from the "low Irish," and was with his family hereafter to be in the ranks of the swell set and best blood. Fortune was his name, and verily the Fortunes were in the swim.

The Art of Disappearing

by John Talbot Smith (New York, Cincinnati: Benziger Brothers, 1899)

The son of Bernard Smith, a railroad worker, and Brigid (O'Donnell) Smith, John Talbot Smith was born in Saratoga, New York, in 1855. After attending the Christian Brothers school in Albany, he went into a seminary in Toronto, and was ordained a priest into the diocese of Ogdensburg in 1881. Smith worked at a small mission on Lake Champlain until 1889, when his superiors recognized his literary potential by releasing him from his mission duties and allowing him to pursue a writing career in New York City. He lived in New York for twenty years – editing the weekly literary periodical The Catholic Review *from 1889 to 1892, founding the Catholic Summer School of America and the Catholic Writers and Actors Guilds, serving as chaplain to several organizations, and writing history and fiction. He died in Dobbs Ferry, New York, in 1923.*

Like Father Hugh Quigley before him, Smith made fictional use of his pastoral mission settings and experiences. Serialized in The Catholic World *in 1880, his first novel,* A Woman of Culture: A Canadian Romance, *depicts Irish life in Canada and has as its climax an Orange/Green riot on St. Patrick's Day on the streets of Toronto. Next came* Solitary Island *(1888), a story of religious enlightenment set among the Thousand Islands of the St. Lawrence River.* Saranac: A Story of Lake Champlain *(1892) dramatizes Irish and French-Canadian tensions in a small Adirondack community, and* His Honor the Mayor: Tales of the Puritan and His Neighbors *(1891) collects stories that examine similar cultural collisions in Ontario, New York, and New England.*

Smith's last, most ambitious, and most accomplished novel was The Art of Disappearing. *Set in New England, New York, and Ireland, this book contains detailed renderings of Irish and Irish-American daily life in the 1860s and 1870s; while also incorporating a number of touchstone public events, including the failed Fenian rising in Ireland in 1867 and the dedication of St. Patrick's Cathedral in New York City in 1879. In the climactic chapter excerpted here, the dying Fenian Owen Ledwith engages his old friend Monsignor O'Donnell in a sophisticated discussion of the thorny Irish debate between nationalism and religion. Visible from Ledwith's window, the nearly completed cathedral is both the catalyst for a vision of Catholic triumphalism and the compelling symbol of Irish-American achievement.*

Monsignor came often, and then oftener when Owen's strength began to fail rapidly. The two friends in Irish politics had little agreement, but in the gloom of approaching death they remembered only their friendship. The priest worked vainly to put Owen into a proper frame of mind before his departure for judgment. He had made his peace with the Church, and received the last rites like a believer, but with the coldness of him who receives necessities from one who has wronged him. He was dying, not like a Christian, but like the pagan patriot who has failed: only the shades awaited him when he fled from the darkness of earthly shame. They sat together one March afternoon facing the window and the declining sun. To the right another window gave them a good view of the beautiful cathedral, whose twin spires, many turrets, and noble walls shone blue and golden in the brilliant light.

"I love to look at it from this elevation," said Monsignor, who had just been discoursing on the work of his life. "In two years, just think, the most beautiful temple in the western continent will be dedicated."

"The money that has gone into it would have struck a great blow for Erin," said Ledwith with a bitter sigh.

"So much of it has escaped the yawning pockets of the numberless patriots," retorted Monsignor dispassionately. "The money would not have been lost in so good a cause, but its present use has done more for your people than a score of the blows which you aim at England."

"Claim everything in sight while you are at it," said Owen. "In God's name what connection has your gorgeous cathedral with any one's freedom?"

"Father dear, you are exciting yourself," Honora broke in, but neither heeded her.

"Christ brought us true freedom," said Monsignor, "and the Church alone teaches, practices, and maintains it."

"A fine example is provided by Ireland, where to a dead certainty freedom was lost because the Church had too unnatural a hold upon the people."

"What was lost on account of the faith will be given back again with compound interest. Political and military movements have done much for Ireland in fifty years; but the only real triumphs, universal, brilliant, enduring, significant, leading surely up to greater things, have been won by the Irish faith, of which that cathedral, shining so gloriously in the sun this afternoon, is both a result and a symbol."

"I believe you will die with that conviction," Ledwith said in wonder.

"I wish you could die with the same, Owen," replied Monsignor tenderly. They fell silent for a little under the stress of sudden feeling.

"How do men reason themselves into such absurdities?" Owen asked himself.

"You ought to know. You have done it often enough," said the priest tartly.

Then both laughed together, as they always did when the argument became personal.

"Do you know what Livingstone and Bradford and the people whom they represent think of that temple?" said Monsignor impressively.

"Oh, their opinions!" Owen snorted.

"They are significant," replied the priest. "These two leaders would give the price of the building to have kept down or destroyed the spirit which undertook and carried out the scheme. They have said to themselves many times in the last twenty years, while that temple rose slowly but gloriously into being, what sort of a race is this, so despised and ill-treated, so poor and ignorant, that in a brief time on our shores can build the finest temple to God which this country has yet seen? What will the people, to whom we have described this race as sunk in papistical stupidity, debased, unenterprising, think, when they gaze on this absolute proof of our mendacity?"

Ledwith, in silence, took a second look at the shining walls and towers.

"Owen, your generous but short-sighted crowd have fought England briefly and unsuccessfully a few times on the soil of Ireland . . . but the children of the faith have fought her with church, and school, and catechism around the globe. Their banner, around which they fought, was not the banner of the Fenians but the banner of Christ. What did you do for the scattered children of the household? Nothing, but collect their moneys. While the great Church followed them everywhere with her priests, centered them about the temple, and made them the bulwark of the faith, the advance-guard, in many lands. Here in America, and in all the colonies of England, in Scotland, even in England itself, wherever the Irish settled, the faith took root and flourished; the faith which means death to the English heresy, and to English power as far as it rests upon the heresy.

"The faith kept the people together, scattered all over the world. It organized them, it trained them, it kept them true to the Christ preached by St. Patrick; it built the fortress of the temple, and the rampart of the school; it kept them a people apart, it kept them civilized, saved them from inevitable apostasy, and founded a force from which you collect your revenues for battle with your enemies; a force which fights England all over the earth night and day, in legislatures, in literature and journalism, in social and commercial life . . . why, man, you are a fragment, a mere fragment, you and your warriors, of that great fight which has the world for an audience and the English earths for its stage."

"When did you evolve this new fallacy?" said Ledwith hoarsely.

"You have all been affected with the spirit of the anti-Catholic revolution in Europe, whose cry is that the Church is the enemy of liberty; yours, that it has been no friend to Irish liberty. Take another look at that cathedral. When you are dead, and many others that will live longer, that church will deliver its message to the people who pass: 'I am the child of the Catholic faith and the Irish; the broad shoulders of America waited for a simple, poor, cast-out people, to dig me from the earth and shape me into a thing of beauty, a glory of the new continent; I myself am not new; I am of that race which in Europe speaks in divine language to you pigmies of the giants that lived in ancient days; I am a new bond between the old continent and the new, between the old order and the new; I speak for the faith of the past; I voice the faith of the hour; the hands that raised me are not unskilled and untrained; from what I am judge, ye people, of what stuff my builders are made.' And around the world, in all the capitals, in the great cities, of the English-speaking peoples, temples of lesser worth and beauty are speaking in the same strain."

Honora anxiously watched her father. A new light shone upon him, a new emotion disturbed him; perhaps that old hardness within was giving way. Ledwith had the poetic temperament, and the philosopher's power of generalization. A hint could open a grand horizon before him, and the cathedral in its solemn beauty was the hint. Of course, he could see it all, blind as he had been before. The Irish revolution worked fitfully, and exploded in a night, its achievement measured by the period of a month; but this temple and its thousand sisters lived on doing their good work in silence, fighting for the truth without noise or conspiracy.

"And this is the glory of the Irish," Monsignor continued, "this is the fact which fills me with pride, American as I am, in the race whose blood I own; they have preserved the faith for the great English-speaking world. Already the new principle peculiar to that faith has begun its work in literature, in art, in education, in social life. Heresy allowed the Christ to be banished from all the departments of human activity, except the home and the temple. Christ is not in the schools of the children, nor in the books we read, nor in the pictures and sculptures of our studios, nor in our architecture, even of the churches, nor in our journalism, any more than in the market-place and in the government. These things are purely pagan, or worthless composites. It looks as if the historian of these times, a century or two hence, will have hard work to fitly describe the Gesta Hibernicorum, when this principle of Christianity will have conquered the American world as it conquered ancient Europe. I tell you, Owen," and he strode to the window with hands outstretched to the great building, "in spite of all the shame and suffering endured for His sake, God has been very good to your people, He is heaping them with honors. As wide as is the power of England, it is no wider than the influence of the Irish faith. Stubborn heresy is doomed to fall before the truth which alone can set men free and keep them so."

Ledwith had begun to tremble, but he said never a word.

"I am prouder to have had a share in the building of that temple," Monsignor continued, "than to have won a campaign against the English. This is a victory, not of one race over another, but of the faith over heresy, truth over untruth. It will be the Christ-like glory of Ireland to give back to

England one day the faith which a corrupt king destroyed, for which we have suffered crucifixion. No soul ever loses by climbing the cross with Christ."

Ledwith gave a sudden cry, and raised his hands to heaven, but grew quiet at once.

The priest watched contentedly the spires of his cathedral.

"You have touched heart and reason together," Honora whispered.

Ledwith remained a long time silent, struggling with a new spirit. At last he turned the wide, frank eyes on his friend and victor.

"I am conquered, Monsignor."

"Not wholly yet, Owen."

"I have been a fool, a foolish fool, – not to have seen and understood."

"And your folly is not yet dead. You are dying in sadness and despair almost, when you should go to eternity in triumph."

"I go in triumph! Alas! if I could only be blotted out with my last breath, and leave neither grave nor memory, it would be happiness. Why do you say, 'triumph'?"

"Because you have been true to your country with the fidelity of a saint. That's enough. Besides you leave behind you the son born of your fidelity to carry on your work —"

"God bless that noble son," Owen cried.

"And a daughter whose prayers will mount from the nun's cell, to bless your cause. If you could but go from her resigned!"

"How I wish that I might. I ought to be happy, just for leaving two such heirs, two noble hostages to Ireland. I see my error. Christ is the King, and no man can better His plans for men. I surrender to Him."

"But your submission is only in part. You are not wholly conquered."

"Twice have you said that," Owen complained, raising his heavy eyes in reproach.

"Love of country is not the greatest love."

"No, love of the race, of humanity, is more."

"And the love of God is more than either. With all their beauty, what do these abstract loves bring us? The country we love can give us a grave and a stone. Humanity crucifies its redeemers. Wolsey summed up the matter: 'Had I but served my God with half the zeal with which I served my king, He would not in mine age, have left me naked to mine enemies.'"

He paused to let his words sink into Ledwith's mind.

"Owen, you are leaving the world oppressed by the hate of a lifetime, the hate ingrained in your nature, the fatal gift of persecutor and persecuted from the past."

"And I shall never give that up," Owen declared, sitting up and fixing his hardest look on the priest. "I shall never forget Erin's wrongs, nor Albion's crimes. I shall carry that just and honorable hate beyond the grave. Oh, you priests!"

"I said you were not conquered. You may hate injustice, but not the unjust. You will find no hate in heaven, only justice. The persecutors and their victims have long been dead, and judged. The welcome of the wretched into heaven, the home of justice and love, wiped out all memory of suffering here, as it will for us all. The justice measured out to their tyrants even you would be satisfied with. Can your hate add anything to the joy of the blessed, or the woe of the lost?"

"Nothing," murmured Owen from the pillow, as his eyes looked afar, wondering at that justice so soon to be measured out to him. "You are again right. Oh, but we are feeble . . . . but we are foolish . . . . to think it. What is our hate any more than our justice . . . . both impotent and ridiculous."

There followed a long pause, then, for Monsignor had finished his argument, and only waited to control his own emotion before saying good-by.

"I die content," said Ledwith with a long restful sigh, coming back to earth, after a deep look into divine power and human littleness. "Bring me tomorrow, and often, the Lord of Justice. I never knew till now that in desiring Justice so ardently, it was He I desired. Monsignor, I die content, without hate, and without despair."

If ever a human creature had a foretaste of heaven it was Honora during the few weeks that followed this happy day. The bitterness in the soul of Owen vanished like a dream, and with it went regret, and vain longing, and the madness which at odd moments sprang from these emotions. His martyrdom, so long and ferocious, would end in the glory of a beautiful sunset, the light of heaven in his heart, shining in his face. He lay forever beyond the fire of time and injustice.

Every morning Honora prepared the little altar in the sick-room, and Monsignor brought the Blessed Sacrament. Arthur answered the prayers and gazed with awe upon the glorified face of the father, with something like anger upon the exalted face of the daughter; for the two were gone suddenly beyond him. Every day certain books provided by Monsignor were read to the dying man by the daughter or the son; describing the migration of the Irish all over the English-speaking world, their growth to consequence and power. Owen had to hear the figures of this growth, see and touch the journals printed by the scattered race and to hear the editorials which spoke their success, their assurance, their convictions, their pride.

Then he laughed so sweetly, so naturally, chuckled so mirthfully that Honora had to weep and thank God for this holy mirthfulness, which sounded like the spontaneous, careless, healthy mirth of a boy. Monsignor came evenings to explain, interpret, put flesh and life into the reading of the day with his vivid and pointed comment. Ledwith walked in wonderland. "The hand of God is surely there," was his one saying. The last day of his pilgrimage he had a long private talk with Arthur. They had indeed become father and son, and their mutual tenderness was deep.

Honora knew from the expression of the two men that a new element had entered into her father's happiness.

"I free you from your promise, my child," said Ledwith, "my most faithful, most tender child. It is the glory of men that the race is never without such children as you. You are free from any bond. It is my wish that you accept your release."

She accepted smiling, to save him from the stress of emotion. Then he wished to see the cathedral in the light of the afternoon sun, and Arthur opened the door of the sick-room. The dying man could see from his pillow the golden spires, and the shining roof, that spoke to him so wonderfully of the triumph of his race in a new land, the triumph which had been built up in the night, unseen, uncared for, unnoticed.

"God alone has the future," he said.

Once he looked at Honora, once more, with burning eyes, that never could look enough on that loved child. With his eyes on the great temple, smiling, he died. They thought he had fallen asleep in his weakness. Honora took his head in her arms, and Arthur Dillon stood beside her and wept.

The Stepmother

by Kate McPhelim Cleary, *McClure's Magazine* 17 (September 1901)

Kate McPhelim was the daughter of Irish immigrants who met and married in New Brunswick. Widowed with three small children, her mother took the family back to Ireland for a time, then to Philadelphia, and finally to Chicago, where Kate attended St. Xavier's Convent School and began selling her poems to periodicals at the age of thirteen. As with Finley Peter Dunne, Chicago journalism was important to her development as a writer. In fact, at one time her whole family was working for the Chicago Tribune *— her mother contributing poems and essays; her brother Edward, dramatic criticism; brother Frank, general reporting; and Kate, short stories. In 1884, at the age of twenty-one, Kate married Michael T. Cleary and accompanied him to the Nebraska prairie town of Hubbell to set up in the lumber business. There, Kate Cleary had six children, attained distinction as a cook (contributing to* Good Housekeeping *magazine), kept a hospitable, book-laden home (known throughout the area as a cultural haven), and continued to publish fiction and poetry. In 1898 the family returned to Chicago, where business reverses forced her to turn out potboilers at the rate of a short story a day. Cleary's better fiction was, however, published widely in respected journals such as* Century, Cosmopolitan, Harper's, Lippincott's, *and* McClure's *magazines, and she was negotiating with Houghton, Mifflin Company to publish a collection of her stories before her death in 1905 in her forty-second year.*

Reflecting her own odyssey, Cleary's best fiction deals with the lives of Irish Americans in Chicago and in rural Nebraska. The Nebraska stories are an effective antidote to the anti-city pastoralism of Mrs. Sadlier's Con O'Regan *and the Irish Catholic colonization movement propagandists, who believed that moving to the country would solve all Irish-American ills. At their best, Cleary's pictures of the Middle-western rural alternative have the powerful bleakness of Hamlin Garland's* Main Traveled Roads, *that 1891 collection of fictional revisions of the agrarian myth.*

"The Stepmother" is a good example. The focus is the second wife of Oliver Carney, a luckless, lazy, and selfish man who has fled business failures in the East to try his hand at farming in Nebraska, and who now fills his empty days with drinking to mitigate his sense of failure. A former schoolteacher with lively, hopeful ideas, the second Mrs. Carney has been drained by years of drudgery and loneliness. The story takes place on Memorial Day, which Mrs. Carney is resigned to spending alone, as her courting stepson Dan has elected to take a neighboring farm girl to town for the festiv-

ities, thereby ignoring the fact that no one has visited the farm since Christmas and his stepmother hasn't been to town for over a year.

The story has two strong points. First, Cleary evokes the hardness and dullness of Nebraska farm life, the terms of which are especially harsh for this intelligent former teacher. A terrifying dust storm at the end of the story reinforces the picture of an alien environment, inimical to normal social intercourse. Second, Cleary presents the emotional impoverishment that seems to follow from the bleak physical setting. There is little communication in the Carney family, and when his stepmother has one of her "heart spells," Dan Carney first helps and soothes her and then feels "ashamed of the compassionate impulse which had temporarily mastered him." Cleary's generalization about Nebraska Irish farmers is reinforced in much twentieth-century fiction by the emergence of a similar trait among other Irish Americans – the inability to express positive emotions, even among family members.

> The world is filled with folly and sin,
>   And love must cling where it can, I say,
> For beauty is easy enough to win –
>   But one isn't loved every day!
>   *– Owen Meredith*

"**Y**ou are going in town to the Memorial services, Dan?" questioned the woman. Her voice was appealing.

The young fellow standing in the doorway shifted his position impatiently. He was twenty-three, tall and brawny. Years of labor on the farm had developed his limbs and toughened his muscles. Later in life he would be stooped and shambling, as are those who follow the plow and guide the harrow after the days of youthful manhood have passed. Now he was straight and stately, and the colossal symmetry of his frame was good to look upon. His cotton shirt, falling loose at the neck, revealed a triangle of sunburnt skin. His low-browed, strong-featured face was copper-red also. The jaw was heavy – the chin square. The blue eyes he turned on the woman had the sullenness of one who expects opposition.

"Yes. I'm a-goin'."

"In the new buggy?"

He nodded. There was a silence which she waited wistfully for him to break. As he said nothing, she picked up the sewing which lay in her lap.

"I was hoping I could get to go," she said, speaking in the plaintive monotone produced by colorless years of self-repression and self-denial. "I've been every time when I could take or leave the children. It's a year since I've been to town." Her needle was suspended. She looked afar over the boundless expanse of prairie with weary eyes. "My father and brother are buried on the hill there. Little Ruby – she's there, too. She died when she wasn't but eight. She was the greatest child for flowers! The weeds even were flowers to her. I guess she'd know if there were some put on her grave."

Again there was silence, she sending him eager, furtive glances; he staring out where an ocean of oats tossed turbulently in the glaring sunshine.

"Even if the celebration brings sad thoughts," she went on, "it's kind of cheerful, too. There's so many folks in town. There's the flags – and the music. The girls have new hats and dresses. It's sociable-like. There hasn't been a soul to this house since Christmas. Then it was only some campers whose wagon broke down. But it seemed good to see them, even."

"Look here, mother," he broke out. "I know you ain't got much pleasure. I'd like you could fix to go. But as for me drivin' you in – well, I promised to take Chastina Marks."

She said nothing, but the look that quivered out on her face made him set his teeth hard for an instant. Then, with a scarlet blotch burning on either thin cheek, she took up her sewing again, and went on stitching – stitching.

The home of the Carneys was a forlorn place. There was no timber in that region. The small, shabby house perched upon the bluff was exposed to the bitter winds of winter and to the almost more malignant furnace blasts of summer. It was nineteen years since Oliver Carney had married for the second time. Then, he and his two sturdy boys had sadly needed the ministrations of a woman. The girl he married was young and romantic. She pitied him. She mistook her exquisite sympathy for the divine passion itself. When he traded his business in the East for a rocky Nebraska farm, and went to live where his lack of experience and the capricious climatic conditions together conspired against him, the outcome was despondency and futile regret. He not only failed to do one thing well; he succeeded in doing many things ill. He credited Fate with peculiar perversity toward himself – with an almost personal antagonism. Dyspepsia, that grim demon evoked by farmhouse viands, became a constant torment. Insomnia duly followed. Pessimism, the prompt hand-maid of these, waited upon them. So he became gloomy and unreasonable, except when his depression was temporarily merged in the maudlin amiability of liquor.

It was upon the woman, however, that the burdens of failure pressed most heavily. She had been a brave and gallant young creature, but the cowardice and shirking selfishness of the man she married ate into the core of her being like an acid.

None knew better than she that work from long before light on winter morns, and from the first streak of pearl in summer skies, was hard. She knew that poverty was a rabid, a relentless thing. She knew that it made petty those who would be great and generous; that it fettered hands which would fain be extended in royal generosity; that none might scale its ramparts which barred out possible ambitions – pleasures – joys! But these she accepted – the poverty and the toil. At the melancholy of inertia surrounding her she rebelled. She dreaded its contagion. She refused to have her heritage of hope wrested from her. She would not live in an atmosphere of rayless foreboding. She denied the right of one man to condemn her to profound and enduring discontent. She was not one of those who succumb to adversity willingly. So she made a hard fight. Occasionally she conquered – less frequently as the years went by. The struggle told on her. She lost expectancy of expression and elasticity of step. Childbearing and child-rearing were part of her handicapped existence.

Now a fresh fear had arisen. What if Dan were to marry – Dan, upon whom they all depended, rather than upon the moping, misanthropic father!

"Dan?" Her voice sounded strange to herself, and she waited until she could speak as usual. "Dan, what would we all do without you?"

She had been a school teacher in her youth, and she spoke with a correctness and a precision which, although marred by occasional idioms, still distinguished her speech from the lingual slovenliness of the Western farm woman.

"Oh, I guess you'd git along!" A dull, slow color had crept into his face. "It's goin' to be a good year. Dick could take my place."

Dick – take – his place! He was thinking, then – he was going to —

"We – we can't depend on Dick!" she murmured. A vision of Dick rose before her – gay, pleasure-loving, inconsiderate Dick! She smiled – a sad smile. "I didn't think Chastina was the kind of girl you'd take a fancy to, Dan."

He swung around.

"What," he demanded, "have you got agin her?"

Her work fell on her lap. She clasped her thin, knobby-jointed hands upon it, and looked up at her stepson. She was a frail little body, gowned in the everlasting print wrapper of the prairie housekeeper. Her large hazel eyes were bright – too bright. She breathed quickly. She had lost two of her front teeth. To have them replaced would be an extravagance not to be considered. Frequently when speaking she lifted her hand with a nervous gesture and covered her mouth.

"She's frivolous, Dan. She likes admiration – and pretty clothes —"

"Is that all? What girl don't, mother?"

"It seems to me," she went on hurriedly, "that your—your marriage to her would be a–a mistake! Think it over a bit —"

"Think it over!" he burst out. "Mother, you didn't use to want to stand in my way? Don't you s'pose I have thought it over? Do you think I'm goin' to be dray horse for all's here – two of 'em as well able to work as me – all the born days of my hull life!"

The hot May sun streamed down on him. She could see his great chest rising and falling, and the muscles of his arms working under the worn sleeves of his shirt.

"You have more than your share of the work!" she admitted. Her voice failed her again. A stray sunbeam glinted on her needle – an idle needle just then. "And – I don't want to stand in your way, Dan. Only – you've always seemed like my boy – the only boy I ever had! Maybe I'm saying this to you about Tina because – because I want to keep you." Her hungry eyes never left his face. "Perhaps I'm – I'm just making excuses. Perhaps — "

The scarlet blotches faded in her cheeks. She picked up her sewing again, but the hands trembled over the coarse cotton cloth. She could not ply the glittering little implement she held. Suddenly she went deathly pale. She lay back, drawing her breath in short, soft gasps.

"Mother!" cried the young fellow. "Mother!"

"It's nothing," she panted. "Nothing."

But her lips took on a bluish tinge, and after a faint shiver she lay quite still. He dashed out to the well for water, brought it to her, forced her to swallow it. He watched her anxiously, all his sullenness gone, as she shuddered back to consciousness.

"I didn't mean to rile you, mother," he said. "But seems like I couldn't bear to have you comin' between Chastina an' me."

He had dropped on one knee beside her chair in a bewilderment of dumb and clumsy penitence.

"I know it's hard for you," she murmured. "You are young – and it's hard for you."

The tired tears were slipping down her cheeks.

"It ain't dead easy for you, mother."

"Oh, don't think of me!"

"We don't. We've got out of the way of thinking of you."

Her little skinny arm lay near him. It never occurred to him to give it a gentle touch. They are chary of caresses – the prairie people. Perfunctory kisses are given at the marriage feast or before the burial – but even these are few and far between. He stumbled to his feet, ashamed of the compassionate impulse which had temporarily mastered him. The woman rose, too.

"It's time to get supper," she said. "They'll be in soon."

But as she crossed the kitchen to set her work aside she suddenly put her hand to her breast – stood still.

One stride and Dan was beside her.

"You're not forgittin' what the doctor said?" he questioned. "That if you got scairt – or – or hurt, an' had another heart spell you was like – like to — "

She flashed around on him. Suddenly her face was young, yearning, eager.

"Oh," she cried breathlessly, "oh, I *was* forgetting! Do you think— " But as suddenly as it had come the brilliance waned. She shook her head. "No – I shall not die – not soon," she said.

She went on filling the little rust-red stove with cobs. Dan did not offer to assist her. The attitude of a young Western farmer to his mother is that of an Indian to his squaw. All domestic drudgery properly pertains to her.

"I'll go out an' take a look at the young peach trees," he said. "They're comin' on fine. This'll be the second year of bearin'. There ought be enough made out'n 'em to pay dad for the hogs the cholery got."

"What you talkin' about?" rasped a dolorous voice. "Them peaches? They'll be some, maybe. But the nursery man fooled me on the settin's. He didn't give me the Baltimore beauties I bought off'n him – on'y the common kind. An' the common kind is dreadful plenty. It's the best that fetches the price. Every one's again me. Every one cheats me. I allus had the worst luck of any one I ever knowed."

He sank into the only comfortable chair the room afforded, a limp heap of inactive humanity. He watched the woman preparing supper.

"There's them," he announced placidly, arousing himself from a trance of indolent content.

"Them" came tumbling in, a riotous, roystering, healthy brood. They laughed, and mocked, and fought, and burst into peals of laughter. The head of the house regarded them with bland interest.

"Seems like," he remarked, "I ain't never so happy as when I a-sittin', so to speak, in the bosom of my fambly."

His conciliatory manner was one to incite distrust. His wife sent him a swift glance.

"Have you been to town?" she asked.

He declared that he had not been to town. That even if he had she knew better than to suppose that he would go into the Owl-King – or near the Owl-King, or —

Dick, perfumed, pomaded, and in his Sunday best, came clattering down the ladderlike stairway.

"Hurry up, mother. I'm goin' in town to a strawberry festival at the Methodist Church. Here, Dolly, you got your supper. You let me set there."

Dolly protested with a howl. Dick picked her up and deposited her on the floor, where she appeared to shrink together like a collapsible drinking cup.

When Dan came in from his aimless tramp through the orchard the owner of the farm was sunk in stertorous oblivion. The last child had been tucked in bed. The last utensil had been washed and set aside. And the woman, sitting by the kitchen table, in the dull light of the kerosene lamp, was sewing, stitching into Dan's denim shirt rebellion, regret, resentment–love. That one unselfish love of all loves!

Chastina Marks was waiting for Dan when he drove up. She was a slender, brown-haired girl, clad in the inevitable white lawn and fluttering ribbons of the prairie belle. She was not pretty, but she was charming. There was a fresh wholesomeness about her as pleasant as the scent of wild-plum blossoms. Her quiet eyes held a look of reserve. They were eyes which might, indeed,

> Keep back a daring lover,
> Or comfort a grieving child.

"I'm late." He had jumped down and was helping her into the buggy. "It's a fine morning, but I'm afraid it's going to blow up a bit."

She looked away to the horizon with the keen and prescient vision of those who are prairie-born.

"It will be a dust storm, I think."

The little town presented its usual Memorial Day appearance, which was that of festivity – festivity, however, the most seemly and decorous. But – as Dan's stepmother had remarked – the flags, flowers, music, the groups promenading in their finest attire, the uniforms of the band of bent veterans, the gold-lettered badges of the Women's Relief Corps, the importance and celerity of the few officials on horseback, the forming of the parade, the deliberate progress to the church, the singing, the speeches, even the bulging baskets in the back of the wagons, were "sociable-like."

Dan enjoyed neither the day nor the propinquity of the girl he loved. His brow was contracted. He spoke seldom. His companion wondered – silently. She was wise enough to know that to question a secretive man is to invoke a lie.

The dust storm she had prophesied did come. At first there was only the most infantile, – the most ineffectual little breeze. Then tiny spirals of dust rose in the country roads. Suddenly the tawny spirals were as tall as waterspouts. The increasing wind, bellowing up from Kansas, blew the dust into a curtain – a wall – an encompassing, enveloping fog. Dan, urging his horses homeward, tried to protect Chastina. He pulled up the buggy top. He drew the linen robe over her lap. He gave her his silk handkerchief to tie over her eyes. But the man does not live who can combat a Nebraska dust storm. The yellowish powder sifted in through the joints of the canopy. It stung the flesh like the bites of myriad infinitesimal insects. It grimed the lap-robe and the girl's white gown. It maddened the old farm horses until they were mettlesome as pastured colts. It pierced, and penetrated, and choked, and blinded. And all the time the wind sent the buggy careening, screeched in the ears of its occupants, and howled in its fury after each rare pause to take breath. All the time, too, the sun blazed down – a great blotch of deep orange seen through saffron clouds.

"I shan't let you out at your house," Dan shouted. "I'll take the short cut to our place. There is something I want to tell you."

The violence of the storm was spent when they turned into the narrow road that zigzagged towards the desolate house on the bluff. Dan slackened rein. At last he could make himself heard.

"Tina," he blurted out, "I asked you to marry me. I didn't know then – anyways I didn't think. But I s'posed we could git married this fall. Now –

well, now we can't. I've thought it over good an' hard – an' we can't. I got to stick by mother awhile longer. Maybe this year maybe all next, too. I don't s'pose now you'll want to keep comp'ny with me no longer. But," doggedly, "I got to stick by mother."

She turned her grave eyes on him. The illimitable love in them dazzled him. His heart plunged.

"I wouldn't think much of you," she said, "if you didn't stick by your mother after all she's done for you. My mother often told me before she died how strong and pretty Mis' Carney was when she first come out to Nebraska. She said how nice she kep' you an' Dick – always good clothes an' the best of everything for you, when she didn't have a stuff dress to her back. I'll wait for you, Dan."

"Tina!" he cried. "Tina!" he ventured again. But the pain in his throat precluded speech. He yelled to the horses. They forged ahead.

Suddenly Tina leaned forward – clutched his arm.

"Look, Dan, look! What's wrong? The children are running down the bluff. They're comin' this way. An' your father – he's beckonin'! There's Mis' Harrowsby – I know her cape – an' Mis' Peterson. Hurry – hurry!"

"Oh, my God!" muttered Dan.

The world seemed to reel away from him. Tina's hand steadied him. Tina's voice recalled him. All at once he was standing up – was lashing the horses.

"I wish I'd taken her!" the girl heard him cry. "I wish to God I'd taken her! She wanted so to go in this Memorial Day!"

"Hush, Dan! Hush, dear! It will be all right!"

Some one was at the horses' heads. He hurled himself out of the buggy – was in the house.

"We don't know just how it happened," one of the whispering group in the kitchen was saying. "She was alone when the storm came up."

"She went out to drive the young calves under shelter," interposed another.

"A loose scantlin' struck her in the side," volunteered a third. "She ain't been real strong of late anyhow. That heart trouble's awful onreliable. The doctor? Can't git him. He's over in Kansas. Mis' Peterson knows well as him, though. She 'lows there ain't anythin' to be done."

Dan pushed by them into the little poor best bedroom. His stepmother lay in the pine bedstead. The patchwork quilt was drawn to her chin. He fell on his knees beside her. His head dropped on his clenched hands. His shoulders were heaving. She lifted one weak arm and laid it around his neck.

"Look at – me – Dan."

He lifted his haggard eyes to hers, which were swept and luminous.

"Dan," went on the voice, which seemed to come from a distance, "I'm – I'm sorry for what I said – about Tina. She is dear – she is good – like her mother before her."

"Mother – she is here."

"Yes – I can see her now. I am glad – very glad. But – Dan."

A woman came in, insisting the sufferer should not speak. The work-worn hand was imperious then as any which ever swayed a scepter. At its light motion the intruder left the room.

"Dan – where are you? Listen!"

"I am listening, mother."

"Don't make Tina's life – too hard! Women are not fitted – to bear – as much as – men. They – must – bear – more. Men love women, only – they – don't understand. This is Memorial Day." Her hand found his rough head and rested there. "I hope you'll remember – every Memorial Day – about Tina. And that a woman isn't always – well – or happy – just because she keeps on her – feet – and doesn't – complain. And let her know – you –"

Grayness swept over her face like an obliterating billow.

"Mother!" he sobbed hoarsely. "Mother!"

The bed shook to the beat of his breast.

"Little Dan," she was saying softly. "No – I can't think he's my stepson. He's my boy." The hand on his head moved caressingly. "Such pretty – pretty curls! My boy – the only boy I ever had."

Then she was whispering about Ruby, the little sister who had died when she wasn't but eight. The little child who had loved all flowers – to whom the weeds were flowers.

Lalor's Maples

by Katherine E. Conway (Boston: The Pilot Publishing Co., 1901)

*Born in Rochester, New York, in 1853, Katherine Conway began a career in jour-
nalism there, then moved on to Buffalo, and in 1883 finally settled in Boston, where
she became an assistant editor of the* Pilot, *under John Boyle O'Reilly. The* Pilot *circle
of writers, including Conway, O'Reilly, James Jeffery Roche, and Louise Imogen
Guiney, was the first significant literary coterie in Irish America. With the encouragement of O'Reilly, himself a gifted poet, novelist, critic, and editor, Conway wrote several Christian self-help guides, much genteel-sentimental poetry, a collection of short
stories, and two novels,* The Way of the World and Other Ways *(1900) and*
Lalor's Maples. *Her fiction contains the mixture of realism and sentimentality characteristic of much work around the turn of the century by writers who found themselves
caught and confused between* Heidi *and* Maggie: A Girl of the Streets. *That mixture is evident in* Lalor's Maples, *which is her most realistic book, probably because
it is based in part on Conway's own life. (Rochester becomes Baychester, and the main
character is the convent-educated, journalist-daughter of a newly rich Irish-American
contractor.)*

*The best chapter in this novel is the first, which is reprinted here. Before the stereo-
types begin to accumulate, before the plot starts to tangle, Conway gives us a perfect set-
piece description of the rise to middle-class respectability of an Irish immigrant family.
John Lalor is an intelligent builder with the instincts of an architect. Sixteen years from
his first job as a construction worker, he has his own contracting business, three hundred men under him, and is thinking of running for mayor. The time is the late 1860s
and he is thirty-nine years old.*

*To validate and celebrate his success, Lalor builds a new house on Baychester's best
street, River Avenue, which has lately been undergoing a population shift from old-line
Yankees to newly wealthy Irish. Through the chapter the relating of Lalor's past runs
parallel to a detailed description of the building of his house: from the pouring of a
foundation so large that one critical onlooker compares it to the town hall, to an inven-
tory of the rooms and furnishings, which include patterned carpets, mahogany and
horsehair chairs, and a mantelpiece Madonna "won at a church fair." All of this rings
true, as does the culminating scene, in which, on his first evening in the new house,
John Lalor softly touches the keys of his new piano and thinks of his penniless landing
at New York sixteen years before. The completed house is a valid symbolic embodiment*

of the Lalor family's social and economic rise. Unfortunately, the novel soon bogs down in a mire of genteel-romantic stylistic passages and wild turns of plot, but the house, named "Lalor's Maples," remains its saving grace. As a central symbol it anchors the book and provides the one sustained realistic focus.

In this conception Conway was probably influenced by William Dean Howells's The Rise of Silas Lapham, *which she must have known as the novel all Boston was talking about after its publication in 1885. The sharpest literary chronicler of American middle-class life in the Gilded Age, Howells recognized that the private dwelling was in his time the most obvious measuring rod of social position. So it is that the building of his new house on the fashionable "water side of Beacon Street" proclaims Silas Lapham's progress from poor Vermont beginnings to success as a paint manufacturer in Boston. Howells is critical of the Lapham family's embrace of materialism, and Lapham's moral rise at the end is made to follow from his self-ordained economic ruin.*

Conway was unable to sustain this much realism. Although the Lalor family also suffers a great calamity, her novel ends with a melodramatic resurrection of surpassing implausibility. And yet, although they prove too hot for Conway to handle, serious questions about Irish-American family life do get asked here for the first time. Mrs. Mary Lalor is a woman whose dominance creates a crippling imbalance in the family power structure, and her acquisitive obsessions with the house and respectability result in a perversion of values that nearly destroys her husband. The character of the dominant mother and the central symbol of the house presented in Lalor's Maples *recur often enough in subsequent Irish-American fiction to be considered archetypal.*

Moving into the New House

> This hearth's our own,
> Our hearts are one –
> And peace is ours forever.
> *– Gerald Griffin*

The Lalors were the last of the new people to build on River Avenue. We say new, not that the earlier builders who had discovered the possibilities of this noblest of Baychester's ways, about three decades before our story opens, were of so very ancient lineage; but because an advance of twenty-five or thirty years beyond the general average, in the matter of money and education, means a great deal in the social life of a young city.

They had taken up large lots when land was cheap, and built, far back from the street among the towering trees preserved from the old forests, those spacious and imposing brick and stone residences that gave so much distinction to River Avenue, especially on the water side, nearing the Lower Falls.

John McFarland, who had made much money in canal contracts, sometimes, of a fine Sunday afternoon, drove down the Avenue with his good-looking and businesslike wife. She had made money on her own account, by accompanying her husband on his contracts and boarding his foremen. Both were wont to cast longing glances at Pritchard Place, Chittenden Grove, Langevin Oaks, and others of the then new and beautiful residences of the pioneers of dignified and easy living in this section of Baychester, and even at the vacant lots in their neighborhood.

John McFarland's name was good now on as big a check as e'er a Pritchard or Langevin ever drew, as his wife said, truly and fondly. But Mrs. McFarland feared that the families above-named might not be neighborly, and she and her worthy spouse would not enjoy isolation, however splendid.

When, however, financial ruin overswept the Chittendens, the McFarlands bought the Grove, moved into it and renamed it. Then Peter Daly, who had also grown rich on the canal, took the vacant lot adjoining, and built as big a brick house as his neighbor's; while the Sullivans, who had made a competence out of their great stone quarries at Deer's Head, acquired an eligible site across the way; and if they could not build a finer residence, at least, as their grounds were capable of more artistic effects, they terraced them down to the river, built a summerhouse on the bluff, and, as the boys grew up, a pier and a boathouse.

Soon after came the Burkes, the Blakes, the O'Connors, the Thompsons, and the Prendergasts, all of whom had outgrown simultaneously the two-story frame houses with green blinds and door-gardens, on sundry respectable but modest side streets, which represented the intermediate stage in their social evolution.

The Avenue did not suffer from this influx of new families, whose heads were not to the manor born. Langevin's Oaks was not a whit better kept than Sullivan's Riverside, and if McFarland Grove differed at all in its external aspect from Chittenden Grove, the change was gain.

The early Irish settlers in Baychester were a sturdy, self-respecting lot, most of whom had brought their handicrafts and a little schooling with them, and money enough to push in from the seaboard to the western part of the state – no short nor cheap journey in the ante-railroad days.

There were even two or three physicians of Old World training, the senior of whom had visited Abbotsford and spoken with Sir Walter Scott; and there was at the outset a fine old schoolmaster, who gave in his own house, to a carefully selected class of boys, a good mathematical training and a smattering of the classics. But in the day of my story Mr. Æneas O'Gorman had retired from active life, and Bradley College claimed the sons of rich or ambitious households.

The keenest newspaper paragraphist had found among the new residents of River Avenue scant material for jokes about the newly rich. It seemed to be the case of good blood run under for a time with most of them; and coming into enlarged educational and social opportunities, they adapted them-

selves to concomitant gentler living with marvellous ease, and not more snob-
bery than had marked the "Yankees" – for so the original New England settlers were familiarly called – at the corresponding stage of their social evolution.

It should be mentioned, however, that the aforesaid McFarlands, Burkes,
Blakes, and O'Connors, for all of a decent pride in their name and race, had
less consciousness of the fitness of their reversion to a higher social plane than
had the Lalors, or, rather, Mrs. Lalor; though the Lalors were the last to
revert, so to speak.

After John Lalor's house on the Avenue was well under way, according
to plans revised by his wife, the latter had remarked with feeling to a humble
friend:

"Indeed, Mrs. McCribbin, 'tis a fine house, as you say, that John Lalor is
building for me; but what is it to the house that he took me from!"

"Thrue for you, ma'am," assented the complaisant Mrs. McCribbin,
though she had as much knowledge of Mrs. Lalor's maiden home as she had
of the palace of the Grand Lama of Thibet. That lady, however, was at the
moment planning the removal of sundry articles of furniture and half-worn
carpets and bedding, which were unfit for the new house, to Mrs.
McCribbin's lowly domicile, and the latter had no readier way of manifesting
her appreciation.

Some of the new builders of more stately mansions on the Avenue had
left the outgrown shells of their old habitations in remote parts of the city; but
John Lalor's social progression had been compressed into a shorter time than
that of any of his fellows, and its successive stages were in plain sight of its culmination.

He had first established himself, with his wife and baby, in a tiny one-
story white cottage, embowered in "matrimony," southernwood, hollyhocks,
and morning-glories, on a short street which crossed the Avenue, running
southward to the river and northward to the great canal.

He had chosen the north side, and having sufficient land, enlarged his
house as the increase in his flock demanded, buying meantime, as occasion
offered and his rising fortune permitted, all the vacant land behind the houses fronting on the Avenue, until his possessions neighbored an eligible site in
line. A rambling wooden cottage, built by an early settler, but now long
untenanted, encumbered it. The back garden abounded in plum and pear
and cherry trees, and across the front lawn, making an unbroken carpet of
shade when the summer sun shone, stretched four magnificent maple trees.

John Lalor would have preferred the water side of the Avenue, but he
could not have bought land through in the same fashion to utilize in his business. Besides, there were the children to be considered, and Mrs. Lalor knew
that if there was a river running at the end of their own back yard, her children, being so much more contrary than anybody's else, would never draw

breath till they had drowned themselves, in spite of all the stone fences and iron railings in town.

So the old cottage in which Moses Trueman and Thankful, his wife, had reared their fourteen children under the sternest Puritan discipline, was dismantled and carried away to make room, as poor old Trueman said in the bitterness of his invincible prejudice, for "the growth of popery in this free land."

In the soft May days John Lalor proudly laid the foundation of the house which he expected to abide in for maybe thirty years, and pass on to a succession of John Lalors, reaching, like Malcolm's line, to the crack of doom. The foundations were broad and deep. "You'd have thought it was a town hall he was building," said a critical onlooker. But few criticised, where many praised and congratulated; for John Lalor's rapid progress was a matter of local pride. It was an honest progress, too; and marked by many a generous deed along its way. He was the idol of his workingmen – who fifteen years before had been his fellow-workers – and, altogether, one of the most popular men of his race and faith in Baychester.

The little Lalors spent all their time between school sessions, and most of the sunny days of the long vacation, watching the brick walls rise. When the maples were reddening in late September the new house was roofed in, and its future little residents had the unspeakable joy of risking life and limb on skeleton staircases and the rafters of unfloored rooms, till the workmen preferred a unanimous petition to "herself," setting forth that they would hold themselves guiltless of certain calamities sure to happen, if "them imps of mischief" were not kept from under their feet.

So for a time the interdict was observed; especially while the maternal threat was fresh in their minds that the new house might be sold to strangers in the event of the persistent disobedience of those for whom it was building; and the little Lalors contented themselves with feasting their eyes upon its external grandeur, and relating their daydreams of the new life which was to be theirs directly they moved in.

Progress to the Avenue had been marked heretofore, in the child-lives at least, by such a sundering of old ties – the distance of a few squares and the playmates of the new environment inevitably estranging the migrators from their previous associations – that the little Lalors' companions of Lime Street, who were to remain in their native obscurity, sadly forecast the separation and its consequences.

"When you move into your new house you'll be Big-Bugs, and you won't play with us any more."

But Mildred Lalor, while not disclaiming the impending evolution of her family into Big-Bugs, solemnly promised that it would make no difference in their friendships; and to give immediate effect to her pledges of loyalty, took a party of her mates on a tour of inspection of the new house – the interdict having lapsed with the departure of the carpenters and glaziers – from the furnace-room and great concrete-floored storeroom in the basement, to the cupola, from the front windows of which they could see away across the river.

Long before the maples had budded again the painters and decorators had put the last touches to the interior, and the little Lalors, wild with antici-pation, though rather unkempt in attire, owing to the preoccupation of their elders with the moving, watched the unloading of the new furniture, and held their breaths with awe at the sight of many objects of which even Mildred barely knew the names.

The day came, at last, when the Lalors, big and little, followed the new furniture into the new house. It was on a late February day that the transit was accomplished, for John Lalor wished to be settled down and at home to his friends on election day, the first Tuesday in March.

Though they all might have walked across lots to take possession, this humbler progress was left to the children and dependents. For his wife, John Lalor harnessed his own low-covered buggy, and having taken her, clothed in her new and fine black cashmere, and with their youngest child and only son in her arms, from the front door of the house they were vacating, drove proudly around the corner, and conducted her to the stately entrance of her new abode.

Mrs. McCribbin, who had been awaiting them, had the double doors open in a trice, and resplendent in a white apron with a bib, covering almost entirely her portly person, curtsied to them, as she was wont "at home" in her girlhood to the landlord.

"Wisha, welcome to yez both, and it's proud I am, ma'am, to see you in a home worthy of you, wid a man to match it, and a fine boy, the image of his father, to keep up the name after yez, please God."

Hardly had they shaken hands with Mrs. McCribbin, in acknowledgment of the triple compliment of her greeting, than a loud peal at the side door on the broad, pillared porch, on which the dining-room opened, announced the three little girls, convoyed by Winnie Blackitt, the maid. After much rubbing of little feet on the mat, and very self-conscious giggles at their own grandeur as they crossed the charmed threshold, they were at last in the NEW HOUSE, and for some time after their entrance, the small brother joining his best efforts to his sisters, "you couldn't hear your ears," as Mrs. McCribbin said, for their joy in taking possession.

They followed at the heels of their father and mother on a tour of the house, sitting down on all the new chairs, warming themselves at every reg-ister, and looking at their rosy countenances in every mirror, as if expectant of some wondrous change in their lineaments, now that they had been duly installed and officially recognized as "Big-Bugs."

Presently their curiosity was satisfied, and their joy reached a stage where a safety-valve was an absolute necessity; so, duly muffled up against the frosty evening air, they rejoined their waiting playmates in the great barn-lot to describe, not without a touch of condescension, the splendors of their new home; while Mrs. Lalor went to the kitchen to superintend the preparation of an evening meal worthy of the occasion.

John Lalor, left alone, paced the long, lofty parlors, renewing his pleasure in every detail of their furnishing, while his heart swelled with the pride of gratified ambition.

To you, dear twentieth-century reader, with your polished floors and Oriental rugs and centrepieces, this interior upon which our friend gazed, of the late '60's of the last century, had hardly been pleasing.

The carpet was of a pale gray ground, patterned with great vases of slate-color, from which pink and blue flowers and pale green garlands overflowed. The walls and cornices were very faintly tinted – the merest ghost of rose-color.

It was the day of "sets" of furniture, and in all the other new houses on the Avenue a set of crimson velvet, at least for the front parlor, was of rigor.

But Mrs. Lalor, with a glimmer of artistic taste far in advance of her time, had declared against parlor sets at least, and had boldly disposed amid the mahogany and horse-hair of her old parlor, sundry comfortable new loung-ing-chairs and divans in rep of harmonious tints, and set up an old but well-polished centre-table with claw-feet, and an escritoire with brass knobs to match in the back parlor.

There was the usual full length gold-framed mirror between the windows of the front parlor, over the marble mantel a copy of the Madonna della Sedia in oils, not badly done, either, which Mrs. Lalor had won at a church fair, and on each mantel a pair of tall porcelain vases. As yet there were only long white shades at the windows.

All other decorations were delayed until Margaret, the oldest hope of the house of Lalor, should return from the convent wherein she was a boarding-pupil for her graduate year.

But just as it was, in the fitful radiance from the fire of cannel coal in the grate in the back parlor, it was to John Lalor more beautiful than the salon of a ducal palace in the style of *Louis Seize*.

His eyes rested with fond approval on every object, and as childlike as the children, now that he was unseen, he lounged a while in every one of the easy-chairs, and even touched softly the keys of the piano.

Not yet sixteen years since he had landed a poor young immigrant in New York City, wise enough to "declare his intentions" as to American citi-zenship on landing, but with barely enough money to take him to Baychester, and set up housekeeping with his wife and child, in a room or two. Not six-teen years since he had been working gladly by the day for whomsoever would have him, and for modest wage, till a famous builder discovered the treasure he had in this young skilled workman who had learned his handicraft in the best of European schools, and mixed brains of the finest quality with all he wrought.

And now with his fortieth birthday more than six months away, he was the owner of this stately residence, and of lands and houses besides yielding revenue enough, as he mused tenderly, to bring up his family in comfort, if God should see fit to take him.

And he who ignominiously lost his job in England a little more than sixteen years before, because of the irresistible impulse of his Irish blood towards political agitation, was now a political power in this beautiful city of free America, with every one of his three hundred workmen joyfully voting as one man the ticket of his choice!

What was there beyond the hope of a man still young, who had achieved so much in the short years behind him? Mayor of Baychester? Why not? – at least when he felt he could afford to put his business behind this ambition? And as for Jack – why, he might easily be governor of the state – or . . .

"Oh, if I had the education that Jack will have!" he sighed.

He thought of his dainty little convent girls, with their sweet voices and fastidious tastes. Margaret, his foreign-born, his little immigrant, the oldest of his flock, would be coming home in June with her graduate's laurel wreath and gold medal.

His mind travelled back to his own laborious boyhood; the frequent migrations of his family, his brief, rudimentary and oft-interrupted school days, now in some English town, anon in some Scotch or Irish village. He did not realize the splendid abilities that had made it possible for him to learn the three "R's" under such fragmentary and imperfect tutelage, and to grasp so quickly, once he had penetrated the mysteries of print, all that he read of history and political systems. True, there was a tradition of education in his family, and a few of his numerous kith and kin had attained the priesthood. But was he the first of his line to feel those mysterious stirrings of the blood that made his heart beat loudly at the sight of great architecture; or brought a mist before his eyes when he set out to his work over a country road in the spring sunrise, and saw a robin on a hawthorn bush, whistling its blithe little heart out?

The double parlors faded from his sight, and his convent girls from the world of fact. Again he lived through that unforgettable leave-taking. His handsome, ambitious young wife – better born and bred than he, as he proudly acknowledged, was by his side; she held their little immigrant in her arms; while his mother – the little, dark, thin mother of many sons, with her last babe at her breast, clung to him in the deep, tearless grief of her conviction that her first-born was going beyond her hand's touch and her eye's delight forever.

He was standing before the grate now, gazing intently at the fitful fire-light.

A little warm hand stole softly into his. He turned quickly. Was it the little, thin, dark mother, renewed in her first youth in happier fortunes? He had never noticed before his mother's aspect in Mildred. But there it was – the short, straight, slight figure – the clear, unflushed, brunette skin, the dusky hair, the large, lustrous eyes. The little girl smiled up shyly at him, with the same wonderful brightening and beautifying of the whole face that he remembered in his mother's smile.

"Oh, papa," she whispered, "I am so proud of you!"

His eyes dimmed as he touched the soft hair of this little daughter, who had never made bold with him like the rest, but only looked up to him, silently and from a distance, with those big, worshipping eyes.

"We mustn't forget to thank God, little girl," he said, remembering that he had forgotten.

Mrs. Lalor served a supper as substantial as well might be on a Lenten evening, when they had had "only a bite" at noon, and dispensed steaming dishes of stewed oysters to her flock with a proud face and a steady hand.

Towards the end of the meal a small covered dish was set before her.

"Why, what's this?" she cried, as she lifted the cold cover.

"A sugar-plum for yourself, Mary," said her husband, laughing like a boy, as she lifted out a long, carefully folded paper – the deed of the house.

"I took you from a good house, Mary, and I've always planned to give you back as good for it," he said softly.

Her maiden home, long magnified by the enchantment of distance, suddenly shrank to its true proportions before Mary Lalor's eyes, which glowed gently under a happy mist, as she pressed her husband's hand. Not for worlds would she have been so wanting in matronly dignity as to kiss him before the children!

Mrs. McCribbin and Winnie Blackitt and Dinny Martin (John Lalor's first workman), who was waiting in the kitchen for "a word wid the master," were all called in to drink a toast to the new house and the mistress.

"And the master, long life to him, and I'm prouder of him than if it was meself," added loyal Dinny.

Margaret Lalor came home in June and arranged the ornaments – people had not learned to speak of bric-a-brac then – and filled the new photograph album with pictures of contemporary celebrities on both sides of the Atlantic, and taught the children to speak of the "drawing-room," the "blue room," the "rose room," the "north room," etc.

She had the pictures of Washington and O'Connell and Archbishop

Hughes, which had previously graced the parlor in Lime Street, hung up in her father's den, which she called the library.

Then she got her cards:

Miss Lalor,
"The Maples," River Avenue.

She impressed upon the minds of her young sisters and the little brother, who, in turn, impressed it upon their mates, that the new house was "The Maples," and was never to be otherwise alluded to; and the father and mother fell in with the idea, as they did with most of those which emanated from Margaret's imperial young mind. So "The Maples" it became to the family. But the youth of the neighborhood devised a variant on Margaret's title. They called it "Lalor's Maples." The name "took," so to speak, and Lalor's Maples it has remained, even unto this day.

The Exiles

by Harvey J. O'Higgins, *McClure's Magazine* 26 (March 1906)

Known in his day as "the prose laureate of the commonplace man," Harvey O'Higgins was an interesting, prolific writer who is all but forgotten today. Born in London, Ontario, in 1876, he attended the University of Toronto for a while, then left to become an urban journalist, at first in Toronto and then in New York City. Around 1900, he began to get stories and topical articles placed in leading American magazines, such as Scribner's, Collier's, *and* McClure's. *He went on from there to produce several volumes on contemporary issues, in collaboration with experts in various fields. These included studies of the effects of the urban environment on young people* (The Beast, *1910), of Mormonism* (Under the Prophet in Utah, *1911), and of the new phenomenon of psychoanalysis* (The Secret Springs, *1920). O'Higgins continued to write fiction, and his best novels were two sympathetic studies of American women,* Julie Crane *(1924) and* Clara Barron *(1926). He also collaborated in the writing of several plays, including a popular dramatization of Sinclair Lewis's* Main Street *in 1921. Known for his generosity toward younger writers, O'Higgins was active in the Authors' League right up until his death in 1929.*

"The Exiles" is one of O'Higgins's earliest published stories. It is representative of his valuable contribution as an early chronicler of the lower-middle-class urban Irish, the "clerks, and bookkeepers, shopgirls, and working women" of New York, as O'Higgins himself describes them in another story. (By 1914, he had become so identified with this genre as to prompt an article in Current Opinion *on "The Man Who Writes Irish Stories.") His stories are often flawed with the touch of sentimentality, but they give us important detail about the daily lives of this transitional Irish-American group, which was just then reaching for the bottom rung of the ladder of respectability. In "The Exiles," servant girl Annie Freel is deceived with tragic consequences by a man who marries another, and O'Higgins delivers a harsh judgment on New York's treatment of the Irish.*

The street was a narrow lane of asphalt between two walls of brownstone house-fronts; and these two walls were so exactly alike that each seemed to be staring, with all its shutterless windows, across the roadway at the other, in the dumb amazement of a man meeting his double. Both were ruled lengthwise in the same four rows of windows. Each window was like all its fellows.

All were arranged as regularly in line as the inch-marks on a yardstick; and at every third window in the lowest row, a house was marked off – as if it were a foot on the rule – by the projection of a brownstone stoop, from which a flight of steps led down to the sidewalk.

It had once been a street of homes; and, in its prosperous days, its stiff monotony must have realized the ideal of the lives that were lived there then according to the strictest conventions of respectability. But now it had fallen into shabbiness and disrepair, and its set, methodical air seemed only proper to such a street of boarding-houses where the conduct of life was chiefly an affair of sub-dividing identical days into sleeping, waking, and eating, joylessly, by the clock.

It was to this street that the dining-room maid in Mrs. Henry's boarding-house had to look for entertainment whenever she was tired of her round of cooking, serving, and washing-up. She was an Irish girl; and her name was Annie Freel; and her cheeks were still as fresh as pinks from the breezes of Donegal. She had the physique of a milkmaid and a rustic gracefulness of good health that was almost beautiful by contrast with the background of Mrs. Henry's faded dining-room – a background of rusty steel engravings in tarnished gilt frames, hung on a yellowed wall-paper that made the whole room look as if the innumerable meals that had been served there had given it the complexion of a dyspeptic.

She was sitting beside the grated basement window, peeling potatoes into a dish-pan, but she kept an eye on the "area" and the street; and whenever the wheels of a wagon sounded on the pavement; she stopped her work to watch it pass behind the fat, stone spindles of the area balustrade. The thermometer on the window frame marked 92°, and her face was wet. There were heat rings under her eyes; and her eyebrows were drawn in a frown that made no wrinkle on a forehead that had never been broken to worry. Whenever she looked away from the window, she glanced anxiously at the clock; it marked a quarter past eleven, and the groceries had not come.

She let her hand fall idle into the cool water of the pan, and stared at the dust floating in the sunlight.

The cook called hoarsely from the kitchen: "Annie!"

She started. "Yis?"

"What're ye at?"

"Peelin' pitaties."

"What's makin' ye so noisy?"

Annie looked down at her hands without answering.

"Why don't ye sing no more these days?" The voice was querulous.

Annie poised a potato to her knife and blushed to the tops of her ears. "It's too warrm," she said.

A pan banged in the kitchen. "Warrm, d'ye call it? I call it drippin' danged hot!"

The girl did not reply; and the cook, after grumbling to herself for a while, resigned herself to a stifled silence.

A delivery wagon came clattering up the street, swung into the gutter, and pulled up with a jerk; and Annie dropped her potato and watched eagerly. When she saw a strange man climb down the wheel, she put her dish-pan on the deep window-sill and stood back from the light to regard him with a look of distress. He bustled down into the area and threw all his weight on a tug at the bell.

"Glory be!" the cook cried to her. "What's that?"

She did not answer. She went to the door and took the basket without raising her eyes from it.

"The grocery man!" the cook greeted her in the kitchen. "Does he want to pluck the bell out be the root! That's not Jawn?"

Annie shook her head. "No," she said vacantly, and turned to empty the basket on the serving table.

The cook studied a moment on the tone of that "No"; and then, taking up the chopper, she attacked the meat in the wooden chopping-bowl with vicious blows. She had the arm of a butcher – short but powerful – and a body of the same build; her hair was a greasy grey; her face was the flat-nosed type of slant-jawed Irish, that is so pathetically like an ape's.

Annie went out with the empty basket, but this time she met the man's eyes with a look of inquiry that held him until she could ask: "Where's Mister Boland now?"

He grinned. "Jack? Oh, he's quit. He's got married. I don't know where he is."

She released her hold of the basket, her face as blank as a bewildered child's.

"Jack'd sooner marry than work," he laughed. He added over his shoulder as he went, "Hot, ain't it?"

She shut the basement door, and stood for a long time with her fingers in the iron lattice, gazing out at the area with set eyes. When she turned back to the dining-room, she groped her way blindly through the dark hall. And when she sat down to her work again, her hands went about it mechanically under the fixed mask of her face.

"Is 't the heat that's worryin' ye?" the cook asked at their luncheon. "Sure I know it is," she persisted, at the girl's listless denial. "It's bad weather fer young blood. Me own ould skull's splittin' like the shell of a hard-boiled egg. Phew! Go in an' lay yersilf down, that's a good child. It's out 'n the fields y' ought to be, stackin' hay, 'stid of stewin' in a kitchen here. Go on, Annie, gurl, an' rest yersilf."

Annie went. In the little bedroom that opened off the kitchen, she stretched herself flat on her back and lay stiff. The pillow was hot to her head. She put her cold hand on her burning forehead, and her eyes settled in a wild stare on a picture of Christ that was tacked on the wall at the foot of the bed, with the heart in the open breast flaming red in a yellow aureole.

The cook muttered over her work: "Please God 't will let up a bit t' night. . . . What's happened that boy Jawn, I wonder. The young thief! She's been lookin' fer 'm fer a week past. . . . Phew, but it 's hot! . . . If he's playin' games with her, I'll break his back."

The city baked its bricks and stones in a scorching sunlight all the afternoon, till the streets were as hot and dry as a kiln. Then with the slanting of the sun, a mist as warm as steam began to gather in from the Bay; the faint breeze that had been fluttering along on the housetops feebly, fell among the chimneys; the plumes of steam rose from the elevator buildings straight in the still air. The thick dusk closed down smothering all.

Annie came white from her room. She blundered from pan to pan in the fat-smoke of the kitchen, helping the cook. Dazed and stupid, in the glare of the dining-room, she served greasy food to the tables and poured ice-water in a dream. Swaying over the pan of steaming dishes – at the sink where the roaches gathered to the sound of trickling water – she washed a thousand glasses, cups and saucers, plates and spoons, knives, forks, pans and pots, deaf to the kindly garrulity of the cook who helped her. When it was done, she went back to her bed again. "Ah, go away, Mary," she said wearily. "Go away an' let be."

Mary took the kitchen rocking-chair and carried it out resolutely to the area. "As sure 's my name's Mary McShane," she promised herself, "I'll break the back o' that boy, Jawn! Here's Saturda' night, an' no sight of 'm since this day week. Let 'm come now. Let 'm come. I'll give 'm a piece o' me mind." And she sat down with her arms crossed to wait for him.

There was a fluttering of white skirts here and there on the porches across the road, where some boarders were sitting out; men dragged past with their straw hats in their hands and their coats on their arms; the clang of trolley gongs and the iron hum of trains on the elevated railroad came to her drowsily. She relaxed to an easier posture and began to fan herself with her apron as she rocked. Both motions ceased together. She closed her eyes.

She was awakened by an insistent "I say, cook! Cook!" and started up to see the young man whom she knew as "Mr. Beatty of the top-floor rear," leaning over her. He said, "What's wrong with Annie?"

"Annie?" she gasped, wide awake. "Saints in Hiven —"

"Oh, it's nothing," he laughed. "She seemed to be acting rather strangely. Anything wrong?"

She put her hands up to rub her eyes in a pretense of sleepiness. "Ye scart the heart out o' me," she evaded him. "I was dreamin'."

He waited.

"Annie?" she said. "Sure, she's worried, poor gurl, be the heat. She's not well. She's not well, at all."

"Well," he replied, "she seemed cool enough just now. She went out in a heavy jacket. . . . She asked me to answer the door bell for her. I was sitting on the steps there, having a smoke."

"Gone out? Gone out, is she? Ay, indeed, thin!" She settled back in her chair. "She must've gone out to meet that Jawn of hers. To be sure! That's it, to be sure. I thought 'twas sick she was. How 're ye standin' the heat yersilf?"

Her voice was transparent, sly. He sat down on the window sill, amused. "Not so bad. But this is hotter than Ireland, cook."

"Ireland?" She made an exaggerated gesture of despair. "Ireland!" She folded her hands in an eloquent resignation. "I was just dreamin' I was back to it. Aw, dear, dear! Will I never ferget it?"

He laughed. He asked in a bantering tone: "Would you like to go back?"

"Me?" she cried sharply. "Sure, what fer? What's to go back to? Naw, naw. Whin ye're ould there's no goin' back to the young days – excipt while ye sleep. An' it's the sorry wakin' ye have."

"That's true," he said, to humor her.

"It is," she replied, unmollified, "but little enough ye know of it. Ye'll learn whin ye're a dodderin' ould man with no teeth to grip yer pipe to." She nodded at a memory of her own grandfather, drowsing before the peat fire of an evening, under the soot-blackened beams of the kitchen, with his pipe upside down in his mouth.

Beatty smiled. The talk of this old woman of the basement's underworld – with her plaintive Irish intonation and her comic Irish face and her amusing Irish "touchiness" – was as good as a play to him. "How long have you been out?" he asked.

"Long enough to learn better. Fourty year an' more."

"Well, why did you come then?"

She turned on him. "God knows! Why did I? Why did Annie gurl? Well may ye ask!" She tossed her head resentfully. "Beca'se roasted pitaties an' good buttermilk were too poor fer proud stummicks. Beca'se we wud be rich, as they tol' us we wud, here in Ameriky. An' what are we? The naygurs o' the town, livin' in cellars, servin' thim that pays us in the money that we came fer, an' gettin' none o' the fair words an' kindness we left behind. Sure at home they're more neighborly to the brute beasts than y' are here to the humans." She looked out at the stifling street. "We're strangers in a strange land, as Father Tierney says. We're a joke to yez, an' that's the best ye'll iver make of us."

He sobered guiltily and looked down at his feet.

"An' Annie!" she broke out, "the simple crature, ust to big gossoons o' boys that swally their tongues whin they go coortin' an' have niver a word to say – what's she to make o' this grinnin' Jawn of hers with all his blether? I know him. He's the mate of a lad that came acrost me the first year I was out, with his hat on the corner of his head an' the divil in 's eye. An' he talked with me an' walked with me an' called me candy names, till there was nuthin' but the sound of his voice in me ears, an' the look of his smile in me eye the whole livelong day till he came again of an evenin'." Her voice broke. "Faith, the time he kissed me first – at the gate that was – I ran into the house trimblin' and blushin' wi' the fear an' the delight of it, me hans shakin' so I cud scarce get me clo's off me to git into me bed, and layin' a-wake weepin' an' smilin' tegither all night long to think of it. That's the sort of fool I was. Th' angils jus' come to Hiven were no happier. . . . I was come to th' ither place before I was done with him. . . . Poor Annie! Poor gurl!"

He looked at her, silenced and ashamed. She wiped her cheeks with her apron and sighed under a load of anxiety for Annie. He tried to think of something to say in apology and reassurance; and glancing from her, at a loss, he saw a dark figure climbing the stone steps, silhouetted against a street light. "There!" he whispered. "Is n't that – Yes it is. She's coming back. She has n't met him. . . . That's all right now. You must n't let her go out again."

"Thank Hiven," the cook said fervently. "I been keepin' her from goin' out with him any night these four weeks. She's a mere child, raised in inno-cency. 'Twas not like her to steal out so."

"There must be something wrong with her," he suggested.

"There is that," she said. "There's somethin' wantin' to her an' she'll niver find it in this town, though she seek it iver so. A home of her own back o' the boor-trees – an' a dip o' bog fer to plant her pitaty slips in – an' a scraw fer her fire an' her man toastin' his big feet at it, an' the baby crawlin' between the legs of his chair, an' the neighbors droppin' in to gossip an' spit in the blaze – she'll niver find it here! Niver, if she has my luck! An' it's powerful small satisfaction she'll get of writin' home to thim that has it, tellin' thim the big wages she earns an' sendin' thim money to Christmas – powerful small!"

While she had been talking, Beatty had seen a policeman stop to look up at the door and then saunter back toward his street corner. And Beatty was still frowning watchfully at the steps when he heard the cook say, "Whur've ye been to, Annie?" He turned to see the girl standing behind the grated base-ment door.

In a thick, blurred voice, fumbling slowly over her words, she replied: "Is that – is that – Jawn?" And Beatty's pipe clicked suddenly on his teeth.

"No, 'tis not," the cook answered. "Go back to yer bed. He'll not come t' night now. 'Tis too late."

"Is it?" she asked, in the simple tones of a child. "Is it too late, Mary?"

"It is that. Go to bed, gurl. Ye're tired out."

"Oh?" she said softly. "It's too late"; and she disappeared in the darkness. Beatty caught a quick breath. "W-what is it? What's the matter with her?" The cook answered wearily: "I've told ye, sor, but ye'll not understan'."

"But there's something wrong with her," he said huskily. "That's not her natural voice."

"Let be, boy," she replied. "Her trouble's come to her. We can do naught fer her now." She added, more gently: we're like a cat with our sores, sor. 'Tis best to let us go off be oursilves an' lick thim. . . . She'll be quiet now. . . . It must've been hot down town this day."

"Yes," he sighed. "I thought — I thought perhaps the heat had affected her. The papers are full of deaths and prostrations."

She nodded and nodded. After a silence, she said: "No doubt. The heat, too. Are y' a Noo Yorker born?"

He cleared his throat to answer: "No. A Canadian. An exile, like yourself."

"Ay," she said. "This is a great town fer young men. Ye get yer chanct here."

He did not reply, and she did not speak again. For a long time, they sat silent. Then they began to talk in low tones of anything but the thoughts that were in both their minds, until a stealthy rustle at the basement door brought them around with a start to see Annie, all in white, fumbling at the latch. She got the door open and drifted out into the light, bare-footed. Beatty stiffened at the sight of her face. The cook started up and caught her by the arm. She swung unsteadily. "That's me money," she said tonelessly; and Beatty heard the ring of coins on the area paving.

"Annie! Annie!" the cook cried.

"An' that's me purse," she said, dropping it.

The cook threw her arms about her. "Annie! Annie, dear! What's this fer? What ails ye, gurl?"

She put a hand down to loosen the cook's arm from her side. "'Twill burn ye," she said. "Me heart's all afire there, like the pi'ture." A bit of silver fell from her sleeve and tinkled at her feet. She looked down at it. "I put it by fer Jawn. . . . What's become of Jawn? Jawn?"

The cook backed her to the rocking-chair and forced her to sit down. "Dang yer Jawn!" she cried. "Will ye drive us all daft?"

It was then, for the first time, she got the light on the girl's face — a face set like stone, while the eyes shifted and wept — and she wailed: "Ach, Annie darlin'," and dropped on her knees beside her. "Is it come to this, gurl? Dear Lord, what 've they been doin' to ye? Look at me. Look at me, child."

Annie was staring at Beatty, and he was sitting cold with horror on the window-sill. "Who's that?" she said. "Good evenin' sir," she smiled. "Ye 're late with the groc'ries." She got no answer. "Look at 'm, Mary," she said fearfully, and put her hand up to her eyes, and peered at him through her fingers. "He glowers at me so."

"Aw, now," the cook pleaded. "Aw now, Annie gurl. Don't be takin' on. 'Tis Mister Beatty from the top floor, an' what'll he be thinkin' of ye, talkin' such like foolishness." She whispered: "Have wit, child. Put down yer hands.

Listen to me. Listen. They'll be takin' ye away. They'll shut y' up in Bellevue fer mad. Have ye no sinse lift?"

Beatty had risen heavy-kneed and stumbled to the basement door. "I'll bring – I'll bring the doctor," he stammered, and ran in for his hat.

The cook had not heard him, but when she looked around she knew what had happened, and she jumped up in a panic, "Quick! Quick!" she cried. "They're comin'"; and fell on her knees to gather up the scattered money in her apron. "Go to bed, gurl! Ach, Annie, Annie," she cried despairingly.

Annie was rocking in the chair, crooning and talking to herself. The cook caught her by the arm, pulled her to her feet and hurried her indoors. "Whist! Whist!" she pleaded. "Quit yer nonsinse, Annie. Ah, quit it – quit it! Wud ye let yerself be taken to the madhouse? Ah, God ha' mercy — "

She dragged the girl back to the kitchen, and had her in bed and frightened into silence when Beatty returned with the doctor from next door. "She's better now," she said suavely, meeting them in the dining room. "'Twas but a touch o' the sun, doctor."

He looked at her. She stood blinking and shifting her small eyes. "What did you do for her?"

She began to stammer: "W-what did I do fer her? Why, to be sure, I–I–"

"Take me to her," he ordered.

She gave Beatty a look of hate and despair and led into the kitchen.

Beatty did not follow. He steadied himself against the old marble mantle of the dining-room, and mopped his face and neck weakly with his handkerchief.

When the doctor reappeared, he ordered: "Call an ambulance. Bellevue Hospital. Be quick, now! Be quick!"

Beatty edged slowly to the door. "I won't!" he gasped, and ran upstairs and locked himself in his room.

———

"You'll have to get your breakfast at a restaurant, Mr. Beatty," Mrs. Henry, the boarding-house mistress told him next morning. "My cook has left me."

"What for?" he asked guiltily.

She shrugged her shoulders and shook her head. "The maid that waits on the table took ill last night. She was delirious – out of her mind – positively violent when the ambulance came for her. The doctor ordered it. I couldn't keep her here. How could I? Who's to look after her here? The work has to be done, and — "

"How is she?" he interrupted.

"She had a sunstroke or I don't know what. I was too upset last night –. We had a terrible time with her. I don't know what it was. It must 've been a sunstroke. We had an awful scene."

"How is she?"

"Well," she said, in a sort of defiance, "she died early this morning in the hospital. . . . And Mary," she cried, "accuses me of murdering her. And she packed up her trunk and left at six o'clock this morning, without even waiting for her wages. I never heard of such a thing. It's the most absurd" – She laughed brokenly. "These Irish servant girls ——"

He looked away with a sickly smile. "I know," he said. "I know."

Mr. Dooley's Bridgeport Chronicle (1893-1898)

by Finley Peter Dunne

> *I know histhry isn't thrue, Hinnissy, because it ain't like what I see ivry day in Halsted Sthreet. If any wan comes along with a histhry iv Greece or Rome that'll show me th' people fightin', gettin' dhrunk, makin' love, gettin' married, owin' th' grocery man an' bein' without hard-coal, I'll believe they was a Greece or Rome, but not befure. Historyans is like doctors. They are always lookin' f'r symptoms. Those iv them that writes about their own times examines th' tongue an' feels th' pulse an' makes a wrong dygnosis. Th' other kind iv histhry is a post-mortem examination. It tells ye what a counthry died iv. But I'd like to know what it lived iv.*

So speaks Mr. Martin Dooley, Chicago's aging immigrant saloon-keeper/philosopher, the remarkable creation of Irish America's first literary genius, Finley Peter Dunne. Born to immigrant parents on Chicago's Irish West Side in 1867, this boy was encouraged in reading and the life of the mind by his mother, Ellen Finley Dunne, and his older sister Amelia, a teacher in the Chicago schools.

In June 1884, fresh out of high school and 16 years old, Peter Dunne took a job as a cub reporter for the Chicago Telegram. *Eight years and five increasingly responsible positions later, he was editorial chairman at the* Chicago Evening Post. *It was there, in October 1893 at the ripe old age of 26, that Dunne imagined himself into the character of Martin Dooley. Almost immediately, his 750-word monologues (delivered to genial politician John McKenna or long-suffering millworker Malachi Hennessy) became a Saturday evening Chicago tradition. The last in a series of dialect experiments for his creator, Mr. Dooley succeeded Colonel Malachi McNeery, a fictional downtown Chicago bar-keep whom Dunne had invented to provide weekly commentary during the World's Fair of 1893. Unlike the cosmopolitan McNeery, Dunne placed Mr. Dooley's saloon on Archer Avenue on the city's South Side, in the Irish working-class neighborhood known as Bridgeport.*

Between 1893 and 1900, when Dunne moved on to New York and a different sort of career as a satirist of our national life, some 300 Dooley pieces appeared in Chicago newspapers. Taken together, they form a coherent body of work, in which a vivid, detailed world comes into existence – a self-contained immigrant/ethnic culture with its own customs, ceremonies, "sacred sites," social pecking order, heroes, villains, and victims. The Chicago Dooley pieces constitute the most solidly realized ethnic neighborhood in nineteenth-century American literature. With the full faith of the literary realist, Dunne embraced the common man as proper subject and created sympathetic, dignified, even heroic characters, plausibly grounded in a few city blocks of apartments, saloons, factories, and churches.

Moreover, characters, places, and community are all embodied in the vernacular voice of a sixty-year-old, smiling public-house man, the first such dialect voice to transcend the stereotypes of "stage Irish" ethnic humor. Indeed, the key to Dunne's amazing ability to create the illusion of a speaking voice grounded in place that still rings true lies in the coming together in these newspaper columns of oral tradition and the written word. These are, after all, transcribed renderings of imagined conversational speech, much of it inspired by stories that had been told to the young Peter Dunne by his parents and their generation of immigrants, in whom the Irish oral tradition was still very much alive. In fact, the Chicago Dooley pieces constitute a rare and marvelous hybrid form. Composed under deadline with imperative spontaneity, these pieces are actually closer to talk than writing. Dunne's body of work is truly transitional, bridging the gap between Irish storytelling and American printed short fiction to create, from fall 1893 through early 1898, an astonishing four-year window into the world of nineteenth-century Irish Chicago. This was a great achievement for Dunne and an even greater gift to those who were living in Chicago's immigrant/ethnic world in the 1890s. Telling stories maintains communal ties with one's origins, past, and shaping world view – crucially important ties when the place from which these have sprung lies an ocean away.

Separately numbered, the Dooley pieces collected here are arranged thematically, as follows:

• Preserved community memories of the Great Hunger (piece 1), the crossing from Ireland (2), the disillusioning early years in America (3), and the Irish in the Civil War (4);

• Vignettes of daily life in Bridgeport in the 1890s, including a parish fair (5) and the parochial school graduation of "Hennessy's youngest" (6);

• Three pieces illustrating the dignity and heroism of Bridgeport people: old Shaughnessy, whose family history reads like an O'Neill tragedy in miniature (7), fireman Shay, whose pride drives him to extraordinary bravery (8), and fireman Mike Clancy, a tragic victim of hubris (9);

• Studies both comic and serious of the effects on the Irish of the painful process of assimilation: the family crisis over naming the tenth Hogan baby (10), troubles in the Donahue home brought on by the acquisition of a piano (11), and the disastrous lives of two young Bridgeport criminals (12, 13), that prompt Mr. Dooley to muse that "sometimes I think they'se poison in th' life iv a big city;

• Pointed analyses of the most visible and controversial career option for the Irish *in American cities in the nineties – politics, including the example of a model campaign for alderman (14) and the capsule biography of a ruthless ward boss (15);*

 • *Examinations of the tragi-comic American contribution to the movement to free Ireland from British rule: a sympathetic meditation on the paradox of Irish accomplishment abroad and failure at home (16), and a broadly satiric report on the amazingly inept "Tynan plot" against Queen Victoria and the Russian Czar (17);*

 • *A final group of pieces that exemplify Dunne's strong writing in the tradition of Jonathan Swift's "savage indignation" – stories from ethnic nineteenth-century cultures of poverty: a small child sent out for beer in a snowstorm (18), the suffering of workers' families during the 1894 Pullman Strike (19), tragic confrontations between ailing and destitute Bridgeport Irish and Polish families and the Illinois Central Railroad (20, 21), and the hard life and death of a proud Galway woman whose flight from famine at home ends with starvation in Chicago (22).*

1. The Necessity of Modesty among the Rich: A Tale of the Famine

On February 10, 1897, the Bradley-Martins of Troy, New York, hosted the most expensive private party ever given, a masked ball at the Waldorf-Astoria, New York City, the cost of which was estimated at nearly $370,000. As the country was then mired in a severe economic depression, many people criticized the timing of this ostentatious display of wealth. "Pether th' Packer" was an Irish "hanging judge," and Hennessy's opening question was prompted by the fact that one of Bridgeport's aldermen around this time was named Charles Martin.

"I wondher," said Mr. Hennessy, "if thim Bradley-Martins that's goin' to give th' ball is anny kin iv th' aldherman?"

"I doubt it," said Mr. Dooley. "I knowed all his folks. They're Monaghan people, an' I niver heerd iv thim marryin' into th' Bradleys, who come fr'm away beyant near th' Joynt's Causeway. What med ye think iv thim?"

"I was readin' about th' Prowtestant minister that give thim such a turnin' over th' other night," said Hennessy. Then the Philistine went on: "It looks to me as though th' man was wr-rong, an' th' Bradley-Martins was right. Faith, th' more th' poor can get out iv th' r-rich, th' better f'r thim. I seen it put just r-right in th' paper th' other day. If these people didn't let go iv their coin here, they'd take it away with thim to Paris or West Baden, Indiana, an' spind it instid iv puttin' it in circulation amongst th' florists an' dhressmakers an' hackmen they'll have to hire. I believe in encouragin' th' rich to walk away fr'm their change. 'Tis gr-reat f'r business."

Mr. Dooley mused over this politico-moral proposition some time before he said: –

"Years ago, whin I was a little bit iv a kid, hardly high enough to look into th' pot iv stirabout on th' peat fire, they was a rich landlord in our part iv Ireland; an' he ownded near half th' counthryside. His name was Dorsey, –

Willum Edmund Fitzgerald Dorsey, justice iv th' peace, mimber iv Parlymint.

"I'll niver tell ye how much land that man had in his own r-right. Ye cud walk f'r a day without lavin' it, bog an' oat-field an' pasthure an' game preserves. He was smothered with money, an' he lived in a house as big as th' Audjitoroom Hotel. Manny's th' time I've seen him ride by our place, an' me father'd raise his head from th' kish iv turf an' touch his hat to th' gr-reat man. An' wanst or twict in th' month th' dogs'd come yelpin' acrost our little place, with lads follerin' afther in r-red coats; f'r this Dorsey was a gr-reat huntsman, bad scran to his evil face.

"He had th' r-reputation iv bein'a good landlord so long as th' crops come regular. He was vilent, it's thrue, an' 'd as lave as not cut a farmer across th' face with his whip f'r crossin' th' thrail iv th' fox; but he was liberal with his money, an', Hinnissy, that's a thrait that covers a multitude iv sins. He give freely to th' church, an' was as gin'rous to th' priest as to th' parson. He had th' gintry f'r miles around to his big house f'r balls an' dinners an' huntin' meetin's, an' half th' little shopkeepers in th' neighborin' town lived on th' money he spent f'r th' things he didn't bring fr'm Dublin or London. I mind wanst a great roar wint up whin he stayed th' whole season in England with his fam'ly. It near broke th' townsfolk, an' they were wild with delight whin he come back an' opened up th' big house.

"But wan year there come a flood iv rain, an' th' nex' year another flood, an' th' third year there wasn't a lumper turned up that wasn't blue-black to th' hear-rt. We was betther off than most, an' we suffered our share, Gawd knows; but thim that was scrapin' th' sod f'r a bare livin' fr'm day to day perished like th' cattle in th' field.

"Thin come th' writs an' th' evictions. Th' bailiffs dhrove out in squads, seizin' cattle an' turnin' people into th' r-road. Nawthin' wud soften th' hear-rt iv Dorsey. I seen th' priest an' th' 'Piscopal ministher dhrivin' over to plead with him wan night; an' th' good man stopped at our house, comin' back, an' spent th' night with us. I heerd him tell me father what Dorsey said. 'Haven't I been lib'ral with me people?' he says. 'Haven't I give freely to ye'er churches? Haven't I put up soup-houses an' disthributed blankets whin th' weather was cold? Haven't I kept th' shopkeepers iv th' town beyant fr'm starvin' be thradin' with thim an' stayin' in this cur-rsed counthry, whin, if I'd done what me wife wanted, I'd been r-runnin' around Europe, enj'yin' life? I'm a risidint landlord. I ain't like Kilduff, that laves his estate in th' hands iv an agint. I'm proud iv me station. I was bor-rn here, an' here I'll die; but I'll have me r-rights. These here people owes their rent, an' I'll get th' rent or th' farms if I have to call on ivry rig'mint fr'm Bombay to Cape Clear, an' turn ivry oat-field into a pasture f'r me cattle. I stand on th' law. I'm a just man, an' I ask no more thin what belongs to me.'

"Ivry night they was a party on th' hill, an' th' people come fr'm miles around; an' th' tinants trudgin' over th' muddy roads with th' peelers behind thim cud see th' light poorin' out fr'm th' big house an' hear Devine's band playin' to th' dancers. Th' shopkeepers lived in clover, an' thanked th' lord f'r a good landlord, an' wan that lived at home. But one avnin' a black man be th' name iv Shaughnessy, that had thramped across th' hills fr'm Galway just in time to rent f'r th' potato rot, wint and hid himself in a hedge along th' road with a shotgun loaded with hardware under his coat. Dorsey'd heerd talk iv the people bein' aggrieved at him givin' big parties while his bailiffs were hustlin' men and women off their holdin's; but he was a high-handed man, an' foolish in his pride, an' he'd have it no other way but that he'd go about without protection. This night he rode alongside th' carredge iv some iv his frinds goin' to th' other side iv town, an' come back alone in th' moonlight. Th' Irish ar-re poor marksmen, Hinnissy, except whin they fire in platoons; but that big man loomin'up in th' moonlight on a black horse cud no more be missed thin th' r-rock iv Cashel. He niver knowed what hit him; an' Pether th' Packer come down th' followin' month, an' a jury iv shopkeepers hanged Shaughnessy so fast it med even th' judge smile."

"Well," said Mr. Hennessy, "I suppose he deserved it; but, if I'd been on th' jury, I'd've starved to death befure I'd give th' verdict."

"Thrue," said Mr. Dooley. "An' Dorsey was a fool. He might've evicted twinty thousan' tinants, an' lived to joke about it over his bottle. 'Twas th' music iv th' band an' th' dancin' on th' hill an' th' lights th' Galway man seen whin he wint up th' muddy road with his babby in his arrums that done th' business f'r Dorsey." (February 6, 1897)

2. The Wanderers

Mr. Dooley's version of the archetypal crossing narrative strikes an eloquent balance between comic and tragic aspects of the trauma of emigration.

"Poor la-ads, poor la-ads," said Mr. Dooley, putting aside his newspaper and rubbing his glasses. "'Tis a hard lot theirs, thim that go down into th' say in ships, as Shakespeare says. Ye niver see a storm on th' ocean? Iv coorse ye didn't. How cud ye, ye that was born away fr'm home? But I have, Jawn. May th' saints save me fr'm another! I come over in th' bowels iv a big crazy balloon iv a propeller, like wan iv thim ye see hooked up to Dempsey's dock, loaded with lumber an' slabs an' Swedes. We watched th' little ol' island fadin' away behind us, with th' sun sthrikin' th' white house-tops iv Queenstown an' lightin' up th' chimbleys iv Martin Hogan's liquor store. Not wan iv us but had left near all we loved behind, an' sare a chance that we'd iver spoon th' stirabout out iv th' pot above th' ol' peat fire again. Yes, by dad, there was wan, – a lad fr'm th' County Roscommon. Divvle th' tear he shed. But, whin we had parted fr'm land, he turns to me, an' says, 'Well, we're on our way,' he says. 'We are that,' says I. 'No chanst f'r thim to turn around an' go back,'

he says. 'Divvle th' fut,' says I. 'Thin,' he says, raisin' his voice, 'to 'ell with th'
Prince iv Wales,' he says. 'To 'ell with him' he says.

"An' that was th' last we see of sky or sun f'r six days. That night come
up th' divvle's own storm. Th' waves tore an' walloped th' ol' boat, an' th'
wind howled, an' ye cud hear th' machinery snortin' beyant. Murther, but I
was sick. Wan time th' ship 'd be settin' on its tail, another it'd be standin' on
its head, thin rollin' over cow-like on th' side; an' ivry time it lurched me
stummick lurched with it, an' I was tore an' rint an' racked till, if death come,
it 'd found me willin'. An' th' Roscommon man, – glory be, but he was dis-
thressed. He set on th' flure, with his hands on his belt an' his face as white as
stone, an' rocked to an' fro. 'Ahoo,' he says, 'ahoo, but me insides has torn
loose,' he says, 'an' are tumblin' around,' he says. 'Say a pather an' avy,' says
I, I was that mad f'r th' big bosthoon f'r his blatherin' on th' flure. 'Say a
pather an' avy,' I says; 'f'r ye're near to death's dure, avick.' 'Am I?' says he,
raising up. 'Thin,' he says, 'to 'ell with the whole rile fam'ly,' he says. Oh, he
was a rebel!

"Through th' storm there was a babby cryin'. 'Twas a little wan, no more
thin a year ol'; an' 'twas owned be a Tipp'rary man who come fr'm near
Clonmel, a poor, weak, scarey-lookin' little divvle that lost his wife, an' see th'
bailiff walk off with th' cow, an' thin see him come back again with th' process
servers. An' so he was comin' over with th' babby, an' bein' mother an' father
to it. He'd rock it be th' hour on his knees, an' talk dam nonsense to it, an'
sing it songs, 'Aha, 'twas there I met a maiden down be th' tanyard side,' an'
'Th' Wicklow Mountaineer,' an' 'Th' Rambler fr'm Clare,' an' 'O'Donnel
Aboo,' croonin' thim in th' little babby's ears, an' payin' no attintion to th'
poorin' thunder above his head, day an' night, day an' night, poor soul. An'
th' babby cryin' out his heart, an' him settin' there with his eyes as red as his
hair, an' makin' no kick, poor soul.

"But wan day th' ship settled down steady, an' ragin' stummicks with it;
an' th' Roscommon man shakes himself, an' says, 'to 'ell with th' Prince iv
Wales an' th' Dook iv Edinboroo,' an' goes out. An' near all th' steerage followed; f'r th' storm had done its worst, an' gone on to throuble those that
come afther, an' may th' divvle go with it. 'Twill be rest f'r that little Tipp'rary
man; f'r th' waves was r-runnin' low an' peaceful, an' th' babby have
sthopped cryin'.

"He had been settin' on a stool, but he come over to me. 'Th' storm,' says
I, 'is over.' 'Yis,' says he, ''tis over.' ''Twas wild while it lasted,' says I. 'Ye may
say so,' says he. 'Well, please Gawd,' says I, 'that it left none worse off thin
us.' 'It blew ill f'r some an' aise f'r others,' says he. 'Th' babby is gone.'

"An' so it was, Jawn, f'r all his rockin' an' singin'. An' in th' avnin' they
burried it over th' side into th' say, an' th' litle Tipp'rary man wint up an' see
thim do it. He see thim do it." (February 16, 1895)

3. Gold-Seeking: Illusions about America

The day before this piece appeared, news of fabulous discoveries of gold in the Yukon broke in the Chicago papers. Mr. Dooley's immediate reaction was to cast doubt on all such accounts, by recalling his own youthful illusions about America and describing the pernicious effects that wealth would have on Hennessy.

"Well, sir," said Mr. Hennessy, "that Alaska's th' gr-reat place. I thought 'twas nawthin' but an iceberg with a few seals roostin' on it, an' wan or two hundherd Ohio politicians that can't be killed on account iv th' threaty iv Pawrs. But here they tell me 'tis fairly smothered in goold. A man stubs his toe on th' ground, an lifts th' top off iv a goold mine. Ye go to bed at night, an' wake up with goold fillin' in ye'er teeth."

"Yes," said Mr. Dooley, "Clancy's son was in here this mornin', an' he says a frind iv his wint to sleep out in th' open wan night, an' whin he got up his pants assayed four ounces iv goold to th' pound, an' his whiskers panned out as much as thirty dollars net."

"If I was a young man an' not tied down here," said Mr. Hennessy, "I'd go there; I wud so."

"I wud not," said Mr. Dooley. "Whin I was a young man in th' ol' counthry, we heerd th' same story about all America. We used to set be th' tur-rf fire o' nights, kickin' our bare legs on th' flure an' wishin' we was in New York, where all ye had to do was to hold ye'er hat an' th' goold guineas 'd dhrop into it. An' whin I got to be a man, I come over here with a ham and a bag iv oatmeal, as sure that I'd return in a year with money enough to dhrive me own ca-ar as I was that me name was Martin Dooley. An' that was a cinch.

"But, faith, whin I'd been here a week, I seen that there was nawthin' but mud undher th' pavement, – I larned that be means iv a pick-axe at tin shillin's th' day, – an' that, though there was plenty iv goold, thim that had it were froze to it; an' I come west, still lookin' f'r mines. Th' on'y mine I sthruck at Pittsburgh was a hole f'r sewer pipe. I made it. Siven shillin's th' day. Smaller thin New York, but th' livin' was cheaper, with Mon'gahela rye at five a throw, put ye'er hand around th' glass.

"I was still dreamin' goold, an' I wint down to Saint Looey. Th' nearest I come to a fortune there was findin' a quarther on th' stthreet as I leaned over th' dashboord iv a car to whack th' off mule. Whin I got to Chicago, I looked around f'r the goold mine. They was Injuns here thin. But they wasn't anny mines I cud see. They was mud to be shovelled an' dhrays to be dhruv an' beats to be walked. I choose th' dhray; f'r I was niver cut out f'r a copper, an' I'd had me fill iv excavatin'. An' I dhruv th' dhray till I wint into business.

"Me experyence with goold minin' is it's always in th' nex' county. If I was to go to Alaska, they'd tell me iv th' finds in Seeberya. So I think I'll stay here. I'm a silver man, annyhow; an' I'm contint if I can see goold wanst a year, whin some prominent citizen smiles over his newspaper. I'm thinkin' that ivry man has a goold mine undher his own dure-step or in his neighbor's pocket at th' farthest."

"Well, annyhow," said Mr. Hennessy, "I'd like to kick up th' sod, an' find a ton iv goold undher me fut."

"What wud ye do if ye found it?" demanded Mr. Dooley.

"I – I dinnaw," said Mr. Hennessy, whose dreaming had not gone this far. Then, recovering himself, he exclaimed with great enthusiasm, "I'd throw up me job at th' gas-house an' – an' live like a prince."

"I tell ye what ye'd do," said Mr. Dooley. "Ye'd come back here an' sthrut up an' down th' sthreet with ye'er thumbs in ye'er armpits; an' ye'd dhrink too much, an' ride in sthreet ca-ars. Thin ye'd buy foldin' beds an' piannies, an' start a reel estate office. Ye'd be fooled a good deal an' lose a lot iv ye'er money, an' thin ye'd tighten up. Ye'd be in a cold fear night an' day that ye'd lose ye'er fortune. Ye'd wake up in th' middle iv th' night, dhreamin' that ye was back at th' gas-house with ye'er money gone. Ye'd be prisidint iv a charitable society. Ye'd have to wear ye'er shoes in th' house, an' ye'er wife'd have ye around to rayciptions an dances. Ye'd move to Mitchigan Avnoo, an' ye'd hire a coachman that'd laugh at ye. Ye'er boys'd be joods an' ashamed iv ye, an' ye'd support ye'er daughters' husbands. Ye'd rack-rint ye'er tinants an' lie about ye'er taxes. Ye'd go back to Ireland on a visit, an' put on airs with ye'er cousin Mike. Ye'd be a mane, close-fisted, onscrupulous ol' curmudgeon; an', whin ye'd die, it'd take half ye'er fortune f'r rayqueems to put ye r-right. I don't want ye iver to speak to me whin ye get rich, Hinnissy."

"I won't," said Mr. Hennessy. (July 17, 1897)

4. The Blue and The Gray

On Memorial Day of 1895, a monument to the Confederate dead was dedicated at Oakwoods Cemetery, Chicago. An Evening Post headline declared that "Blue and Gray Clasp Hands." Colonel James Mulligan was the much revered leader of Chicago's Irish regiment in the Union Army.

"A-ho," said Mr. Dooley, "th' blue an' th' gray, th' blue an' th' gray. Well, sir, Jawn, d'ye know that I see Mulligan's regiment off. Sure I did. I see thim with me own eyes, Mulligan marchin' ahead with his soord on his side, an' his horse dancin' an' backin' into th' crowd; an' th' la-ads chowlder arms an' march, march away. Ye shud've been there. Th' women come down fr'm th' peeraries with th' childher in their arms, an' 'twas like a sind-off to a picnic. 'Good-by, Mike.' 'Timothy, darlin', don't forget your prayers.' 'Cornalius, if ye do but look out f'r th' little wans, th' big wans'll not harm ye.' 'Teddy, lad, always wear ye'er Agnus Day.' An', whin th' time come f'r th' thrain to lave, th' girls was up to th' lines; an' 'twas, 'Mike, love, ye'll come back alive, won't ye?' an' 'Pat, there does be a pair iv yarn socks in th' hoomp on ye'er back. Wear thim, lad. They'll be good f'r ye'er poor, dear feet.' An' off they wint.

"Well, some come back, an' some did not come back. An' some come back with no rale feet f'r to put yarn socks on thim. Mulligan quit down somewhere in Kentucky; an' th' las' wurruds he was heard to utter was, 'Lay me down, boys, an' save th' flag.' An' there was manny th' other that had nawthin' to say but to call f'r a docthor; f'r 'tis on'y, d'ye mind, th' heroes that has somethin' writ down on typewriter f'r to sind to th' newspapers whin they move up. Th' other lads that dies because they cudden't r-run away, – not because they wudden't, – they dies on their backs, an' calls f'r th' docthor or th' priest. It depinds where they're shot.

"But, annyhow, no wan iv thim lads come back to holler because he was in th' war or to war again th' men that shot him. They wint to wurruk, carryin' th' hod 'r shovellin' cindhers at th' rollin' mills. Some iv thim took pinsions because they needed thim; but divvle th' wan iv thim ye'll see paradin' up an' down Ar-rchey Road with a blue coat on, wantin' to fight th' war over with Schwartzmeister's bar-tinder that niver heerd iv but wan war, an' that th' rites iv sivinty-sivin.* Sare a wan. No, faith. They'd as lave decorate a confeatherate's grave as a thrue pathrite's. All they want is a chanst to go out to th' cimitry; an', faith, who doesn't enjoy that? No wan that's annything iv a spoort.

"I know hundhreds iv thim. Ye know Pat Doherty, th' little man that lives over be Grove Sthreet. He inlisted three times, by dad, an' had to stand on his toes three times to pass. He was that ager. Well, he looks to weigh about wan hundherd an' twinty pounds; an' he weighs wan fifty be raison iv him havin' enough lead to stock a plumber in his stomach an' his legs. He showed himsilf wanst whin he was feelin' gay. He looks like a sponge. But he ain't. He come in here Thursdah night to take his dhrink in quite; an' says I, 'Did ye march to-day?' 'Faith, no,' he says, 'I can get hot enough runnin' a wheelbarrow without makin' a monkey iv mesilf dancin' around th' sthreets behind a band.' 'But didn't ye go out to decorate th' graves?' says I. 'I hadn't th' price,' says he. 'Th' women wint out with a gyranium to put over Sarsfield, the first born,' he says.

"Just thin Morgan O'Toole come in, an' laned over th' ba-ar. He's been a dillygate to ivry town convention iv th' Raypublicans since I dinnaw whin. 'Well,' says he, 'I see they're pilin' it on,' he says. 'On th' dead?' says I, be way iv a joke. 'No,' he says; 'but did ye see they're puttin' up a monnymint over th' rebels out here be Oakwoods?' he says. 'By gar,' he says, ''tis a disgrace to th' mim'ries iv thim devoted dead who died f'r their counthry,' he says. 'If,' he says, 'I cud get ninety-nine men to go out an' blow it up, I'd be th' hundherth,' he says. 'Yes,' says I, 'ye wud,' I says. 'Ye'd be th' last,' I says.

---

*[These riots were skirmishes between state militiamen and striking railroad workers in Bridgeport in the summer of 1877.]

"Doherty was movin' up to him. 'What rig'ment?' says he. 'What's that?' says O'Toole. 'Did ye inlist in th' army, brave man?' says Pat. 'I swore him over age,' says I. 'Was ye dhrafted in?' says th' little man. 'No,' says O'Toole. 'Him an' me was in th' same cellar,' says I. 'Did ye iver hear iv Ree-saca, 'r Vicksburg, 'r Lookout Mountain?' th' little man wint on. 'Did anny man iver shoot at ye with annything but a siltzer bottle? Did ye iver have to lay on ye'er stummick with ye'er nose burrid in th' Lord knows what while things was whistlin' over ye that, if they iver stopped whistlin', 'd make ye'er backbone look like a broom? Did ye iver see a man that ye'd slept with th' night befure cough, an' go out with his hooks ahead iv his face? Did ye iver have to wipe ye'er most intimate frinds off ye'er clothes, whin ye wint home at night? Where was he durin'th' war?' he says. 'He was dhrivin' a grocery wagon f'r Philip Reidy,' says I. 'An' what's he makin' th' roar about?' says th' little man. 'He don't want anny wan to get onto him,' says I.

"O'Toole was gone be this time, an' th' little man laned over th' bar. 'Now,' says he, 'what d'ye think iv a gazabo that don't want a monniment put over some wan? Where is this here pole? I think I'll go out an' take a look at it. Where'd ye say th' la-ad come fr'm? Donaldson? I was there. There was a man in our mess – a Wicklow man be th' name iv Dwyer – that had th' best come-all-ye I iver heerd. It wint like this,' an' he give it to me." (June 1, 1895)

5. A Parish Fair at St. Honoria's

"Jawn, d'ye know who's th' most pop'lar man in St. Honoria's parish?" asked Mr. Dooley.

"The little priest ought to be," said Mr. McKenna.

"Well, iv coorse, we ba-ar him. Th' most pop'lar man in th' parish is Cornelius J. Costigan. He bate th' aldherman and Aloysius Regan. He did that.

"I like Fa-ather Hogan, though he an' Fa-ather Kelly does be at outs over th' Nicene council an' th' ma-an Hopkins put to wurruk on th' r-rid bridge. So whin he come over with tickets f'r th' fair an' I seen he had a game leg fr'm toddlin' around in th' snow makin' sick calls I bought two an' wint over th' closin' night – 'twas las' Sathurday.

"'Twas a gr-rand fair. They had Roddy's Hibernyun band playin' on th' cor-rner an' th' basement iv th' church was packed. In th' ba-ack they had a shootin' gall'ry where ye got five shots f'r tin cints. Hogan, th' milkman, was shootin' whin I wint in an' iverybody was out iv th' gall'ry. He missed eight shots an' thin he thrun two lumps iv coal at th' ta-arget an' made two bull's-eyes. He is a Tipp'rary man an' th' raison he's over here is he hit a polisman with a rock at twinty ya-ards – without sights.

"I'd no more thin inthered th' fair thin who should come up but Malachi Dorsey's little girl, Dalia. 'Good avnin,' she says. 'Won't ye take a chanst?' she says. 'On what?' says I. 'On a foldin' bed,' says she. 'Faith, I will not,' I says. 'I'll take no chances on no foldin' bed,' I says. 'I was locked up in wan wanst,' I says, 'an' it took a habees corpis to get me out,' I says. She lift me alone afther that, but she must've tipped me off to th' others f'r whin I come away I stood to win a doll, a rockin' chair, a picture iv th' pope done by Mary Ann O'Donoghue, a deck iv ca-ards an' a tidy. I'm all right if th' combination comes out ayether way fr'm th' rockin' chair to th' doll 'r th' tidy. But I wuddent know what th' divvle to do if I sh'd catch th' pope iv R-rome an' th' ca-ards.

"Th' booths was something iligant. Mrs. Dorsey had th' first wan where she sold mottoes an' babies' clothes. Next to hers was the ice crame layout, with the Widow Lonergan in cha-arge. Some wan touted big Hinnisy again it. He got wan mouthful iv it an' began to holler: 'F'r th' love iv hivin' won't some wan give me a cup iv tay,' he says. 'Me insides is like a skatin' rink.' He wint over an' shtud be th' fire with his coattails apart till th' sexton put him out.

"Acrost th' hall was th' table f'r church articles, where ye cud get 'Keys iv Hevin' an' 'St. Thomas a Kempises' an' ros'ries. It done a poor business, they tell me, an' Miss Dolan was that sore at th' eyesther shtew thrade done be Mrs. Cassidy next dure that she come near soakin' her with th' 'Life iv St. Rose iv Lima.' 'Twas tur-r-rible.

"But I wanted to tell ye about th' mos' poplar ma-an. Iv coorse ye know th' ga-ame. Ye've been agin it. Well, they had th' stand in th' middle iv th' flure an' 'twas bossed be Donnigan, th' lawyer. Donnigan is prisidint iv th' Young Married Min's Sodality an' dhraws all th' thrade iv th' parish; he's gettin' rich. Th' names iv th' candydates was on th' blackboord – th' aldherman, Costigan an' Regan. Ye know Regan. Reel estate man. Costigan has made enough conthractin' to be thinkin' iv movin' away, an' th' aldherman was bound to win. Regan is fr'm Kildare, Costigan's a black-hear-rted villain fr'm th' County Mayo an' th' aldherman come fr'm Wexford, though a dacint man. He married a towny iv mine. She was second cousin iv me wife's second cousin, Judy Flynn.

"Th' votes dhropped in mighty fast till iliven o'clock an' thin they poored in. Poor Doheny come fr'm threatin' th' ba-and an' he wint up to vote. 'How much?' says he. 'Fifty cints,' says Donnigan. ''Tis not enough,' says Doheny. 'Niver liss thin a dollar.' He'd hear-rd, d'ye mind, that th' candydates was spindin' money f'r votes an' he'd made a conthract f'r to bring down a lodgin' house. He was that mad.

"Each wan iv th' three had some wan to place his money. Donnigan kept thim runnin' for more. O'Malley'd come r'rushin' up with a bunch iv bills an' roar 'Wan hundhred votes f'r Costigan!' In a minyit they'd be two more rolls undher Donnigan's nose. 'Wan hundhred an' fifty f'r th' aldherman!' 'Wan hundhred an' thirty-five f'r Regan!' Whin we seen odd numbers comin' we knowed Regan was down. He begun borryin' fr'm his frins an' thin he dhropped out intirely, lavin' th' race to Costigan an' th' aldherman. He made an assignmint th' nex' day. Whin th' polls closed th' Mayo man had him beat be two votes, an' half th' people left in disgust."

"For why?" asked Mr. McKenna.

"F'r why?" said Mr. Dooley, scornfully. "Th' idee that anny rayspict'ble parish sh'd allow a May-o man to go around wearin' a diamond stud an' boastin' himself th' mos' pop'lar man! I tell ye what, Jawn, 'tis goin' too far. I'll not knock anny church, d'ye mind, but I'll say this here an' now, that manny nice people was that angry they wint to th' Frinch church, where they cudden't undherstand th' announcement, th' nex' day." (December 29, 1894)

6. A Parochial School Graduation

A transfer of customs from Ireland is evident at this graduation ceremony – in the musical entertainment, the recitation of the sentencing speech of Irish patriot Robert Emmet, and the award of a copy of William Carleton's Willy Reilly *(1855), which is not a religious book but a popular novel of Irish rural life. Toward the end, Mr. Dooley compares the Hennessy boy's oratorical stance to that of a notorious Chicago after-dinner speaker, "Macchew P." Brady.*

"I wint up las' night to th' school hall to see Hinnissy's youngest grad-jooate," said Mr. Dooley. "He's a fine la-ad that, an' they do be thinkin' iv makin' a priest iv him. I shouldn't wondher if he'd be a good wan. He's doin' nothin' all th' livelong day but readin' 'Th' Lives iv th' Saints' an' 'Saint Thomas a Kempis.' A fine lad."

"Was it any good?" asked Mr. McKenna.

"It was a pretty good show," said Mr. Dooley. "Near ivry wan along th' r-road was there an' had their best clothes on thim. Father Kelly was th' busyest man ye iver see. He met all th' ol' folks at th' dure an' give thim th' glad hand. 'Twas: 'Ye have a smart boy there, Mrs. Murphy,' an' 'Niver mind about Tim, Mrs. Cassidy. There's worse nor him, an' he's th' divvle an' all at figgers.' Thin he was lecturin' Brother Aloysius about th' way th' stage was fixed up with thim little Christmas trees that grows on'y in tubs, an' hoistin' th' curtain an' lightin' th' footlights till his collar was th' color iv that sponge – an' as wet.

"Th' first number on th' program was th' speech that Robert Immitt made whin they was goin' to hang him. 'Tis a warm speech an' Grogan's boy had to say it. He come out lookin' red an' nervous, an' old man Grogan had a front seat an' begun to applaud most uproaryous. That rattled Micky all th' more an' his voice sounded like wan ye'll hear over a tiliphone whin he said, 'Oh, dear an' vinrated shades iv me departed fathers.' He thrun his hands in th' air an' begun snappin' his fingers. 'Mike,' whispers Grogan fr'm th' front seat. 'Ye'er mitts,' he says. 'Drop ye'er mitts. Mike,' he says louder, 'ye'er mitts,' he says. 'Drop thim,' he says. 'Stop snappin' ye'er fingers,' he says. Thin raisin' his voice he bawls, 'Mike, what in th' name iv goodness d'ye think ye'er doin' – defindin' Ireland or shootin' craps?' Th' boy was overcome with emotion an' Mrs. Grogan wint home.

"They was other things done be th' lads. Wan iv th' Kelly boys played 'Kathleen Mavourneen' on a flute his father bought f'r him an' th' Saint Ignatius Quartet sang 'Row, Brothers, Row,' that they'd practiced undher me window Sundah nights till I cud near sing it mesilf. Thin they was a conversation bechune young Dimpsey, Hannigan's Jawnny an' little Tommy Casey. Tommy Casey was a good young man an' Dimpsey was th' divvle an' Jawnny Hannigan was a good angel, d'ye mind. Dimpsey was tryin' to lure Tommy Casey away. 'Come,' he says, 'enjoy ye'erself while ye'er life lasts,' he says. 'Ye'll be dead a long time,' says Dimpsey, 'an' ye might as well have a good time now.' 'But,' says Jawnny Hannigan, 'what availeth a man if he gain th' whole wurruld an' lose his own sowl,' he says. 'Will ye desert me f'r a few days iv vice knowin' that ye'er immortial sowl will be denied happiness to come an' will be condimmed to atarnal torture.' 'Nit,' says Tommy Casey – an' ye sh'd've seen Father Kelly's face! He was that mad with rage. I dinnaw what he done to Casey, but th' good angel had a black eye this mornin' f'r puttin' him up to it.

"Thin they was a thrajeedy an' all th' lads took th' parts iv play-acthors. 'Twas a hot play; young Murphy was attimpting to walk through the forest whin up comes Malachi Cassidy. 'What,' says Malachi, 'you here?' 'Yis,' says the Murphy kid, 'an' what woulds't with me?' he says. 'What woulds't with me?' 'Die, caitiff,' says Malachi, givin' him a wallup with a tin soord. 'Twas in th' play f'r Murphy to be croaked, but he refused to die, an' his father stood up an' roared across th' hall: 'Look here, Cassidy, ye put that boy up to that,' he says. 'I'll not have it,' he says. Father Kelly ran to th' front iv th' stage, an' says he: 'Murphy,' he says, 'if ye don't be quite an' make that la-ad lay down an' die,' he says, 'I'll excommunicate th' both iv ye,' he says. An' he'd iv done it there an' thin. So th' play wint on.

"Afther th' play Hinnissy's youngest spoke his piece. He come out wearin' a long black coat an' a white nicktie an' read his speech with his hand tucked in th' coat like Macchew P. He said that he was lookin' th' future square in th' eye, an' though th' past was bad he'd thry to do the bist he cud f'r th' wurruld. What was needed to be done, he said, was f'r young min to take up th' battle iv life an' fight it out coorajously. He'd been very busy at school for some years, but now that he'd gradjooated he thought he'd have time to put things in ordher. He tipped off a whole lot to us. Father Kelly hung a medal to him an' give him two prizes – relijous books – 'Th' Life iv Pope Boniface' an' 'Willy Reilly.'

"His father come over with me afther th' intertainment an' he looked blue. 'What's th' matther with ye?' says I. 'Does it remind ye iv ye'er own boyhood days,' I says, 'whin ye was gradjooated be th' toe iv th' hidge school-masther's boot?' I says. 'No,' says he. "Tis not that,' he says. 'I was on'y thinkin' afther hearin' Joe's o-ration,' he says, 'that I've lived a misspent life,' he says. 'I niver give care nor thought to th' higher jooties iv citizenship,' he says. 'Mebbe,' he says, 'I had to wurruk too hard,' he says. 'Go home,' says I. 'I'm goin' to close up,' I says." (July 6, 1895)

7. Shaughnessy

"Jawn," said Mr. Dooley in the course of the conversation, "whin ye come to think iv it, th' heroes iv th' wurruld, – an' be thim I mean th' lads that've buckled on th' gloves, an' gone out to do th' best they cud, – they ain't in it with th' quite people nayether you nor me hears tell iv fr'm wan end iv th' year to another."

"I believe it," said Mr. McKenna; "for my mother told me so."

"Sure," said Mr. Dooley, "I know it is an old story. Th' wurruld's been full iv it fr'm th' beginnin'; an' 'll be full iv it till, as Father Kelly says, th' pay-roll's closed. But I was thinkin' more iv it th' other night thin iver befure, whin I wint to see Shaughnessy marry off his on'y daughter. You know Shaughnessy, – a quite man that come into th' road befure th' fire. He wurruked f'r Larkin, th' conthractor, f'r near twenty years without skip or break, an' seen th' fam'-ly grow up be candle-light. Th' oldest boy was intinded f'r a priest. 'Tis a poor fam'ly that hasn't some wan that's bein' iddycated f'r the priesthood while all th' rest wear thimsilves to skeletons f'r him, an' call him Father Jawn 'r Father Mike whin he comes home wanst a year, light-hearted an' free, to eat with thim.

"Shaughnessy's lad wint wrong in his lungs, an' they fought death f'r him f'r five years, sindin' him out to th' Wist an' havin' masses said f'r him; an', poor divvle, he kept comin' back cross an' crool, with th' fire in his cheeks, till wan day he laid down, an' says he: 'Pah,' he says, 'I'm goin' to give up,' he says. 'An' I on'y ask that ye'll have th' mass sung over me be some man besides Father Kelly,' he says. An' he wint, an' Shaughnessy come clumpin' down th' aisle like a man in a thrance.

"Well, th' nex' wan was a girl, an' she didn't die; but, th' less said, th' sooner mended. Thin they was Terrence, a big, bould, curly-headed lad that cocked his hat at anny man, – or woman f'r th' matter iv that, – an' that bruk th' back iv a polisman an' swum to th' crib, an' was champeen iv th' South Side at hand ball. An' he wint. Thin th' good woman passed away. An' th' twins they growed to be th' prettiest pair that wint to first communion; an' wan night they was a light in th' window of Shaughnessy's house till three in th' mornin'. I raymimber it; f'r I had quite a crowd iv Willum Joyce's men in, an' we wondhered at it, an' wint home whin th' lamp in Shaughnessy's window was blown out.

"They was th' wan girl left, – Theresa, a big, clean-lookin' child that I see grow up fr'm hello to good avnin'. She thought on'y iv th' ol' man, an' he leaned on her as if she was a crutch. She was out to meet him in th' avnin'; an' in th' mornin' he, th' simple ol' man, 'd stop to blow a kiss at her an' wave his dinner-pail, lookin' up an' down th' r-road to see that no wan was watchin' him.

"I dinnaw what possessed th' young Donahue, fr'm th' Nineteenth. I niver thought much iv him, a stuck-up, aisy-come la-ad that niver had anny-thing but a civil wurrud, an' is prisident iv th' sodality. But he came in, an' married Theresa Shaughnessy las' Thursdah night. Th' ol' man took on twin-ty years, but he was as brave as a gin'ral iv th' army. He cracked jokes an' he made speeches; an' he took th' pipes fr'm under th' elbow iv Hogan, th' blind-man, an' played 'Th' Wind that shakes th' Barley' till ye'd have wore ye'er leg to a smoke f'r wantin' to dance. Thin he wint to th' dure with th' two iv thim; an' says he, 'Well,' he says, 'Jim, be good to her,' he says, an' shook hands with her through th' carredge window.

"Him an' me sat a long time smokin' across th' stove. Fin'lly, says I, 'Well,' I says, 'I must be movin'.' 'What's th' hurry?' says he. 'I've got to go,' says I. 'Wait a moment,' says he. 'Theresa 'll' – He stopped right there f'r a minyit, holdin' to th' back iv th' chair. 'Well,' says he, 'if ye've got to go, ye must,' he says. 'I'll show ye out,' he says. An' he come with me to th' dure, holdin' th' lamp over his head. I looked back at him as I wint by; an' he was settin' be th' stove, with his elbows on his knees an' th' empty pipe between his teeth." (March 28, 1896)

8. Images of Policemen vs. Firemen

The day after a grain elevator explosion in which five firemen were killed and fifty-one injured, Dunne wrote this piece, comparing the images of Chicago's police and fire departments. The tragedy occurred during the unpopular governorship of John R. Tanner, and the "Three medal," for which Fireman Shay is recommended, is the Tree medal, given annually to the Chicago fireman performing the most heroic act in the line of duty.

"How is it," asked Mr. Dooley, "that whin a fireman dies th' whole city mourns an' whin a polisman dies all annywan says is: 'Who's th' first iligible on th' list?' How is it?"

"I dinnaw," said Mr. Hennessy, "but 'tis so."

"No doubt iv it," continued Mr. Dooley. "I think th' reason is we're bumpin' too much into th' polis foorce. If we was to see thim on'y goin' by in th' get-ap wagon, with th' horses chargin' along an' th' gong ringin', we'd play thim f'r pop'lar heroes. A polisman always looks good whin he's goin' by in a hurry. But whin he gets out iv th' chariot an' goes to bat he's no man's frind, an' anny citizen is entitled to move things fr'm th' roof on his head. He mixes in with th' populace an' familyarity breeds contempt, as Shakespeare says. Now 'tis altogether diffrent with th' fireman. No wan is on really intimate terms with him. We may call him by his first name an' play dominoes with him or pitch horseshoes behind th' barn, but we have a secret feelin' that he's a shuperior person that it's not safe to take liberties with. Ye may be settin' in th' injine-house with a fireman as calm an' frindly as ye plaze, an' it's 'Ye'er move, Tom,' an' 'There goes ye'er king row, Felix,' but lave th' ticker buzz wanst an' the gong ring an' ye've suddenly lost equality. Over goes th' boord, out come th' horses an' it's 'Get out iv th' way, there, blast ye,' an' 'All right, Misther Casey.' I niver see th' day whin I felt just right in th' prisince iv a man in a helmet. Did ye iver know a fireman to be slugged? Or robbed? Niver. Th' toughest thief that iver roamed th' sthreets 'll lave alone a lad with a brown sthraw hat an' silver buttons. If I was Tanner an' wanted to be pop'lar I'd hire a fireman to go around with me.

"How can it be anny other way? There used to be a man up here be th' name iv Duggan, an', havin' a large fam'ly, he lived on th' fifth flure iv th' Flaherty Buildin' near the roof. He was a jealous man whin he was dhrunk, an' that was sometimes, an' he used to roar about th' aisy life iv th' firemen. 'Here,' he says, 'am I, a man with a good hot intilleck condimned to wurruk in th' broilin' sun shovellin' coal f'r wan sivinty-five a day,' he says, 'while th' likes iv ye set in ye'er aisy cheers,' he says, 'smokin' ye'er pipes, with nawthin' to do,' he says, 'but decide who's th' champeen dominoes player,' he says. 'Fr'm morn to night ye don't do a tap iv wurruk, an' I an' th' likes iv me pay ye f'r it,' he says. He talked this way in th' injine house day an' night an' th' lads laughed at him an' wint on playin'. On'y wan man didn't like th' talk. He was a dark man be th' name of Shay with a big horseshoe mustache, an' he used to eat half iv it off ivry time Duggan made his speech. I seen he was achin' f'r Duggan's throat, but it's a rule iv th' departmint that mimbers 'r not allowed f'r to lick civilyans. They can lick polisman, if they're able to, but not citizens.

"Th' Flaherty flats took fire wan night an' bein' consthructed f'r poor people out iv nice varnished pine an' cotton waste they burned up without anny loss iv time. Duggan counted his childher an' found wan missing. He had a good manny – twelve or thirteen, I think – but he needed thim all in his business. He counted again an' again, but there was still wan short, an' afther awhile he figured it was th' baby, be th' name iv Honoria. She's a great big girl now – with red hair. Whin Duggan found he was shy a chip he proceeded to throw fits on th' sthreet an' wanted to go into th' buildin', which wud've been th' end iv him, f'r he was full iv rum and wud've burned like a celluloid collar. Cap Kenny iv thruck twenty-nine heerd his ravin' and wanted to know what ailed him. 'He's short a kid,' said th' polisman that was holdin' him be

th' hair. Kenny begun cursin' like a tug captain, an' in less thin a minyit he
was shinnin' up a ladder with three or four others, among them bein' our
frind Shay. Th' cap wint in first an' stayed in five minyits an' had to be carrid
out. Thin two others staggered to th' window an' was dhragged out be th' legs.
But Shay stuck. We waited an' waited, with all th' pipes playin' on th' wan
window, an' fin'lly th' Connemara man come out carryin' something in his
ar-rums. Glory be, but he was a sight. He was as black as a lump iv coal an'
he had no more hair on him thin a lookin'-glass. He slid out to th' ladder an'
climbed down, scornin' assistance. Th' women gathered around him, weepin'
an' callin' on all th' saints in th' catalogue to bless him, an' th' men swore an'
ran to get dhrinks. But Shay paid no attintion to thim. He pegged th' baby at
a sthrange woman an' walked over to Duggan. 'What ye said to me las'
Choosdah night,' he roared, 'was a lie, an' I'm goin' to club ye'er head off.'
An' he fell on th' weepin' father an' wud've kilt him. Cap Kenny pulled him
away, an' Shay, lookin' ashamed to death undher th' soot, saluted. 'Pipeman
Shay,' says th' cap, 'I will recomind ye f'r th' Three medal,' he says, 'but I fine
ye five days' pay f'r lickin' a civilyan,' he says. 'Lord help us, I hope Swenie*
won't hear iv this,' he says.

"That man Shay used to come into my place an' play forty-fives with me.
But d'ye suppose I cud challenge his count as I do other people's, or ask to
cut his ca-ards?"

"Ye'd be afraid he'd lick ye," suggested Mr. Hennessy.

"That was wan reason," said Mr. Dooley. (August 7, 1897)

9. The Popularity of Firemen

*A second Chicago fire-fighting tragedy prompted this piece, which opens with Mr.
Dooley naming the four firemen who had died the day before in a downtown factory
and warehouse blaze.*

"O'Donnell, Sherrick, Downs, Prendergast," Mr. Dooley repeated slowly.
"Poor la-ads. Poor la-ads. Plaze Gawd, they wint to th' long home like thrue
min. 'tis good to read th' names, Jawn. Thanks be, we're not all in th' council.

"I knowed a man be th' name iv Clancy wanst, Jawn. He was fr'm th'
County May-o, but a good man f'r all that; an', whin he'd growed to be a big,
sthrappin' fellow, he wint on to th' fire departmint. They'se an Irishman 'r
two on th' fire departmint an' in th' army, too, Jawn, though ye'd think be
hearin' some talk they was all runnin' prim'ries an' thryin' to be cinthral
comitymen. So ye wud. Ye niver hear iv thim on'y whin they die; an' thin,
murther, what funerals they have!

---

*[Chicago Fire Chief Denis Swenie.]

"Well, this Clancy wint on th' fire departmint, an' they give him a place in thruck twenty-three. All th' r-road was proud iv him, an' faith he was proud iv himsilf. He r-rode free on th' sthreet ca-ars, an' was th' champeen handball player f'r miles around. Ye shud see him goin' down th' sthreet, with his blue shirt an' his blue coat with th' buttons on it, an' his cap on his ear. But ne'er a cap or coat 'd he wear whin they was a fire. He might be shiv'rin' be th' stove in th' ingine house with a buffalo robe over his head; but, whin th' gong sthruck, 'twas off with coat an' cap an' buffalo robe, an' out come me brave Clancy, bare-headed an' bare hand, dhrivin' with wan line an' spillin' th' hose cart on wan wheel at ivry jump iv th' horse. Did anny wan iver see a fireman with his coat on or a polisman with his off? Why, wanst, whin Clancy was standin' up f'r Grogan's eighth, his son come runnin' in to tell him they was a fire in Vogel's packin' house. He dhropped th' kid at Father Kelly's feet, an' whipped off his long coat an' wint tearin' f'r th' dure, kickin' over th' poorbox an' buttin' ol' Mis' O'Neill that'd come in to say th' stations. 'Twas lucky 'twas wan iv th' Grogans. They're a fine family f'r falls. Jawn Grogan was wurrukin' on th' top iv Metzri an' O'Connell's brewery wanst, with a man be th' name iv Dorsey. He slipped an' fell wan hundherd feet. Whin they come to see if he was dead, he got up, an' says he: 'Lave me at him.' 'At who?' says they. 'He's deliryous,' they says. 'At Dorsey,' says Grogan. 'He thripped me.' So it didn't hurt Grogan's eighth to fall four 'r five feet.

"Well, Clancy wint to fires an' fires. Whin th' big organ facthry burnt, he carrid th' hose up to th' fourth story an' was squirtin' whin th' walls fell. They dug him out with pick an' shovel, an' he come up fr'm th' brick an' boards an' saluted th' chief. 'Clancy,' says th' chief, 'ye betther go over an' get a dhrink.' He did so, Jawn. I heerd it. An' Clancy was that proud!

"Whin th' Hogan flats on Halsted Sthreet took fire, they got all th' people out but wan; an' she was a woman asleep on th' fourth flure. 'Who'll go up?' says Bill Musham. 'Sure, sir,' says Clancy. 'I'll go'; an' up he wint. His captain was a man be th' name iv O'Connell, fr'm th' County Kerry; an' he had his fut on th' ladder whin Clancy started. Well, th' good man wint into th' smoke, with his wife faintin' down below. 'He'll be kilt,' says his brother. 'Ye don't know him,' says Bill Musham. An' sure enough, whin ivry wan'd give him up, out comes me brave Clancy, as black as a Turk, with th' girl in his arms. Th' others wint up like monkeys, but he shtud wavin' thim off, an' come down th' ladder face forward. 'Where'd ye larn that?' says Bill Musham. 'I seen a man do it at th' Lyceem whin I was a kid,' says Clancy. 'Was it all right?' 'I'll have ye up before th' ol' man,' says Bill Musham. 'I'll teach ye to come down a laddher as if ye was in a quadhrille, ye horse-stealin', hamsthringin' May-o man,' he says. But he didn't. Clancy wint over to see his wife. 'O Mike,' says she, ''twas fine,' she says. 'But why d'ye take th' risk?' she says. 'Did ye see th' captain?' he says with a scowl. 'He wanted to go. Did ye think I'd follow a Kerry man with all th' ward lukkin' on?' he says.

"Well, so he wint dhrivin' th' hose-cart on wan wheel, an' jumpin' whin he heerd a man so much as hit a glass to make it ring. All th' people looked up to him, an' th' kids followed him down th' sthreet; an' 'twas th' gr-reatest priv'lige f'r anny wan f'r to play dominos with him near th' joker. But about a year ago he come in to see me, an' says he, 'Well, I'm goin' to quit.' 'Why,' says I, 'ye'er a young man yet,' I says. 'Faith,' he says, 'look at me hair,' he says, – 'young heart, ol' head. I've been at it these twinty year, an' th' good woman's wantin' to see more iv me thin blowin' into a saucer iv coffee,' he says. 'I'm goin' to quit,' he says, 'on'y I want to see wan more good fire,' he says. 'A rale good ol' hot wan,' he says, 'with th' win' blowin' f'r it an' a good dhraft in th' ilivator-shaft, an' about two stories, with pitcher-frames an' gaso-line an' excelsior, an' to hear th' chief yellin': "Play 'way, sivinteen. What th' hell an' damnation are ye standin' aroun' with that pipe f'r? Is this a fire 'r a dam livin' pitcher? I'll break ivry man iv eighteen, four, six, an' chem'cal five to-morrah mornin' befure breakfast." Oh,' he says, bringin' his fist down, 'wan more, an' I'll quit.'

"An' he did, Jawn. Th' day th' Carpenter Brothers' box factory burnt. 'Twas wan iv thim big, fine-lookin' buildings that pious men built out iv cel-luloid an' plasther iv Paris. An' Clancy was wan iv th' men undher whin th' wall fell. I seen thim bringin' him home; an' th' little woman met him at th' dure, rumplin' her apron in her hands." (November 23, 1895)

10. Naming the Hogan Baby

One of the Hogan children mentioned here was probably born between January and March, 1880, while Irish leader Charles Stewart Parnell was touring America to raise funds for the Irish National Land League.

Mr. Dooley yawned. "You look tired," said Mr. McKenna.

"I am that," said Mr. Dooley. "I was at Hogan's christenin' las' night an' 'twas 2 o'clock befure me an' Kelly come down th' road singin': 'Iv a-hall th' towns in I-er-land, Kil-a-kinny f'r me-e-e-e.'"

"Have Hogan another?"

"He have; th' tinth. An' 'twas near to breakin' up th' family. Ye know th' time we seen Hogan comin' out iv th' sicond story window in his shir-rt-sleeves. That was whin he said they was no such a saint in th' catalogue as Aloysius. He wanted f'r to na-ame th' kid befure this wan Michael. 'Twas named Aloysius an' th' family calls it Toodles, I belave. Be hivins, Hogan have growed gray haired an' bald thryin' f'r to inthrodjooce th' name iv Michael or Bridget in th' family. Michael was his father's name an' Bridget was his mother's, an' good names they ar-re; none better. Th' first wan was a boy an' afther Mrs. Hogan had th' polis in 'twas called Sarsfield. Th' second was a girl an' 'twas called Lucy, d'ye mind? Lucy! Yes, by dad, Lucy Hogan.

Thin they was Honoria an' Veronica an' Arthur an' Charles Stewart Parnell, bor-rn durin' the land lague, an' Paul an' Madge an' William Joyce Hogan, an' th' ol' ma-an all this time tryin' f'r to edge in Michael or Bridget.

"Well, Hogan does be gettin' on in years now an' whin th' last come an' th' good woman was sthrong enough f'r to walk around, says he: 'Whin ar-re ye goin' to christen little Mike,' he says. 'Little who?' says she. 'Little Mike,' he says. 'Little Mike Hogan,' he says, 'th' kid.' 'There'll be no little Mikes around this house,' says she, 'unless they walk over me dead body,' she says. Jawn, she's County May-o to th' backbone. 'D'ye think I'm goin' to sind th' child out into th' wurruld,' she says, 'with a name,' she says, 'that'll keep him from anny employmint,' she says, 'but goin' on th' polis for-rce,' she says. 'Mike is a good name,' says Hogan. ''Twas me fa-ather's,' he says, 'an' he was as good as anny.' 'Don't tell me about ye'er father,' says she. 'Didn't I know him,' she says, 'carryin' around a piece iv ol' chalk,' she says, 'atin' wan ind iv it f'r heartburn an' usin' th' other ind iv it to chalk up for-rty-fives scores on th' table,' she says. 'I had a cousin a priest,' says Hogan. 'Match that if ye dahr.' 'Ye had wan a lamplighter,' says she. 'Me mother's brother kep' a cow,' he says. 'Not afther th' polis found it out,' says Mrs. Hogan. ''Twas me aunt Ayleonara's.' That thrun Hogan, but he come back sthrong. 'Ye'll be namin' no more children iv mine out iv dime novels,' he says. 'An' ye'll name no more iv mine out iv th' payroll iv th' bridge depar-rtmint,' says she. Thin Hogan wakened. 'What ar-re ye goin' to call it?' he says. 'Augustus,' says she. An' be hivins 'twas Augustus th' priest give it. Th' poor, poor child!

"We had th' divvle's own time gettin' it anny name, bedad. Terence Kelly was th' god fa-ather, an' he insisted on carryin' th' kid to th' church. He lost his prisince iv mind whin he come to where O'Connor is puttin' up a house an' started f'r to climb th' ladder with th' kid over his chowlder. Thin whin he was standin' at th' rail he put th' big hand iv him out an' says, 'Hello, Mick; how's thricks?' to th' good man. They're cousins, d'ye mind. Ye should've seen th' look th' soggarth* give him.

He got aven though. Kelly couldn't f'r th' life iv him say the confeetjoor. 'Ye hathen,' says th' soggarth. 'Ye standin' up f'r an innocent baby,' he says, 'whin ye don't know ye'er prayers,' he says. 'Take this book,' he says, 'an' go over in th' cor-rner an' larn it,' he says. 'Twas scand'lous. Kelly delayed th' game near an hour an' forty minutes.

"And where was Hogan all this time?" asked Mr. McKenna.

"He didn't come an' no wan seen him at th' house. I wint into th' Dutchman's on me way home f'r to tell him th' election was over an' I found Hogan there thryin' to tell Schmittberger that they had a new kid at th' house an' that they called him Angostura Bitthers Hogan." (November 17, 1894)

---

*[Gaelic for "priest."]

11. The Piano in the Parlor

In 1890 Edward Harrigan produced a popular musical, Reilly and the Four Hundred, *about the social pretensions of the "lace-curtain" Irish. The hit song of the show contained a chorus that applies to this Dooley piece: "There's an organ in the parlor, to give the house a tone / And you're welcome every evening at Maggie Murphy's home."*

"Ol' man Donahue bought Molly a pianny las' week," Mr. Dooley said in the course of his conversation with Mr. McKenna. "She'd been takin' lessons fr'm a Dutchman down th' sthreet, an' they say she can play as aisy with her hands crossed as she can with wan finger. She's been whalin' away iver since, an' Donahue is dhrinkin' again.

"Ye see th' other night some iv th' la-ads wint over f'r to see whether they cud smash his table in a frindly game iv forty-fives. I don't know what possessed Donahue. He niver asked his frinds into the parlor befure. They used to set in th' dining-room; an whin Mrs. Donahue coughed at iliven o'clock, they'd toddle out th' side dure with their hats in their hands. But this here night, whether 'twas that Donahue had taken on a tub or two too much or not, he asked thim all in th' front room, where Mrs. Donahue was settin' with Molly. 'I've brought me frinds,' he says, 'f'r to hear Molly take a fall out iv th' music-box,' he says. 'Let me have ye'er hat, Mike,' he says. 'Ye'll not feel it whin ye go out,' he says.

"At anny other time Mrs. Donahue'd give him th' marble heart. But they wasn't a man in th' party that had a pianny to his name, an' she knew they'd be throuble whin they wint home an' tould about it. ''Tis a melodjious insthrument,' says she. 'I cud sit here be the hour an' listen to Bootoven and Choochooski,' she says.

"'What did thim write?' says Cassidy. 'Chunes,' says Donahue, 'chunes. Molly,' he says, 'fetch 'er th' wallop to make th' gintlemen feel good,' he says. 'What'll it be, la-ads?' 'D'ye know "The Rambler fr'm Clare"?' says Slavin. 'No,' says Molly. 'It goes like this,' says Slavin. 'A-ah, din yadden, yooden a-yadden, arrah yadden ay-a.' 'I dinnaw it,' says th' girl. ''Tis a low chune, annyhow,' says Mrs. Donahue. 'Misther Slavin ividintly thinks he's at a polis picnic,' she says. 'I'll have no come-all-ye's in this house,' she says. 'Molly, give us a few ba-ars fr'm Wagner.' 'What Wagner's that?' says Flanagan. 'No wan ye know,' says Donahue; 'he's a German musician.' 'Thim Germans is hot people f'r music,' says Cassidy. 'I knowed wan that cud play th' "Wacht am Rhine" on a pair iv cymbals,' he says. 'Whisht!' says Donahue. 'Give th' girl a chanst.'

"Slavin tol' me about it. He says he niver heerd th' like in his born days. He says she fetched th' pianny two or three wallops that made Cassidy jump out iv his chair, an' Cassidy has charge iv th' steam whistle at th' quarry at that. She wint at it as though she had a gredge at it. First 'twas wan hand an' thin th' other, thin both hands, knuckles down; an' it looked, says Slavin, as if she was goin' to leap into th' middle iv it with both feet, whin Donahue jumps up. 'Hol' on!' he says. 'That's not a rented pianny, ye daft girl,' he says. 'Why, pap-pah,' says Molly, 'what d'ye mean?' she says. 'That's Wagner,' she says. 'Tis th' music iv th' future,' she says. 'Yes,' says Donahue, 'but I don't want me hell on earth. I can wait f'r it,' he says, 'with th' kind permission iv Mrs. Donahue,' he says. 'Play us th' "Wicklow Mountaineer,"' he says, 'an' threat th' masheen kindly,' he says. 'She'll play no "Wicklow Mountaineer,"' says Mrs. Donahue. 'If ye want to hear that kind iv chune, ye can go down to Finucane's Hall,' she says, 'an' call in Crowley, th' blind piper,' she says. 'Molly,' she says, 'give us wan iv thim Choochooski things,' she says. 'They're so ginteel.'

"With that Donahue rose up. 'Come on,' says he. 'This is no place f'r us,' he says. Slavin, with th' politeness iv a man who's gettin' even, turns at th' dure. 'I'm sorry I can't remain,' he says. 'I think th' wurruld an' all iv Choochooski,' he says. 'Me brother used to play his chunes,' he says, – 'me brother Mike, that run th' grip ca-ar,' he says. 'But there's wan thing missin' fr'm Molly's playin',' he says. 'And what may that be?' says Mrs. Donahue. 'An ax,' says Slavin, backin' out.

"So Donahue has took to dhrink." (April 20, 1895)

12. The Idle Apprentice

On October 11, 1895, Henry "Butch" Lyons, a twenty-seven-year-old Chicagoan of Irish descent, was hanged at the county jail for a murder committed during a robbery attempt the previous February. The crowd around the jail was reported to be the largest since the execution of the Haymarket anarchists in 1887. A Times-Herald editorial claimed that Lyons, the son of "a drunkard" and "a poverty-stricken working woman," was first sent to the bridewell (city jail) at the age of nine, and that his subsequent criminal career included two hundred arrests, twenty-one terms in the bridewell, and one term in the state penitentiary. The editorial concluded with the question, "Did he have a fair chance?" The day after the hanging, this Dooley piece appeared.

"They scragged a man to-day," said Mr. Dooley.

"They did so," said Mr. McKenna.

"Did he die game?"

"They say he did."

"Well, he did," said Mr. Dooley. "I read it all in th' pa-apers. He died as game as if he was wan iv th' Christyan martyrs instead iv a thief that'd hit his man wan crack too much. Saint or murdherer, 'tis little difference whin death comes up face front.

"I read th' story iv this man through, Jawn; an', barrin' th' hangin', 'tis th' story iv tin thousan' like him. D'ye raymimber th' Carey kid? Ye do. Well, I knowed his grandfather; an' a dacinter ol' man niver wint to his jooty wanst a month. Whin he come over to live down be th' slip, 'twas as good a place as iver ye see. Th' honest men an' honest women wint an' come as they pleased, an' laid hands on no wan. His boy Jim was as straight as th' r-roads in Kildare, but he took to dhrink; an', whin Jack Carey was born, he was a thramp on th' sthreets an' th' good woman was wurrukin' down-town, scrubbin' away at th' flures in th' city hall, where Dennehy got her.

"Be that time around th' slip was rough-an'-tumble. It was dhrink an' fight ivry night an' all day Sundah. Th' little la-ads come together under sidewalks, an' rushed th' can over to Burke's on th' corner an' listened to what th' big lads tol' thim. Th' first instruction that Jack Carey had was how to take a man's pocket handkerchief without his feelin' it, an' th' nex' he had was larnin' how to get over th' fence iv th' Reform School at Halsted Sthreet in his stockin' feet.

"He was a thief at tin year, an' th' polis'd run f'r him if he'd showed his head. At twelve they sint him to th' bridewell f'r breakin' into a freight car. He come out, up to anny game. I see him whin he was a lad hardly to me waist stand on th' roof iv Finucane's Hall an' throw bricks at th' polisman.

"He hated th' polis, an' good reason he had f'r it. They pulled him out iv bed be night to search him. If he turned a corner, they ran him f'r blocks down th' sthreet. Whin he got older, they begun shootin' at him th' minyit they see him; an' it wasn't manny years befure he begun to shoot back. He was right enough whin he was in here. I cud conthrol him. But manny th' night whin he had his full iv liquor I've see him go out with his gun in his outside pocket; an' thin I'd hear shot after shot down th' sthreet, an' I'd know him an' his ol' inimy Clancy 'd met an' was exchangin' compliments. He put wan man on th' polis pension fund with a bullet through his thigh.

"They got him afther a while. He'd kept undher cover f'r months, livin' in freight cars an' hidin' undher viadocks with th' pistol in his hand. Wan night he come out, an' broke into Schwartzmeister's place. He sneaked through th' alley with th' German man's damper in his arms, an' Clancy leaped on him fr'm th' fence. Th' kid was tough, but Clancy played fut-ball with th' Finertys on Sundah, an' was tougher; an', whin th' men on th' other beats come up, Carey was hammered so they had to carry him to th' station an' nurse him f'r trile.

"He wint over th' road, an' come back gray an' stooped. I was afraid iv th' boy with his black eyes; an' wan night he see me watchin' him, an' he says: 'Ye needn't be afraid,' he says. 'I won't hurt ye. Ye're not Clancy,' he says.

"I tol' Clancy about it, but he was a brave man; an' says he: "'Tis wan an' wan, an' a thief again an' honest man. If he gets me, he must get me quick.' Th' nex' night about dusk he come saunterin' up th' sthreet, swingin' his club an' jokin' with his frind, whin some wan shouted, 'Look out, Clancy.' He was not quick enough. He died face forward, with his hands on his belt; an' befure all th' wurruld Jack Carey come across th' sthreet, an' put another ball in his head.

"They got him within twinty yards iv me store. He was down in th' shadow iv th' house, an' they was shootin' at him fr'm roofs an' behind barns. Whin he see it was all up, he come out with his eyes closed, firin' straight ahead; an' they filled him so full iv lead he broke th' hub iv th' pathrol wagon takin' him to th' morgue."

"It served him right," said Mr. McKenna.

"Who?" said Mr. Dooley. "Carey or Clancy?" (October 12, 1895)

13. On Criminals: Petey Scanlan

The young Irish American in this piece is related to a real Chicago criminal – one Daniel Carroll. A Times-Herald *editorial a week after his arrest for murder claimed that "from his earliest childhood he has lived a hunted life, like the dogs and cats of the alleys. When he committed some petty offense he was sent to the bridewell, and when released was watched as a suspect. The wonder is that he ever tried to earn an honest living." This Dooley piece appeared a day or two after Carroll's arrest. It may have been the most popular of Dunne's pieces in Chicago in the nineties; one Catholic priest used it as the text for a yearly sermon, and Studs Lonigan's father recalled it in his front-porch revery near the beginning of James T. Farrell's trilogy: "But life was a funny thing, all right. It was like Mr. Dooley said, and he had never forgotten that remark, because Dooley, that is Finley Peter Dunne, was a real philosopher. Who'll tell what makes wan man a thief, and another man a saint?"*

"Lord bless my sowl," said Mr. Dooley, "childher is a gr-reat responsibility, – a gr-reat responsibility. Whin I think iv it, I praise th' saints I niver was married, though I had opporchunities enough whin I was a young man; an' even now I have to wear me hat low whin I go down be Cologne Sthreet on account iv th' Widow Grogan. Jawn, that woman'll take me dead or alive. I wake up in a col' chill in th' middle iv th' night, dhreamin' iv her havin' me in her clutches.

"But that's not here or there, avick. I was r-readin' in th' pa-apers iv a lad be th' name iv Scanlan bein' sint down th' short r-road f'r near a lifetime; an' I minded th' first time I iver see him, – a bit iv a curly-haired boy that played tag around me place, an' 'd sing 'Blest Saint Joseph' with a smile on his face like an angel's. Who'll tell what makes wan man a thief an' another man a saint? I dinnaw. This here boy's father wurrked fr'm morn till night in th' mills, was at early mass Sundah mornin' befure th' alkalis lit th' candles, an' niver knowed a month whin he failed his jooty. An' his mother was a sweet-faced little woman, though fr'm th' County Kerry, that nursed th' sick an'

waked th' dead, an' niver had a hard thought in her simple mind f'r anny iv
Gawd's creatures. Poor sowl, she's dead now. May she rest in peace!

"He didn't git th' shtreak fr'm his father or fr'm his mother. His brothers
an' sisters was as fine a lot as iver lived. But this la-ad Petey Scanlan growed
up fr'm bein' a curly-haired angel f'r to be th' toughest villyun in th' r-road.
What was it at all, at all? Sometimes I think they'se poison in th' life iv a big
city. Th' flowers won't grow here no more thin they wud in a tannery, an' th'
bur-rds have no song; an' th' childher iv dacint men an' women come up hard
in th' mouth an' with their hands raised again their kind.

"Th' la-ad was th' scoorge iv th' polis. He was as quick as a cat an' as
fierce as a tiger, an' I well raymimber him havin' laid out big Kelly that used
to thravel this post, – 'Whistlin'' Kelly that kep' us awake with imitations iv a
mockin' bur-rd, – I well raymimber him scuttlin' up th' alley with a score iv
polismin laborin' afther him, thryin' f'r a shot at him as he wint around th'
bar'rns or undher th' thrucks. He slep' in th' coal-sheds afther that until th'
poor ol' man cud square it with th' loot. But, whin he come out, ye cud see
how his face had hardened an' his ways changed. He was as silent as an animal, with a sideways manner that watched ivrything. Right here in this place
I seen him stand f'r a quarther iv an hour, not seemin' to hear a dhrunk man
abusin' him, an' thin lep out like a snake. We had to pry him loose.

"Th' ol' folks done th' best they cud with him. They hauled him out iv
station an' jail an' bridewell. Wanst in a long while they'd dhrag him off to
church with his head down: that was always afther he'd been sloughed up f'r
wan thing or another. Between times th' polis give him his own side iv th'
sthreet, an' on'y took him whin his back was tur-rned. Thin he'd go in the
wagon with a mountain iv thim on top iv him, swayin' an' swearin' an'
sthrikin' each other in their hurry to put him to sleep with their clubs.

"I mind well th' time he was first took to be settled f'r good. I heerd a
noise in th' ya-ard, an' thin he come through th' place with his face dead gray
an' his lips just a turn grayer. 'Where ar-re ye goin' Petey!' says I. 'I was jus'
takin' a short cut home,' he says. In three minyits th' r-road was full iv polismin. They'd been a robbery down in Halsted Sthreet. A man that had a grocery sthore was stuck up, an' whin he fought was clubbed near to death; an'
they'd r-run Scanlan through th' alleys to his father's house. That was as far
as they'd go. They was enough iv thim to've kicked down th' little cottage
with their heavy boots, but they knew he was standin' behind th' dure with
th' big gun in his hand; an', though they was manny a good lad there, they
was none that cared f'r that short odds.

"They talked an' palavered outside, an' telephoned th' chief iv polis, an'
more pathrol wagons come up. Some was f'r settin' fire to th' buildin', but no
wan moved ahead. Thin th' fr-ront dure opened, an' who shud come out but
th' little mother. She was thin an' pale, an' she had her apron in her hands,
pluckin' at it. 'Gintlemin,' she says, 'what is it ye want iv me?' she says.

'Liftinant Cassidy,' she says, "tis sthrange f'r ye that I've knowed so long to make scandal iv me befure me neighbors,' she says. 'Mrs. Scanlan,' says he, 'we want th' boy. I'm sorry, ma'am, but he's mixed up in a bad scrape, an' we must have him,' he says. She made a curtsy to thim, an' wint indures. 'Twas less than a minyit befure she come out, clingin' to th' la-ad's ar-rm. 'He'll go,' she says. 'Thanks be, though he's wild, they'se no crime on his head. Is there, dear?' 'No,' says he, like th' game kid he is. Wan iv th' polismin stharted to take hold iv him, but th' la-ad pushed him back; an' he wint to th' wagon on his mother's ar-rm."

"And was he really innocent?" Mr. McKenna asked.

"No," said Mr. Dooley. "But she niver knowed it. Th' ol' man come home an' found her: she was settin' in a big chair with her apron in her hands an' th' picture iv th' la-ad th' day he made his first c'munion in her lap." (June 13, 1896)

14. A Model Campaign for Alderman

William Jennings Bryan had just made his "Cross of Gold" speech and been nom-
inated for president when Dunne wrote this piece in July 1896. William J. O'Brien
represented Bridgeport in the city council from 1889 to 1893 and again from 1897 to
1899. Mr. Dooley is his only biographer. O'Brien's opponent is the namesake of Irish
nationalist leader William Smith O'Brien, who was transported to Australia after the
rising of 1848.

"D'ye know," said Mr. Dooley, "that histhry repeats itself, as th' good book says. An' th' more I hear iv th' young man Bryan th' more I wish he was bor-rn a dumby, though if he had been he'd 've wore his ar-rms down to a stump befure now thryin' to make himsilf undherstud.

"I mind th' first time Willum J. O'Brien r-run f'r office, th' Raypublicans an' th' Indypindants an' th' Socialists an' th' Prohybitionist (he's dead now, his name was Larkin) nommynated a young man be th' name iv Dorgan that was in th' law business in Halsted Sthreet, near Cologne, to r-run again' him. Smith O'Brien Dorgan was his name, an' he was wan iv th' most iloquint young la-ads that iver made a speakin' thrumpet iv his face. He cud holler like th' impire iv a base-ball game; an', whin he delivered th' sintimints iv his hear-rt, ye'd think he was thryin' to confide thim to a man on top iv th' Audiotorium tower. He was prisidint iv th' lithry club at th' church; an' Father Kelly tol' me that, th' day afther he won th' debate on th' pen an' th' soord in favor iv th' pen, they had to hire a carpenter to mend th' windows, they'd sagged so. They called him th' boy or-rator iv Healey's slough.

"He planned th' campaign himsilf. 'I'll not re-sort,' says he, 'to th' ordin'ry methods,' he says. 'Th' thing to do,' he says, 'is to prisint th' issues iv th' day to th' voters,' he says. 'I'll burn up ivry precin't in th' ward with me iloquince,' he says. An' he bought a long black coat, an' wint out to spread th' light.

"He talked ivrywhere. Th' people jammed Finucane's Hall, an' he tol' thim th' time had come f'r th' masses to r-rise. 'Raymimber,' says he, 'th' idees iv Novimb'r,' he says. 'Raymimber Demosthens an' Cicero an' Oak Park,' he says. 'Raymimber th' thraditions iv ye'er fathers, iv Washin'ton an' Jefferson an' Andhrew Jackson an' John L. Sullivan,' he says. 'Ye shall not, Billy O'Brien,' he says, 'crucify th' voters iv th' Sixth Ward on th' double cross,' he says. He spoke to a meetin' in Deerin' Sthreet in th' same wurruds. He had th' Sthreet-car stopped while he coughed up reemarks about th' Constitution until th' bar-rn boss sint down an' threatened to discharge Mike Dwyer that was dhrivin' wan hundherd an' eight in thim days, though thransferred to Wintworth Avnoo later on. He made speeches to polismin in th' squad-room an' to good la-ads hoistin' mud out iv th' dhraw at th' red bridge. People'd be settin' quite in th' back room playin' forty-fives whin Smith O'Brien Dorgan'd burst in, an' addhress thim on th' issues iv th' day.

"Now all this time Bill O'Brien was campaignin' in his own way. He niver med wan speech. No wan knew whether he was f'r a tariff or again wan, or whether he sthud be Jefferson or was knockin' him, or whether he had th' inthrests iv th' toilin' masses at hear-rt or whether he wint to mass at all, at all. But he got th' superintindint iv th'rollin'-mills with him; an' he put three or four good fam'lies to wurruk in th' gas-house, where he knew th' main guy, an' he made reg'lar calls on th' bar-rn boss iv th' sthreetca-ars. He wint to th' picnics, an' hired th' or-chesthry f'r th' dances, an' voted himsilf th' most pop'lar man at th' church fair at an expinse iv at laste five hundherd dollars. No wan that come near him wanted f'r money. He had headquarthers in ivry saloon fr'm wan end iv th' ward to th' other. All th' pa-apers printed his pitch-er, an' sthud by him as th' frind iv th' poor.

"Well, people liked to hear Dorgan at first, but afther a few months they got onaisy. He had a way iv breakin' into festive gatherin's that was enough to thry a saint. He delayed wan prize fight two hours, encouragin' th' voters prisint to stand be their principles, while th' principles sat shiverin' in their cor-rners until th' polis r-run him out. It got so that men'd bound into alleys whin he come up th' sthreet. People in th' liquor business rayfused to let him come into their places. His fam'ly et in th' coalshed f'r fear iv his speeches at supper. He wint on talkin', and Willum J. O'Brien wint on handin' out th' dough that he got fr'm th' gas company an' con-ciliatin' th' masses; an', whin iliction day come, th' judges an' clerks was all f'r O'Brien, an' Dorgan didn't get votes enough to wad a gun. He sat up near all night in his long coat, makin' speeches to himsilf; but tord mornin' he come over to my place where O'Brien sat with his la-ads. 'Well,' says O'Brien, 'how does it suit ye?' he says. 'It's sthrange,' says Dorgan. 'Not sthrange at all,' says Willum J. O'Brien. 'Whin ye've been in politics as long as I have, ye'll know,' he says, 'that th' roly-boly is th' gr-reatest or-rator on earth,' he says. 'Th' American nation in th' Sixth Ward is a fine people,' he says. 'They love th' eagle,' he says, 'on th' back iv a dollar,' he says. 'Well,' says Dorgan, 'I can't undherstand it,' he says. 'I med as manny as three thousan' speeches,' he says. 'Well,' says Willum J. O'Brien, 'that was my majority,' he says. 'Have a dhrink,' he says." (July 18, 1896)

15. A Brand from the Burning: A Political Biography

In order to avoid prosecution, Tammany Hall leader Richard Croker left New York secretly in May 1894. A month later he turned up in Europe, where he was to spend the next three years. Mr. Dooley responded to the news of Croker's flight with this biographical sketch of a Bridgeport boss.

"I see be th' pa-apers," said Mr. Dooley, "that Croker have flew th' coop. 'Tis too bad, too bad. He wa-as a gr-reat man."

"Is he dead?" asked Mr. McKenna.

"No, faith, worse thin that; he's resigned. He calls th' la-ads about him, an' says he: 'Boys,' he says, 'I'm tired iv politics,' he says. 'I'm goin' to quit it f'r me health,' he says. 'Do ye stay in, an' get ar-rested f'r th' good iv th' party.' Ye see thim mugwumps is afther th' Boss, an' he's gettin' out th' way Hogan got out iv Connock. Wan day he comes over to me fa-ather's house, an' says he, 'Dooley,' he says, 'I'm goin' to lave this hole iv a place,' he says. 'F'r why?' says th' ol' man; 'I thought ye liked it.' 'Faith,' says Hogan, 'I niver liked a blade iv grass in it,' he says. 'I'm sick iv it,' he says. 'I don't want niver to see it no more.' And he wint away. Th' next mornin' th' polis was lookin' f'r him to lock him up f'r stealin' joo'lry in the fair town. Yes, by dad.

"'Tis th' way iv th' boss, Jawn. I seen it manny's th' time. There was wanst a boss in th' Sixth Wa-ard, an' his name was Flannagan; an' he came fr'm th' County Clare, but so near th' bordher line that no wan challenged his vote, an' he was let walk down Ar-rchey Road just 's though he come fr'm Connock. Well, sir, whin I see him first, he'd th' smell iv Castle Garden on him, an' th' same is no r-rose gyranium, d'ye mind; an' he was goin' out with pick an' shovel f'r to dig in th' canal, – a big, shtrappin', black-haired lad, with a neck like a bull's an' covered with a hide as thick as wan's, fr'm thryin' to get a crop iv oats out iv a Clare farm that growed divvle th' thing but nice, big boldhers.

"He was a de-termined divvle though, an' th' first man that made a face at him he walloped in th' jaw; an' he'd been on th' canal no more thin a month before he licked ivry man in th' gang but th' section boss, who'd been a Dublin jackeen, an' weighed sixteen stone an' was th' 'ell an' all with a thrip an' a punch. Wan day they had some wurruds, whin me bold Dublin man sails into Flannagan. Well, sir, they fought fr'm wan o'clock till tin in th' night, an' nayther give up; though Flannagan had th' best iv it, bein' young. 'Why don't ye put him out?' says wan iv th' la-ads. 'Whisht,' says Flannagan. 'I'm waitin' f'r th' moon to come up,' he says, 'so's I can hit him right,' he says, 'an' scientific.' Well, sir, his tone was that fierce th' section boss he dhropped right there iv sheer fright; an' Flannagan was cock iv th' walk.

"Afther a while he begun f'r to go out among th' other gangs, lookin' f'r fight; an', whin th' year was over, he was knowed fr'm wan end iv th' canal to th' other as th' man that no wan cud stand before. He got so pop'lar fr'm lickin' all his frinds that he opened up a liquor store beyant th' bridge, an' wan night he shot some la-ads fr'm th' ya-ards that come over f'r to r-run him. That made him sthronger still. When they got up a prize f'r th' most pop'lar man in th' parish, he loaded th' ballot box an' got th' goold-headed stick, though he was r-runnin' against th' aldherman, an' th' little soggarth thried his best to down him. Thin he give a cock fight in th' liquor shop, an' that atthracted a gang iv bad men; an' he licked thim wan afther another, an' made thim his frinds. An' wan day lo an' behold, whin th' aldherman thried f'r to carry th' prim'ries that'd niver failed him befure, Flannagan wint down with his gang an' ilicted his own dilligate ticket, an' thrun th' aldherman up in th' air!

"Thin he was a boss, an' f'r five years he r-run th' ward. He niver wint to th' council, d'ye mind; but, whin he was gin'rous, he give th' aldhermen tin per cint iv what they made. In a convintion, whin anny iv th' candydates passed roun' th' money, 'twas wan thousand dollars f'r Flannagan an' have a nice see-gar with me f'r th' rest iv thim. Wan year fr'm th' day he done th' aldherman he sold th' liquor shop. Thin he built a brick house in th' place iv th' little frame wan he had befure, an' moved in a pianny f'r his daughter. 'Twas about this time he got a dimon as big as ye'er fist, an' begun to dhrive down town behind a fast horse. No wan knowed what he done, but his wife said he was in th' r-rale estate business. D'ye mind, Jawn, that th' r-rale estate business includes near ivrything fr'm vagrancy to manslaughter.

"Whativer it was he done, he had money to bur-rn; an' th' little soggarth that wanst despised him, but had a hard time payin' th' debt iv th' little church, was glad enough to sit at his table. Wan day without th' wink iv th' eye he moved up in th' avnoo, an' no wan seen him in Bridgeport afther that. 'Twas a month or two later whin a lot iv th' la-ads was thrun into jail f'r a little diviltry they'd done f'r him. A comity iv th' fathers iv th' la-ads wint to see him. He recaved thim in a room as big as wan iv their whole houses, with pitchers on th' walls an' a carpet as deep an' soft as a bog. Th' comity asked him to get th' la-ads out on bail.

"'Gintlemen,' he says, 'ye must excuse me,' he says. 'I am too busy f'r to engage,' he says, 'in such matthers.' 'D'ye mane to say,' says Cassidy, th' plumber, 'that ye won't do annything f'r my son?' 'Do annything,' says Flannagan. (I'll say this f'r him; a more darin' man niver drew breath; an', whin his time come to go sthandin' off th' mob an' defindin' his sthone quar-ry in th' rites iv sivinty-siven, he faced death without a wink.) 'Do?' he says, risin' an' sthandin' within a fut iv Cassidy's big cane. 'Do?' he says. 'Why,' he says, 'yes,' he says; 'I've subscribed wan thousand dollars,' he says, 'to th' cit-izen's comity,' he says, 'f'r to prosecute him; an',' he says, 'gintlemen,' he says, 'there's th' dure.'

"I seen Cassidy that night, an' he was as white as a ghost. 'What ails ye?' says I. 'Have ye seen th' divvle?' 'Yes,' he says, bendin' his head over th' bar, an' lookin' sivinty years instead iv forty-five." (May 12, 1894)

16. The Irishman Abroad

Mr. Dooley had few illusions about the climate for revolution in Ireland in the 1890s, and he refuted the Irish-American rhetorical patriots convincingly with this explanation of the paradox of Irish accomplishment abroad and failure at home. Austrian premier Count Taafe had been in the news recently, and an Irish Home Rule bill had passed the British House of Commons on September 1, 1893, only to be reject-ed by the House of Lords.

Mr. Dooley laid down his morning paper, and looked thoughtfully at the chandeliers.

"Taaffe," he said musingly, – "Taaffe – where th' divvle? Th' name's familiar."

"He lives in the Nineteenth," said Mr. McKenna. "If I remember right, he has a boy on th' force."

"Goowan," said Mr. Dooley, "with ye'er nineteenth wa-ards. Th' Taaffe I mane is in Austhria. Where in all, where in all? No: yes, by gar, I have it. A-ha!

> "But cur-rsed be th' day,
> Whin Lord Taaffe grew faint-hearted
> An' sthud not n'r cha-arged,
> But in panic depa-arted."

"D'ye mind it, – th' pome be Joyce? No, ye gom, not Bill Joyce n'r Dan Corkery n'r Tommy Byrnes. Joyce, th' Irish pote that wrote th' pome about th' wa-ars whin me people raysisted Cromwell, while yours was carryin' turf on their backs to make fires for th' crool invader, as Finerty says whin th' sub-scriptions r-runs low.* 'Tis th' same name, a good ol' Meath name in th' days gone by; an' be th' same token I have in me head that this here Count Taaffe,

---

*[Dr. Robert Dwyer Joyce, physician, poet, and immigrant to Boston, published *Legends of the Wars in Ireland* (1868) and many other books. John Finerty edited the Chicago Irish nationalist week-ly paper, *The Citizen*.]

whether he's an austrich or a canary bur-rd now, is wan iv th' ol' fam'ly. There's manny iv thim in Europe an' all th' wurruld beside. There was Pat McMahon, th' Frinchman, that bate Looey Napoleon; an' O'Donnell, the Spanish jook; an' O'Dhriscoll an' Lynch, who do be th' whole thing down be South America, not to mention Patsy Bolivar. Ye can't go annywhere fr'm Sweden to Boolgahria without findin' a Turk settin' up beside th' king an' dalin' out th' deck with his own hand. Jawn, our people makes poor Irishmen, but good Dutchmen; an', th' more I see iv thim, th' more I says to mesilf that th' rale boney fide Irishman is no more thin a foreigner born away from home. 'Tis so.

"Look at thim, Jawn," continued Mr. Dooley, becoming eloquent. "Whin there's battles to be won, who do they sind for? McMahon or Shur'dan or Phil Kearney or Colonel Colby. Whin there's books to be wrote, who writes thim but Char-les Lever or Oliver Goldsmith or Willum Carleton? Whin there's speeches to be made, who makes thim but Edmund Burke or Macchew P. Brady? There's not a land on th' face iv th' wurruld but th' wan where an Irishman doesn't stand with his fellow-man, or above thim. Whin th' King iv Siam wants a plisint evenin', who does he sind f'r but a lively Kerry man that can sing a song or play a good hand at spile-five? Whin th' Sultan iv Boolgahria takes tea, 'tis tin to wan th' man across fr'm him is more to home in a caubeen thin in a turban. There's Mac's an' O's in ivry capital iv Europe atin' off silver plates whin their relations is staggerin' under th' creels iv turf in th' Connaught bogs.

"Wirra, 'tis hard. Ye'd sa-ay off hand, 'Why don't they do as much for their own counthry?' Light-spoken are thim that suggests th' like iv that. 'Tis asier said than done. Ye can't grow flowers in a granite block, Jawn dear, much less whin th' first shoot 'd be thrampled under foot without pity. 'Tis aisy f'r us over here, with our bellies full, to talk iv th' cowardice iv th' Irish; but what would ye have wan man iv thim do again a rig'ment? 'Tis little fightin' th' lad will want that will have to be up before sunrise to keep th' smoke curlin' fr'm th' chimbley or to patch th' rush roof to keep out th' March rain. No, faith, Jawn, there's no soil in Ireland f'r th' greatness iv th' race; an' there has been none since th' wild geese wint across th' say to France, hangin' like flies to th' side iv th' Fr-rinch ship. 'Tis on'y f'r women an' childher now, an' thim that can't get away. Will th' good days ever come again? says ye. Who knows! Who knows!" (November 4, 1893)

17. The Tynan Plot

In September 1896, a New York Irishman, P. J. P. Tynan, was arrested in France for having fomented a "Fenian-Russian Nihilist" plot to assassinate Queen Victoria and the Czar, who was about to visit England. According to British detectives, Tynan had planned to tunnel under Buckingham Palace and blow it up. He was quickly released after having been identified as the notorious eccentric who had written a 700-page book claiming responsibility for the Dynamite Campaign of the early 1880s and the murder of Lord Frederick Cavendish in Dublin's Phoenix Park in 1882. It was also reported that Tynan had been publicizing his plot for years in New York saloons. Coincident with the Tynan affair was the return to America of three Irish Americans who had been imprisoned in England since 1883 for dynamite conspiracy. Dunne responded to all of the press coverage with this tour-de-force Dooley piece.

"Well," said Mr. Dooley, "th' European situation is becomin' a little gay."

"It 'tis so," said Mr. Hennessy. "If I was conthrollin' anny iv the gr-reat powers, I'd go down to th' Phosphorus an' take th' sultan be th' back iv th' neck an' give him wan, two, three. 'Tis a shame f'r him to be desthroyin' white people without anny man layin' hands on him. Th' man's no frind iv mine. He ought to be impeached an' thrun out."

"Divvle take th' sultan," said Mr. Dooley. "It's little I care f'r him or th' likes iv him or th' Ar-menyans or th' Phosphorus. I was runnin' over in me mind about th' poor lads they have sloughed up beyant f'r attimptin' to blow up Queen Victorya an' th' cza-ar iv Rooshia. Glory be, but they'se nawthin' in the wide wurruld as aisy to undherstand as a rivoluchonary plot be our own people. You'll see a lad iv th' right sort that'd niver open his head fr'm wan end iv th' year to th' other; but, whin he's picked out to go on a mission to London, he niver laves off talkin' till they put him aboord th' steamer. Here was Tynan. They say he had a hand in sindin' Lord Cavendish down th' toboggan, though I'd not thrust his own tellin' as far as th' len'th iv me ar-rm. Now he figured out that th' thrue way to free Ireland was to go over an' blow th' windows in Winzer Palace, an' incidentally to hist th' queen an' th' Rooshian cza-ar without th' aid iv th' elevator. What this here Tynan had again th' Rooshian cza-ar I niver heerd. But 'twas something awful, ye may be sure.

"Well, th' first thing th' la-ads done was to go to Madison Square Garden an' hold a secret meetin', in which thim that was to hand th' package to th' queen and thim that was to toss a piece iv gas pipe to his cza-ars was told off. Thin a comity was sint around to th' newspaper offices to tell thim th' expedition was about to start. Th' conspirators, heavily disgeesed, was attinded to th' boat be a long procission. First come Tynan ridin' on a wagon-load iv nithroglycerine; thin th' other conspirators, with gas-pipe bombs an' picks an' chuvvels f'r tunnellin' undher Winzer Castle; thin th' Ah-o-haitches; thin th' raypoorthers; thin a brigade iv Scotland Ya-ard spies in th'ga-arb iv polismin. An' so off they wint on their secret mission, with th' band playin' 'Th' Wearing' iv th' Green,' an' Tynan standin' on th' quarther deck, smilin' an' bowin' an' wavin' a bag iv jint powdher over his head.

"No sooner had th' conspirators landed thin th' British gover'mint begun to grow suspicious iv thim. Tynan was shadowed be detictives in citizens' clothes; an', whin he was seen out in his backyard practisin' blowin' up a bar'l that he'd dhressed in a shawl an' a little lace cap, th' suspicions growed. Ivrywhere that Tynan wint he was purshooed be th' minions iv tyranny. Whin he visited th' house nex' dure to th' queen's, an' unloaded a dhray full iv explosives an' chuvvels, the fact was rayported to th' polis, who become exthremely vigilant. Th' detectives followed him to Scotland Yard, where he wint to inform th' captain iv th'conspiracy, an' overheard much damming ividence iv th' plot until they become more an' more suspicious that something was on, although what was th' intintions iv th' conspirators it was hard to make out fr'm their peculiar actions. Whin Tynan gathered his followers in Hyde Park, an' notified thim iv the positions they was to take and disthributed th' dinnymite among thim, th' detectives become decidedly suspicious. Their suspicions was again aroused whin Tynan asked permission iv th' common council to build a bay window up close to th' queen's bedroom. But th' time to act had not come, an' they continted thimselves with thrackin' him through th' sthreets an' takin' notes iv such suspicious remarks as 'Anny wan that wants mementoes iv th' queen has on'y to be around this neighborhood nex' week with a shovel an' a basket,' an' 'Onless ye want ye'er clothes to be spoiled be th' czar, ye'd best carry umbrellas.' On th' followin' day Tynan took th' step that was needed f'r to con-vince th' gover'mint that he had designs on the monarchs. He wint to France. It's always been obsarved that, whin a dinnymiter had to blow up annything in London, he laves th' counthry. Th' polis, now thoroughly aroused, acted with commindable promptness. They arristed Tynan in Booloon f'r th' murdher iv Cavendish.

"Thus," said Mr. Dooley, sadly, "thus is th' vengeance f'r which our beloved counthry has awaited so long delayed be th' hand iv onscrupulious tyranny. Sthrive as our heroes may, no secrecy is secure against th' corruption iv British goold. Oh, Ireland, is this to be thy fate forever? Ar-re ye niver to escape th' vigilance iv th' polis, thim cold-eyed sleuths that seem to read th' very thoughts iv ye'er pathriot sons?"

"There must have been a spy in th' ranks," said Mr. Hennessy.

"Sure thing," said Mr. Dooley, winking at Mr. McKenna. "Sure thing, Hinnissy. Ayether that or th' accomplished detictives at Scotland Yards keep a close watch iv the newspapers. Or it may be – who knows? – that Tynan was indiscreet. He may have dhropped a hint of his intintions." (September 19, 1896)

18. The Grady Girl Rushing the Can

Appearing at the onset of the harsh "Black Winter" of 1893-94, this piece complemented an Evening Post *series on "The Children of the Poor" that ran around the same time.*

Up in Archey road the streetcar wheels squeaked along the tracks and the men coming down from the rolling-mills hit themselves on their big chests and wiped their noses on their leather gloves with a peculiar back-handed stroke at which they are most adept. The little girls coming out of the bakeshops with loaves done up in brown paper under their arms had to keep a tight clutch on their thin shawls lest those garments should be caught up by the bitter wind blowing from Brighton Park way and carried down to the gashouse. The frost was so thick on the windows of Mr. Martin Dooley's shop that you could just see the crownless harp on the McCormick's Hall Parnell meeting sheet above it, and you could not see any of the pyramid of Medford rum bottles founded contemporaneously with that celebrated meeting.*

Still, signs of warmth and good cheer were not lacking about the Dooley establishment. One sign in particular, a faded one and time worn, bearing a legend touching upon Tom and Jerry, hung from the door. It met the eye of the Hon. John McKenna standing on the streetcar platform and conversing with the driver upon the benefits to civilization only possible under the mayoralty of George Brains Swift. Mr. McKenna hopped from the car and went in to find Mr. Dooley sitting comfortably behind the tall stove which was steaming from the reservoir atop. Mr. Dooley was partaking contentedly of an aromatic mixture of a golden color, slightly flecked with Vandyke brown, in which a bit of lemon peel was floating.

"Is it cold out, I dinnaw?" said Mr. Dooley, laying down his glass.

"Oh, no," said Mr. McKenna, rubbing his ear; "it isn't cold. I dropped in to get an umbrella. I'm afraid I'll get sunstruck if I go along without one."

"I didn't know," said Mr. Dooley, calmly chasing the lemon peel around with the spoon. "It isn't cold in here, Jawn, and by gar as long as it isn't, 'tis not mesilf'd poke me nose out to learn th' timphrature. Some idjuts iv me acquaintance kapes a thermomter about to tell how cold it is, but f'r me, Jawn, I'd as soon have a mad dog in th' house. There was a man be th' name iv Denny that kep' th' block below Finucane's, an' he bought a thermomter f'r to tell how cold it was, an', by gar, th' poor, deluded man 'd be r-runnin' out fr'm morn till night to take a pike at th' thermomter, an' him in his shirt sleeves. Wan day he tuk noomony in th' lungs and died, Gawd rest him, in three days. I wint to his wake. They waked him in beer, but annyhow thim Dennys was always low people. Wan iv thim is a polisman now. It's dam'd little I care how cold it is so long as I have this here fire baychune me an' th' frost. Zaro or twinty daygrees below zero an' wan lump iv coal in that there shtove, and it's all akel to Dooley. I can plant mesilf in this chair an' say to mesilf: 'Come on winter; I'm here before ye.' Thin to think iv th' poor divvles out in th' night, tortured an' sufferin' with th' cold an' nothin' to cover thim an' protect thim fr'm th'frost – Jawn, there's no divarsion more cheerin'.

---

*[Charles Stewart Parnell had visited Chicago in February, 1880.]

Bedad, half th' philo-sophy iv life is in knowin' that some wan is sufferin' whin ye're on aisy street. It is, so it is."

A rattle at the door and a short cry caused Mr. Dooley to pause and listen and finally to toddle out grumbling complaints about the Donohue goat, whose only divarsion was to batter down the tenements of dacint people. As he opened the door his grumbling ceased, and presently he came in carrying something that looked like a rather large parcel of rags, but on close inspection turned out to be a very small girl carrying a very big can.

"Glory be to Gawd," said Mr. Dooley, setting the little girl down in the chair. "Glory be to Gawd, an' did ye iver see th' likes iv that? Luk at her, Jawn, th' unfortunate chick, lyin' out there froze in this murdhrin' night with a can in her hand. Who are ye, poor thing? Let me take a luk at ye. By gar, I thought so. 'Tis Grady's kid – Grady, th' villain, th' black-hearted thafe, to send th' poor choild out to her death. Don't stand there, ye big numbskull, like a cigar store injun starin'. Go over an' fetch that can iv milk. Musha, musha, ye poor dear. Naw, naw, don't wipe ye'er nose on me apron, ye unmannerly crather. Give me a towel, Jawn, fr'm in under th' shilf where thim Angyostooria bitthers stands. There ye are. Don't cry, dear. Does ye'er – what th' 'ell's baby talk f'r feet, Jawn?"

"Tootsy-wootsies," said Mr. McKenna proudly.

"Does ye'er tootsy-wootsies hurt ye, avick? Dhrink that an' ye'll be as warm as two in a bed."

Mr. Dooley stood with hands on his hips and saw the little Grady girl laving her purple nose in the warm milk. Meantime he narrated the history of her father in forcible language, touching upon his failure to work and provide, his bibulous habits and his tendency toward riotous misconduct. Finally, he walked behind the bar and set out the glasses, as his custom was for closing time. He placed the cash drawer in the small iron safe in the corner and tucked a $5 bill in his vest pocket. Then he turned out the lights in the window and put on his overcoat.

"Where are you going?" asked Mr. McKenna.

"I'm goin' over to lick Grady," said Mr. Dooley.

"Then," said Mr. McKenna, "by heavens," he said, "I'll go with you."

And they marched out together, with the little Grady girl beween them. (November 25, 1893)

19. The Pullman Strike: What Does He Care?

George Pullman's employees had walked out in the first place because prices in company stores and rents on their company-owned houses at Pullman, Illinois, had not been reduced after lay-offs and salary cuts were announced in May, 1894. After the strike was broken, these policies remained unchanged, and reports began to come back from the company town of widespread destitution, even starvation, among the workers and their families. As the situation grew worse, and Pullman still refused to capitulate, Dunne responded with this powerful personal attack. In his biography of Dunne, Elmer Ellis recounts the reaction to this piece at the Post: *"When the typesetter ran off his proof . . . he passed it about the composing room, and later when Dunne stepped into the room for a moment, the typesetters started to drum their sticks on their cases, and then broke into the more customary applause of handclapping. . . . Dunne remembered it as one of the great thrills of his life" (Mr. Dooley's America [New York: Knopf, 1941], 86).*

"Jawn," said Mr. Dooley, "I said it wanst an' I sa-ay it again, I'd liefer be George M. Pullman thin anny man this side iv Michigan City. I wud so. Not, Jawn, d'ye mind, that I invy him his job iv runnin' all th' push-cart lodgin'-houses iv th' counthry or in dayvilopin' th' whiskers iv a goat without dis-playin' anny other iv th' good qualities iv th' craythur or in savin' his taxlist fr'm th' assissor with th' intintion iv layin' it befure a mathrimonyal agency. Sare a bit does I care f'r thim honors. But, Jawn, th' la-ad that can go his way with his nose in th' air an' pay no attintion to th' sufferin' iv women an' child-her – dear, oh, dear, but his life must be as happy as th' da-ay is long.

"It seems to me, Jawn, that half th' throuble we have in this vale iv tears, as Dohenny calls Bridgeport, is seein' th' sufferin' iv women an' little childhren. Th' men can take care iv thimselves, says I. If they can't wurruk let thim go on th' polis foorce an' if they can't go on th' polis foorce let thim fol-low th' advice big Pether Hinnissy give th' Dutchman. 'I dinnaw vat to do,' sa-ays th' Dutchmen. 'I have no money and I can get no wurruk.' 'Foolish man,' says Hinnissy. 'D'ye know what th' good book says? To those that has nawthin' something will be given,' he sa-ays; 'an' those that has a lot,' he sa-ays, 'some wan'll come along with a piece iv lead pipe,' he sa-ays, 'in a stockin',' he sa-ays, 'an' take what they got away,' he sa-ays. 'D'ye see that big man over there?' he sa-ays, pointin' to Dorgan, the rale estate man. 'Go over an' take him be th' neck an' make him give up.' Well, sir, th' German, bein' like all iv th' ra-ace but Hesing,* was a foolish la-ad, an' what does he do but follow the joker's advice. Sure Dorgan give him a kick in th' stummick, an' whin he got out iv th' hospital he wint to th' bridewell, an', by dad, I'm thinkin' he was betther off there than most poor divvies out iv it, f'r they get three meals a da-ay, av'n if there ain't no toothbrushes in th' cells.

"But as I said, Jawn, 'tis not th' min ye mind; 'tis th' women an' childhren. Glory be to Gawd, I can scarce go out f'r a wa-alk f'r pity at seein' th' little wans settin' on th' stoops an' th' women with thim lines in th' fa-ace that I seen but wanst befure, an' that in our parish over beyant, whin th' potatoes was all kilt be th' frost an' th' oats rotted with th' dhrivin' rain. Go into wan iv th' side sthreets about supper time an' see thim, Jawn – thim women sittin'

---

*[Washington Hesing, owner-editor of the German-language newspaper, the *Illinois Staats-Zeitung*, and former Postmaster of Chicago.]

at th' windies with th' babies at their breasts an' waitin' f'r th' ol' man to come home. Thin watch thim as he comes up th' sthreet, with his hat over his eyes an' th' shoulders iv him bint like a hoop an' dhraggin' his feet as if he carried ball an' chain. Musha, but 'tis a sound to dhrive ye'er heart cold whin a woman sobs an' th' young wans cries, an' both because there's no bread in th' house. Betther off thim that lies in Gavin's crates out in Calv'ry, with th' grass over thim an' th' stars lookin' down on thim, quite at last. An' betther f'r us that sees an' hears an' can do nawthin' but give a crust now an' thin. I seen Tim Dorsey's little woman carryin' in a loaf iv bread an' a ham to th' Polack's this noon. Dorsey have been out iv wurruk f'r six months, but he made a sthrike carryin' th' hod yistherday an' th' good woman pinched out some vittles f'r th' Polacks."

Mr. Dooley swabbed the bar in a melancholy manner and turned again with the remark:

"But what's it all to Pullman? Whin Gawd quarried his heart a happy man was made. He cares no more f'r thim little matthers iv life an' death thin I do f'r O'Connor's tab. 'Th' women an' childhren is dyin' iv hunger,' they says. 'Will ye not put out ye'er hand to help thim?' they says. 'Ah, what th' 'ell,' says George. 'What th' 'ell,' he says. 'What th' 'ell,' he says. 'James,' he says, 'a bottle iv champagne an' a piece iv crambree pie. What th' 'ell, what th' 'ell, what th' 'ell.'"

"I heard two died yesterday," said Mr. McKenna. "Two women."

"Poor things, poor things. But," said Mr. Dooley, once more swabbing the bar, "what th' 'ell." (August 25, 1894)

20. Mrs. Mulligan and the Illinois Central Railroad

This piece was prompted by the refusal of President Fish of the Illinois Central to have pedestrian crossings installed over his railroad's lakeside tracks.

"Jawn," said Mr. Dooley, "I had Hinnissy in with me las' night. He's a smart ol' buck wanst in awhile. He tol' me he's goin' to get up a new caddychism. It'll go like this: 'Who made ye?' 'Th' Illinye Cinthral made me.' 'An' why did it make ye?' 'That I might know it, love it, an' serve it all me days.' Be hivins, 'twould be a good thing. They's naw use teachin' th' childher what ain't thrue. What's th' good iv tellin' thim that th' Lord made th' wurruld whin they'll grow up an' find it in th' possission iv th' Illinye Cinthral?

"Th' ma-an that does be at th' head iv th' r-road is a man be th' name iv Fish. I don't know what Fish he is, but he's no sucker. He was a jood down in th' City iv New York an' th' Frindly Sons iv Saint Pathrick or th' Ivy Leaf Plisure Club or some other organization give a party an' this here Fish he wanted f'r to be th' whole thing in it – wanted f'r to take th' tickets an' have th' ba-ar privilege an' lade th' gr-rand ma-arch, d'ye mind. 'Naw,' says they.

'Naw. Ye can't be th' whole thing.' 'Thin,' says th' man-Fish, 'I quit ye.' An'
he come out here to run th' Illinye Cinthral.

"Well, he's runnin' it. He's runnin' th' Illinye Cinthral, an' he's runnin' th'
earth, an' he's got an irne fince around th' lake, an' if he has his way he'll be
puttin' th' stars in a cage an' chargin' ye two bits f'r a look at thim – Show
ye'er ticket to th' ma-an at th' gate.

"Jawn, I don't care no more f'r Lake Michigan than th' likes iv you cares
f'r th' tin commandments. They're all right, but ye don't use thim. In tin years
I've set me eyes on it but twict, an' I on'y see it now as it comes out iv that
there faucet. Whin I want what Hinnissy calls eequathic spoorts I goes over
here to th' r-red bridge an' takes a ride with Brinnan. But there's thim that
uses it an' they say 'tis good f'r babies.

"Ye mind th' Mulligans – thim that lives over beyant Casey's – th' little
quite man with th' r-red whiskers. He wurruks hard, but all he's been able to
lay up is throuble an' childher. He has tin iv thim old an' young, an' th' last
come is sick an' feverish. I seen th' good woman rockin' it wan day on th'
stoop, an' says I: 'How's th' kid?' 'Poorly, thank ye,' says she. 'He seems
throubled be th' heat. 'Tis mortial hot,' she says. 'Why don't ye take him
where 'tis cool?' I says. 'I'm goin' to to-morrah, praise Gawd,' she says. 'I'm
goin'to take him down an' give him a r-ride around on th' steamboat. Th' doctor tells me th' lake air 'll make him right,' she says. ''Tis ixpinsive,' she says.
'Five cints on th' boat, but 'tis betther than to have th' poor chick sufferin' an'
I'm goin' to do it.'

"Ye see, she'd been brought up on th' ol' caddychism an' thought Gawd
ownded th' wurruld, an' she'd niver heerd tell iv th' man-Fish. So I see her
goin' off downtown with th' baby in her arms, shieldin' its face fr'm th' blazin'
sun, bright an' early. How she found her way across th' city I dinnaw. F'r
mesilf, I'd as lave attimpt to cross hell as State sthreet. I was r-run over be a
gripca-ar th' last time I was there. But annyhow she got across to where she
cud see th' blue wather iv th' la-ake an' th' crib that Tom Gahan built. 'Twas
there she found who ownded th' wurruld. She wint along th' irne fince lookin'
f'r a gate an' they was no gate. Thin she wint into th' little deepo an' says she:
'I want to go over to thim boats,' she says. 'Ye'll have to buy a ticket beyant,'
says th' man. 'An' how much is it?' says she. 'Tin cints,' says th' man. 'But,'
says she, 'I've on'y th' fifteen left,' she says, 'an' th' boat costs tin cints,' she
says. 'Lave me in,' she says. 'I can't help it,' says th' man. ''Tis me ordhers,
'he says. Ye see, th' man-Fish had tol' thim not to let annywan go to his lake,
th' wan he made, d'ye mind, on th' sicond day. An' there she stood, peerin'
through th' irne fince an' lookin' out at th' lake – at th' Illinye Cinthral's lake
– an' glory be, I suppose she didn't undherstand it, but no more does she undherstand why it is f'r some to live off th' fat iv th' land an' f'r her on'y to bear
childher an' see thim die or go to th' bad.

"She come home afther awhile whin th' baby got cross again. I seen her that night. 'Did ye like th' lake?' I says. 'I didn't go,' she says. 'F'r why?' says I. 'Th' Illinye Cinthral wudden' let me,' she says. 'I think it'd done th' baby good,' she says. 'He's onaisy tonight. Maria,' says she, 'will ye take Tiddy while I cuk ye'er father's supper?'

"So I think with Hinnissy they'll have to make a new caddychism, Jawn. I hope th' Illinye Cinthral 'll be kinder to Mulligan's baby in th' nix' wurruld than it's been in this, f'r unless me eyes have gone back on me, they'll be another sthring iv crape on Mulligan's dure tomo-rah mornin'." (August 10, 1895)

21. Charity and Education: An Immigrant Shot for Stealing Coal

On January 21, 1897, the Times-Herald *claimed that "Chicago's poor are starving within sight of relief," while political red tape was holding up the dispensation of supplies. Two days later, amid rumors that Mayor George Swift was about to issue a proclamation on the relief crisis, a* Times-Herald *editorial described the city in these terms:*

> *. . . when ill-clad, half-famished shapes confront us on the streets; when the cold pinches the denizens of hovels and tenements, when the children in a thousand squalid homes cry for sustenance, when women fight for bread at the county agent's door, and able-bodied men swarm on the railway tracks, eagerly bagging fragments of coal – this crisis is not to be met with perfunctory measures.*

That night, Mr. Dooley told the story of one of those coal-pickers, a Polish immigrant named Sobieski.

Mr. Dooley put a huge lump of soft coal into the gaping stove and whacked it to pieces with a little iron poker. Then he composed himself luxuriously before the blaze and said "Slanthu" to his friend Mr. Hennessy.

"How low did ye say th' glass was?" he asked.

"Four below," said Mr. Hennessy. "I near froze me ears comin' over here."

"R-rum," said Mr. Dooley. "R-rum'll be th' death iv ye, Hinnissy. 'Tis nat'ral f'r me to dhrink. I have it at me elbow. But 'tis a vice with you, an' anny man that'd lave a comfortable home an' th' society iv his fam'ly on a night like this f'r to put that into his face that steals away his feet is a sot, an' no mistake."

"Well, annyhow," said Mr. Hennessy, not at all abashed by the sarcasm, "I'm betther off than manny a man that has nayether home nor rum."

"Faith, ye ar-re," said Mr. Dooley. "They'se no wan had to get out a rile proclamation f'r ye. They'se manny ways iv dealin' with th' poor. Wan is th' ol' fashioned way that prevails among th' poor thimsilves iv packin' away some potatoes an' a pound iv tay an' a side iv bacon in a basket an' takin' it around to th' poorer an' rayturnin' to tell what furniture they had in th' house. Another is th' organized charity that on'y helps thim that can prove that whin they had money they didn't spind it f'r food an' other luxuries but put it by f'r a rainy day. Th' new way is f'r to have th' mayor issue a proclamation callin' upon people f'r to give freely to th' destitute. I haven't heard that th' Whole Thing has donated a bar'l iv axle grease f'r to comfort th' afflicted.* Mebbe he has a betther scheme. I shudden't be surprised if he'd set aside th' income fr'm th' Union loop to keep wan fam'ly each year. They'd hardly be enough; but ivry little bit helps, ye know.

"Me own scheme iv charity, Hinnissy, d'ye mind, is to duck whin I can, but whin a case comes up in front iv me eyes so that it hur-rts, d'ye mind, to give what I got an' ask no questions. I look on th' thing th' way an' ol' frind iv mine be th' name iv Hogan did. He was comin' up on th' late car wan night an' th' on'y other passenger was a big, r-rough-lookin' man. As th' conducter passed through th' car he dhropped a nickel. He didn't notice it, but Hogan an' th' other did, an' whin th' conductor got out on th' platform th' big man an' Hogan med a grab f'r it. They reached th' flure together, clinched an' rolled around, an' finally th' big man got on top an' thried to put Hogan's head in th' fire. Hogan hollered quits. 'Do I get it?' says th' big man. 'Sure,' says Hogan. 'If ye want it that bad ye ought to have it.' So be me with th' la-ads on th' street. Anny man that's so far gone that he'll ask ought to have. Besides, I feel this way about it, Hinnissy: Supposin' I was in that fix, wud I r-run up on a man in th' sthreet an' stick out a blue hand an' say: 'Can't ye help another young feller to get a meal?' Not on ye'er life. I'd steal a sock an' a small piece iv lead pipe somewhere, an' I'd not be particular about th' sock, an' I'd stand in th' corner iv an alley an' when a man come along that looked more thin 38 cints I'd tap him wanst if 'twas th' last act iv me degraded career, I wud so. I regard it as th' hite iv civility whin a man asks me f'r money instead iv takin' it away fr'm me. Th' money most people pay in charity is no more thin six per cint on what they steal, annyhow.

"But iv coorse ye can't get people to look at it that way. Ye didn't know a man named Sobieski, that lived down be Grove sthreet, did ye? Ah-ha! Well, he was not so bad, afther all. He's dead, ye know. Last week. Ye see, this here Sobieski had no more sinse thin a grasshopper. He arned enormous wages f'r a man with eight childher – wan twinty-five a day, half a week in good times, sidintary imploymint carryin' pigs iv steel at th' mills. Bimeby th' saviors iv their counthry, believin' th' market was overstocked, shut down an' left time and grocers' bills heavy on Sobieski's hands. Th' col' weather come on, an' Sobieski grew tired iv inaction. Also th' childher were freezin' to

---

*[Chicago Mayor Swift ("th' Whole Thing") was associated with a company that manufactured axle grease.]

death. So he put a bag on his shoulder an' wint over to th' railway thracks to pick up some coal. Wan man can't pick up much coal on th' railway thracks, Hinnissy, but it is an unpardonable crime, just th' same. 'Tis far worse thin breakin' th' intherstate commerce act. Anny offense again' a railway company is high threason, but pickin' up coal is so villainous that they'se no forgiveness f'r th' hidyous wretch that commits it.

"Sobieski walked along th' thracks, gettin' a chunk here an' there, till a watchman seen him, an' pintin' a revolver at him, called 'Halt!' Sobieski didn't know th' English language very well. 'Dam Pole' was about his limit, an' he had that thrained into him be th' foreman at th' mills. But he knew what a revolver meant, an' th' ignorant fool tur-rned an' run with his three cints' worth iv coal rattlin' at his back. Th' watchman was a good shot, an' a Pole with heavy boots is no tin-second man in a fut race. Sobieski pitched over on his face, thried to further injure th' comp'ny be pullin' up th' rails with his hands, an' thin passed to where – him bein' a Pole, an' dyin' in such a horrible sin – they'se no need iv coal iv anny kind.

"That shows wan iv th' evils iv a lack iv idyacation," Mr. Dooley continued. "If Sobieski had known th' language ——"

"He'd a halted," said Mr. Hennessy.

"He wud not," said the Philosopher. "He'd niver been there at all. While th' watchman was walkin' knee-deep in snow, Sobieski'd been comfortably joltin' th' watchman's boss in a dark alley downtown. Idyacation is a gr-reat thing." (January 23, 1897)

22. Organized Charity and the Galway Woman

The winter of 1896-97 was the worst in recent memory for the poor of Chicago. On November 30, 1896, the Bureau of Associated Charities estimated that eight thousand families were destitute. As that figure grew larger, the situation was aggravated by a cold wave that struck in early December and held on until February. Accelerating demands for food and fuel soon swamped the city's relief bureaucracy, and Chicago faced a life-and-death crisis. In this piece Dunne attacks the self-defeating regulations of the city's Relief and Aid Society with a grim vignette set in an earlier hard winter, that of 1874.

"Whin th' col' spell comes along about Chris'mas time," said Mr. Hennessy, opening the stove door and lighting a small piece of paper which he conveyed to the bowl of his pipe with much dexterity, just snaring the last flicker with his first noisy inhalation, "whin th' col' weather comes on I wish thim Grogans down in th' alley'd move out. I have no peace at all with th' ol' woman. She has me r-runnin' in night an' day with a pound of tay or a flannel shirt or a this-or-that-or-th'-other thing, an' 'tis on'y two weeks ago, whin th' weather was warrum, she tol' me Mrs. Grogan was as ongrateful as a cow an' smelled so iv gin ye cud have th' deleeryum thremens if ye sat with her f'r an hour."

"What ye shud do," said Mr. Dooley, "is to get ye'er wife to join an organized charity. Th' throuble with her is she gives to onworthy people an' in a haphazard way that tinds to make paupers. If they'se annything will make a person ongrateful an' depindent it's to give thim something to eat whin they're hungry without knowin' whether they are desarvin' iv th' delicate attintion. A man, or a woman ayether, has to have what ye may call peculiar qualifications f'r to gain th' lump iv coal or th' pound iv steak that an organized charity gives out. He must be honest an' sober an' industhrious. He must have a frind in th' organization. He must have arned th' right to beg his bread be th' sweat iv his brow. He must be able to comport himself like a gintleman in fair society an' play a good hand at whist. He must have a marridge license over th' pianny an' a goold-edged Bible on th' marble-topped table. A pauper that wud disbelieve there was a God afther thrampin' th' sthreets in search iv food an' calmin' an onreasonable stomach with th' east wind is no object iv charity. What he needs is th' attintion iv a polisman. I've aften wondhered why a man that was fit to dhraw a ton iv slate coal an' a gob iv liver fr'm th' relief an' aid society didn't apply f'r a cabinet position or a place in a bank. He'd be sthrong f'r ayether.

"I mind wanst there was a woman lived down near Main sthreet be th' name iv Clancy, Mother Clancy th' kids called her. She come fr'm away off to th' wist, a Galway woman fr'm bechune mountain an' sea. Ye know what they ar-re whin they're black, an' she was worse an' blacker.* She was tall an' thin, with a face white th' way a corpse is white, an' she had wan child, a lame la-ad that used to play be himsilf in th' sthreet, th' lawn bein' limited. I niver heerd tell iv her havin' a husband, poor thing, an' what she'd need wan f'r, but to dhrag out her misery f'r her in th' gray year sivinty-foor, I cudden't say. She talked to hersilf in Gaelic whin she walked an' 'twas Gaelic she an' th' kid used whin they wint out together. Th' kids thought she was a witch an' broke th' windows iv her house an' ivry wan was afraid iv her but th' little priest. He shook his head whin she was mintioned an' wint to see her wanst in awhile an' come away with a throubled face.

"Sivinty-foor was a hard winter f'r th' r-road. Th' mills was shut down an' ye cud've stood half th' population iv some iv th' precints on their heads an' got nothin' but five days' notices out iv thim. Th' nights came cold, an' bechune relievin' th' sick an' givin' extremunction to th' dyin' an' comfortin' th' widows an' orphans th' little priest was sore pressed fr'm week's end to week's end. They was smallpox in wan part iv th' wa-ard an' diphtheria in another an' bechune th' two there was starvation an' cold an' not enough blankets on th' bed.

---

*[The adjective "black" connotes grim seriousness, strong will, and pride.]

"Th' Galway woman was th' las' to complain. How she iver stud it as long as she did I lave f'r others to say. Annyhow, whin she come down to Halsted sthreet to make application f'r help to th' Society f'r th' Relief iv th' Desarvin' Poor she looked tin feet tall an' all white cheek bones an' burnin' black eyes. It took her a long time to make up her mind to go in, but she done it an' stepped up to where th' reel-estate man Dougherty, cheerman iv th' comity, was standin' with his back to th' stove an' his hands undher his coat tails. They was those that said Dougherty was a big-hear-rted man an' give freely to th' poor, but I'd rather take rough-on-rats fr'm you, Hinnissy, thin sponge cake fr'm him or th' likes iv him. He looked at her, finished a discoorse on th' folly iv givin' to persons with a bad moral charackter an' thin turned sudden-ly an' said: 'What can we do f'r ye?' She told him in her own way. 'Well, me good woman,' says he, 'ye'll undherstand that th' comity is much besieged be th' imporchunities iv th' poor,' he says, 'an' we're obliged to limit our alms to thim that desarves them,' he says. 'We can't do anything f'r ye on ye're own say so, but we'll sind a man to invistigate ye're case, an',' he says, 'if th' ray-poort on ye'er moral charackter is satisfacthry,' he says, 'we'll attind to ye.'

"I dinnaw what it was, but th' matther popped out iv Dougherty's head an' nayether that day nor th' nex' nor th' nex' afther that was annything done f'r th' Galway woman. I'll say this f'r Dougherty, that whin th' thing come back to his mind again he put on his coat an' hurried over to Main sthreet. They was a wagon in th' sthreet, but Dougherty took no notice iv it. He walked up an' rapped on th' dure, an' th' little priest stepped out, th' breast iv his overcoat bulgin'. 'Why, father,' he says, 'ar-re ye here? I jus' come f'r to see —— ' 'Peace,' said th' little priest, closin' th' dure behind him an' takin' Dougherty be th' ar-rm. 'We were both late.' But 'twas not till they got to th' foot iv th' stairs that Dougherty noticed that th' wagon come fr'm th' county undertaker, an' that 'twas th' chalice made th' little priest's coat to bulge." (December 5, 1896)